CW01507533

Praise for Tessa Harris

'The beauty of the Italian countryside is a stunning backdrop for an ugly war of betrayal, cruelty and love . . . a must for all fans of WW2 fiction'
Mandy Robotham

'I was completely immersed in this book from start to finish'
Kathleen McGurl

'Packed with atmosphere, this wartime resistance drama is a thrilling, chilling close-up of the battle to save Italy'
Sarah Steele

'Gripping, compelling and beautiful'
Emma Cowell

'I was swept away by this heart-rending, gripping page-turner set in beautiful Tuscany'
Annie Lyons

'Beautifully written and immaculately researched, with characters that jump off the page. I couldn't put it down!'
Lana Kortchik

TESSA HARRIS read History at Oxford University and has been a journalist, writing for several national newspapers and magazines, for more than thirty years. She is the author of 13 published historical novels. Her debut, *The Anatomist's Apprentice*, won the Romantic Times First Best Mystery Award 2012 in the USA. She lectures in creative writing and is married with two children and a grandson. She lives in the Cotswolds.

Facebook: Tessa Harris Author
X: @harris_tessa

Also by Tessa Harris

Beneath a Starless Sky
The Light We Left Behind
The Paris Notebook
The Tuscan Daughter

The Florence Sisters

TESSA HARRIS

ONE PLACE. MANY STORIES

HQ
An imprint of HarperCollins*Publishers* Ltd
1 London Bridge Street
London SE1 9GF

www.harpercollins.co.uk

HarperCollins*Publishers*
Macken House, 39/40 Mayor Street Upper,
Dublin 1 D01 C9W8
This edition 2025

1
First published in Great Britain by HQ,
an imprint of HarperCollins*Publishers* Ltd 2025

Copyright © Tessa Harris 2025

Tessa Harris asserts the moral right to be identified as the author of this work.
A catalogue record for this book is available from the British Library.

ISBN: 9780008640521

This novel is entirely a work of fiction. The names, characters and incidents
portrayed in it are the work of the author's imagination. Any resemblance to
actual persons, living or dead, events or localities is entirely coincidental.

All rights reserved. No part of this publication may be reproduced, stored
in a retrieval system, or transmitted, in any form or by any means,
electronic, mechanical, photocopying, recording or otherwise,
without the prior permission of the publishers.

Without limiting the author's and publisher's exclusive rights, any unauthorized
use of this publication to train generative artificial intelligence (AI) technologies
is expressly prohibited. HarperCollins also exercise their rights under Article
4(3) of the Digital Single Market Directive 2019/790 and expressly reserve this
publication from the text and data mining exception.

Printed and bound in the UK using 100% Renewable
Electricity by CPI Group (UK) Ltd

This book contains FSC™ certified paper and other controlled sources to ensure
responsible forest management.

For more information visit: www.harpercollins.co.uk/green

For Theo, with love

'What is art, but life upon the larger scale, the higher?'
Elizabeth Barrett Browning

Prologue

Florence

August 3, 1944

Flashes of light pulsed across the southern night sky, and ash drifted on the air like snow. The distant hills were dotted with fires and the guns were growing louder. The power plant was out of action and the city had been plunged into darkness, although now and again the gibbous moon would appear from behind gathering clouds. Down there, somewhere, lay the Arno; the Allies' last barrier. All six of its bridges were shackled by mines and awaiting their cruel fate. It looked like the Germans planned to blow them up throughout the night. Angelina could hardly believe that by morning they may all be gone.

Turning her head towards the direction of the Ponte Vecchio, she felt her heart ache at the thought of its destruction. Out of all of the bridges, with its beauty and grace and history, surely even the Nazis could find just a little pity in their cruel and callous hearts to save it? It was then that the thought hit her. *The portrait of the young woman.* She wondered if it was still there on the bridge. The prospect of it being lost to civilisation forever was very real – yet one more victim of this terrible war.

She squinted at her watch in the moonlight. *Eight minutes to ten.* Eight minutes until the first explosion. Her stomach was in knots. Her head hurt and her heart pounded; each beat marking another second closer to destruction. Deafened by her own trepidation, she didn't hear the footsteps behind her. It was only when the moon showed its face for a moment, and a shadow loomed behind her, that she whipped round, realising she wasn't alone. Instinctively, she took cover, hoping whoever it was hadn't seen her.

But then she saw him, and panic welled inside her as he moved through the darkness towards her. There was nowhere to hide. A thick wooden stick had propped open the trapdoor. She'd grabbed it on the way up, knowing it would make a weapon. As she flattened herself against the chimney stack, she felt the weight of it in her hand. Closer. He drew closer, glass crunching under his feet. She readied herself to take a swipe. Raising her arm to shoulder height she held her breath and struck blindly, but hard.

The night of the bridges had begun.

PART ONE

Chapter 1

Florence

June 1940

'Good heavens,' exclaimed a rather startled elderly lady, abruptly pulling a hearing trumpet from her ear. 'What's that racket?'

Lady Felstein's companion, Agatha Fortescue-Smythe, slightly younger but with an air of invincibility, glared at her through lorgnettes. 'I'm sure I can't hear anything,' she replied, taking a sip of Earl Grey. She resumed her conversation with the other ladies at the table, although sitting by her, Angelina, her great-niece, could most definitely hear something. The sound was growing louder by the minute.

It was a sweltering Monday afternoon in the city and members of the English Ladies' Arts Appreciation Society had convened as usual in the Gran Caffè Doney. But the whirring overhead fans were having little effect on the hot, close air, and the heat only added to the young woman's terrible sense of foreboding. For a while now, Lina – as she liked to be known, although her aunt's circle insisted on calling her by her full name – had sensed the city was simmering. She half expected it to boil over at any moment.

If Italy joined the war, as most predicted, it wasn't only millions of lives that would be endangered. Florence was considered the cradle of the western Renaissance and centuries of priceless art risked destruction, too. Summers spent in the city as a child had led to her own passion for art and a degree at university in London. Her love of the Renaissance was one of the reasons she'd returned – that and to be with her formidable great-aunt, who'd so encouraged and inspired her in the first place.

Still, Agatha refused to be put off her stride. 'So, I asked the ambassador what might happen to all the works of art in the city, should Italy enter the war. "Surely," I said to him, "Signor Mussolini must be sensitive to his responsibilities for the preservation of the priceless masterpieces in his care."'

As the founder, chairwoman and all-round director of the English Ladies' Arts Appreciation Society, Agatha headed one of the very few expatriate groups still found in Italy. In her late seventies and less than five feet in height, she possessed the energy of a woman half her age and several inches taller. With a slightly arthritic finger in every proverbial English pie in Florence, she would throw herself into 'cultural projects' with all the gusto of an opera singer at La Scala.

'What a tragedy it would be if a single fresco were to be destroyed,' she added, taking another sip of tea.

Outside the noise continued to grow with such speed that it almost drowned out the drone of English tongues.

'It's the Blackshirts,' said Lina. As the older women gossiped merrily away in their leghorn straw hats and floral frocks, she'd been quietly observing passers-by on the Via de Tornabuoni. She'd noticed several young men wearing black armbands. They were Mussolini's fascist supporters.

'The Blackshirts,' repeated Agatha, wiping crumbs from her chin. '*We've* nothing to fear from them. Those brutes are only interested in other Italians.'

'What's that they're shouting?' asked Lady Felstein, her waxen face becoming slightly alarmed.

'English out!' volunteered the elegantly coiffed Mrs Clutterbuck, looking distinctly uncomfortable.

Alarm spread across Miss Marjorie Harrowby's thin face as a terrible prospect reared in front of her. A mild-mannered spinster, she always wore a fresh flower in her hair – a rose today – and angling her head towards Agatha she asked, 'What if the Uffizi Gallery was bombed to smithereens?'

Agatha raised her brow, clearly picturing the alarming scenario in her mind's eye. 'Quite so. Centuries of paintings and sculptures. And as for the Botticellis – the world would be a poorer place without his *Primavera*.'

While the other ladies nodded their heads in agreement, Lina grew increasingly concerned. She'd seen the fascist propaganda leaflets and graffiti on British-owned buildings, where Queen Victoria's portrait once hung with pride. The genteel *A Room with a View* world of E M Forster had long disappeared, but the more senior members of the English community clung on to their old ways in the city they'd called home for much of their lives. They simply had nowhere else to go. Nor did she, for that matter. Her late father was Italian. Her mother, English. She guessed that made her fire and ice, part fiery Italian, part coolly reserved English. After her mother's second marriage to a very unwelcoming Scottish laird, she'd completed a doctorate in England before returning to the place of her birth. She loved Florence and everything about it.

'Perhaps we should leave,' Lina suggested, the sensible English in her coming to the fore. Her hand rose as she gestured to the waiter for the bill.

'Really, Angelina dear, one mustn't let oneself be bullied by these thugs,' Agatha chided from beneath the brim of her dark blue hat.

Just then, a dapper gentleman in cream flannels, a pink tie, and a matching handkerchief, appeared at the café entrance.

As soon as he whipped off his hat, Lina recognised a red-faced Rodney Ponting. He was the only honorary male member of the arts appreciation society. He was also one of the few men Agatha saw as a suitor for her niece, even though he didn't seem to show the least interest in the opposite sex.

'Oh, ladies. Dear ladies,' he addressed them, dabbing the sweat off his brow. Clutching his Panama hat by its rim he told them, 'Something rather awful has just happened, I'm afraid.'

'Good heavens. Do enlighten us, Mr Ponting,' Agatha invited, looking mildly askance.

The dapper little man took a deep breath. 'I've just come from the Piazza della Repubblica.' He gulped. 'Mussolini has declared war on Britain and France.'

Even though it was half expected, a collective gasp went round the table.

'So, it is as we feared,' Agatha shot back.

'Nasty piece of work,' growled widowed Mrs Clutterbuck, fingering her pearls. 'Never did like him.' She was a Yorkshire woman and always spoke her mind.

'My word,' gasped Miss Harrowby.

Lady Felstein's attention was, however, otherwise engaged. She'd just spotted someone else approaching the table. Heads turned to watch a woman in her middle years, with dark, cropped hair and implausibly white teeth, striding towards them.

'Well, Miss Giltrap looks rather pleased with herself,' observed Mrs Clutterbuck. She reached for her fan and fluttered it furiously.

Lina switched round to catch sight of the American – another honorary member of the arts appreciation society. Dressed in her ubiquitous men's trousers and brogues, round her neck she wore her trusty Rolleiflex camera.

'History in the making out there, ladies, and I got some great shots,' she announced with a dazzling grin. Then, suddenly aware that no one else shared her excitement, she shook her head sheepishly. 'I'm sorry but it's not every day war gets declared.'

'And for that we are most grateful,' Agatha assured her, haughtily.

The announcement only compounded Lina's anxiety. War, she feared, couldn't be brushed away like cake crumbs, but her aunt and the other ladies seemed unable to grasp its full implications. They lived in their own little world. More immediately, however, a quick glance through the café's long windows confirmed the angry crowd she'd heard was now just outside on the street.

'I really do think—' Lina began. But she didn't finish because at that precise moment a large rock came hurtling through the café window, shattering the glass and narrowly missing Mrs Clutterbuck as it landed just inches away. Miss Harrowby screamed. Lady Felstein gasped. And Lina leapt to her feet as shards showered their table.

The frock-coated waiters scattered like startled penguins, running hither and thither, checking on their clients, while two more ran outside to see if they could spot the culprit.

'Is everyone all right?' asked Lina, her eyes darting around the café. Several customers were now on their feet. Others sat in shocked silence.

'Goodness. I think so,' replied Miss Harrowby, not quite grasping what had just happened. Miss Giltrap helped her shake broken glass from her kid gloves on the table.

'Aunt Agatha?'

Agatha had turned the colour of the clotted cream in front of her. Still, she managed to nod. 'Of course,' she replied, as if it would take more than a mere missile to put her off her stride. Mr Ponting tried to help her up, but she fought him off with the white parasol she always carried. 'I can manage perfectly well on my o—'

'Good God!' cried an alarmed Mrs Clutterbuck.

Lady Felstein's right hand flew up to her cheek when she saw her companion's expression. It came down with blood on her fingers. She'd been cut by flying glass.

'I suggest we leave immediately,' said Lina. 'Lady Felstein needs attention.'

Agatha tutted but agreed, almost as if the whole terrifying episode was a minor inconvenience. 'My tea had gone cold anyway.'

So had the blood in Lina's veins. As soon as they stepped outside onto the street, the women would become like lambs, and unless they could find an alternative exit, they were about to throw themselves to the wolves.

'This way, ladies,' said Signor Rossi, the moustachioed head waiter, valiantly appearing at their table to come to their rescue. 'The back door.' He gestured to the far end of the café.

Through the windows, Lina could see the gathering crowd was growing bigger by the minute. University students carried banners and placards displaying the now familiar fascist emblem. 'We need to get away from here as quickly as we can.'

By now a patch of the white napkin used to stem the flow of blood from Lady Felstein's cheek was bright red, while outside the crowd continued to chant.

'*Inglesi! Inglesi!*'

As the cries grew louder, the little party joined the stream of other alarmed English customers exiting through the back door. Signor Rossi was directing everyone into a narrow passageway leading to the inferno of a kitchen. From there it was out through a beaded curtain into a cobbled alley. Three waiters then guided their patrons safely onto a side street, away from the mob.

'You will be safe now, yes?' asked the head waiter.

'*Grazie, Signor Rossi,*' Lina replied, not dwelling on what may have happened if they had left by the main entrance. In fact, her future in the city, and that of Agatha and her circle, had been abruptly thrown into doubt. All she was sure of was that now Italy had declared war on Britain, every Englishman and woman had become the enemy.

Chapter 2

September 1940

'I'm sorry. I can give you no more,' said Edoardo Bernini with a shake of his well-oiled head. If only someone handed him a thousand lira every time he repeated that phrase, he'd be a rich man by now. But like everyone else, his finances had nose-dived with the threatened war that had recently become a reality for Italy.

A pale, wrinkled face peeped out at him from a mink coat that appeared far too big for its wearer. Even though it was late September, the Florentine sun remained unforgiving. *Why is this woman wearing a mink coat when it's still so hot outside?* Edoardo thought to himself, unless it was to keep her most valuable possessions as close as she possibly could.

The elderly woman's thin lips turned down. She seemed both offended and dismayed; offended that she was having to sell her late husband's art collection at all and dismayed that the offer she'd just received was so very low.

Over the past few weeks, there'd been a stream of clients – mainly Jewish, like this old lady – into the Bernini Gallery. But none of them had wanted to buy. They'd all seen what was happening to their fellow Jews in Germany and Poland and knew

11

they could be next. Their paintings, jewels and furs could be passports to safety. They hoped their cash would buy their freedom, and sometimes, their lives. Edoardo had seen a few good pieces, but buyers were thin on the ground and right now he didn't have the money to invest.

'Surely, you can stretch to a little more. My husband ...' There were tears in the widow's eyes as she studied the oil painting in its magnificent gilt frame. It was by an eighteenth-century painter whose work ordinarily fetched a decent price at auction.

'Few are buying at the moment, *signora*,' Edoardo explained, tugging at his starched shirt cuffs. 'I am sorry.' He gave her one of his '*I would love to help you, but that is my final offer*' smiles he'd cultivated over the years. He used it a lot these days, even though it pained him. Reluctantly, the old woman turned, the painting still under her arm, and left the gallery to meet her uncertain fate. He, on the other hand, knew exactly what he planned to do.

As soon as she was out of sight, Edoardo grabbed his fedora from the rack, locked the gallery and ventured out onto the Via Porta Rossa on his way to see the podesta – the mayor of Florence. The summons the previous day had set alarm bells ringing. Cesari Manzano was Mussolini's right-hand man in the city. When he called you, you not only jumped, you scrambled through barbed wire and scaled high walls.

Less than half an hour later Edoardo was sitting in an office in the Palazzo Vecchio, watching an electric fan thrash against the September heat as it raged all around. It was fighting a losing battle. The room faced south and was in direct sunlight. Flicking a handkerchief from the breast pocket of his well-cut suit, Edoardo dabbed his forehead. It wouldn't do to be seen sweating. It could be taken as a sign of weakness.

Through the open door the art dealer saw Manzano's massive bulk approach via an ante room. He brought to Edoardo's mind the bronze statue of *Il Porcellino*, the wild boar so beloved of tourists in the new market. If you rubbed its snout, and placed a coin in its mouth, water would pour out. Yes, there were definite similarities, and both always exacted their price.

A young woman with blonde hair, in a tight pencil skirt, leaned over a drawer in a filing cabinet. As he passed, the podesta patted her backside. Edoardo saw her wince, but when she glanced back at her boss, it was with a fake smile.

'Ah, Signor Bernini.' Manzano lumbered into the office. He was twenty minutes late for the meeting but didn't apologise. Mussolini had personally put his stooge in charge of Florence and with such power came control of the city's vast art collections. Edoardo knew both the podesta and Il Duce shared an ignorance of the subject, while understanding the power it could command. A dangerous combination.

'Has Silvia got you something to drink? Water, coffee, brandy? Food?'

The girl glanced through the door at Edoardo. They'd swapped words – and looks – on his arrival. Satisfying Manzano's appetite was clearly part of her job.

'*Gelato!* This heat calls for *gelato*, don't you think? Get me a dish of vanilla and chocolate!' the podesta called through. 'You want some?'

'No, but thank you,' Edoardo replied with a false smile. He knew this wasn't a social visit. Even though he had followed the fascist party line, his late father had always been wary of this man. He'd never said why, although Edoardo knew he'd had some dealings with him over art.

'I expect you're wondering why I asked you here,' said Manzano, plumping himself down at his desk. Since Italy had joined the war on Germany's side, he'd exchanged his ill-fitting suit for a new fascist uniform. 'Our paths do not often cross, Signor Bernini,' he went on, loosening the top fastener of his uniform tunic. Edoardo could see the tight collar left red marks where it chaffed against his bullish neck.

'True.'

'But of course I knew your father.'

'Yes, but everyone knew my father, Excellency.' *Or at least knew of him, thought Edoardo.*

Manzano made an odd grunting sound. 'Shame what happened to him. He was a good party man. He just got greedy.'

The dealer worked his jaw but held his tongue. His father's death was like a wound that wouldn't heal.

'And now I am to give you the chance to restore the fortunes of the family business.'

Edoardo's head shot up. 'I'm sorry. I don't follow.'

'I'm not one to bear grudges, Bernini. Unlike some people, I shan't hold your father's past against you.' He tilted his head. 'And, of course, I am sure you will want to serve Il Duce in whatever way you can.'

Edoardo nodded, even though he was aware it was a loaded question. Immediately after his father's death, it had been hard to build back the business. He'd just about clambered his way out of the dark hole when war was declared. The past few months had been testing for him, to say the least. He needed to stay on the right side of the law – the fascist law at least.

Manzano licked his lips as his secretary walked through the door with a dish of *gelato*. She set it down, together with a long spoon, in front of him and handed him a napkin. He tucked it into the top of his tunic like a baby's bib.

Edoardo nodded. 'Of course,' he replied, while at the same time wondering why he'd really been summoned to this meeting. This man, devouring *gelato* with gusto when so many of his citizens were going hungry, had an agenda. He always did. *His father had warned him that Manzano never gave without wanting something of at least twice the value in return.* And then it came.

'As you know Herr Hitler was most impressed with our art collection at the Uffizi Gallery when he visited a couple of years ago. He told Professor Loggi he had fallen in love with our city and its culture.'

Edoardo and his father were in the welcoming party for the Nazis. How could he ever forget standing next to the Führer, trying not to inhale the fetid stench of the German's breath as he leered at Botticelli's *Primavera, Allegory of Spring*? The way his piercing blue eyes lusted after the scantily clad mythological figures as they celebrated the most vibrant season, had been unsettling. 'I remember his visit well. The Führer was most taken,' he agreed.

The podesta took another spoonful of *gelato* – chocolate this time. 'He was particularly interested in the Cranachs, of course.'

Of course, thought Edoardo. Lucas Cranach the Elder was best known for his portraits of Hitler's fellow countrymen, of German princes and leaders of the Protestant Reformation, not to mention his seductive women. His paintings had been in the Medici collection for almost four hundred years. Everyone in the art world had known for a while that Adolf Hitler and his deputy Hermann Goering were casting their greedy eyes over great works of European art. Since the Nazis had overrun Paris, Reichsmarschall Goering, who also happened to be the head of the Luftwaffe, was a regular visitor to the Jeu de Paume Museum. Through the grapevine, Edoardo had heard he was helping himself to whatever he fancied to furnish Carinhall, his hunting lodge near Berlin.

Even so, what Manzano said next came as a shock. 'In fact, the Führer was so taken with Florence, he asked Il Duce if they might hold a meeting here again.'

Edoardo jolted in his seat. 'The Führer? He plans to return?'

Manzano grinned as he reached for a sheet of paper on his desk and waved it in the air. 'Indeed, and, as you and your father proved yourself worthy last time, I would like you to be a member of the official escort again.' He looked down at the itinerary. 'How does dinner at the Palazzo Medici Riccardi sound? I am sure Herr Hitler will have questions about the frescoes, and you, with your fluent German and expert knowledge, will be the one to answer them.'

Despite the heat, a cold shiver ran down Edoardo's spine. Manzano might have noticed because his smile dissolved.

'You should be flattered I have chosen you, Signor Bernini, especially after your father's betrayal.'

Admittedly the thought of escorting Hitler again left him a little off balance. The offer was so unexpected. 'I am, sir. Honoured, in fact,' he returned, holding a steady gaze and sounding confident.

The podesta nodded. 'Good,' he said, fixing the dealer with an odd look. 'I liked him. Your father, I mean. I did all I could to help him, you know.'

No. Edoardo didn't know. Eighteen months on and he still knew virtually nothing about his father's dealings or the circumstances surrounding his death. He continued to hold Manzano's gaze, even though it was as intense as the sun on his face through the open window.

'And I would hate to see his son make the same mistakes,' the podesta added.

There was a definite threat in Manzano's tone. *If he refused, would one of the Blackshirt gangs roaming round the city just happen to choose his gallery as a target?* Edoardo wondered. He arranged his mouth into a smile. Defying this man was futile, not to mention dangerous. Is this what happened to his father? Had he found himself in an impossible situation and paid the ultimate price?

'As I said, your Excellency. I will be honoured to accompany the Führer.' While the words didn't leave his mouth lightly, he was sure he could somehow turn the situation to his advantage. His father taught him opportunities came from overcoming obstacles. It was all part of the game, even though when Manzano was involved, he already knew it was a dangerous one.

The podesta slapped the desk with his palms, rattling the spoon in his *gelato* dish. 'Good, that's settled,' he said, rising with difficulty from his seat. 'You will be briefed shortly.'

Edoardo nodded. 'Thank you, sir,' he replied and turned to

find the secretary holding the door for him.

'Oh, and Bernini,' Manzano called after him.

'Podesta?' A knot tightened in his stomach as he swivelled round.

'Make sure *you* don't let me down.'

Chapter 3

'Wake up! Wake up! We've no time to lose!' Agatha's croaky voice sounded in Lina's ear.

A needle of white light lanced through half-open bedroom shutters of Villa Mimosa. At first, she thought she might be dreaming but when she felt the sheets being wrenched from her bed, she sat bolt upright. Her aunt loomed over her as she rubbed sleep from her eyes.

'Donna says they're looting the Uffizi,' Agatha declared, clearly in battle mode. 'We must stop them at once!'

'What? I … Who?' Lina babbled incoherently. She'd slept badly. In fact, ever since war was declared three months before, sleep had been hard to come by. It was as if a black cloud had drifted across Italy's sun, blocking out all light and colour. And now, it seemed Donna, the maid and a regular purveyor of gossip, was the harbinger of more alarming news.

Flinging open the wardrobe, Agatha pulled out the first clothes hanger she found. 'Come, come. Hurry up, dear,' she urged, casting a critical eye over a pale blue suit with a peplum jacket. Lina had long ago ditched the floral patterns, favoured by Agatha and her circle, for sharply cut suits. 'This'll do,' she announced, flinging it on the bed. 'Downstairs in five minutes.'

Lina muttered a mild expletive to herself in Italian but managed to plant her feet onto the marble floor tiles. The shock of the cold under her soles helped clear her head a little. Her septuagenarian aunt may be a whirlwind, but by any standard, this show of strength was a hurricane. Agatha had exited the room even before she'd had time to protest, but over the past few months she'd grown used to her bluster. Her great-aunt's no-nonsense Victorian attitude had driven her mad at first, of course, but she'd learned to cultivate a resilient smile and pay lip service to whatever she said to keep the peace. Outside the walls of Villa Mimosa world leaders may be battling it out, but inside, Lina was keen to ensure harmony reigned.

'Yes, Aunt,' she mumbled as she heard footsteps power along the landing and down the stairs.

After she'd splashed her face with cold water, she peered in the mirror to drag a comb through her thick, dark hair. She knew she'd been lucky to live in Italy. A lot of girls from her old boarding school in England would now be wearing military uniforms, not the latest Milan fashions. Returning to Florence after spending much of her childhood in grey England, was like someone turning on an electric light bulb in a dark room. Everything that surrounded her was so full of colour, vibrant and alive, including Agatha, who'd welcomed her so enthusiastically when her own mother had remarried and wanted nothing more to do with her.

Her aunt was waiting for her in the hall. Lina grabbed her hat and plonked it unthinkingly on her dark head, but Agatha cleared her throat. 'We may be at war, but we mustn't let standards drop,' she remarked, straightening the pillbox before handing her niece her white kid gloves.

'Of course not,' Lina replied, replacing the urge to snap back with just a hint of sarcasm. She decided now was not the time to launch a challenge.

The Uffizi Gallery was less than a half hour on foot from Villa

Mimosa, the charming residence Agatha had occupied for the past forty years. With its cool white facade and lush gardens, the villa was a welcome oasis of calm in contrast to the city centre. There, suspicion and anxiety hung in the air, and the secret police, the OVRA, were a constant presence, not to mention the thuggish Blackshirts.

'Is this really wise?' Lina asked, struggling to keep up. Despite a bad knee, Agatha had practically broken out into a trot along the Via Romana.

'Wise? What do you mean?' asked her aunt.

'Well' – Lina drew breath – 'if they, whoever they may be, are looting the Uffizi, how can we stop them?'

Agatha brandished the white parasol that barely left her side and replied, 'With this, of course.'

She really is incorrigible, Lina thought.

On they marched towards the city centre, and no sooner had they reached the Piazza della Signoria than the hive of activity outside the Uffizi Gallery became apparent. Men in brown overalls buzzed around waiting trucks, hefting crates and what appeared to be huge canvasses.

'So, it's true!' gasped Agatha.

It certainly appeared to Lina that several artworks were being removed from the gallery, although she wasn't as keen to rush to judgement as her aunt. But Agatha didn't hesitate. Drawing her parasol like a sword, she entered the fray.

'I say! I say, you there!' she cried to two passing workmen. They did their level best to ignore her. Boxes were piled high outside the gallery and unprotected canvasses processed in front of them at an alarming rate.

One of the men, however, did stop in front of them but just looked at Agatha and smirked. '*Eh, Georgio. Gli Scorpioni!*' he called to his friend.

Lina stiffened. The *Scorpioni* was the unkind name the Florentines gave her great-aunt's group of elderly English women, who were all either single or widowed. They'd remained in the city long after most of their compatriots had left because of the Great War. They had a reputation for being condescending and unfriendly, with a sting in their tail. The fact that they always marked British celebrations like the King's birthday and St George's Day, which just happened to be Shakespeare's birthday, too, did nothing to endear them to the fascist authorities either. Even she found them infuriating at times. Being so set in their English ways made them an easy target for ridicule, and for the Blackshirts.

Agatha didn't help herself, either. 'Where are your superiors?' she called truculently, wielding her parasol.

Lina tried to calm her. 'Please, Aunt. I'm sure they're acting perfectly properly. We just need to find …' Forlornly she looked around for someone in authority.

'Mind how you go!' Agatha cried. 'Take care, will you?!' she yelled above the running engines of the trucks. 'Angelina, dear,' she pleaded, continuing to flit from crate to crate like a demented bird. 'Can you find out what's going on?' It didn't help that despite being resident in Italy for more than fifty years, Agatha had never made any effort to learn the language. 'They're surely not emptying the gallery. All those Giottos and Botticellis! Where are they taking them?'

Lina asked one of the porters, in Italian, what was going on. 'They're not looting, Aunt,' she assured her as a marble sculpture was paraded before them. 'Just taking precautions because of the war.'

Agatha looked bewildered. 'But where will everything go?' As she spoke, her heavily lidded eyes scanned the piazza in front of the gallery. 'Surely someone is in charge?'

Just then a gentleman, who despite the heat was wearing a deerstalker hat, tweed jacket and knickerbockers, came on the scene. He carried a cane and walked stiffly.

'Ah!' exclaimed Agatha, her arm raised as if flagging down a taxi. 'Professor Loggi', she called, then under her breath to Lina she muttered, 'Just the man.'

The professor, Superintendent of Collections in Tuscany, raised his hat to reveal a frill of silver hair stretching from ear to ear around a bald pate. 'Good day, Mrs Fortescue-Smythe', he greeted.

'Professor Loggi', replied Agatha, with a bob of her head. 'Do you know why these louts are manhandling such priceless treasures?'

Bemused by her indignation, the professor took a breath. 'My dear Mrs Fortescue-Smythe, I can assure you that these "louts" know exactly what they are doing. They are acting on my orders.' He inclined towards her confidentially, putting all his weight on his walking stick, and nodded. 'They are going away for safe-keeping.'

'Safekeeping?' repeated Agatha, a startled look on her face. 'Safekeeping where exactly?'

'Several secure castles have been selected in remote areas outside the city', confided Loggi. He slid a playful look at Lina. 'It is an enormous task, keeping track of all the treasures, and we're very short-staffed. But work goes on behind the scenes. It's all very *hush-hush*.' His forefinger tapped the side of his nose.

Agatha's mouth formed an 'o' but no sound came out. For once she seemed not exactly embarrassed, noted Lina, but a little chastened.

'Thank you for clearing that up, Professor', said Lina, filling the void left by her nonplussed great-aunt. 'It's comforting to know someone is taking care of all these precious artworks.'

True to form, Agatha didn't remain quiet for long. 'I don't think you've met my great-niece, Professor. This is Dr Angelina Leone.' She nudged Lina. 'She is considered an authority on Cranach the Elder, you know', she declared, adding under her breath, 'although why she studies a German painter in Italy, I'll never understand.'

Despite having olive skin, Lina felt the blood rise to her cheeks. Her dark complexion was something she'd inherited from the

Italian father she'd barely known; that together with brown eyes, wavy brown hair and, rather helpfully, Anglo-Italian citizenship.

'Dr Leone?' repeated Loggi, impressed. 'Yes, indeed. I read your paper,' he replied, smiling courteously at Lina from under a neat moustache. 'A fascinating study.'

She was flattered. She'd only completed her doctorate a couple of years before, but her reputation in the field of academia seemed to be spreading.

The professor flicked back to Agatha. 'I'm sure you must be very proud,' he said, a twinkle in his eye. Lina knew she was, although sometimes she thought a rich society husband and grandchildren would probably make her prouder.

He paused then and narrowed his eyes as if a thought had unexpectedly come to him. 'In fact, I plan to visit one of the repositories shortly,' he said, touching his temple. 'Castello Di Montegufoni. A few kilometres south of here.'

Lina frowned. 'But isn't travel banned, Professor?' she asked.

He shrugged. 'This is official business; I am fortunate in that I can come and go freely. So, would you ladies care to join me?' he suggested, smiling at Agatha. 'Just to set your minds at rest.'

Surely, he can't be flirting with her? thought Lina.

If that were the case, then her aunt was a welcome recipient. The lines around her eyes crinkled in a smile. 'That would be most satisfactory, Professor,' she replied. Without so much as a look at Lina she accepted the invitation, adding, 'Thank you. We'd like that very much.'

Chapter 4

Lina was relieved when Professor Loggi's battered green Lancia finally pulled up outside the ancient walls of Castello Di Montegufoni. Being rolled about like a barrel in the back seat, as the car lurched and bounced over dusty Tuscan hills, had left her feeling decidedly sick. Agatha fared a little better, although Lina noticed her hat needed righting after it slipped to one side.

'So, here we are,' said the professor, cranking on the handbrake.

Up until a few weeks ago the medieval castle was home to an eccentric English antiquarian but had since been sequestered by the Italian government as a storage facility for artworks. Professor Loggi opened the passenger door with a broad smile for Agatha, before helping Lina alight. She looked up at the ochre-coloured towers of the fortress as she slid out of the vehicle. It was a beautiful, if rather austere, building, surrounded by dark green fingers of cypress trees.

Theirs was not the only vehicle parked outside. Lina counted four military lorries, with another one wheezing up the hill, a cloud of dust in its wake. A short distance from the trucks, in the shade of oleander bushes, there was also a red Alfa Romeo.

The professor caught Lina's curious look, then frowned when he followed her gaze and spotted the sports car. 'There's only one person I know who drives a car like that,' he muttered.

The three of them made their way up to the castle entrance. They were greeted by an armed guard, who recognised the professor with a smile. After a formal salute he said, 'One of your colleagues is already here, sir.'

'He is not my colleague,' the professor replied dismissively, reaching into his breast pocket for a pen to sign the visitors' register. 'He is an acquaintance.' Plainly, Professor Loggi was not a fan of the driver of the sports car, who'd beaten them to the castle that morning. Underlining his name with a flourish, the professor went inside. 'This way, ladies,' he beckoned.

Passing through the central courtyard of the castle, they remained on the ground floor to enter a series of chambers illuminated by large windows. A constant stream of soldiers carrying paintings flowed past them, directed by an officer. To Lina's dismay, she noticed many of them weren't protected in any way but were simply stacked upright against the walls. One of the men, struggling under the weight of a hugely cumbersome wooden panel dropped his corner. The air filled with curses.

'An Uccello!' gasped Agatha when she realised what was at stake. The professor rushed forwards to look for damage. Mercifully, it seemed none was done.

'Take more care,' Loggi growled at the clumsy soldier. From the insolent expression on his face, Lina doubted the man would.

Still in a state of nervous anxiety, the women followed the soldiers into the next room. There the professor led them to the far left-hand corner.

'Is it really necessary to bring all these pieces from Florence, Professor? I remember you once told me the safest place for a painting is on a w—' But Agatha didn't finish what she was about to say. They'd all stopped in front of a large painting that needed no introduction. For the second time in as many minutes Agatha gasped, and Lina stood statue-still. It may have been painted against a dark background, but the work's luminescence made it stand out from all the others.

'*Primavera*,' murmured Agatha, immediately entranced. 'One of the greatest pieces of Western art.' There was reverence in her voice as she took a few steps nearer.

The professor beamed. 'Magnificent, yes?'

'Yes,' Lina agreed, speaking for Agatha who seemed to have fallen under the painting's spell. Of course, they'd both seen the Botticelli painting many times at its home in the Uffizi, but never so close. Never so intimately.

'Will you have it covered? Protected in some way?' asked Lina, concerned for the artwork's safety. It could easily be damaged by damp or mould, or crack in the heat.

'All in good time,' replied the professor, still gazing at the painting. 'All in good time,' he assured her just as another painted wooden panel, which looked suspiciously like a Ghirlandaio to Lina, was deposited unceremoniously alongside the *Primavera*.

'It doesn't seem right,' muttered Agatha, coming round from her daze. 'This painting. All these wonderful treasures …' She lifted her gaze and looked around the lofty room. Crates were abandoned in no particular order. Poplar panels – the wood favoured by Renaissance artists – were leaning upright against each other, while some were angled like dominoes, poised to topple over at any minute. Then there was the temperature to consider, not to mention the humidity. Both of which were crucial to a painting's preservation, and neither were controlled.

'It is not ideal by any means, but it is the best we can do, dear lady,' replied Loggi. 'We have to save on blankets and straw, I fear.'

Agatha tutted loudly. But said nothing. For once it seemed she was going to hold her tongue, even though Lina could tell she was most disturbed by the makeshift arrangement.

As another painting joined the Ghirlandaio, the professor shepherded the women towards the door. On the way out he said to Lina, 'As a Cranach expert I'm sure you'd like to see a couple we have here,' he said. Scratching his head, he muttered, 'Yes, now where might they be? Perhaps …' He gestured to the next salon. 'Follow me, ladies, if you please.' No sooner had they entered the room, than Loggi stopped in his tracks.

A younger man in a well-cut light-grey suit and fedora was crouching in front of a medium-sized portrait, making notes in a pocketbook.

'There you are, Bernini,' called the professor, approaching him. 'I was told you were here.'

Edoardo stood upright and whipped off his hat to reveal his strikingly handsome face and large, deep-set eyes with long lashes.

'Professor, good morning. I'm glad to see you.'

Loggi seemed unsettled by the meeting. 'Then fortune has smiled on you,' he replied, although there was no smile on his lips. Seeing Edoardo's gaze fall on the two ladies, he was duty-bound to introduce them. Turning to Lina and Agatha he said, 'Signor Bernini, this is Mrs Fortescue-Smythe, and her great-niece, Signorina Leone.'

Edoardo bowed formally. 'I am delighted to meet you both,' he replied, his white teeth now showing in the wake of a disarming smile. But he switched back quickly into a businesslike mode. 'Professor, I was wondering—'

'Bernini?' interrupted Agatha. She wasn't prepared to let him off so lightly. 'Of the Bernini Gallery?'

'Yes, signora,' replied the dealer. Lina noted his expression snagged on her words, as if anticipating a sting in the dowager's tail. It turned out he was right to be concerned.

Looking at the younger man disapprovingly, Agatha said, 'I hope you're not planning on removing anything from here, young man!'

Lina cringed. Her great-aunt's comment implied Signor Bernini was up to no good. By the look on his face, he, too, was taken aback, but recovered himself and forced out a laugh.

'Quite the opposite,' he replied. 'I am sure we are all here because of our wish to protect the city's masterpieces.'

Agatha didn't reply, but Lina saw her exchange a knowing look with her host. The dealer, nevertheless, ploughed on undaunted. Turning to the professor he said, 'I wondered if we might talk in private.'

Loggi turned, but Lina could see he was unhappy. 'Ladies, please feel free to browse at your leisure. I shall return shortly, but in the meantime I'm sure Signorina Leone will find the Cranachs most interesting.'

As the professor and the art dealer disappeared into another chamber, Lina and Agatha continued to marvel at the paintings, even though they were concerned about their protection – concerns that were soon justified.

'Look at this,' said Lina, shaking her head at a portrait of a bearded nobleman. 'And here,' she cried, switching her attention to another painting featuring the figure of Venus. The Cranachs had both been abandoned in a mouldy corner.

'There's nothing to protect them,' Lina complained as, a few moments later, she caught sight of Signor Bernini on his way out. He was looking troubled. He saw her, too, and raised his hat, but this time there was no disarming smile, no flash of white teeth as at their introduction.

Loggi followed hot on his heels but stopped at the door to watch the younger man power down the castle steps. The professor turned then and remarked to Agatha, standing close behind, 'A wolf in sheep's clothing.'

'Like father, like son, I suppose,' she agreed, watching Bernini stride to his car.

Lina remained silent, as she, too, observed the dealer jump into his Alfa Romeo. He drove off, spinning his wheels and churning up a plume of dust as he went. Whoever this debonair man was, he not only had a temper, but a past, too. Both her great-aunt and Professor Loggi were hostile towards him. Clearly, they felt he wasn't to be trusted. But why?

Chapter 5

October 1940

It rained on the day of Adolf Hitler's second visit to Florence. Those who mistrusted the German Führer murmured it was as if all Raphael's angels were shedding tears at having to welcome the devil into their midst. Most Florentines, however, went out to greet him. Edoardo Bernini was one of them. For the past week streets had been swept, beggars taken away and swastikas draped on official buildings alongside the banners and flags emblazoned with the *fleur-de-lys* of Florence. The Führer had arrived by train earlier and been whisked to a concert. He was currently meeting Mussolini and various ministers in the Palazzo Vecchio before dinner at the Palazzo Medici Riccardi.

Knotting his tie in front of the mirror in the apartment above the gallery, Edoardo knew he needed to look his best. Appearances were everything, but he kept being distracted by the reflection of his father's portrait on the wall behind. He'd chosen to sketch him in pen and ink, sitting in his favourite high-backed chair, looking distinguished with wings of hair bracketing high cheekbones and deep-set eyes. At the time Edoardo had been pleased with his efforts, blissfully unaware that Henrico Bernini was stealing art from the city's museums. Studying Fine Art in Germany meant he had no idea what his father got up to in his absence.

Five o'clock and still the rain fell. Taking an umbrella, Edoardo walked to the palazzo, skirting the thousands of excited, flag-waving citizens squeezed into the square, waiting to cheer the two leaders when they appeared on the balcony. Despite the downpour, it was a remarkable spectacle.

On arrival, Edoardo presented his papers to a guard at the entrance and was allowed to pass. Once inside, he was met by a pompous official who asked him to wait in a modest room – modest compared with most of the rooms, it didn't have any frescoes on its walls and ceiling. Edoardo glanced at the clutch of notes in his hand. He knew a thing or two about the Luca Giordano masterpieces adorning the palazzo's great salons and started to refresh his memory. But then the recollection of his visit to Castello Di Montegufoni returned. The encounter with Professor Loggi's guests had been awkward. The old woman was quite formidable, and far too outspoken, quite typical of the English he'd met, but her niece, Signorina Leone, had caught his attention. With that hair and those eyes, she looked pure Italian, but there was something intriguing about her, as if something smouldered under that cool exterior.

An hour or so later, word came of the Führer's imminent arrival. 'Signor Bernini.' A voice called his name. He looked up to see the pompous official again. 'It is time.'

Edoardo's stomach clenched. He wanted to get this over with; do what was asked of him and no more. The welcoming party was already lined up in the gallery, whose walls and ceiling were designed to show off the glories of the Medici family. He joined the others and a few minutes later Hitler and Mussolini appeared side by side. Podesta Manzano, his massive chest covered with undeserved medals, followed behind. Progressing along the line, the leaders shook hands with various officials and dignitaries. Edoardo stiffened as they drew nearer, every sinew of his body straining to look confident and in control.

'This is Signor Bernini, Führer. He studied Fine Art in Berlin,' said Manzano when he reached Edoardo. 'He and his father escorted you to the Uffizi on your first visit.'

The familiar reek wafted in front of Edoardo as Hitler looked deep into his eyes. Was that a flicker of recognition? Edoardo couldn't be sure as his lips jerked into a smile and he shook the Führer's cold hand.

'I'm sure you are aware the Riccardi family moved to Florence from Cologne in the fourteenth century. They were German,' Hitler remarked in an even voice. There was a difficult pause until Mussolini, at his side, laughed at the remark. Manzano joined in.

Il Duce waved a hand. 'So, all these frescoes were commissioned by a German, you say!' he cried, patting Hitler playfully on the back. 'Very good, my friend. Very good.'

Did Hitler have his eyes on Giordano's frescoes, as well as the Cranachs, Edoardo wondered? There seemed no limits to the Führer's claims on Florence's art.

Mercifully, as the schedule was running late, there was no time for a full tour of the palazzo as planned. Hitler seemed duly impressed by what he saw, but the frescoes were not his priority. At the dinner table Edoardo sat five places away, so wasn't included directly in any conversation. After short speeches at the end of dinner, it was time for Hitler to get back on his train.

They all stood as the official party left the dining room. Relieved the ordeal was over, Edoardo decided he needed a cigarette. But when he reached into his pocket, he remembered he'd left the packet in the anteroom where he'd waited earlier on. He excused himself from the dull curator he'd been sitting next to and found his way back. But before he did, he happened to glance into another salon where the door remained ajar. There, to his surprise, he caught a glimpse of Mussolini. He stopped and doubled back to see he was still with Hitler. The two men were standing in front of an easel admiring a portrait – a Renaissance portrait of a man by the looks of it, although he couldn't be sure.

Careful not to arouse suspicion from the guard posted outside, Edoardo craned his neck to see the leaders nodding and shaking hands. Two of Hitler's aids then picked up the painting. As they approached the door, Edoardo walked on. Had Il Duce just given the Führer a souvenir of his visit? One of the city's masterpieces? It certainly looked that way. If he'd wanted a cigarette before, after what he'd just seen, Edoardo needed one.

The day after Hitler's visit, Lina came downstairs to find Agatha in the morning room of Villa Mimosa. Over her usual toast and marmalade – much harder to come by since war was declared – she was staring at a copy of a special souvenir edition of Florence's official fascist newspaper *Il Bargello*. Below the headline that the Führer's visit had coincided with Mussolini's invasion of northern Greece, something else in the fascist newspaper had grabbed her attention, even though she could barely read a word of Italian.

'Did Donna bring that?' asked Lina, pouring herself coffee.

Agatha looked up distractedly. 'What, dear? Oh, yes. Yes, she did. She said despite the rain, the city was packed for that dreadful little man's visit yesterday.' Since the start of the London Blitz, Agatha always referred to the German Führer in derogatory terms. When she returned to study the newspaper, Lina saw her eyes were fixed on a particular photograph on an inside page.

'Something interesting?' she asked, tilting her head to focus.

Once more her aunt looked up, only this time she was frowning. Then, jabbing the newspaper, she shunted it across the polished table, a look of disgust on her face. Lina took the copy and scrutinised the photographs. It wasn't long before she saw what had so irked Agatha. Taken at the Palazzo Medici Riccardi, there was one that showed Adolf Hitler shaking hands with a young man who looked vaguely familiar. Lina glanced up.

'Is that the dealer we met at Montegufoni? Signor Bernini?' she asked.

'Indeed, it is,' Agatha replied, looking down her nose at the newspaper as if it were giving off an offensive odour. 'Cosying up to the Nazis now, but then I shouldn't be surprised. He'd sell his own soul if he could be guaranteed a large cheque in return.'

'I see,' replied Lina, suddenly recalling her encounter with the dealer at the castle. At the time she'd found him very … what would be the word? *Enigmatic*. But according to Agatha and Professor Loggi, he was a man of few principles and only out for himself. Returning to the unsettling image, it seemed they could be right. In an odd sort of way, as if she'd expected more of this dark, handsome stranger, she couldn't help but feel let down.

Chapter 6

As the strains of a Puccini opera drifted from the gramophone through his apartment, Edoardo lit a cigarette, but he'd barely had time to slump into an armchair before the doorbell rang. He wasn't expecting anyone. He listened to Signora Bianchi's husky voice echoing downstairs. A moment later the matronly, black-clad housekeeper was at the salon door.

'Signor Manzano is here to see you,' she announced, before her hawkish gaze noticed Edoardo didn't have an ash tray for his cigarette. She tutted and reached for one from a sideboard. 'How many times?' she grumbled under her breath. She'd worked for his late father for several years and still treated him like a child.

As the housekeeper set down a pewter ashtray with a clatter, the dealer frowned. Why would Manzano visit him personally?

'Show him up, if you please,' he replied. 'And see to it we're not disturbed,' he added.

He stubbed out the cigarette and stood to lift the needle off the record, just as Manzano appeared on the threshold. His great, untidy bulk filled the doorway.

'Sir. An honour. Please, take a seat,' said Edoardo. 'Brandy?'

'Why not?' The podesta clumped to a nearby chair and sat, watching Edoardo pour his drink from a decanter on a sideboard.

'Have one for yourself, too,' he said. 'Then we can toast your success together.'

Confused, Edoardo frowned. He handed Manzano his drink. 'I'm not sure what you mean.'

A grin stretched the podesta's large mouth. 'You made quite an impression on the Führer yesterday,' he said, taking a gulp.

Edoardo shrugged as he poured himself a brandy. 'But I hardly spent any time with Herr Hitler. His schedule did not permit it,' he replied, adding, 'regrettably.'

The podesta shook his head. 'No. No. The Führer was taken with your manner, your knowledge and, of course, your excellent command of the German language.'

Edoardo sat opposite Manzano. 'That's most generous of the Führer, but I—'

'In fact, he was so impressed,' Manzano cut in, 'that he recommended you to his deputy.'

Edoardo, taking a sip of his brandy, spluttered. 'I'm sorry.'

'Apparently *Reichsmarschall* Goering has been looking for someone trustworthy in the city for a while now.'

The words crashed into Edoardo's skull. 'I don't follow.'

'He needs someone to assist him.'

'Assist him?' repeated Edoardo. 'In what exactly?'

Manzano took another gulp of brandy. 'We live in unusual times.' He shrugged. 'Friends must stick together. As a dealer yourself, you understand the need to make trade-offs.'

Edoardo narrowed his eyes. *Where was all this leading?* 'Trade-offs?' he repeated.

Manzano grunted as he leaned forwards. 'The *Reichsmarschall* wants you to oversee an operation for him.'

'Me?' Edoardo couldn't hide his surprise.

'Yes. There is a consignment that needs to be supervised.'

'A consignment? A consignment of what?'

The podesta shook his bullish head. It was clear he didn't want to say too much. 'It's just a question of travelling with the merchandise and seeing it safely delivered. That is all you need to know.'

Now the muscles in Edoardo's neck stiffened as the nature of this *merchandise* occurred to him. Was Goering about to start stealing art from Italy just as he was already doing in France? 'But surely …' he began, yet Manzano was adamant.

'There is no need for you to know, my friend. Suffice to say you play by the rules, and you will be rewarded handsomely.' He drained his glass and heaved himself up from the chair to hold out a hand. 'That is the deal. I trust you will accept it.'

Silently, Edoardo regarded the hand held before him. If he didn't take it, the OVRA could make life very difficult for him indeed. His father would have seen it as a unique opportunity, no doubt. An offer from one of the Third Reich's most powerful leaders. Money was to be made and much more besides, refusal wasn't an option. So why not? As the podesta's hot hand was presented to him, he decided he'd take it with enthusiasm. He'd be foolish not to seize the chance.

'I will let you have details of the rendezvous when I know them myself,' Manzano told him, lumbering towards the door. 'Oh, and Bernini.' He turned.

'Yes.'

'You will need your passport.'

Three weeks later, towards midnight on the appointed day, a car pulled up outside the Bernini Gallery. Edoardo slid into the back seat next to Manzano. The car smelled of cheap perfume. He imagined the podesta had just dropped off one of his mistresses. A glass screen was drawn behind the driver so their conversation couldn't be overheard.

'So, now will you tell me where we are going?' Edoardo asked. He wasn't nervous. Just curious. He wanted to see for himself if the rumours were true.

'You'll see soon enough,' replied the podesta, tucking into a focaccia, wrapped in paper. 'You've brought your passport as instructed?'

In reply Edoardo took it from his pocket and waved it with a smile.

They drove on in silence until a few minutes later they arrived at the stockyard, at Florence's central railway station. The curfew meant the place was virtually deserted apart from a few guards and *Carabinieri* on patrol along the ill-lit concourse and platforms. As they pulled up, Manzano wiped his greasy fingers on his handkerchief and brushed the crumbs off his uniform. The driver first opened Manzano's door, then Edoardo's, just as the loud rumble of a large military truck pulled up outside the freight depot.

'Right on time,' said the podesta with a smug smile. 'Come.'

The two men strode over to the depot's high metal gates. The guards saluted. They were expected. An unmarked goods train was already waiting, the doors to one of its wagons wide open. Edoardo thrust his hands into his jacket pockets. The night was chilly, and he shivered.

'Here we are,' replied Manzano, turning to follow a trolley loaded with crates as it overtook them. Several soldiers appeared from nowhere to unload the large wooden boxes into the waiting freight wagon.

Edoardo nodded. 'Do they contain what I think they do?'

Manzano's rubbery lips twitched. 'If you're thinking a few paintings, a couple of sculptures, and the odd ancient object, then yes, you are right.'

Even before Hitler's second visit to the city, there'd been talk of valuable artefacts mysteriously disappearing, and now he'd seen a painting being gifted to the Führer with his own eyes, this illicit looting no longer surprised him.

'Goering has requested these?' he asked calmly. He guessed the consignment would probably be heading for the *Reichsmarschall*'s hunting lodge, near Berlin.

'Yes.'

'So, I am going to Germany?'

'Austria,' Manzano replied. 'Innsbruck, to be precise. Easier that way and there is minimal paperwork. No customs declarations and no *notifica*.'

Edoardo nodded his acceptance, while holding down his surprise. *Notifica* were orders prohibiting certain artworks of cultural importance from leaving Italy. He'd had one placed on a sculpture he'd sold to an English buyer once, unaware of its provenance. But now Germany seemed to be looting Italy's treasures with Mussolini's blessing. 'And,' Manzano carried on, 'the import tax has been already paid by our Ministry of Foreign Affairs. So much easier that way.'

The dealer was thankful they were standing in the shadows so Manzano couldn't see the look on his face. *The Italian government was sanctioning the removal of its own artworks, but paying tax for the Germans?* That was on another level. As an opportunist himself, he almost admired the audacity of it.

'There must be a lot of work involved, sourcing these pieces. I hope there is some benefit for you, podesta,' said Edoardo disingenuously. He knew Manzano wasn't doing this just to cosy up to the Germans.

Throwing back his head, the podesta laughed. 'You mean what's in it for you?' he asked. 'Just like your father.'

Edoardo shrugged.

'You'll get commission on each shipment. We'll discuss details later.' He raised his hand as a crate trundled past and the guard stopped. Tapping on the wooden lid, he said, 'Sealed, you see. They are to arrive that way. They must remain unopened. That is why you are required to travel with them.'

Edoardo patted down his overcoat. He needed a cigarette. Manzano offered him one of his from a silver case, then pressed his lips together in a line. 'Discretion, Bernini,' he said. 'As a dealer, you must appreciate the need to be discreet when such valuable pieces are at stake.'

'I understand,' he replied.

It was an eight-hour journey to the Austrian border, to Innsbruck. Edoardo reckoned he should be back in Florence the following evening. All the same, he didn't relish the journey, but long before Manzano handed him his papers, he knew the die was cast.

Chapter 7

December 1940

A letter was waiting on a silver salver on the hall table at Villa Mimosa when Lina arrived home from the Uffizi. Ever since war was declared she'd been keeping her head down, researching her book on Lucas Cranach at the university library, and hoping to avoid catching the eye of the fascist authorities. She'd witnessed a colleague being beaten up by the secret police simply for being Jewish and had heard all manner of horror stories from students. And now this. It was what she had been dreading for a while. In Britain, thousands of Italians had already been banished to internment camps on the Isle of Man. *Could this be the payback?*

'A *fascista* came,' Donna explained, emerging from the kitchen wiping her hands on her apron. She was the only remaining servant in the household.

'A *fascista*?' It was Agatha. As unfortunate timing would have it, she'd just arrived home and caught Lina with the letter in her hand. Relieving herself of her unfashionably large hat in front of the hall mirror, she frowned when she saw it. 'Oh, dear, that looks rather official.'

Lina was holding the envelope as if it were an unexploded

bomb. It was stamped with the fascist emblem and addressed to
I Residenti Inglesi. When Britain was at war with Italy anything
marked 'The English Residents' spelled trouble. She'd hoped to
open it in private, but Agatha's sudden arrival left her little choice.

'Well, aren't you going to open it?'

'I suppose I'd better,' Lina replied, taking a paper knife and
slitting the top edge of the envelope. Inside was a typewritten
letter in Italian. Her mouth went dry as she translated aloud.

To Whom It May Concern,

*In light of current hostilities, all British citizens must report to the
Palazzo Vecchio within the next seven days to register their details
for internment. Failure to do so will result in immediate arrest.*

Cesari Manzano (Podesta of Florence)

The message couldn't be clearer.

'Internment?' repeated Agatha, shock puckering her face. 'Oh,
my goodness. It makes us sound like common criminals.'

Lina suspected the other women had received similar letters.
Now it was the turn of the British to be interned in Italy and she
doubted whether the fascists would have any regard at all for the
welfare of their charges, especially the old and infirm.

'You don't think they'd do that to us, do you?' asked Agatha,
reaching for the console table to steady herself. 'Oh, my dear,
they couldn't possibly do that, could they?'

Underneath her aunt's formidable exterior, Lina knew there
was a vulnerability she tried, and usually succeeded, to hide. She'd
lost her husband Reginald seven years ago – not to mention a
daughter in infancy – and although proving herself capable and
independent, Lina could tell her bravura was only for show.

'Don't worry,' she replied, putting an arm around Agatha's slight
frame. 'There's probably been some mistake.' Despite her soothing
words, it was obvious to her that Manzano and his minions were
keen to rid the city of 'enemy aliens'. Knowing how the fascists
worked, it was only a matter of time before the English ladies,
too, were carted off to some godforsaken camp and left to rot for

the duration of the war.

As she guided her aunt to an armchair, Lina felt her birdlike body trembling. Although she'd never admit it, Agatha Fortescue-Smythe was afraid.

'Perhaps I could go and have a word at the town hall,' Lina suggested. After all, having dual citizenship put her in a unique position. 'There's surely been some misunderstanding. You've lived here for most of your life. So have the other ladies. You're practically Italian,' she said, even though none of them spoke Italian and rather looked down on Florentines. 'Given the circumstances, they might make an allowance,' she said, hoping to reassure, even though she herself very much doubted it.

The courtyard of the magnificent Palazzo Vecchio was a scene of biblical chaos straight out of a Renaissance fresco. Yet among the haggard men, the anxious women and the bawling babies, there were several faces Lina recognised from the Gran Caffè Doney. Among those waiting in line to register were Lord and Lady Strathmore and their butler from Oxford. Mr and Mrs Witherspoon, who used to run a boarding house in the Via Panzani, were there too, as was Mr Bevan, the owner of the English bookshop forced to close the year before. He and his wife were desperately trying to keep their four young children and a dog – a long-haired, little mongrel – under control. There was another queue for French citizens, too. But everyone waiting in line had something in common. They all looked as if they were facing the Final Judgement.

'Signorina Leone.' Above the general hum of voices, Lina heard her name. She turned. Rodney Ponting was standing in line, fanning himself with his Panama. 'Are you here to register?' he asked.

She shook her head, knowing how fortunate she was to possess dual nationality. 'No. No, I'm here to see if I can ask for an exemption for my aunt and the other English ladies,' she replied.

It was hard to make herself heard over the noise of the Bevans' yapping dog.

A look of alarm pulled Mr Ponting's face tight. 'But isn't internment like house arrest, or have I got that wrong?' He leaned in. 'You don't think they're going to lock us in some terrible camp, do you?'

Lina's lips twitched. 'I'm sure they wouldn't do that,' she said, stretching her mouth into a smile, but inside she feared that was exactly what the fascists planned. 'If you'll excuse me …' She decided to take a leaf out of her aunt's book. *Go straight to the top if you want results*, Agatha would always say. So, seeing the chaos, she determined to speak with Podesta Manzano directly. Of course, she only knew him by reputation, and, on the Florentine grapevine, she'd heard he was boorish and corrupt and had only risen to power because he was a childhood friend of Mussolini's. But all Italians loved to do deals, Lina told herself. Hopefully, he was no exception.

The directory on the wall told her the podesta's office was upstairs. Even though the thought of negotiating with such a man intimidated her, she'd tackled some crusty old academics in her time and told herself he wouldn't be that different. She also dared to imagine he might possess a shred of decency. Was it too much to ask him to make an exception for a group of vulnerable, elderly ladies who posed no threat at all?

She'd just taken her first steps towards the vast monumental staircase when the Bevans' dog let out an unearthly yowl. Whipping round, she saw a bundle of fur flying through the air and hitting a nearby wall. The poor creature had just felt the full force of a fascist boot. The Bevan children wailed at the sight and rushed to help the stunned pet. Several people shook their heads in shock and a few even left the queue to see what was going on. A sense that something unacceptable had just happened seemed to ripple down the lines and voices were raised. The guard became the object of abuse. Women started shouting at him and he went on the defensive, grabbing his rifle from his shoulder and aiming at the small crowd gathering round him. Another guard came to his aid, followed by another, all with their rifles pointed at the uneasy crowd

Seeing the mayhem deteriorate, Lina decided to take advantage of the chaos. While the guards were distracted, she hurried directly up the staircase and down the corridor to arrive unchallenged at the podesta's office.

'Podesta Manzano is a very busy man,' said his secretary, seated in the small anteroom. With her very low-cut blouse, Lina doubted the young woman had been recruited for her office skills alone. She glanced through the open door to see a heavily built man with a polished, hairless head who could've stepped straight out of a Caravaggio. He was taking a telephone call.

'Then shoot over their heads,' she heard him say. Was the situation in the courtyard spiralling out of control?

Switching back to the secretary, Lina persisted. 'I appreciate that,' she said, 'but I was hoping he might be able to see me.'

The secretary was, however, adamant. 'I'm sorry, signorina. You will have to write to him for an appointment.'

Lina took a deep breath to argue her case further, but just then the office door opened wide, and the gap was filled by Podesta Manzano.

'Is there a problem?' he asked, his eyes locking on to hers.

The secretary broke in. 'This woman wishes to speak with you, sir. I told her—'

His rubbery lips stretched into a leering smile and Lina noticed a flake of pastry at one corner. 'You told her that I always make time for a beautiful woman, I hope,' he replied. 'Come in, please, Signorina …'

'Leone,' Lina replied, as she stepped inside the office feeling like a Christian about to confront a lion at the Coliseum. The large chaise longue covered in silk cushions and the scent of cheap perfume did nothing to reassure her. This was a mistake.

A terrible mistake. What could she have been thinking?

'What is it you wished to see me about, *signorina*?' Manzano asked, shutting the door firmly behind her and gesturing to a chair in front of his desk.

Her throat was clogged with misgivings. She cleared it with a cough. 'It's about this,' she replied, fumbling in her handbag for the official letter. 'I'm here on behalf of my great-aunt Mrs Fortescue-Smythe and her English friends.'

Manzano glanced at the letter before tossing it aside. It landed near a plate with a half-eaten pastry on it. 'The *Scorpioni*, yes?' he asked.

Lina cringed at the nickname. She also wondered how he'd heard of them, but then again, the women's eccentricities were widely known in the city. She might have known pleading on their behalf would meet with derision. There was little sympathy for them. 'They are foreigners. They need to register,' he said dismissively, easing himself into his chair. 'But you … you are not English,' he added with a wink.

'I'm half English, half Italian,' she replied self-consciously, not returning his gaze. This meeting was not going well.

'You are too beautiful to be English,' he came back.

Lina took a deep breath. 'I'd rather we talked about the English ladies, if you don't mind,' she continued, the tension mounting in her chest. 'They're worried they might be sent away, you see.' She hesitated to say the word *interned*, but Manzano had no such qualms.

'Sent away? Interned, you mean? But of course,' he replied, waving a fat hand in the air. She supposed they were just names on a list to him. Not real people, with real feelings and lives. His bald head glinted in the winter sunshine streaming through the window as he added, 'They could be spies, traitors, for all I know.'

Lina felt her stomach convulse at the accusation. 'I can assure you they are no such thing, sir,' she protested. 'They are all in their seventies and eighties and take no interest in Italian politics.'

The podesta threw back his head and laughed. 'And why should you care about these old women?'

Those 'old women' as he called them, were her family now. They were all she had and, despite the fact some of them were grumpy and self-opinionated, deep down she knew their hearts were in the right place. She felt fiercely protective of them. 'As I said, my aunt is among them,' she replied.

Manzano narrowed his eyes that were barely visible under his thick brows. 'You say you are half English.'

Lina shifted uncomfortably in her seat. 'My mother is English. My father was Italian, but I have dual nationality.'

'I see. You are a fortunate young woman.' His gaze was playing on her face and travelling south, making her feel even more uncomfortable. He leaned back in his chair. 'So, what is it that you want of me, signorina?' He picked up a linen napkin from his desk.

Perhaps now she might get somewhere. 'I would very much like you to make an exemption for the ladies, because of their age,' she replied, unable to take her eyes off Manzano's bulbous fingers as he wiped them suggestively one by one on his napkin in front of her.

'Would you indeed? And if I did show them mercy?'

Her head shot up. 'If you did?' He wanted a trade-off. A deal. No wonder Agatha always warned her against Italian men.

'What would you give me, Signorina Leone? I am a reasonable man, but naturally I would want something in return for the women's freedom.'

Lina feared this might happen. She had to think quickly. English logic overrode her Italian urge to slap this ogre's face. 'I could … I could …' She cast around the room as if looking for an object that might inspire her and found it on the wall next to the portrait of Il Duce. 'I could verify your paintings,' she blurted.

Manzano's brows lifted, while his bullish neck retracted. 'And what do you know about art?' he sneered.

'I know about Renaissance art.'

'Renaissance art?' he repeated with a smirk.

'I have studied it for many years,' she replied calmly, clamping down her natural anger, both Italian and English, at this man's arrogance.

'Well, well,' the podesta chuckled. 'So, not just a pretty face.' His fingers drummed on his desk. 'Experts in this field are in demand at the moment, with so many artworks in transit. Forgers are having a field day.'

Lina gulped down her repulsion. 'If it meant you would guarantee my great-aunt and her friends would not be arrested and interned, I could assist you.'

A laugh now, deep and slow, as if Manzano were picturing her leaning over him at his desk. She pictured him, too, and the idea of being close enough to feel his breath on her skin filled her with disgust. There had to be a way out, but she would think of it later. Right now, if it meant Agatha and the others would be saved from an internment camp, where the hardship could kill them, she had to risk it.

Manzano's hands slapped the desk with a dull thud. 'Very well, Signorina Leone, we have a deal,' he told her, reaching across the desk to shake her hand. His was hot and clammy as it gripped hers. Forcing herself to look at him squarely to show her professionalism, Lina felt his grip tighten. Now she knew what it was like to sell your soul to the devil.

All was quiet in the courtyard when Lina made her way back down the staircase. The lines of anxious families had disappeared. She'd no idea where they'd gone. There was no sign that less than half an hour before, the space had been rammed with people. It was only when she was about to leave through the main door that she noticed a bright red smear on the tiles where the Bevans' little dog had stood barking.

Chapter 8

The Brancacci Chapel inside the church of Santa Maria del Carmine was a place of peace and quiet; normally somewhere to engage in prayer and contemplation and marvel at the glorious frescoes that adorned its walls. On this chilly winter afternoon, however, the silence of the chapel was broken by an unlikely assemblage. It was a Friday, and every Friday afternoon the English Ladies' Arts Appreciation Society would meet in a pre-arranged venue to learn about a particular aspect of Renaissance art.

War was spreading like a virus and had already changed many things. All the city's English hotels, bookshops and tearooms had been forced to close and Lina had learned several British citizens were already interned. When she'd broken the news of her meeting with Podesta Manzano to Agatha and the others, she hadn't been entirely honest. She told them she'd come to some sort of arrangement but hadn't gone into detail.

'Oh, my dear. That's wonderful. I knew you'd be able to talk sense into this podesta, or whatever he calls himself,' Agatha had said over tea the following afternoon at the Villa Mimosa.

'We can't thank you enough.' Miss Harrowby beamed, clasping her hands.

'No, no, we can't,' agreed Lady Felstein.

All the women were most grateful for Lina's intervention without having the slightest notion of the price Manzano wished to exact from her. Of course she didn't intend to pay it, but at that moment, she had no idea how she could possibly extricate herself from his grasp without sacrificing the women's freedom. In fact, news of their exemption made Agatha even more determined to plough on with her weekly attempts to 'educate' her circle of friends about Renaissance art.

That afternoon, Agatha planned to offer the ladies her considered critique of *The Expulsion*, Masaccio's fresco depicting Adam and Eve's fall from grace. The usual crowd was present; Miss Harrowby, whose asthma was clearly plaguing her again, Mrs Clutterbuck, dressed in all her finery, and Lady Felstein who, looking serene in azure blue silk, stood at the front so she could hear what Agatha said. Mr Ponting had excused himself with a headache. Last to arrive, but by no means least, came the American, Miss Gloria Giltrap, complete with camera. As ever, she was keener on photographing the frescoes than listening to Agatha's talk.

Fortunately, there were few visitors to the chapel that day. The ladies, all covering their heads with hats or black mantillas as the church required, entered via three marble steps, and now formed a little circle around Agatha. Lina was always careful to keep to the back. That way, if her attention just happened to stray, she might avoid her aunt's public disapproval.

Agatha was exhorting everyone to gaze up at the scene in the Garden of Eden when Adam and Eve were expelled. Eve looked so deeply distressed at being cast out of paradise that Lina found it hard not to be moved.

'Ladies, we see here a prime example of …' As Agatha waxed lyrical about Masaccio's use of light and perspective, Lina's gaze started to flit around the chapel. The pews were dotted with elderly women in black, kneeling in prayer. She supposed many of them had lost husbands and sons in the Great War and now their daughters would soon be losing their husbands and sons, too. But just as her heart ached at the thought, she spotted a man lighting a votive candle in a nearby side chapel. Edoardo Bernini.

She watched him make the sign of the cross and stand thoughtfully staring at the candle flame, head bowed, before kneeling in a nearby pew. After their last encounter, Lina had been left wondering why he'd had some sort of disagreement with Professor Loggi. But if she was being perfectly honest, she'd also just wanted to see him again. There was something mysterious, something dangerous about him, that attracted her. How had the professor described him? *A wolf in sheep's clothing.* Then, of course, there'd been the photograph of him shaking Hitler's hand in the newspaper. But in the report, he was described as 'an art expert'. She supposed he'd had no choice if he was asked to meet the German Führer. Agatha had warned her away from him, of course, but to Lina a warning was as good as a challenge. *You always were a stubborn child*, was one of her great-aunt's mantras whenever they disagreed.

She turned back to Agatha, still in full flow. Now was a good time. She slid quietly away from the group towards the pews where the art dealer knelt in prayer. His eyes, however, were clearly not closed, because as she walked slowly towards him, he lifted his gaze. Lina looked away pretending not to notice him, but just as she passed, he whispered her name.

'Signorina Leone!'

Switching round quickly, she realised he was out of the pew and standing behind her. She feigned shock. 'Signor Bernini.'

'I'm sorry. I didn't mean to startle you, but we met at the Castello Di Montegufoni.'

Of course he didn't have to remind her where they had met. She wouldn't ever forget that first meeting. But her English half told her to play it cool.

'I remember,' she replied calmly when her heart was beating wildly. 'What are you doing here?' His gaze dipped for a moment and Lina realised she shouldn't pry. Inquisitiveness, or just down-right nosiness. It was another trait she seemed to have picked up from Agatha. 'Forgive me, I didn't …'

'It would have been my father's birthday. He passed almost two years ago.'

'I'm sorry,' she replied, seeing a sadness in his eyes, but then she remembered Agatha's cryptic comment to Professor Loggi. *Like father, like son.* She'd wondered at the time what she'd meant but when she'd pressed her later, she'd clammed up and refused to speak on the matter.

He nodded. 'And you?'

Lina smiled and turned her head towards the Brancacci Chapel. Agatha was pointing animatedly at the fresco depicting the expulsion to her – reasonably attentive – audience. 'My great-aunt—' began Lina, but she stopped when an old woman further along the pew cast a frown and lifted her finger to her lips. Edoardo nodded apologetically and retreated into the shadows. Lina followed.

'She is an expert in Renaissance art?' he asked, casting in the direction of the chapel.

'Yes. Yes, she is,' Lina replied. For some reason she felt awkward. 'You're welcome to come and listen,' she suggested in a whisper.

He pulled an amused face at the idea. 'I hardly think—' he began, as if an elderly English woman could teach him anything, but then, realising his attitude had offended, he stopped abruptly.

'It's amazing what one can learn with an open mind,' she shot back.

There was a hint of humility when he smiled at her again, but then looking beyond her, he said, 'I think you are being summoned.'

Lina tracked his gaze to see Agatha was indeed beckoning her vigorously.

'Yes. Yes, I am,' she said, frostily. 'Good day, Signor Bernini.'

He bowed gallantly. 'Good day, Signorina Leone.'

Agatha was clearly displeased when she'd realised Lina had strayed.

'What were you doing? Did I see you with a man?' she interrogated as soon as the little party began to break up a few minutes later. Perhaps it was because she'd witnessed the damage Lina's drunken Italian father had wrought, leaving a four-year-old girl and her mother destitute, that made her so infuriatingly protective. It certainly explained how one withering look from Aunt Agatha's watchful eyes was enough to send any Italian suitor running a mile.

Lina knew her aunt wouldn't like it, but she answered truthfully anyway. 'I was talking to Signor Bernini.'

Agatha snatched at a breath. 'Bernini.'

'Yes,' replied Lina, sticking to her guns. 'He was lighting a candle for his father. I couldn't ignore him.'

'I've told you before, you may be a grown woman, but you'd do well to keep away from that man, my dear. If he's anything like his father, he is trouble. You understand?'

Lina nodded, even though she wasn't the one who needed reminding she was a grown woman. But she was also acutely aware this handsome, dashing Italian with a murky past wasn't liked by either Professor Loggi or her great-aunt, even though Agatha only had her best interests at heart. Or thought she had. Yet Lina found herself inexplicably drawn to 'that man' and not just because of his good looks. That afternoon she'd certainly witnessed his arrogance, but she'd also seen a softer side to him, an openness, that made her dare to believe he couldn't be that bad a person. 'Yes, Aunt,' she replied. Of course she understood Agatha was warning her to keep away from Edoardo Bernini, but it didn't mean she had to obey.

Chapter 9

The bell on the *duomo* tolled eleven o'clock as the ladies filed out of the chapel. It was a chilly, but bright day in January and they weren't the only people in the Piazza del Carmine. Alongside the pigeons, the ladies of the Arts Appreciation Society also had the misfortune to share the square with a group of young men dressed in black, brandishing banners displaying the familiar fascist emblem. Lina was reminded of the unpleasant episode at the Gran Caffè Doney in the summer. What's more, their numbers were increasing by the minute.

'Perhaps we ought to go back into the chapel,' she suggested.

'Nonsense,' came Agatha's quick riposte. 'We've as much right as anyone to walk the streets.'

The group was swelling into a crowd. It started to move along the square, becoming noisier as it went. The women were hardly inconspicuous in their hats and outdated dress, not to mention their speech. Someone spotted them. Barely had they set foot out of the church's main door when someone shouted '*Inglesi!*' quickly followed by another.

Alarmed, Lina looked round to see if they could make a quick getaway behind the back of the church when, to her horror, she noticed a young thug loop his arm under Miss Harrowby's.

'Wait! No!' she cried, as he dragged the terrified woman along. A split second later another student was manhandling a startled Lady Felstein.

Everything was happening so quickly. Switching to her left, Lina saw Miss Giltrap clutching on to her camera as two urchins tried to wrestle it off her. Equally alarming was the sight of Agatha raising her white parasol in anger at a young hooligan who'd started jostling her.

'Get away from me, you beast!' she cried.

'Aunt Agatha!' Lina yelled over the crowd just as the familiar leghorn hat disappeared into the sea of chaos. 'Agatha!' she cried, pushing her way towards her flailing aunt. All she could see was the hat being worn by one of the hoodlums.

The situation was out of control. Lina had to find an escape route, but before she could, an arm snaked around her waist. Pivoting quickly, she saw an older man leering at her. A finger jabbed her ribs and rough hands thrust her into the tide of marchers heading northwards up the main street. People pressed all around her, shoving her in the back and chanting at the tops of their voices, '*Il Duce! Il Duce!*' The sound was deafening. As she was carried along, Lina caught the occasional glimpse of Mrs Clutterbuck and Lady Felstein in the swirling current, but she'd lost sight of Miss Harrowby long ago and as for Aunt Agatha, she seemed to have sunk without trace.

The shattering of glass as a missile hurtled through a nearby shop window triggered a cheer. The marchers veered left, funnelling into a narrow street and an elbow dug into Lina's ribs. She was packed in so tightly on all sides, breathing was hard. Lifting her face up all she could see was a square of startlingly blue sky above. The crowd's chants hammered against her skull, and she started to feel faint, but then another chant from nearby cut the air like a stiletto.

'*Inglesi! Gli Scorpioni!*'

A shock charged through her when she heard the call. Shaking off the dizzy feeling, she craned her neck to see the student in Agatha's hat was just up ahead. She watched him barge his way down an even narrower alley to the right, followed by two or three other young men. As the crowd continued to surge forwards, a few students peeled off. It was then Lina realised Mrs Clutterbuck and Miss Harrowby were with them; their hats at cocked angles and faces alarmed. They were being singled out, separated from the rest.

It was the side of Florence that tourists never saw. The narrow street had opened out into a small filthy square, plastered in posters, and stinking from an overflowing drain. Lines of washing hung across it and they were being corralled inside. Scanning the area she could see Lady Felstein, now bareheaded, and poor Miss Harrowby, the camelia she'd worn in her hair trampled underfoot, looking distraught.

'No!' screamed Lina, recoiling as a young man in a fez grabbed her arm. 'Leave me alone!' she cried.

Up ahead Agatha's umbrella was still aloft, waving drunkenly in the air. Another four men were breaking away from the main group, chanting, '*Gli Scorpioni!*' The next thing she heard was a voice she knew so well bark above the mayhem. 'Get away from me, you brute!'

An initial wave of relief swept over Lina at seeing Agatha, but it was immediately replaced by terror when she realised Agatha was pinioned against a wall. The men were pumped up on adrenaline, like boxers about to enter the ring. Some were jeering at them. Others were shaking angry fists. They were joined by another two who blocked off the narrow alleyway to the street beyond. The women were trapped, and Lina dreaded to think what the men planned to do. If they had any hope of escape, she needed to create a distraction. But how?

As the tension within the peeling terracotta walls rose, the courtyard became a pressure cooker. Even though the air was cold, the atmosphere was at boiling point. Lina searched frantically for another way out but found none. Somehow, she needed to marshal the ladies together. They'd be safer that way. She was just about to reach out to Agatha when a shove in her back hurled her forwards. Luckily, she managed to put her hands out to stop her face hitting the stone wall ahead. Even so, she felt a searing pain in her palm as a sharp stone cut into her skin. Blood trickled in a thin stream from her left hand. Seeing it, Miss Harrowby let out a scream, and no amount of reassurance from Lina would calm her.

'You bastards!' joined in Mrs Clutterbuck shaking her clenched fists at their attackers.

The sight of Lina's blood seemed to trigger a free-for-all.

'How dare you?' Agatha yelled, taking a swing with her brolly at the nearest student. But he replied with a lunge, making a grab for her garnet choker. Mrs Clutterbuck, too, was pounced on by scavengers eager to plunder the rings on her fingers.

The students were laughing manically. They poked fun at Lady Felstein, whirling her around in a mock polka. Miss Harrowby, too, had long ago lost her stick and was propping herself up on some steps, wailing as one of the men tried to drag her to her feet. Another had found Agatha's hat, now distinctly battered, and put it on his head before trying to take her in his arms, while one wielded her parasol like a baton.

Lina knew they were completely at the mercy of these thugs. As one of the men approached her with a wild grin on his face, she stepped back, her heart racing. She was working out how to defend herself if they pinned her against the wall when a loud voice cut through the chaos. '*Eh, basta!* Stop!'

The thug shifted round. A well-dressed man in a fedora appeared at the mouth of the courtyard, gesticulating with long, outstretched arms.

Lina brushed back the strand of hair that had fallen across her face to steal a better look.

'Signor Bernini,' she muttered, as he continued to shout at the attackers.

'*Why are you bothering these women?*' Lina heard. '*Now leave them alone and go home or I will report you personally to the podesta. I'm sure he will take a dim view of your behaviour.*'

The tension was broken. The young men swapped glances, and the one brandishing Agatha's parasol threw it onto the cobbles. 'We've had our fun!' Lina heard one say. He wiped his streaming nose with the back of his hand. The student in the fez switched round once again, a scowl still on his face. But after a moment, his breath steadied, and he launched a gob of spittle onto the cobbles, presumably to show his contempt for the English women. Then, one by one, they pared away and either skulked off or jogged on to rejoin the main march.

While poor Miss Harrowby struggled to her feet; Mrs Clutterbuck salvaged a ring discarded on the ground; Lady Felstein tugged at her silk jacket; and Agatha retrieved her battered hat, Lina found herself watching the art dealer approach.

'Ladies, are you all right?' he asked, offering a helping hand to Miss Harrowby. 'I am so sorry. What a shameful thing.' Bending low, he handed back Mrs Clutterbuck her handbag and checked on Agatha before his attention switched to Lina. He grimaced when he saw the blood on her sleeve and noticed her palm.

'And your hand, signorina?' He took it in his.

Lina didn't answer straightaway. The shock of his touch held her tongue, as he produced a laundered handkerchief from his jacket pocket and dabbed away the blood. When she finally spoke, her voice came out thin and reedy.

'We can't thank you enough, *signor.*'

Edoardo flashed her a smile. 'Think nothing of it, *signorina*,' he said before he turned to the other women. 'Shameful,' he repeated, this time in English. 'The war between our countries is no excuse.'

Agatha, her wiry grey hair dishevelled, and her lace blouse torn at the neck, regained her composure.

'Well, Signor Bernini, although we are grateful to you, we could have managed very well on our own.' With that she drew back her shoulders and said to the others, 'Come along now, ladies.'

Lina, embarrassed by her aunt's behaviour, stepped in apologetically. 'We are all most grateful to you, *signor*,' she assured Edoardo.

Their rescuer shook his head. 'Not a problem,' he replied in English, raising his hat to her. 'Think nothing of it.'

But Lina did think something of it. It was all very well Agatha deluding herself. She may be a strong, independent woman, but there was no question Signor Bernini had saved them all from humiliation, injury and worse. Despite her great-aunt's terse manner, Lina for one, would be eternally grateful.

'Angelina!'

Agatha was calling.

'I must go, *signor*,' she told Edoardo awkwardly, then realising she still held his bloodied handkerchief in her hand, she thrust it forwards.

Seeing the dark stains, he hesitated, and she rolled her eyes and withdrew it. 'My apologies. I'll get it laundered,' she said.

'Only on the condition you return it to me in person,' he replied, with a wry smile.

Lina felt the heat rise in her neck. 'I suppose that's only fair. Yes,' she agreed, a tingling sensation coursing through her. 'Yes, I will do that.'

'Angelina, will you come along?' Agatha grew increasingly impatient.

'Good day to you, Signor Bernini,' she said. 'Coming, Aunt,' she called, and despite the ordeal she'd just experienced, she hurried towards the rest of the group with a spring in her step.

Chapter 10

For a second time Podesta Manzano called at Edoardo's apartment unannounced. On this occasion it was to see how the latest Austrian trip had gone. Edoardo had now made two. He'd settled himself in the same chair as before and had just poured the podesta a brandy.

'It went according to plan,' the dealer replied, handing his uninvited guest a drink.

'Good,' said Manzano, watching Edoardo help himself to a brandy. 'That's right. Make it a large. You deserve it after the challenging day you've had.'

Edoardo frowned. 'I'm not sure what you mean.'

The podesta snorted. 'I heard on the grapevine that you played the hero to the *Scorpioni*.'

Edoardo stiffened. *Had the OVRA been behind today's attack on the English women?* he wondered. 'Word travels fast,' he said.

'It does when I have a man trailing you.' The podesta's small eyes slid towards the window.

'And why would you think that necessary?' asked Edoardo, now seated opposite.

'I make it a rule that as far as business is involved,' replied the podesta, 'Herr Goering needs to be able to trust those who work for him one hundred per cent.'

Edoardo felt his shoulders tighten but outwardly he remained calm. 'That is fair enough,' he said.

'So, tell me.' The podesta leaned as far forwards as his belly allowed. 'How did you just happen to be in the women's vicinity when they were attacked?'

The questioning was taking a line Edoardo did not appreciate. 'I was in the Brancacci Chapel. It would have been my father's birthday. I lit a candle for the repose of his soul.'

Manzano coughed out a laugh. 'How very touching. And the young one, Signorina Leone, just happened to cross your path.'

'That's the size of it, yes. We went our separate ways, but a little later, when I heard the mob shouting, I realised what was happening and intervened.'

'Very gallant of you.'

Edoardo looked deep into his glass. 'I did what any decent man would do. If I hadn't, they—'

'And now they are indebted to you, are they not?'

The dealer's head jerked up. 'No. They owe me nothing.'

'Come, come. You are too modest, like your father. But also, like your father, you can spot an opening. A weakness. The girl could be most useful.'

'The girl?' queried Edoardo.

'Yes, *the girl*,' Manzano smirked. 'Half Italian. Half English. Don't pretend she doesn't make the blood race through your veins. I am sure she could be persuaded to volunteer useful information about the British.' He let out a lecherous laugh and touched the side of his nose.

Edoardo was puzzled. 'How do you know her?'

The podesta swigged his brandy and winked. 'She came to me the other day, imploring me to save the old women from internment. It was very amusing watching her grovel. She practically begged me to ravage her there and then. I left her wanting for the time being. But she will have contacts, traitors sympathetic

60

to the enemy. Members of the Tuscan Liberation Committee, for example. Don't you agree?' An unnerving smile rippled his lips. 'All I need do is lock up her dear old English ladies if she doesn't cooperate.'

Edoardo arched a brow. The Tuscan Liberation Party was the main anti-fascist opposition party in the city that had been forced underground long ago. 'So right now you don't plan to intern them?'

Manzano shrugged. 'Again, as a dealer you must know it is best to keep several plates spinning at the same time. The girl's collateral could come in handy.'

Edoardo thought of Lina. Of course he found her physically attractive, but there was something else about her; a strangely appealing seriousness not usually found among the people he knew. He nodded slowly. 'I see,' he replied, planting a broad smile on his tanned face. He'd gone from being Hitler's guide to Goering's courier, and now, it seemed, to Manzano's right-hand man in a very short space of time. He was in deeper than he'd imagined, and he could use it to his advantage.

Manzano wagged a fat finger and chuckled. 'No man would walk away from that girl,' he said. 'Consider getting to know Signorina Leone one of the perks of the job.' He took another slug of brandy. 'And if she's of no use, well,' he mused, 'she and those old women are easily disposed of.'

Chapter 11

Despite what Agatha called 'that unfortunate incident', the English Ladies' Arts Appreciation Society's next weekly meeting was to go ahead as scheduled. 'We may have been bloodied, but we shall not be bowed,' Agatha told Lina. 'And now that we've been told we won't be interned, we can get on with our lives.'

The ladies were on their way to one of Agatha's favourite haunts – the English Cemetery. It offered an oasis of calm in the busy city. It was also where her daughter had been laid to rest almost forty years before. Jane died of measles, aged ten, and Lina knew her own presence went some way to filling the gaping hole left in her aunt's heart by the little girl's death. Coincidentally, Lina was born on the anniversary of Jane's passing. Her mother had taken it as a sign. The circle of life was continuing, and her baby girl was, she said, a messenger from heaven. 'That's why she named you Angelina,' Agatha had explained one day. 'It gave me great comfort to think my Jane sent you.'

As they walked through the cemetery gates, Miss Harrowby approached Lina. 'We can never thank you enough for what you did the other day,' she told her, clasping her hands together in gratitude.

Lady Felstein was close behind. 'You're our guardian angel,

too,' she cut across. 'Angelina,' she added, with a titter.

'Yes, indeed,' agreed Mrs Clutterbuck.

Lina smiled modestly but shook her head. 'It was Signor Bernini who was our guardian angel,' she replied. She looked to Agatha for her reaction and saw her raise a brow at the mention of Edoardo's name.

As they continued towards their destination – the large marble casket of the celebrated English poet Elizabeth Barrett Browning – Lina just had to ask. The question smouldering on her tongue for days had become too hot to tolerate any longer. 'Why won't you tell me about Signor Bernini?' she demanded as soon as they were out of earshot of the other women.

Agatha sucked air through her teeth, as if Lina had set her some insolvable conundrum. 'You really are better off not thinking about him, my dear,' she insisted.

'But why?' asked Lina, her hot Italian blood simmering just below the surface. 'I'm not a child, Aunt, although you still treat me like one. I have a right to know, surely?'

Puckering her lips Agatha broke her stride. 'If you must, my dear, there was a scandal regarding his father's integrity.'

'A scandal?' repeated Lina. That was not what she'd expected, although she hadn't really known what to expect in the first place.

Agatha forced out an exaggerated sigh and resumed her stride. 'I shall say no more on the subject, save to point out the apple never falls far from the tree.'

Lina frowned. Her aunt was talking in riddles, but she still felt oddly protective towards Signor Bernini. 'Well, I think he's very …' She searched for the right word that wouldn't reflect how intrigued she was by him, '… decent,' she blurted.

Once more Agatha broke her stride and turned to her great-niece. 'Decent?' she queried, before barking out a laugh. 'I'm sure he's very charming,' she replied, before adding, enigmatically, 'but then so was the serpent in Eden.'

Lina thought of Masaccio's distraught Eve in the fresco. Why was she being warned away from the man who'd saved them from a terrible fate at the hands of the Blackshirts, and who seemed so charming, if a touch arrogant? Just like Eve, she was sorely tempted to discover the reason for herself.

While Agatha snored gently in the conservatory later that afternoon, Lina snuck unseen into the laundry room, slipped Signor Bernini's freshly laundered handkerchief into her purse, and made her way to his gallery.

'Signorina Leone.' Edoardo, seated behind a desk, rose. He seemed glad to see her. 'Please, come in,' he said, inviting her further inside.

As she walked towards him, Lina looked around. The space was deceptively large and the ceiling double height. The back of the gallery was flooded with daylight that came through a large window in the roof. Two marble busts, an Etruscan vase and a sculpture of an athlete were displayed alongside half a dozen paintings. Her eyes were immediately drawn to a portrait of a very corpulent courtier, with a frilled collar and one hand on his hip.

'A de Rij?' she asked.

Edoardo came to stand behind her. 'Ah, yes. You know your Renaissance art.'

'A little,' she replied enigmatically, squinting closely at the painting. 'Although I'd say that is a fake. Yes?' She turned to face him.

Edoardo smiled uneasily. 'I prefer to call it a good copy. I can assure you it is sold as such.' He seemed keen to change the subject. 'And you have recovered from the other day?'

'Yes, thank you.' In his presence she found her heart quickening.

'And the ladies?'

'They are still a little shaken.'

'Of course. It was a shocking thing to happen.'

'Yes,' she agreed.

There was a slightly awkward pause as Lina found herself

looking deep into the dealer's large eyes.

'So how can I help you?' Edoardo asked.

'Oh, yes,' she said, suddenly remembering the purpose of her visit. 'I almost forgot,' she said, opening the clasp of her clutch bag. 'I came to return this.' She handed over the clean handkerchief.

'Thank you,' he replied, slipping it into the breast pocket of his jacket and patting it twice. 'But where are my manners? I haven't offered you a coffee or a cognac or ...'

As Lina looked at him, she knew something was happening between them. Something dangerously exhilarating. There was a spark, an energy that she couldn't put into words. Sensing an awkwardness, Edoardo filled the gap. He tugged at his shirt cuffs. 'Look, I know we didn't get off to a great start, but you may hear things about me that give you a bad impression.'

Lina eyed him, willing her heart to stop pounding. 'You mean the reason my aunt and Professor Loggi want me to stay away from you?' She hadn't meant to be so blunt, but the words had just come tumbling out.

He nodded, then palmed the side of his head in thought. 'Well, that's one way of putting it,' he said laughingly. 'Sit. Please.' He directed her to the chair by his desk. She did as he bade. He sat opposite her.

'You see, I inherited this from my father,' he told her, casting around the gallery. 'He was a dealer, too, but he was accused of some, how can I put it ... dubious practices.'

Lina frowned and found herself repeating his phrase. 'Dubious practices?'

Edoardo closed his eyes for a moment. 'He – and I – joined the fascist party, for business, you understand. That was, and still is, the only way to survive these days, but then' – he shrugged – 'it seems he got a little greedy and started to take risks.'

'Risks? I don't follow,' said Lina. She could tell it was hard for him dragging up the past.

He sighed heavily. 'He did wrong and was sentenced to twenty years. But he died of a fever in jail two days later.'

Lina shook her head. Was Edoardo really saying his father was a criminal? So this was why the professor and Agatha treated him with such contempt, even though it was blatantly unfair to blame him for his father's wrongdoing? She was shocked by the revelation. 'I'm so sorry,' was all she could say.

He gave a resigned shrug. 'Reputations lost overnight are not quickly recovered. The sins of the father are visited upon their children and all that.' His lips may have lifted in a smile, but Lina sensed inside he was still raw. He didn't have to confide in her, but she felt flattered that he had.

They stared in silence at each other for a moment. A connection had been made but it was broken by the ring of the telephone. Two, three, four rings. 'Aren't you going to answer it?' Lina asked.

'Do you mind?'

'Of course not.' She reached for her handbag on the desk, but he raised his hand. 'No, please. I won't be long,' he told her, lifting the receiver, still smiling. 'Bernini Gallery.'

Lina heard a woman's voice on the line. A young woman's voice. 'Edoardo?' she said. His head shot up and his eyes locked onto Lina, as if he'd just been branded by a red-hot poker.

'Good afternoon, *signorina*,' he said, formally, cupping his hand around the receiver and turning away. 'Perhaps we could talk later, I'm with a client.'

But Lina was already on her feet. Whoever this woman was, she and Edoardo were in some sort of close relationship that he didn't want her to know about. He must've thought she was born yesterday and now he was referring to her as 'a client'. She'd heard and now seen enough. She would leave.

'Seven, tonight,' she heard Edoardo say, concluding his conversation as Lina turned to go. 'Signorina Leone!' he called.

'I've just remembered an appointment, Signor Bernini,' she shot back, approaching the gallery's door.

'No, please stay.' Edoardo ran in front of her and blocked her way. 'Please.'

'I don't think so,' she replied calmly, while inside her emotions were in a maelstrom. How could she be so stupid as to have feelings for this man? Despite showing kindness towards her, it seemed as though Professor Loggi and Agatha were right. *A wolf in sheep's clothing.* He couldn't be trusted.

'Good day to you, Signor Bernini,' she said. And she walked out of the gallery with her head held high, but trailing uncertainty and bitter disappointment in her wake.

Chapter 12

Another long night stretched before Lina. In Edoardo Bernini she thought she'd found someone who might understand and support her in her isolation. Hadn't there been a spark between them? Surely the stirrings she'd felt weren't entirely one-sided. There was something in his eyes, too, that lifted her up and made her feel as light as thistledown. But then, she told herself, he probably behaved that way with all young women; toying with their emotions, then playing them off against each other. Just when she thought she'd found someone who not only cared about the safety of Florence's treasures, but about its people, he'd let go of her hand and allowed her to come crashing down to earth. No, even though he had set her alight just by standing close, she would not allow herself to be reeled in by his charms.

Still smarting from Edoardo's sting, she was pacing her bedroom floor, when something outside hit her bedroom shutters. The sudden noise brought her back to the moment. Hurrying over to the window, she looked out into the still, dark night. A movement below made her look straight down. Someone was standing under her sill. Lina strained her eyes to see what she thought was a short man.

'Who's there?' she whispered, not wanting to wake Agatha.

It was only when the figure emerged from the shadows into the moonlight, dressed in slacks, that she realised it was Miss Giltrap, the American.

'Can you get down here, Miss Leone? We've got real trouble.'

Lina frowned, her eyes narrowing to focus on her caller. 'Miss Giltrap! What sort of trouble?'

'It's Lady Felstein,' came the reply in a gruff half whisper.

An image of the vulnerable aristocrat, with her ear trumpet and permanently placid look on her lined face, loomed before Lina. 'She's all right, isn't she?'

'She needs our help.' Impatience now crept into Miss Giltrap's tone.

'I'll be right down.'

Slipping on her dressing robe, Lina rushed downstairs. She unlocked the back door and joined Miss Giltrap in the garden.

'What's happened?'

'She's at the *questura*.'

'What?' Lina was shocked. The city's police station was no place for an elderly woman at the best of times.

'Some official went round to hers and told her to go with him,' explained Miss Giltrap.

'On what grounds?'

'Something about her passport.'

'Then it's probably a clerical error. I'm sure it can all be sorted out quite easily,' Lina suggested. She turned to go back inside but felt a tug at her arm.

'Where are you going?' asked the American.

'To tell my aunt, of course. She'll be worried if—'

'There's no time,' Miss Giltrap broke in. 'It's getting kind of crazy.'

'Crazy?' repeated Lina.

'They mentioned something about her being Jewish!'

'Jewish?' Lina flinched. Lady Felstein's late husband was a leading Jewish advocate. Last year the *fascisti* passed a new law to incarcerate Jews of foreign nationality, but it hadn't been strictly enforced – until now.

'In that case we'd better hurry,' she replied.

The *questura* lay in the centre of the city and was marked out by the bars on its windows and, more often these days, by anxious family members outside waiting for news of their arrested loved ones. Even though it was almost midnight, the large reception area was busy with *Carabinieri* herding people around. There was a drunken man railing against Mussolini, two heavily made-up women, and a group of bewildered-looking middle-aged men being corralled in the corner. Most of the action, however, seemed to be centred on the desk where three or four *Carabinieri* were clustered around someone on the floor. They were shouting and cursing at whoever was on the tiles. But an alarmingly familiar voice rose high above all of theirs. Startled, Lina followed it.

'*Scusami! Scusami!*' she cried, tapping on shoulders.

One of the policemen immediately took a step back in surprise. Another followed suit until she managed a clear view of the person at the centre of all the attention.

'Aunt Agatha!' Rushing forwards she added her own voice to the mêlée. 'But I thought you were asleep!' she cried in exasperation, seeing her aunt planted on the floor, parrying any attempt to remove her with her parasol.

'I didn't want to disturb you, my dear.' She looked up and scowled at the men glaring down on her. 'But Lady Felstein's maid told me about her predicament, and I refuse to move until I know where they've taken her,' she said defiantly.

'Taken her?' repeated Lina, aware that four pairs of male eyes were trained on her.

'I'm not budging from this spot until I find out where she is!' Agatha announced. 'And kindly convey my intention to these brutes,' she added, shaking her parasol threateningly to show she meant business.

One or two of the *Carabinieri* laughed at the gesture, but the others seemed very unamused, and Lina knew she'd have to act as the peace broker in this stand-off. At this point she was also very grateful Agatha's grasp of the language was virtually non-existent. In Italian, she asked the assembled officers to forgive her elderly aunt, blaming her erratic behaviour on her medication.

'It's for a heart condition and she sometimes gets a little addled and slightly aggressive,' she explained.

'Argh,' said one of the men, as if a light had just been turned on his own brain. The others nodded their understanding. '*Si. Si*,' said another.

Sensing the sudden change in mood among her captors, Agatha looked to her niece. 'You see, these sort of men just need to be told who's in charge,' she said sternly, blissfully unaware of what they'd just been told.

'Of course,' her niece lied, playing for time. She still had to talk to someone in authority. 'Can I speak with whoever is in charge?' Lina asked one of the officers. '*Per favore*,' she added with a smile and a coquettish tilt of her head.

A *Carabiniere* who seemed to be senior to the others stepped forwards. 'You wait here,' he instructed, before gabbling something to one of his men.

Agatha, following the gist of the instruction, concurred. 'Oh, I'm not going anywhere,' she growled. 'I'll stay here all night if I have to,' she said, crossing her arms. 'I'm not leaving without Lady Felstein.'

'I'm sure we can sort this out,' Lina replied, trying to sound positive. 'We just need to get to the bottom of things.' She glanced at Miss Giltrap nearby, hands in pockets and anxiously chewing her lip.

A moment later, the senior officer received word from his man.

'Commander Parissi will see you in his office, *signorina*,' he announced, showing her to a door at the far side of the hall. Another policeman was waiting to receive her.

'Good. I'll sort this out,' said Agatha, rolling up her sleeves and holding out her hand to Miss Giltrap to help her up from the floor. But as soon as she was upright, the *Carabiniere* shoved her in the chest. 'Not you, old woman. Only her,' he snapped in Italian, leering at Lina.

'Well, I must say!' cried an exasperated Agatha.

'It's all right, Aunt, I'm sure we can come to an agreement,' Lina assured her. She disappeared with the senior policeman.

'I'll be here when you come back,' called out Agatha, as her niece started towards the door.

Miss Giltrap linked her arm through the dowager's in a show of sisterly solidarity. 'Good luck,' she called to Lina.

Commander Parissi rose to greet his young female visitor. Lina took it as a good sign and an even better one when he invited her to sit. A trace of a smile narrowed his eyes, although most of his mouth was hidden by a bushy moustache.

'I understand you want to know about an Englishwoman we are holding,' he began. 'A Jew.'

Lina found his remark troubling, but masked her anxiety with a smile. Charm, rather than aggression, would be a more effective weapon in this case, she thought. 'Yes, some misunderstanding about a passport, I believe. I wonder if I can help clear things up.'

The commander said nothing at first then clasped his hands over his belly. 'Hmm. You are responsible for this woman?'

Lina baulked. 'Technically, no, but—'

'And that old woman?' His head craned towards the door.

'That *old woman* as you call her is my aunt,' she replied indignantly, before correcting herself. 'Well, technically my great-aunt.'

'I know there are other English, too.'

Lina frowned, fearing where this conversation was leading. 'I myself am half Italian, and Miss Giltrap is American, but yes, there are some English in the city.'

'The *Scorpioni*, eh?' he chuckled, stroking his moustache.

She winced and dipped her gaze. 'Some people call them that,'

72

she conceded.

Knowledge of the hated nickname could, she knew, go against the ladies. But, without warning, the commander nodded. 'Then you have saved me a job.'

Lina's head jerked up. 'What do you mean?'

'I've sent my men out to bring them all here,' Parissi told her, jabbing a typed list on his desk with his finger.

'I don't understand,' she protested, but the chief wasn't listening to her. Instead, he cupped a hand round his ear, tuning into a row that seemed to have erupted outside in the corridor and was growing louder by the second. Lina saw him rise and stride across the room to open the door wide. Perfectly framed in the doorway she could see two women of advanced years being manhandled inside the building. To her horror she recognised them. Miss Harrowby and Mrs Clutterbuck were headed to the cells, the latter wearing an expression so ferocious it matched that of the leopard whose skin was now her coat.

'Get your filthy hands off me!' yelled the Yorkshire woman, while her distressed companion tried to hold back tears.

'*Avanti! Avanti!*' cried the two guards, eager to push their noisy charges behind bars.

Noticing Lina standing by the door, Miss Harrowby called out, 'Can't you do something, Miss Leone?' before both women disappeared towards the cells.

Lina stood stunned and powerless. Manzano had gone back on his word, even before she had begun working for him. She should never have trusted him. Pleading with the police chief, she said, 'Surely you don't have to do this? There has to be another way.'

'I have my orders from the podesta,' Parissi shot back. Just as he spoke, more mayhem was unleashed further down the corridor. The voice that cried, 'Get away from me, you brute,' belonged to Agatha. She was also being escorted towards the cells, Lina presumed, to join Miss Harrowby and Mrs Clutterbuck.

'Can't you see they're old and frail?' she begged Parissi, as she rushed out into the corridor to see a heavy iron door closed behind her aunt. Miss Giltrap, trailing in Agatha's wake, was left pummelling the door in vain, crying out, 'You sons of bitches.'

Commander Parissi joined them in the corridor, hands on hips. He shook his head. 'Italy is at war with Britain. These ladies are our enemies and need to be out of the city. They are due to leave in the next twenty-four hours.'

'What? But you can't do that!' gasped Miss Giltrap, turning her fire on the policeman. She started to kick the door leading to the cells. It really wasn't helping matters.

Ignoring the American, he turned to fix Lina with an unyielding glare. 'Unless you can come up with some alternative arrangements, they will be taken by truck to somewhere outside the city.' He looked disdainfully towards the cells. 'For me and my men, they can't go soon enough.'

'Alternative arrangements?' repeated Lina. 'What sort of alternative arrangements?' She might have just spied a chink of light in the darkness.

Parissi scratched the back of his head. 'Ones that mean the *Carabinieri* are no longer responsible for what happens to the *Scorpioni*.' He glanced up at the ceiling and brought his palms together, as if praying for a break.

Lina blinked. 'And if something can be found, does that mean they won't be sent away?' she asked.

The commander shrugged. 'All I know is, I don't want these scorpions here any longer than necessary. The sooner they are out of my jail, and this city, the better.'

'But really, you can't do this,' insisted Lina.

Parissi, however, was adamant. Flinging out an arm towards the exit, he yelled, 'Go! Go now, before you and that American join them behind bars!'

Chapter 13

A cold dawn was breaking over the city as Lina and Gloria Giltrap stumbled out of the *questura*, dazed and exhausted.

The American's apartment was less than half a mile away. 'You want to stay at mine a while?' she asked, her normally tanned complexion looking alabaster in the stark light.

'No, thank you,' said Lina. 'I need to think.' Despite her own fatigue, sleep was the last thing on her mind. She had to find a way out of this terrible mess, or risk losing Agatha and her valiant ladies for good. None of them was in the best of health and all would struggle amid prison squalor. Being locked up alongside women of the night and common thieves would be hard enough for them to bear. But when it came to plucking a small group of elderly Englishwomen from the jaws of a hellish internment camp, that would be infinitely more difficult.

What Lina knew – and perhaps she'd inherited the knowledge from her Italian father – was that bargaining usually yielded more positive results than direct action. Although right now, as she stood in the street listening to the bells of the *duomo* toll six o'clock and watching stray cats search for scraps in the gutter, she couldn't see a way out.

While Miss Giltrap returned to her apartment, Lina set off

towards the *duomo* to figure out her next move. There were a few people about. A priest in a stiff biretta strolled along and nodded as he passed, while two urchins who'd spent the night in a doorway were sent away empty-handed by an irate baker. His curses alerted two *Carabinieri* patrolling nearby, who appeared round the corner in seconds, catching the boys and giving them both a good beating. All Lina could do was close her eyes and take refuge in an adjacent alley. The last thing she needed right now was to be questioned by the police.

Leaning into the shadows, the pounding of her heart drowning out most noise, she waited until she hoped the coast was finally clear. The *Carabinieri* were swaggering, truncheons in hands, down the street. They were men out of a mould. The Manzano mould – exercising their power but giving nothing in return. But then she remembered something Manzano had said to her in his office. *I am a reasonable man, but naturally I would want something in return for the women's freedom.* She'd been vulnerable but had used her wits as a bargaining tool. But now she'd just thought of another untapped resource in her armoury; something that could be used to help the ladies. In that moment, the way opened up in front of her. Edoardo Bernini was a dealer, too. Doubling back in the opposite direction, she told herself she had to push aside all her doubts. Any fears and misgivings needed to be forgotten. She had to swallow her pride. There was no other choice. She would go to the Bernini Gallery.

A tug at the bell rope prompted the opening of upstairs shutters and a man with slightly tousled hair peered down through blurry eyes. Edoardo had only just returned from his third mission to Innsbruck late the night before.

'Signorina Leone? Is that you?'

She looked left and right and nodded, not wanting to attract attention from passers-by.

Edoardo re-emerged at the apartment's front door, next to the gallery. Wearing a silk burgundy dressing gown with a monogrammed pocket, he was shocked to see Lina so early in the morning.

'I'm so sorry to disturb you, Signor Bernini,' she blurted. 'I just didn't know where else to turn.'

'Come in. Come in,' he said, opening the door wide into an inviting hallway. He let Lina pass before he, too, looked down the street to check no one was watching.

The moment they were alone, Lina couldn't hold back. She'd told herself to remain composed, but her Italian passion took over and she launched in straightaway as they stood in the hall. 'Something terrible has happened, Signor Bernini.'

'Please calm yourself, Signorina Leone.'

Lina gulped down more air. 'My Aunt Agatha and all her friends are in the *questura*. They're going to take them to a detention camp in the next twenty-four hours if I can't—'

The art dealer frowned and broke in, 'A detention camp?' He showed her the stairs, and she started to climb them, talking breathlessly as she went.

'Yes. Very soon. Today, maybe. I have to help them. I can't just leave them in jail.'

They reached the marble-tiled landing and just as she turned, Lina saw Edoardo's hand fly to his lips and a finger press against them.

'Wait. Please, signorina. It is still so early.'

For a terrible moment, Lina feared she was right to have misgivings. There was a woman in his bedroom.

He was just about to open some double doors when Signora Bianchi appeared at the landing in a dressing gown, and her grey hair in a long braid on one shoulder. Edoardo glanced at her.

'It's all right, *signora*,' he told her. Then turning to Lina, he explained, 'Signora Bianchi is my housekeeper. She worked for my father, too. You can trust her.'

The woman shot Lina a curious look then tossed her plait over her shoulder, as if a strange female in the Bernini apartment was nothing out of the ordinary and went back to bed. Meanwhile, Edoardo opened the studded double doors into the salon beyond.

'Please.' He gestured her inside a room dominated by huge paintings in gilt frames on its walls. Lina couldn't hide her surprise as she went up to a large canvas of a reclining nude. 'But that's—'

'The *Venus of Urbino*,' he interrupted. 'Yes, but alas, not by Titian.'

She turned with a frown. 'You mean …'

'It's another copy. A good one, but a copy nonetheless.' He smiled. 'In fact, none of the paintings you see are originals, but they are still beautiful, don't you agree?'

'Yes. Yes, they are,' she conceded, even though she was a little surprised that such a renowned art dealer should hang his own walls with copies.

'Take a seat,' he said, showing her to a chaise longue. She nodded and was just about to sit down when she noticed an open sketch pad on the nearby coffee table. On it was a drawing in charcoal. She recognised it instantly, but Edoardo realised his mistake too late. The shock of seeing her own face staring out at her in black made her hesitate.

'An idle hobby,' he mumbled, bundling the pad away into the nearest drawer. 'So, the English ladies are being detained you say,' he began again, changing the subject.

Lina composed herself, smoothing her skirt and taking a deep breath to play for time as she marshalled her thoughts. She fixed Edoardo with a hard glare. He was a dealer, and dealers did deals. Perhaps he could broker one for her. 'The chief of the police said they'll be sent away from the city and interned soon. They're being held in that terrible *questura* and, as you know, they're nearly all over seventy. Some of them are in poor health.' She thought of Lady Felstein's failing hearing and Miss Harrowby's asthma.

Edoardo interrupted her again. 'This is a very serious situation. I can see that, but how do you think I can help the *Scorpioni*?' Lina winced at the nickname but would not be put off her stride. He sat down opposite and she felt herself tense, knowing she would have to play to his ego. First, she would flatter him. 'You saved us all once, and I thought—' She broke off when she realised he was shaking his head.

'I am honoured that your ladies think me – what was it in English? – a knight in shining armour, but I'm sorry to disappoint you. I'm not sure what I can do. You credit me with more power than I have.'

Lina would not be put off. 'But you are a dealer, Signor Bernini. A well-known one. You make deals. That is what you do,' she told him, aware she was sounding as high-handed as her great-aunt. 'You are important, too. You met Hitler.'

The remark prompted an incredulous laugh. 'You want me to make a deal with the German Führer?'

He wasn't taking her seriously, but she could make him change his tune. She shook her head. 'No. Not Hitler,' she replied. 'Manzano.'

Edoardo's eyes widened 'Podesta Manzano?'

'Why not?' Irritation crept into Lina's voice, even though she knew getting what she wanted wouldn't be easy. Nevertheless, she carried on undaunted. 'He is an associate of yours – I saw the newspaper photographs – and you appear to be a good fascist. It seems to me the whole of Italy functions on people in power doing favours for each other.'

Edoardo's smile dissolved. 'You know the British are enemies of Italy.'

'But these women are vulnerable,' she protested. 'The conditions …' Her mind flashed to the look of sheer helplessness on Miss Harrowby's face and consternation on Lady Felstein's. 'I can't let them languish in squalor.'

'You are right there, and I appreciate your concern, but I don't see what I can do,' Edoardo interrupted.

Lina felt his hand on her arm. She looked at it, but instead of comforting her it only spurred her on. While his concern may have been genuine, she still couldn't be sure of his support, so she played her trump card. 'You said your father died in jail, *signor*,' she said unwaveringly. 'You know how squalid those places are.'

Mention of his father's fate cast a shadow across Edoardo's face. She'd hurt him, but she was too focused to care. She certainly wanted his help, but she wasn't going to beg for it. 'And that is why I want to put a proposal to you, *signor*.'

Edoardo's expression changed. Curiosity suddenly replaced sadness, and he leaned towards her. 'A proposal?' His brow arched as he spoke. She could see the cogs of his mind whirring, but she held his gaze. What she was about to suggest could mean the difference between life and death for Agatha and her friends. She had to make her case with all the Italian passion and the English reasoning she could muster. 'Please, *signorina*,' he said. 'Go on. I'm listening.'

Chapter 14

February 1941

The last occasion Edoardo had found himself in Manzano's office had been in the sweltering heat. This time it was freezing cold, but he hoped the chill would thaw when the podesta heard his proposition. As soon as Lina left his apartment, he'd picked up the telephone. His recent mission to Innsbruck had been successful once again. He was in Goering's good books and that meant so was Manzano. He decided to take a chance.

'What you have to say better be good. I've interrupted my breakfast for this,' the podesta huffed, gesturing to the half-eaten plate of prosciutto and eggs on his desk. 'It's the one thing the English do better than us!' he joked, before yelling through to his secretary for coffee for his visitor.

Ignoring Manzano's remarks, Edoardo dived straight in. 'You remember a while back I told you I visited the repository at Castello Di Montegufoni.'

'Yes. You said it was chaos,' replied Manzano with a smirk.

'That's right. No proper security, let alone an inventory system, and the canvasses and panels aren't even being protected from direct sunlight. Loggi has no control.'

Manzano's lips twitched. 'But that is how we like it. That way things get "lost". It suits me, and it should suit you. Just as long as the Cranachs are safe.'

Edoardo persisted. 'But surely we're missing an opportunity.'

The podesta narrowed his eyes. 'What are you driving at, Bernini?'

'I'm thinking we don't want just chaos.'

'No?'

'We want *organised* chaos.' He took out a packet of Muratti and offered the podesta a cigarette, which was declined.

Manzano set down his knife and fork as his secretary – this time in a tight-fitting sweater – brought in another pot of coffee, pouted, and left the room.

'Go on.'

'You said yourself you were short-staffed. Conscription has taken some of your best men, and you have no chance to replace them.' Feeling more confident, Edoardo eased himself back into his chair and lit his cigarette. 'But, if you could pull together a small team of experts to produce a full inventory of not just objects in the Uffizi and Pitti Palace, but in other museums and churches, too, it would surely be of interest to our German allies.'

'Interesting,' said Manzano, taking up his cutlery again.

Edoardo poured himself a coffee and took a sip from the espresso cup set before him. 'I hear that Goering's new taskforce is doing well, especially in the east. The Jews love their art, almost as much as we Florentines. Much of it is now in occupied Paris.'

'It is,' agreed Manzano. 'The *Reichsmarschall* is making almost weekly trips to the Jeu de Paume and taking his pick of the treasures it has to offer.'

'So, we've already established the head of the Luftwaffe doesn't only want to shop for planes. He's in the market for art, too,' said Edoardo. 'He's got a few Florentine pieces, but he's only skimmed the surface.'

'True,' Manzano conceded.

Edoardo leaned forwards. 'If detailed inventories are compiled by experts, it will make it a lot easier for him to lay his hands on Italian pieces that interest him. He won't have to ransack collections before he finds what he really wants.'

'Perhaps.' A slice of cheese was placed thoughtfully in his mouth. Manzano was taking the bait.

'I like it,' he replied, His brain clicking into action was almost audible.

'And as long as these inventories remain in friendly hands, then our own dealings will be much more straightforward.'

'But, tell me, where would I find such people, these experts?'

'There is no need to even look.' He knew he sounded smug.

Manzano scoffed and slapped his desk. 'Don't play games with me Bernini.'

'I'm not, Excellency,' he countered. 'The only problem is these experts are in the *questura* as we speak, and they are there on your orders.'

Manzano's eyes almost bulged out of their sockets. 'You mean the English women, don't you? The *Scorpioni*?'

Edoardo nodded. 'That's exactly who I mean.'

'I ordered them to be rounded up. The girl backed out of a meeting I'd arranged for tomorrow.' There'd been a telephone call to say Dr Leone was ill and, for some reason he could not work out, his secretary hadn't challenged her excuse. His face suddenly darkened. 'No one cancels on me,' he huffed angrily. 'A bad cold! I wasn't going to let her get away with that. She needed to be punished. But you say we could use them in another way?'

'I do.'

Manzano snorted. 'But they are *le nemiche*, the enemy.'

Edoardo shook his head. 'They love our nation. That is why they have made it their home for all these years. They love Italy, but they love art more. They couldn't bear to think of priceless Giottos and Raphaels being damaged or stolen or even destroyed in this war. They would do anything to help preserve them.'

'You are suggesting I set them to work?'

'Exactly. They work or they are interned.'

Manzano blew on his hands then rubbed them together to warm himself. 'And you say they are art experts, like the girl claims to be?'

'Every one of them in the field of Renaissance art.'

'And?' Manzano was interested but wanted more.

'They can work discreetly. In an office in the Uffizi perhaps, under strict supervision, of course, and no one outside the museum, apart from you and I, need ever know what they're doing,' Edoardo suggested.

Manzano's shoulders twitched, and he lengthened his neck approvingly. 'Yes. Yes, I like it. It's an interesting proposition,' he agreed. 'So, when can these women start?'

Edoardo's lips curled at the corners and his thoughts flew to Lina and how she would react to the news. He might just have played a winning hand. The deal could soon be brokered. 'Just as soon as you release them from jail, Signor Manzano.'

Chapter 15

Lina had been sitting by the telephone in Villa Mimosa, desperate for news. A call from Signor Bernini, telling her the meeting with Manzano had gone well, lifted her hopes. She'd remained distant and professional with him, but then she'd heard nothing for twenty-four hours. Agatha's white parasol rested forlornly in the stand by the front door, rescued from the *questura* on that fateful night. Now Lina couldn't wait to reunite it with its owner.

At the sound of a vehicle pulling up in the drive, she rushed to the front door. A police car. Stepping out, Agatha looked weary, but she was back, and Lina greeted her with a hug on the steps. The gamble had paid off. Bernini had acted as a broker and Manzano had accepted the proposal. It was a compromise, but it meant she could hold Agatha in her arms once more, and the threat of internment hanging over all the ladies was lifted.

'Welcome home, dearest aunt,' Lina cried, flinging her arms around Agatha's frail body.

'Oh, I can't tell you how good it is to be back,' she gasped.

'A nice cup of tea will make you feel much better,' Lina assured her aunt, about to guide her through into the salon. But then she noticed the burly *Carabiniere* who'd escorted Agatha stood his ground behind her.

'Is something wrong, officer?' she asked as Donna shepherded her mistress into the hallway.

'I am to give you this,' he said, handing her a sheet of paper.

'What …?' Lina's head started to shake as soon as she saw the first line. 'But I don't understand,' she blurted.

'Those are the conditions of the women's release.'

She scanned the list. '… *to remain under supervision during the day. A curfew between the hours of six in the evening until eight in the morning. No visitors.*'

'They must report to the *questura* every day and stick to the rules,' replied the officer, sternly.

'And if they don't?'

'The penalties will be severe.'

She should have known Manzano would want his pound of flesh from the women, but why hadn't Signor Bernini warned her of the strict conditions they'd be forced to live under? This was not what they had spoken about when she'd met the dealer.

As soon as the officer had gone, Lina hurried back to the salon to see Agatha sitting, exhausted, in her armchair.

She lifted her rheumy eyes. 'So now you know,' she said with an air of resignation. 'We are under house arrest.'

Lina knew she needed to bolster her spirits. Planting a wide smile on her face, she sat by her side and took her cold hands in hers. 'Yes, I know. But it'll be all right. You'll see.' She tried to sound reassuring. 'You're back home and you won't be taken away again. You won't be interned.' She patted Agatha's hand. 'Now, how about that cup of tea?' she suggested.

The horrors of a desolate internment camp had ebbed away, for the time being at least. The conditions of the deal Edoardo Bernini had brokered were not what any of the women wanted, but the members of the English Ladies' Art Appreciation Society could remain in Florence. Anything was better than their banishment, Lina supposed. Nevertheless, Edoardo Bernini's actions still left a slightly bitter taste in her mouth. Trust was something to be earned, she told herself. Right now, the jury in the case of the dashing Italian art dealer was still out.

A rickety old police truck pulled into the drive of Villa Mimosa early the following week. Lina saw it arrive from her bedroom window. For a moment, the vehicle's black exhaust fumes belched out over the flower beds, threatening to suffocate Agatha's beloved English roses. The plan was to ferry the women to the Uffizi Gallery and bring them back to their respective homes at the end of the working day, where they were to remain on pain of imprisonment in a Florentine jail.

A portly guard opened the back doors for Agatha. The other ladies were already inside. They were squeezed onto hard benches normally occupied by prisoners en route to court or jail. Although Miss Harrowby wasn't sporting the usual flower in her hair, she smiled as Agatha settled herself on a bench next to her. Lady Felstein did, however, look even more bewildered than usual.

'Welcome aboard,' greeted Mrs Clutterbuck wearing a loud patterned print in orange and purple. The ladies' mission at the Uffizi might have been top secret, but the Yorkshire woman certainly had no intention of going incognito.

Lina had decided to accompany them, even though she didn't have to. She felt almost maternal towards them, as if she were taking her children for their first day at a new school. Everything was unknown and, quite frankly, nerve-racking. No one was sure how they'd be treated or how they would tackle the enormous task that lay ahead.

It was the first time the women had seen each other since the end of their ordeal in the *questura*, and Lina was glad when Agatha took it upon herself to show leadership once more. Over the noise of the rattling engine, she delivered a speech to rally her society members.

Clearing her throat, she began, 'Ladies, we find ourselves in a rather unusual situation. Thankfully we appear to have avoided internment, and it seems, at long last, our expertise is being valued by the Italian authorities. We must therefore seize this opportunity. As members of the English Ladies' Arts Appreciation Society, we have to ask ourselves why is art important to us? Some of you' – she looked pointedly at Mrs Clutterbuck – 'may allow your attention to stray at times during my lectures, but why is art important to the world?'

Her question was answered with one or two blank faces, or dipped gazes. Lina stepped in. 'Because it knows no boundaries. It transcends everything. It gives meaning to our lives and helps us understand the world and other cultures.'

Agatha's solemn expression dissolved into a smile.

'You are so right, my dear,' she replied, beaming. 'And most eloquently put. At least my lectures haven't been wasted on you.'

Lina smiled wryly, allowing Agatha to take the credit for instilling her with a love of art, while not mentioning the years of study she, herself, had undertaken at university.

There were nods of approval from the other women, as if no one else had ever really considered the question. 'And that is why we must look upon this work we've been ordered to do as putting ourselves at the service of art. We would be failing not only these great artists, but human civilisation if we turned down the chance to preserve their master works for future generations.'

Agatha's speech seemed to lift spirits and persuade Miss Harrowby and Lady Felstein it was their duty to help preserve as many treasures from the depravations of war as possible. Only Mrs Clutterbuck remained a little prickly.

'I'm sure she'll come round,' Lina confided to Agatha, as the truck finally juddered to a halt outside the gallery's back entrance. The doors were opened hastily. No one could see them enter or leave in case questions were asked about the reason for the presence of 'enemies' at the Uffizi. But to everyone's surprise and relief, as soon as the women disembarked, a familiar face was present to greet them.

'Professor Loggi,' cried Agatha, her face lighting up as if she'd seen a vision.

'My dear Mrs Fortescue-Smythe,' he replied, with a more muted smile. 'We meet again.' He took her gloved hand and kissed it. 'I am delighted you and your ladies will be working here. We could certainly do with your help.'

Agatha drew herself up to her full height – all four feet ten – but to Lina she seemed to grow by at least six inches. 'We are here to do our duty as art lovers, Professor.'

'Hear, hear,' agreed Miss Harrowby.

'A noble sentiment,' agreed the professor. 'We are very fortunate to have your skills at hand.'

Agatha beamed at this remark and Lina saw something spark in her eyes as she looked at the professor.

'Perhaps you and the others would care to follow me?' he said with a bow. It sounded as though he was inviting them to afternoon tea, or an elegant soirée, rather than the serious and meticulous work they'd been ordered to undertake.

Professor Loggi led the women along an ill-lit passage towards the basement, then traipsing down some dingy steps, they were all shown into a large, low-ceilinged room, containing row upon row of shelves. Each shelf contained boxes of files, bulging with papers. The smell of neglect gathered like dust on cardboard covers. Instructing a uniformed guard to remain by the door, the professor guided the women over to an area where two single electric bulbs hung forlornly over long tables.

'Ladies, ladies, please,' he said, calling for quiet.

What he was about to say was for their ears only. 'This gallery, along with several others in the city, is home to thousands of paintings, sculptures and other priceless pieces. Some have already gone to repositories for their security, as you know,' he told them, looking pointedly at Agatha. 'But many more remain, and they all need to be recorded. I confess I have not had the staff to do this properly.'

'Up until now,' interrupted Agatha, casting around at the other women for support.

'Quite,' acknowledged Loggi, noticing the nodding heads. 'But things are rather out of control, and it is hard to know what is where. And that of course leaves room for ...' He hesitated. 'Opportunism.'

Agatha nodded, knowing 'opportunism' was a euphemism for theft. 'We understand.'

'So, your role will be vital,' he continued. 'From now on the safety and security of the city's masterpieces will be largely in your hands.'

Lina noted a nervous undercurrent rippled around the room at the thought of such a monumental undertaking. Agatha, however, seemed raring to get going. 'We shan't let you down,' she told the professor. 'Shall we, ladies?'

Even when no one replied, Agatha's enthusiasm seemed undiminished. 'Where will we be working?' she asked.

'This will be your office,' replied the professor, looking around him at the dingy, windowless space. 'You will be expected to return here when you are not supervising the packing and transportation of items. And, of course, you will need to type up receipts into a catalogue, so we know exactly what everything is and where it is being stored.' Loggi pointed to two typewriters lined up on a large table.

Agatha raised a brow. 'A mammoth task, Professor.'

'I fear so,' agreed Loggi.

Undeterred, she took a leaf from Miss Giltrap's book. 'But, if anyone can do it, the English Ladies' Arts Appreciation Society can,' she exhorted, a triumphant fist in the air. There were nods of approval from her audience.

Loggi frowned. 'I'm afraid I am not familiar with the name.'

Agatha smiled. 'It is what our little group calls itself, Professor.' Looking dramatically into the distance and paraphrasing Shakespeare, she added, 'If anyone has the passion and desire to save such treasures for generations to come, it is we band of sisters. *We happy few*. Isn't that right, Angelina?'

Lina smiled weakly and nodded. 'Yes, Aunt,' she agreed, even though she was acutely aware of the enormity of the undertaking before them.

Agatha smiled. 'Oh, yes, the masterpieces of Florence will be safe in our hands.'

Loggi bowed his head. 'That is good to know,' he replied. Then in a half whisper he added, 'And that is why we need to talk. Alone.'

'Oh?' Agatha's brows lifted heavenwards.

'But now is not the time.' He turned to glance at a uniformed official stationed at the door. 'Your guard.' He cleared his throat. 'You will be supervised, I fear.'

'Will we indeed?' mumbled Mrs Clutterbuck with a sceptical look. She may as well have added 'We'll see about that.'

The professor tilted his head towards Agatha and spoke from the corner of his mouth. 'I warn you, Mrs Fortescue-Smythe, the guards have eyes like hawks. Please don't do anything rash.' He looked at his wristwatch. 'Now we shall shortly go up to the first floor,' he continued, addressing all the women. 'The porters are about to load more paintings. There you will each be given a list of works to be transported. It will be your job to make sure they are all listed correctly before they are taken to their various destinations.' He paused and shook his head. 'Of course, the safest place for all these paintings is on the walls of this revered gallery, however, circumstances force us to uproot them to find new homes. I realise it is far from ideal, but I fear we have no choice.' He clapped his hands together. 'Before we go, does anyone have any questions?'

For a moment there was silence. The women seemed too nervous, or too overwhelmed, to say anything, as if a great weight had just been placed on their shoulders. But then Agatha turned and cast around the basement. 'Yes, Professor,' she replied. 'I'd like to know how one gets a cup of tea around here.'

Chapter 16

March 1941

Edoardo sat in the railway carriage, reading a newspaper – a fascist one, of course. This was his fourth journey from Florence to Innsbruck. Once again, he was accompanying a consignment. He'd little idea what was in the crates, apart from knowing they contained priceless artwork worth millions of lire. This time there were four of them, twice as many as before. And unlike his ticket, theirs was one way to Goering's hunting lodge. This time, however, if everything went to plan, not all of them would reach their destination.

The carriage was chilly again, but at least he had it all to himself. He folded his newspaper and ate the cheese panini Signora Bianchi had packed for him. It was stale but at least it was filling. He'd just reached for his newspaper once more when the train slowed a little. The first station. He read the sign. Bologna. By now it was almost midnight, but they were still in Italy. The platform was packed with soldiers. From the looks of them they were fresh from the Front. Several were wounded. Stretchers were lined up on the platform; some of the men looked in bad shape. After much shouting and jostling most of them boarded, but they'd taken their time. Edoardo looked at his watch. The stop had overrun by seven minutes. By the time the guard had blown his whistle the train was eleven minutes behind schedule. Then came the next blow.

The door slid open. 'These free?' asked an officer, a captain by his stripes, pointing at the five empty seats surrounding Edoardo.

Damn, he cursed. 'Of course,' he said.

The captain, his face darkened by thick stubble, was followed by another officer of the same rank, his left hand bandaged. Both looked battle-weary and stank of dirt, sweat and dried blood. Taking two seats opposite Edoardo, they quickly made themselves at home, flanking him with their booted feet on the banquettes and lighting cigarettes. Silently, they regarded him, suspicion and contempt melding in their gazes. Edoardo guessed they wanted to know what a civilian, whose fingernails were clean and whose suit unstained, was doing travelling north. He flicked out his folded newspaper and pretended to read once more, all the while aware of the minutes ticking down.

The halt at Verona an hour later was mercifully quick. Four minutes made up, he told himself. Just seven late. The train picked up speed again. The spinning wheels felt good beneath him. A rush of adrenaline coursed through his veins. Not far till the Austrian border. He glanced at his watch again, then up at his travelling companions. One was asleep but the other was still staring at him. It was no good. He was going to have to move. Opening the briefcase at his feet, he dropped in his folded newspaper, closed the clasp and stood. Reaching up to the luggage rack, he took down his small valise. With a courteous nod to the officers, he slid open the door and walked out of the carriage.

What next?

To his horror, Edoardo found the corridor rammed with troops. Some stood, some, too exhausted to stand, crouched down. Others sat, their legs splayed in front of them. Somehow, he needed to wade through this swamp of human misery to the freight cars at the rear. With his briefcase in one hand and his suitcase in the other, he began his unsteady trek. Clambering over inert bodies, lurching through hostile clusters of men and shouldering insults, he forged ahead. Five carriages and several bruises later, he came to the guard's van. Pulling out his documents from his breast pocket, Edoardo addressed the guard.

'I am authorised to check on the cargo,' he told him, glancing at the crates stacked in the freight car behind him.

The guard, a sullen man with crooked teeth, was seated in a small space portioned from the remainder of the wagon itself. He squinted at the document, then nodded and let Edoardo pass.

There were no lights in the freight car, but the glow from the guard's lamp permeated the gloom. The crates were there, all right, lined up, side by side. Just ready for the taking. It was now up to Edoardo to ensure they could be. From his briefcase, he took out his torch and directed the beam to the slatted sides of the windowless truck. He'd have to get to the far door by the couplings to give the signal. He glanced round. The guard had been joined by another, taller, official and they had just begun a game of cards. Another glance at his watch. He had two minutes to open the far door and flash his torch. He made his move. The wagon lurched, wrong-footing him. He careened into one of the crates but quickly righted himself and carried on, hurtling towards the door. Gripping the handle tight, he held his breath and pulled towards him. It opened a crack, blasting cold, mountain air into his face.

Wedging his body through the opening, he clung on to the safety rail with one hand. There was no way of checking the time, so he signalled regardless. Two quick flashes, a pause, then two more. He'd no idea where he was, but he just kept on flashing in the hope a look-out would see the lights. Then, after what seemed like the longest minute of his life, he felt the train slowing before it braked hard. The screeching sound was deafening as he staggered backwards into the freight car and managed to slam the door. With a final brutal shudder, the locomotive came to an abrupt halt.

The guards were on their feet, playing cards now sprayed all over the carriage floor. 'What's going on?' cried the one with crooked teeth, baffled. The other shrugged in reply and both left their stations to venture down the train. Edoardo followed behind and stopped at the first window he came to. Shouts were coming from the track. Something about a landslide. The line was blocked. A delay!

Rushing back to the freight car, Edoardo knew there wasn't a moment to lose. Shooting back the bolts from the inside, he waited breathlessly in the darkness for the knock. It came a few seconds later and in response he slid the door wide open. Four men in Italian infantry uniform were waiting. They clambered inside and made a beeline for the crates.

'Welcome aboard!' greeted Edoardo, as he helped them into the freight car. Without another word they dragged the first crate of artworks back towards the door, where another two men hefted it off the train and onto a waiting cart. The whole operation took less than five minutes. It went exactly to plan.

Cesari Manzano's bloated face was a worrying shade of purple. Edoardo had never seen the man so enraged. Then again, he mused, the podesta had every right to be. He was pacing up and down his office, gnawing at his clenched fist from time to time. Then he would hammer it down on his desk as soon as another consequence of the train debacle opened up before him like a yawning chasm.

'What am I to tell the Germans?' he quailed. Flinging out both arms, he grabbed his own head, as if he thought it might explode at any moment. Up until then Edoardo had remained silent, staring at the half-eaten dish of olives on the desk. Of course, he'd had to telephone the podesta to report the theft. He was horrified, he said. He'd only grasped what had happened when the soldiers started unloading the crates at Innsbruck Station. Two had disappeared. It was only then the realisation dawned. The 'landslide' must have been a hoax. The thieves stole as many crates as they could, in the time it took to clear the track of a few boulders and send the train on its way again.

'Everyone was fooled,' ventured Edoardo, sticking his head above the parapet. But Manzano quickly shot back. 'And you weren't in the least suspicious? You idiot. You buffoon. And to think I gave you a second chance. You'll be lucky if you don't end up the same way as your father after Goering has finished with you.'

Edoardo had remained grounded until he heard that name spill from Manzano's rubbery lips. Now the room swam as he thought of the punishment the *Reichsmarschall* might exact on him. But the mere thought of it had already prompted a solution. Once more, he lifted his head and spoke.

'Does Herr Goering ever have to know, sir?'

'Your total incompetence is—' Manzano broke off and turned to face Edoardo. 'What did you just say?'

Edoardo chewed his lip then reframed his question. 'The *Reichsmarschall* wasn't made aware how many crates were expected.'

Manzano narrowed his piggy eyes. 'Go on.'

'Only two were stolen, so two were left. These can still be delivered to Carinhall and Herr Goering will be delighted with the consignment and none the wiser.' As soon as he'd finished speaking, Edoardo realised his lip was bleeding. Yet while he could taste a coppery tang on his tongue, he could also smell a breakthrough with the podesta.

Manzano stood bowed behind him, his breath hot on the dealer's neck. 'And you were the only one who knew this had happened?'

'That is correct.'

'And you told no one?'

Edoardo shook his head. 'Of course not, sir. You instructed me that the contents of those crates were to remain secret at all costs. I followed your orders to the letter, sir.'

He heard the podesta inhale deeply then walk around his desk to sit down. Slowly he nodded his head. 'Very well,' he began. 'After all, the crates contained gifts, and it is not for the recipient to question our generosity.' He was talking to himself, justifying his own subterfuge, but Edoardo was happy to play along.

'Quite so, sir,' he agreed. 'We could forget the whole sorry episode.'

Manzano regarded him from the corner of his eye. 'And you think these men were just mountain brigands?'

'I do. There is no way they could have known about the consignment. They were chancing their arm, and they just struck lucky.'

Manzano nodded as if convincing himself that this was the only way out of an unbearably awkward situation. 'Lucky. Yes,' he reiterated.

'It will not happen again, sir. Forewarned is forearmed, as they say,' Edoardo reminded him.

'You're right, yes,' agreed Manzano. 'It must not happen again. We shall double the guards on the next train.'

Edoardo sensed the meeting was coming to an end. He had entered Manzano's office a sacrificial lamb, but he was about to leave it a free man. It was a good outcome. The best he could have hoped for. Even though the podesta was none the wiser, Edoardo had just scored a victory.

Chapter 17

April 1941

A month had passed since the ladies started work at the Uffizi and Agatha's reports seemed favourable. The cataloguing had given them all a purpose and Lina was satisfied with the way things seemed to be running smoothly, even if the war – Mussolini's war – was not.

On her way to the university library that morning, to continue researching Cranach's later life for her biography of him, Lina had purchased a newspaper and stopped for an espresso at a street café. On the front page, despite the article's praise for Il Duce, it was clear Mussolini's men were paying a high price for their attack on Greece. She scanned the rest of the broadsheet but found little else of interest. And as for the item headlined *Landslide Blocks Rails Near Verona*, she didn't even bother to read the accompanying report. In fact, these days, she was finding it hard to concentrate at all, but it wasn't just the ladies' welfare that was playing on her mind. It was Edoardo Bernini. He had done what she'd asked of him by making an arrangement with Manzano. No doubt it hadn't been easy, but he had used his skills and his intellect to help the women avoid internment. Despite the women being placed under house arrest – something that had come as a shock to everyone – she was grateful to him, she truly was. Yet she still couldn't trust him completely.

Their last telephone call had been brief and awkward, and she could tell the dealer had been puzzled by her manner. But when she'd put down the receiver at the end of her conversation, she felt quite wretched. She'd tried to sound in control and strong when all she'd really wanted to do was cry with relief and fling her arms around Edoardo to thank him. There was something about him that fascinated her. Perhaps it was the air of risk that surrounded him, the sense she had that danger and excitement were never far away from him. And that smile of his. She found it hard to get his face out of her mind – seeing him in doorways, on trams, or just sitting in a piazza sipping a coffee. The thought of him was driving her to distraction. There was only one thing for it. She had to see him again; to dispel the bitter taste their last encounter at the gallery had left in her mouth. Who was he trying to fool, calling that woman on the line 'a client'? Draining her cup and folding her newspaper, she rose from the table and decided to pay a visit to the Gallery Bernini.

At his desk, Edoardo Bernini, suave in a well-cut suit, was taking an important telephone call. Podesta Manzano was in a suspiciously good mood. He seemed to have forgotten about the unfortunate incident with the consignment the other day and instead wanted to enquire about the English ladies. 'The *Scorpioni* have started work?' he asked.

Edoardo shrugged. 'I believe so.'

'You have not seen the girl lately?'

Edoardo tensed. 'No, sir. Not for a while.' During the single telephone call, Lina had thanked him for his help in arranging the release of the English women, but nothing more. She'd sounded reserved, aloof. It was if he had served his purpose but now, it appeared, she wanted nothing more to do with him. He wasn't used to being treated like that. Normally he was the one who paid the piper and called the tune when it came to dealing with people, especially women.

Manzano nodded and chuckled. Edoardo could tell he was eating something as he spoke. 'I've been checking up on her, you know. She told me she was an art expert but apparently that pretty head of hers is filled with our friend Cranach the Elder. She may be useful.'

Edoardo feigned surprise. 'In what way?'

'She's offered her services to me,' he replied suggestively.

'Oh?' Edoardo frowned.

'She says she can verify artworks. We can't go giving fakes and forgeries to the *Reichsmarschall* can we?'

'No, of course not,' replied Edoardo.

'I have a couple of tickets for the opera,' Manzano said unexpectedly.

'Opera tickets?' The gesture caught Edoardo by surprise.

'You could take the Leone girl.'

Of course. The podesta, he guessed, would never make such a gesture without there being an ulterior motive.

'See if you can get something out of her.'

Naturally Edoardo wanted to see Lina again, but he'd fought the urge, not wishing to embroil her in his mess. Besides, she'd made it pretty plain she had no interest in him, but perhaps Manzano had just handed him an excuse to reach out to her again. 'Very well,' he said. 'If that is what you wish.'

'It is what I order,' came the reply. 'I will send the tickets by courier later today.'

There was no time for Edoardo to reply before the telephone line went dead. He held the receiver away from his ear and looked at it quizzically. Manzano was up to something, something that involved Lina, and he didn't like it.

Returning the receiver to its cradle, he rose, snatched his coat from a hook and slipped it on as he walked to the front door.

He was contemplating closing the gallery early, but just as he reached for the sign, he saw a young woman wearing dark glasses approach – her hair swathed in a scarf and her frame draped in a shapeless coat. Despite her disguise, he recognised her instantly.

'Silvia!' Quickly he ushered her inside, his eyes darting left and right to check she hadn't been followed. 'What are you doing here?' he snapped. She wasn't supposed to come to the gallery. Ever. 'What's happened?'

'I've got something,' she said nervously, looking beyond Edoardo to his office at the back.

He put an arm around her and felt her body shaking beneath her coat. 'Through here,' he pointed. Once more he glanced back towards the large plate glass gallery window to make sure his unexpected visitor hadn't been followed. At first, he was relieved he couldn't see one of Manzano's secret agents in sight, but then he stood stock still. Someone else was standing on the other side of the pane, looking in and watching aghast at what had just happened between Edoardo and Podesta Manzano's secretary.

For a split second, Lina's incredulous eyes locked on to Edoardo's, her questions searing into his forehead like a brand. Her astonished gaze crippled him. He wanted to explain, to tell her everything, but instead he shook his head and took the anxious young secretary by the shoulders, wheeling her round towards his office, leaving Lina on the cobbles outside, confused, bewildered, and stunned.

When she returned home to Villa Mimosa, Lina was still reeling from seeing Edoardo – the man she'd been so drawn to and had feelings for – with Podesta Manzano's secretary. He'd put his arm around her. If she hadn't seen it with her own eyes, she would never have believed they were lovers. Even though she had no right over him, the sight unsettled her. It seemed like a betrayal, and a sensation she'd never felt before seeped into her veins like poison. His absence had made her soften towards him and once more she had begun to question the prejudice shown by both Professor Loggi and Agatha. But now she realised perhaps her aunt had been right all along. She'd told her Edoardo regarded art as a commodity to be traded like tea or flax. And when it had come to trading the women's freedom, his willingness to give way to Manzano's draconian terms had left her feeling let down. How could she ever let herself be attracted to such a man when he clearly had no soul? And now this – this affair, or fling or whatever it was – with Manzano's secretary whose skills were clearly not limited to typing.

A mixture of bitter disappointment and anger were fighting it out in Lina's head as she returned along the Via de Tornabuoni in an odd sort of daze. She had just reached a junction when from nowhere a voice called into her ear, giving her a fright.

'A penny for your thoughts. That's what you English say, isn't it?'

Lina jumped to see Gloria Giltrap, her white teeth fully exposed in a wide smile, standing at her shoulder.

'Miss Giltrap,' she gasped, palming her chest. 'What are you doing here?'

'My apartment is just around the corner,' she replied. 'Why don't you come in?' She nudged her in the ribs. 'You look like you lost a dollar and found a cent.'

She led the way to a large block and up the stairs to a first-floor apartment.

'Bourbon?' she asked, raising a half-empty bottle of Jack Daniels.

Lina hesitated, but then shrugged. 'Why not?'

As her flamboyant hostess poured the liquor, Lina looked about the spacious salon. The walls, she noted, were lined not with copies of Renaissance, or even famous Florentine art, as in most of the English homes she'd visited in the city, but with photographs. At least a dozen of them had been enlarged and framed. There were shots of all the famous Florentine landmarks like the cathedral, the Vasari Corridor and the Pitti Palace. There were also less well-known buildings and squares too, like the Piazzale Michelangelo. But most intriguing of all were the photographs of frescoes, taken inside churches. Lina recognised Masaccio's *Adam and Eve* immediately. Every exquisite detail had been captured on black-and-white film with startling clarity.

'These photographs,' Lina began as Miss Giltrap handed her a bourbon. 'You took them?'

'Sure, I did,' she replied, looking up at a particularly dramatic image of the *duomo* in a lightning storm. 'And that's what I wanted to talk to you about.' She sat down.

'Oh?' said Lina, settling herself into an armchair.

'Cheers!' Gloria Giltrap raised her glass and took a gulp.

Lina replied by raising her glass and tentatively sipping the fiery liquid.

'Have you heard of the Frick Art Reference Library in New York?' the American began.

A shake of the head. 'No. Should I have?'

'Set up by a friend of mine, Helen Clay Frick,' Miss Giltrap explained. 'Full of photographs and archival records that document the history of Western art. She's been commissioning professionals for years to photograph works of art in private collections. There are thousands of images, some of them of pieces lost in the Great War.'

'I see,' said Lina, impressed.

The American took another slug of bourbon then slouched forwards, her elbows on her knees, 'A few years ago, Helen – Miss Frick – asked an Italian photographer to record notable works of art over here. He went all over the place: Rome, Bologna, Milan, shooting stuff. Did a good job, but since Italy joined in the war, things have gotten difficult for him. He's not allowed to travel like he used to, so I said I'd be happy to take over.'

'You mean …' Lina hesitated. If what she thought Miss Giltrap was saying was true, then she was very interested.

'Yes. The Frick Library wants me to photograph as many

treasures in Florence as I can, and send the images back to the States.'

Lina nodded slowly. 'So that if, God forbid, they are damaged, then there will be a record of them.'

'You got it.'

She smiled. 'That is good news, Miss Giltrap,' she said. Keeping a photographic archive was a wonderful tool in the armoury of conservation. It could be useful in so many ways. The revelation made her feel more optimistic, even though she knew the Jack Daniel's might have something to do with it.

'Hell, if anyone is up to the job, it's me!' replied the American slapping her thigh. 'And call me Gloria, please,' she added.

'Yes, Gloria.' Lina nodded. Miss Giltrap was perfect for the job. Perhaps Agatha was right when she'd declared, after the Blackshirt attack, they could have managed well enough on their own. Going to Signor Bernini and asking him to help the women a second time had made her feel beholden to him. She realised that now. Opposite her, Miss Giltrap was raising her glass.

Lina smiled. 'I'll certainly drink to that,' she said.

Chapter 18

'Signor Bernini.' Lina found her own voice sounded an octave higher than usual when she realised who was on the other end of the telephone line. Only four hours had passed since she'd seen the dealer ingratiating himself with Manzano's brazen secretary. Four hours spent trying to come to terms with the fact that she could never trust the man she imagined falling in love with. It was such a silly, childish notion. Yet here he was again, calling her at Villa Mimosa. Why? He had some secret agenda, she told herself as his voice reached into the hallway.

'What can I do for you?' she asked, aware she sounded frosty.

'I feel I owe you an explanation,' he told her.

'Oh? Why might that be, Signor Bernini?'

A sigh then. 'When you called by the gallery earlier today.' She clenched her teeth, annoyed with herself that he'd spotted her. 'I was with a supplier.'

'A supplier?' she repeated, not knowing whether to laugh or cry. *Did he really take her for such a fool?*

'Yes, Signorina Corvo's father is one of my framers. She came to tell me he'd fallen ill. Seriously ill.'

'One of your framers?' she whispered. The information was delivered with such conviction that she suddenly felt quite wretched. Had she been too quick to jump to conclusions? Just like Agatha? But one of the many lessons she'd also learned from her aunt was to manipulate a man's ego. She took a deep breath. 'You must be mistaken, Signor Bernini. I'd no intention of calling on you. I was running an errand and just happened to glance into your gallery window.'

'Oh. Oh, I'm sorry, my mistake,' he said. 'I thought you might have come to tell me how the ladies were getting on.'

'They are well.' She deliberately sounded distant.

'I'm glad,' came the reply. 'But I still feel I owe you a proper explanation for today, Signorina Leone.'

'Owe me?' she repeated. It was as if this man saw everything in terms of accounting, of balance sheets and income, of expenditure and profit. Or loss.

'I have two tickets for the opera on Saturday night. *Tosca*. Would you do me the honour of accompanying me?'

The question rattled her. An invitation was not what she'd expected. 'The opera?' She hesitated, not because she didn't like opera. She loved it. 'I … I.' So, this was his apology. But should she accept it? Her first instinct was to say no. 'I couldn't possibly,' she replied.

There was a silence down the line. He hadn't been expecting a rejection. She suspected he wasn't used to them – from women at least.

'I'm sorry to hear that,' he said. 'I thought you might be a fan of opera.'

'I am,' she said.

Why didn't she simply say 'no' and put down the receiver? She realised that now, but something had made her stay on the line. There was no pleasure in sensing him squirm. If she were honest with herself, it was just that she wanted to hear his voice and, deep down, of course she did want to go to the opera with him.

'Please, there is no need to explain. I know you don't think very highly of me. I should never—'

'No,' she broke in. Perhaps she had been too quick to jump to conclusions, after all. Too harsh. Perhaps he was telling the truth about Manzano's secretary being his supplier's daughter. If her father was very ill, then maybe she did need comforting. Lina shook her head. She could have overreacted to what she'd seen through the window. She considered giving the dealer the benefit of the doubt, then after a moment replied, 'Very well.'

Another hesitation on the line. 'You mean you'll come?'

'I will.'

'Thank you, Signorina Leone,' he said. 'I'll pick you up at your villa around seven.'

Lina had fielded the call on the telephone on the console table in the hallway. When she put down the receiver, she paused to take in her reflection in the large mirror on the wall facing her. *Tosca.* The tale of a woman who had to make a horrific bargain; surrender herself to a powerful man or have her lover killed. It was a terrible choice and one she prayed she would never have to make herself, so why did she have a dreadful feeling she may have just walked into a trap?

Agatha came out of nowhere and was standing behind her, watching her in the mirror. 'Signor Bernini, I take it,' she said stony-faced.

Lina swallowed hard, then turned. 'You heard.'

'No, but I can tell from your expression, my dear,' replied Agatha. 'You're flustered. Only a young man can make you flustered. A handsome young man who holds an attraction for you.' She was regarding her niece with a weary disappointment, melded with concern. 'Be careful, my dear,' she warned. 'Signor Bernini may be very charming and gallant, but I'm still not sure that man can be trusted.'

The truth was, Lina remained uncertain, too.

Chapter 19

The magnificent Teatro Comunale, decked out in its red velvet and gold livery inside, was magical. For a moment Lina felt she was in a beautiful dream. Soft lights twinkled, diamond necklaces and earrings sparkled, and the women's gowns were breathtaking. But then the fascist uniforms came into view, reminding her she was hovering on the edge of a nightmare. Edoardo wore a dinner suit and Lina a full-length midnight-blue evening gown, but these men, who carried themselves with such an air of arrogance were the same men who kicked dogs, beat up homeless children and arrested defenceless, elderly women. She didn't like to imagine what they did to those who disagreed with their politics.

Edoardo was being a perfect gentleman; sophisticated and charming, but she couldn't help but think that maybe he, too, was just putting on an act. He made no more mention of the encounter she'd witnessed at the gallery. Nor did she, and yet, the current of mistrust remained, taking the shine off what should have been a glittering evening. The shimmering lights and the glint of diamonds wove a magical spell as the orchestra tuned up against a hum of excited conversation. The sense of anticipation was as real as the red velvet drapes on the stage. Yet, even after the performance began, Lina found it hard to concentrate on what was happening on the stage. The scenarios playing out in her own head were even more powerful and unsettling.

When the lights went up for the interval and they left their seats to go to the bar, Lina remained uneasy. Her mouth was dry, but she didn't want Edoardo to sense her discomfort at feeling so out of place.

'So, what do you think of the performance, Signorina Leone?' he asked, with a smile.

'I—' She was going to lie and say she was enjoying it very much, but before she could, someone in the crowd called out Edoardo's name.

'Bernini? Edoardo Bernini?' A tall, broad man with thinning hair towered over them.

The dealer turned and smiled awkwardly. 'Decker! Franz Decker.' He was an associate who dabbled in dealing. They'd met on a business trip to Switzerland. Edoardo knew Decker didn't have any interest in art. He just wanted to make quick money.

The man laughed then turned to Lina and ogled her unashamedly. 'So, you've been busy, I see.' He nudged Edoardo. 'You always were one for the women,' he remarked jokily, as if she wasn't there.

'But what are you doing here?' asked Edoardo, aware of Lina's disapproving glare and trying to change the subject.

'Business, of course.' He dropped his voice and lifted his lips. 'There's money to be made in war and I'm seeing if I can do anything to help my Italian friends.' He dipped his head and raised his glass to a passing general.

Edoardo's hand went to his temple. 'Don't tell me. Armaments, yes?'

Decker smiled. 'Very good. Manufacturing rifles to be precise.' He clapped Edoardo on his back. 'The old man is busy sending regular shipments to Germany.'

'We all make money how we can these days, my friend,' conceded Edoardo, eager to draw the conversation to a close.

Decker parted, vowing to arrange to meet up with the art

dealer soon.

'I'm sorry about that,' apologised Edoardo with a shrug, tugging his shirt cuffs.

In reply, Lina managed to nod graciously. 'I always knew you were well connected, *signor*,' she replied.

'You flatter me,' he said with a smile, but no sooner had he spoken than Edoardo's lips flattened, and a shadow spread over his face. Lina noticed his attention was, once again, being diverted. This time it was by a man in a formal fascist uniform that was too small for him. When she realised who was beckoning him, horror filled her eyes. Manzano.

'We are being summoned,' Edoardo told her. She saw a bead of sweat break out on his forehead.

The panic that had been simmering inside her threatened to boil over. She wanted to bolt for the nearest exit. 'You knew he was going to be here?'

Edoardo looked scandalised. 'Of course not. I would never have brought you if I thought for one moment he was.' He was shaking his head as Manzano beckoned. 'But we have to go over. We can't refuse.'

Each step closer to Manzano felt like walking on hot coals for Lina. She held Edoardo's arm tightly.

'You will join us for a champagne, yes?' said Manzano, standing by a table with a bottle of Krug in an ice bucket. A young brunette in diamonds and a mink stole was already seated.

Although he was speaking to Edoardo, his eyes were firmly set on Lina, and on her cleavage, in particular.

The dealer bowed. 'You are very kind, Excellency,' he replied.

'And Signorina Leone,' said Manzano, leering at her. 'I hope your aunt and the other English ladies are finding the new arrangement satisfactory.'

'The new arrangement?' echoed Lina. That was one way of describing house arrest, she supposed. She glanced at Edoardo, but his eyes urged her to play along.

'Yes, thank you,' she replied as Manzano reached for her gloved hand and brushed it with his slack lips.

'And I have work for you, too.'

The woman with him rolled her eyes, as if she'd witnessed the podesta act the same with a hundred different women. He turned to her and said, 'Signorina Leone is an expert in Renaissance art, darling. She has offered to verify some pieces.' He turned back. 'It's not every day one meets such a combination of beauty matched by knowledge,' he added with a look that turned Lina's stomach.

Despite her repulsion, somehow she mustered a smile, but swiftly switched her gaze to Edoardo as he pulled out a chair and a waiter poured champagne. She'd been hoping he'd make some excuse to leave, but it was too late. As soon as they were seated, the podesta's lethal tongue took aim and fired straight at her.

'I hear you are writing a book on Cranach the Elder, one of Germany's finest painters, Signorina Leone,' said Manzano, slurping his champagne.

She couldn't hide her surprise. Her face fell. He'd been checking up on her.

'I've been studying him for a while, yes,' she acknowledged.

'Tell me, what is his appeal to you?' He threw a smirk in Edoardo's direction, as if he was playing some sort of game with her.

But Lina didn't want to play. Instead, she said simply: 'Weibermacht.'

Manzano looked puzzled. '*Weibermacht?*' he repeated. 'A German word, I presume. I am not familiar.'

'It translates to "Female Power" or "Power of Women",' explained Edoardo, looking directly at Lina.

Her lips lifted slightly as she nodded then locked eyes with Manzano. 'Cranach painted beautiful women – from history, or the Bible or mythology. They all exerted a power over men that led to their doom. Cranach was warning men to beware the she-wolf, Excellency. Fall for her charms and a nasty fate awaits you.'

The podesta laughed nervously and reached for his collar, trying to loosen it a little. Clearly disconcerted by the thought of powerful women, he simpered, 'Of course, he is inferior to our own masters, but worthy of time, I'll grant you. Did you know he is the German Führer's favourite painter, too?'

'So I believe,' replied Lina, forcing her mouth to stretch into a smile.

'And who are we to argue with Herr Hitler?' he joked, but then his features changed abruptly, and his tone turned serious. 'Strangely enough I've heard something on the grapevine, that a portrait that could be a Cranach has become, how can I put it, unexpectedly available.'

'Really?' asked Edoardo, arching a brow. It was clearly news to him.

'Yes. In a villa at Forte dei Marmi.' Manzano leaned in. 'It just happens to be the summer home of an Austrian Jew, who is looking to leave it in safe hands.' He turned to Lina and said pointedly, 'I assured him I knew of an expert to verify the painting's authenticity and, if it is a Cranach, I volunteered to store it safely for him.' The podesta laughed again, this time more heartily. 'Perhaps you would oblige me, Signorina Leone?'

Lina felt the blood leach from her face. 'Me?' she asked, glancing at Edoardo for support. 'You mean you want me to look at it?'

Manzano's laugh rose from the depths of his large belly. 'Come, come, Signorina Leone. We have an arrangement, don't we? Besides, I can think of no one more qualified to authenticate a Cranach.' From the way he looked at her, Lina understood a refusal wasn't an option. She tried to shake away the nightmare enfolding her. Had she really just been asked to authenticate a masterpiece confiscated from a Jew? She thought of Lady Felstein and how, as a Jew of foreign nationality, she was still in danger of imprisonment. It was a battle to keep her rising anger under wraps. But when she hesitated to reply, Manzano took it as a weakness. 'Do I detect a reluctance, signorina?'

She turned to Edoardo as she spoke. 'I … I couldn't possibly. There are others more qualified,' she replied.

'Oh, but you are too modest,' countered Manzano. 'And besides, I am giving you a chance to serve your country, Signorina Leone. The *Scorpioni* are proving themselves useful and I am sure you would wish to do the same.' He slurped more champagne and angled his head. 'Or do you feel more British than Italian?'

A shiver slid down her spine at the implied threat behind the podestà's comment, and she looked to Edoardo once more for support. He must know how abhorrent this proposal was to her. Surely, he would refuse on her behalf. Wouldn't he? But when he spoke, she could barely believe the words that left his mouth.

'I am sure Signorina Leone would be honoured to offer her expertise,' he said with a nod.

'But I—' As soon as she protested, fingers dug sharply into her waist below her silk stole. Edoardo was warning her to keep quiet. If she were Agatha, she'd have delivered a flat refusal and given the podestà a piece of her mind. But Edoardo was telling her to rein in her disdain for Manzano. Reluctantly she obeyed, but inside her anger still simmered at the sight of Edoardo colluding with this lecherous monster.

'Excellent. Then that is settled.' Manzano turned to Edoardo. 'I shall authorise you to accompany the signorina to Forte dei Marmi tomorrow.' Switching back, he eyed Lina triumphantly. 'I am sure you'll find the challenge most interesting, Signorina Leone.'

Manzano offloaded his drained champagne glass onto a passing waiter's tray. The brunette followed suit, darting a hostile glare at Lina. 'You'll be hearing from me,' said the podestà. With those words, he headed off back to the auditorium. The third act was about to begin.

Edoardo looked at Lina to catch her barely controlled contempt.

'What have you just done?' she asked him incredulously. This time, as they returned to the auditorium, she was desperate to avoid brushing against Edoardo. Only two hours ago, she'd been prepared to allow herself to be drawn into his orbit. Now she couldn't even bear to be near him.

'Believe me, I had no idea he'd be here, but let's talk about it later,' Edoardo urged, as an elderly countess with feathers in her hair bumped into him. He took Lina's arm, but she yanked it free.

'I'll thank you not to touch me, Signor Bernini,' she replied through gritted teeth.

A high-ranking general just happened to be passing and glowered at her.

'Don't make a scene, please,' urged Edoardo.

'You've put me in an impossible position, Signor Bernini,' she protested.

'I'm sorry, but I had to,' he told her.

Lina stopped in the aisle and stared at him, statue-still, for a moment, trying to work out whether he was paying lip service in case he was overheard or whether he truly believed what he'd just said. Either way the last act passed before Lina's eyes in a blur. The score battered her brain and every note sung by the soprano chafed and scratched. She simply couldn't blank out the prospect of travelling to Forte dei Marmi on fascist business. As the opera reached its shocking climax, and Tosca mounted a parapet to evade the police, she could see a chilling parallel with her own situation. When the curtain fell, she only hoped she wouldn't be forced to choose between working for the fascists to protect herself and loyalty to her aunt and the English ladies.

The short journey back to Villa Mimosa in the chauffeur-driven car was spent in almost complete silence. Once or twice Edoardo tried to explain his behaviour, but Lina always shut him down immediately. She was too angry to speak. She felt betrayed, and when the limousine drew up outside the villa, she didn't wait to be helped out of the passenger seat.

'Goodnight, Signor Bernini,' she told him, slamming the door hard.

'Goodnight, Signorina Leone,' he called after her. 'I shall return for you tomorrow.'

Lina didn't reply. She was already on the front steps of the villa. As soon as she was inside, Agatha came out of the drawing room only to see her rush up the stairs.

'Did you have a …' Her voice trailed off in the wake of her niece's visible distress.

Upstairs, Lina flung herself face down on her bed. Professor Loggi was right. Edoardo was a sheep in wolf's clothing. He had bared his teeth that evening and handed her over to Manzano on a plate. Her pent-up anger and frustration flowed over into tears. But she wasn't left to cry alone. Agatha sat down on the bed and laid a comforting hand in the small of her back. Watching her niece's shoulders rise and fall with each sob, she said finally, 'I feared this would happen.'

Lina eased herself up on her elbows and twisted to face Agatha. 'I know you warned me against him.'

Agatha sighed. 'His father was not a good man, and, as I said, the apple does not fall far from the tree.' She didn't have to say any more.

Accepting the handkerchief Agatha offered, Lina said, 'Tell me what he did that was so bad, please, Aunt.'

Agatha tutted in exasperation. 'Very well.' She sighed heavily. 'I suppose you ought to know.'

'Know what?' asked Lina, dabbing her eyes.

'Henrico Bernini was arrested for stealing works of art.'

Lina sat upright. 'You mean he was a thief?'

'In court it transpired he had been filching from the city's museums for several months. Small pieces by relative unknowns, granted, but theft is theft.' Agatha's voice cracked, and Lina noticed her aunt's eyes had become glassy. 'He was sentenced to twenty years' imprisonment. It was an open and shut case.'

'I see,' said Lina. She'd understood that Bernini Senior had been sent to prison, but hadn't known why, or if his crime was political or criminal. 'And you're afraid that Edoardo is like him?'

'Yes. Yes, of course, I am.' There seemed no question in Agatha's mind.

Lina thought of her own father. He'd been a complete wastrel, but being aware of that had made her want to do something positive with her own life. It wasn't fair to tar the son with the same brush as his father. What troubled her more was Edoardo's relationship with the vile Manzano. He seemed happy to do his bidding and now he had drawn her into the web, too.

'Oh, dearest Aunt,' she cried, flinging her arms around Agatha's slight frame. 'Thank you,' she murmured. 'I needed to know,' she said, as her own, confused tears fell once more.

Chapter 20

The wheels of the Alfa Romeo crunched on the gravel drive of Villa Mimosa. It was noon and Lina was waiting in the shade. Too angry and upset to sleep, overnight she'd rehearsed what she would say to Edoardo Bernini when he called to take her to Forte dei Marmi.

'I was afraid you wouldn't come,' the dealer remarked. He whipped off his sunglasses and Lina could see concern in his eyes. He walked round the front of the Alfa Romeo to open the passenger door for her. She didn't move when he held it wide, and he looked at her like a puppy who knew it shouldn't have chewed a slipper. 'We need to talk,' he told her.

She flared her nostrils. 'No, Signor Bernini. I'm the one who needs to talk to you.' Inhaling deeply, she launched into her well-rehearsed speech. 'You had no right to force me into this.' She paused, even doubting if she could still confide in him. 'I want no part in supporting the fascists.'

Edoardo closed his eyes for a moment, then nodded. 'I understand you feel that way, Signorina Leone.'

'I do.' It was good to offload some of the intense frustration that jangled her nerves. 'You trapped me into doing this. You know, especially after what happened to my great-aunt and her circle, that I have everything to fear from your fascist masters, and I want no dealings with that vile man Manzano. You've seen the way he looks at me. You know he makes my flesh crawl.'

Edoardo waited until she had finished to reply. 'I hear everything you say, Signorina Leone.' He nodded and walked closer. 'Manzano is a monster.'

His answer shocked her. 'You agree Manzano is evil and yet you—'

The dealer shook his head and lifted a hand. 'It was never my intention to drag you into this. I swear I didn't know the podesta would be at the opera last night, let alone that he would ask you to work for him. But believe me, agreeing to his request was the right thing to do for your own protection. If you had refused there could have been consequences.'

'Consequences?' She looked at Edoardo warily.

'You are only half Italian, *signorina*, and Manzano could easily overlook your paternal heritage and see to it that you also are subjected to harsh restrictions like the other English ladies.' He looked down at his shiny leather brogues, then back up at her. 'There are things … things you should know.'

'What things?'

'Things that cannot be said here,' he replied, casting around towards the villa's gardens. 'I will tell you when I can guarantee we are not being watched,' he told her.

She took a deep breath to stop herself shaking. 'Watched?' she repeated. Never in a thousand years had she thought Villa Mimosa would be under surveillance.

'You mean the OVRA?'

Edoardo pressed his finger to his lips.

'Very well,' she agreed. Edoardo gestured to the passenger seat once more and this time she eased herself into the car. She would force herself to be patient, but his explanation had better be good.

The road from Florence to Forte dei Marmi on the Mediterranean coast was busy with armoured vehicles and trucks. Edoardo had a special pass which enabled him to use his own car to travel within Tuscany. But it still meant he had to deal with rutted roads and endless checkpoints until finally, three hours later, Lina caught her first glimpse of the sea beyond coils of barbed wire and barricades. She couldn't help but smile. After the claustrophobia of the city, the sight of the azure water, fringed by golden sand and palm trees, was a balm for the soul, despite the constant reminders of war along the shore.

'Very beautiful, yes?' shouted Edoardo over the engine noise, turning to her as they drove along the coast road.

She'd swathed her dark hair in a chiffon scarf to hold it in place, but whisps had broken loose on the journey. 'Yes, very,' she replied. The fresh air and the sensation of speed helped banish her anxiety, if only for the duration of the drive.

The strip of road soon became smoother and neatly trimmed verges appeared on one side. Green hedges rose up and offered tantalising glimpses of villas that promised elegance and luxury. Shortly, Edoardo was pulling up at gates flanked by a high wall and guarded by two sentries. He waved his papers and was allowed to pass without further questions.

The driveway wound through a lemon grove and rose a little towards a breathtakingly beautiful pale ochre residence with a tall, central tower.

'So, here we are,' said Edoardo, bringing his sports car to a stop. He made it sound as though they'd arrived at a holiday destination.

'What has happened to the owner?' asked Lina. Edoardo was silent for a moment and from the look on his face, she could tell it was a question he couldn't – or wouldn't – answer.

'I am not sure,' he told her, leaving the possible outcomes to her own imagination. She understood that if the Austrian Jew and his family had made it out of their country hoping to find refuge in their summer villa in Mussolini's Italy, he had been very much mistaken.

Stepping out of the car, Lina took off her sunglasses and looked up at the building. The shutters were closed, and, glancing round the back, she could see barbed wire blocked off the rear terrace. It seemed the luxurious home was now in fascist hands. Two army sentries stood on either side of the elaborate entrance. Edoardo tendered more documentation for inspection, as an Italian officer came to meet them.

'Signor Bernini,' said a squat, broad army officer with a jet-black moustache, shaking Edoardo's hand. 'Captain Rizzio at your service.'

Edoardo smiled. 'This is Dr Angelina Leone, an expert on Cranach. She is here at the behest of Podesta Manzano.'

The captain took a step back. 'Is she, indeed?' he said, as if Lina was an object to be examined. 'Well, well.' He huffed out a bemused laugh and, overcoming his shock that a woman could be an expert at anything apart from bearing children, gestured inside. 'This way, please.'

They were escorted into a large room. The curtains on the long windows were drawn and most of the furniture was hidden under dust sheets. In the centre stood an easel and on it an unseen painting was covered by a large white cloth.

'So here it is,' said the officer. He leaned towards Edoardo. 'I think you'll find she's a looker.' He chuckled to himself, but when Edoardo didn't reply, he said, 'And here's what I think they call the provenance.' He laid a folder on a nearby table. 'Well, I'll leave you to it,' he said and he walked off, his hands clasped behind his back.

Lina let out a sigh of relief as soon as the officer left. She'd no wish to have him there, breathing down her neck as she examined the painting. She gestured to the remaining guard to draw back the curtains and moved closer to it.

'Ready?' asked Edoardo, clasping the cover in his hand.

She nodded and he pulled it away with a flourish.

The sight stunned Lina. Standing in silence, her eyes swept

over the painting with a sense of reverence. Edoardo joined her, as he too studied the portrait wordlessly.

A young woman with dark hair and a piercing gaze stared out at them from a wooden panel. She wore sixteenth-century court dress, and a set of rosary beads were entwined between her slender fingers. A *fleur-de-lys*, the emblem of the city of Florence, was embroidered on her gown. Normally women averted their gaze when they were being painted. But this one was staring out at the painter with an air of confidence. Lina was reminded of the Mona Lisa's smile. Only this young gentlewoman seemed even more self-assured.

For the next few moments, she remained staring at the work, making detailed notes. She took in its beauty and the craftsmanship involved; the way the black background contrasted with the woman's pale complexion, the way her red dress drew out the pink blush on her cheeks, the high collar drawing attention to her breasts. And, of course, there was the emblem painted at the bottom of the portrait. She squinted at it closely, knowing that until 1508 Cranach signed his works with his initials. After that, his patron gave him the winged snake as his *Kleinod*, his personal emblem.

'Now for the provenance,' she said, walking over to the table and opening the folder. But then her face fell. All that it contained was a bill of sale for the painting and a cutting from an Austrian art magazine. The article was in German. Edoardo skimmed it. 'It says the owner bought it at a sale just after the Great War.'

'Not very helpful,' she remarked, taking out a camera from the case around her neck.

'What's this?' asked Edoardo.

She was glad she'd had the foresight to borrow Miss Giltrap's Rolleiflex. 'I thought some shots would help me write my report,' she replied, snapping the portrait from various angles.

The subject, the colours, the brush strokes all reeked of Cranach, and yet she'd never seen the painting before. It wasn't in any exhibition she'd been to or any catalogue she'd studied. It was newly discovered, and a thrill of adrenaline shot through her. Even though she was almost convinced, for appearances' sake she picked up the portrait to examine it more thoroughly. The young woman's facial features may have been romanticised, but it was that confident look that sealed the deal. The way the artist had been given the expression of a classical goddess. It was powerful. It was magnificent.

She lifted the portrait off the easel and took it over to a table by the window where the light was better. Edoardo closed the curtain slightly, so the rays didn't fall directly onto the panel. Lina took out a magnifying glass from her handbag to lean over and scrutinise it further, making notes as she went. Cranach's quick technique with very little underpainting was evident. She turned it over. The panel was poplar wood, favoured by Renaissance painters. There was evidence of glue where the panels had been stuck together, but no woodworm. A good sign.

'Well?' asked Edoardo eagerly.

After less than ten minutes she felt confident enough to announce her verdict. Taking the painting in both hands, she returned it to the easel in the centre of the room, stood up straight and nodded. Her mind was made up. It was undoubtedly a Cranach the Elder. But before she made her announcement, she paused, then shook her head and, to Edoardo's astonishment, said, 'It's not a Cranach.' Her voice was emphatic – and loud enough so the guard would hear.

'What?' Edoardo's body jolted forwards, and he fixed her with a frown. 'It's not? But from your expression—'

'No,' she cut him off, her eyes flaring as she spoke. 'The positioning of the sitter, the hands. They're all wrong.'

Captain Rizzio stepped back into the room. 'You have come to a conclusion?'

She suspected he'd been hovering outside all the time. How else would he have known she'd reached a verdict?

Lina looked round at the officer, then switched back to gaze on the wooden panel. 'I have,' she replied. 'It's a poor imitation, and definitely not a genuine Cranach.'

The captain frowned.

'Let me show you,' she said, inviting him to look in more detail at the work. 'The finger joints under her gloves are all wrong. They're too low. And here …' She pointed to an inconsistency in the pattern on the girl's dress.

'I see what you mean,' he replied, stroking his moustache in thought. He seemed disappointed.

'Lucas Cranach would never make such mistakes.'

'But didn't students sometimes paint for their masters and pass it off as their work?' asked the captain.

Lina sucked in air between her teeth. 'True, but Cranach's emblem is all wrong. And the wood.' She turned the portrait over. 'It's got woodworm in it. It's not poplar. Cranach always painted on poplar,' she lied, still staring at the portrait. 'It's most definitely a fake.'

Rizzio sighed. 'Then you have wasted your time, *signorina*.'

She shook her head and swallowed her principles, replying with a polite smile, 'I am only glad I could be of assistance.'

Another glance at the painting seemed to satisfy the officer and he snapped his fingers at a nearby guard. 'Return this to the wall,' he ordered.

'Not so fast, if you please, sir,' Edoardo called out.

The captain baulked. 'What?'

'I have orders from Podesta Manzano to take the portrait back to Florence with us, no matter Signorina Leone's assessment.'

A sudden frown creased the officer's brow. 'That is most irregular.'

Edoardo nodded as he brought out his wallet and proceeded to count out five hundred lire. 'Irregular, true, but beneficial for you, sir,' he suggested, laying the notes on the table.

The captain glanced over towards the guard, who was

conveniently looking in another direction. Without a word, he shrugged then drew the notes towards him into his own pocket. Clearing his throat, he said, 'I wish you a safe journey back to Florence.'

'Thank you, *Capitano*. You have been most accommodating,' said Edoardo.

As soon as the officer left the room, Lina skewered Edoardo with a quizzical look.

'Please tell me what that was about.'

'You know as well as I do, Signorina Leone, that this painting is genuine.' He pointed to the portrait. 'Now, if you'll please lend me your headscarf.'

'What?'

Edoardo put his finger to his lips. 'Please.' He held out his hand and she placed her chiffon scarf into his palm. Wrapping it around the painting along with the folder containing the cutting and the bill, he tucked it under his arm.

'But you can't just—' she began before she was silenced with a glare and they made their way, unchallenged, out of the villa. Neither of them said another word until they were back at the car.

Chapter 21

'I underestimated you,' said Edoardo, his hands firmly on the steering wheel.

The Alfa Romeo was parked on a remote stretch of the coast overlooking the sea. It was a cool evening, but the sun was setting in a crimson sky. There was a break in the barbed wire where, at the edge of the shore, a brightly coloured fishing boat had just beached. Two fishermen were unloading their catch, tipping silver fish into wooden pales. If it hadn't been for the fact that Lina was confused and angry, an onlooker might think it a romantic scene.

'And I thought I *couldn't* underestimate you enough, Signor Bernini. But I did.'

'The Cranach is genuine.' Edoardo remained staring out over the sea.

Lina shivered as a sharp breeze blew off the water. 'Of course it is.' She turned to him in her seat and shot him an angry glare. 'And you've just stolen it.'

He looked at her then and laughed infuriatingly. It made her want to storm out of the car and walk back to Florence on her own, barefoot if necessary.

'How dare you?' she cried, swivelling back in her seat. 'I only said it wasn't real so that Jewish family could keep what is rightfully theirs and then you … you …' She clenched her fists in frustration.

'Manzano would have kept it anyway, so I've stolen it from him.' He was smiling as he spoke, like a complacent cat.

Lina found herself wanting to wipe the smirk off his handsome face. 'That's it. I've had enough,' she said, reaching for the handle of the car door. 'You sold my aunt and her friends down the river, having them put under house arrest, and now you've done the same to me.'

'No, please,' urged Edoardo, as she flung open the door. 'Where are you going?'

She looked at him then, and at his hand, laid on her sleeve. 'Anywhere. As long as it's away from you.' Turning quickly, she stepped out of the car.

'You've got me all wrong, *signorina*,' he protested.

'Have I?' she asked, slamming the door. 'Am I wrong to think you are an opportunist? A double-dealer and a thief? Not to mention a womaniser.' She spat out the last word, so that a fleck of spittle landed on Edoardo's cheek. He wiped it away deliberately with his finger. 'I never should have trusted you. I should have believed my aunt,' she cried.

Edoardo looked bemused. 'Your aunt? What did she have to say about me?' His tone was half mocking, as if an elderly self-opinionated English woman was no match for him.

'If you must know, she said you were just like your father and not to be trusted.'

This last remark seemed to wound. The smile on Edoardo's lips melted away. He looked straight ahead as the orange sun hung like a huge balloon above the horizon. The fishermen were walking back up the beach, carrying a net between them. 'Then perhaps you'd like to tell your aunt I only bribed the officer to keep the painting safe. I have no intention of holding on to it myself, or selling it, or handing it over to Manzano.'

Lina frowned and tried to steady her rapid breathing. 'So, what do you intend to do with it?'

Edoardo sighed and looked at her straight. 'If you get back into the car, I'll tell you.'

A thousand questions flapped like gulls inside her head, yet for some reason she wanted to believe him; wanted to trust him. She flattened her lips and sighed. 'Very well,' she said, opening the car door and slipping into the passenger seat once more. 'I'm listening.'

With both hands clutching the steering wheel, he turned his head to look at her squarely. 'I shall return it to its rightful owner,' he replied. 'Just as soon as he is able to receive it in person.'

She flashed the dealer another wary look. He was yet to convince her of his good intentions, but there was something in his eyes that made her think there was a grain of truth in his words. Taking a deep breath, she asked, 'And what about me? I've betrayed my country, haven't I? Some might say I'm a traitor.'

'You, a traitor?' Edoardo snorted and turned to look at the view once more, just as the sun touched the horizon. 'It's Manzano who is the traitor. To Italy. To its art. To its people.'

Lina remained uncertain. 'But you work for him?' she flashed back, her pulse quickening. 'I don't understand. I thought you—'

'You thought what?'

Realising that, like Agatha, she was guilty of rushing to judgement, she confessed, 'I thought you were on his side. My aunt said your father—'

Edoardo frowned. 'My father? What's he got to do with this?'

'She told me he was a thief and got sent to jail.'

He flinched then slowly began to nod. 'Well, well,' was all he said at first, as if she'd picked at a scab. 'If it's of any interest to you, I had no idea what he was up to until the court case. I was in Germany on an art scholarship.'

'But he was accused of stealing, yes?' Lina knew she sounded blunt, but she needed to know.

Edoardo took a ragged breath. 'You're right. Artworks. From

127

the city's museums. But I'd no idea that he was involved in anything criminal.' He turned to her, and she saw tears welling in his eyes. 'He betrayed me, too.'

After a moment Lina said, 'I understand.' She thought of her own Italian father; a chancer, too, by all accounts. *A waste of space* was how her mother described him. Agatha had agreed, but from old photographs she preferred to think of him as a charming adventurer. Gazing at Edoardo she said quietly, 'My father didn't get the chance to betray me. He left my mother before I was old enough to know the difference between right and wrong.'

Edoardo shrugged. 'Then perhaps you were fortunate.'

Lina had to agree. Sometimes ignorance was easier to handle than the truth. Inside her, something stirred. Ten minutes ago, she'd loathed this man who sat at her side. She'd thought him a risk taker, a fascist and a thief. Now, by opening his own heart to her, she'd seen someone else. Edoardo's hands were still grasping the wheel of the sports car, and she wanted to reach out to reassure him, but a sudden gust of wind ruffled his slicked-back hair. Lifting his hand, he patted it down and the moment was lost. Instead, they sat in silence watching the fishermen hang out their nets on a wooden frame on the shore, until Edoardo said without warning, 'There is something else you do need to know, Signorina Leone. Something I must tell you.'

Another shiver coursed down Lina's spine. His tone was ominous. 'Tell me what?'

Edoardo inhaled deeply, as if wondering how to frame the secret he was about to divulge. 'It concerns Adolf Hitler.'

Lina coughed out a laugh. 'What?' She narrowed her eyes. 'Please don't tell me the German Chancellor has got something to do with the Cranach?'

Edoardo didn't reply but ploughed on. 'Did you know he was refused admission to the Vienna Academy of Fine Arts?'

It was a strange question, and she was at a loss to understand why Edoardo had asked it. 'What of it?' she shot back.

'Hitler wanted to be a painter, but his work was poor. Even now, he bitterly resents never being recognised as a great artist, so he's decided to take his revenge.'

'Revenge? How?' she repeated, still not taking Edoardo seriously. 'I don't understand how this is relevant to the Cranach.'

He lifted his gaze heavenwards, as if calling on the Almighty to give him strength, as if he felt he needed it for what he was about to say. 'He plans to build what he calls *Das Führermuseum*.'

'*What?*' She let out a nervous laugh.

'A cultural complex in his hometown of Linz, in Austria, full of the most prized works of art. He wants it to be the greatest museum in the world.'

'The greatest museum in the world?' Lina repeated. 'This is some sort of joke, yes?'

Edoardo shook his head. 'I'm afraid it's not.'

She swallowed hard, realising he was deadly serious. Now she understood where Edoardo was leading.

'Why else has he started plundering the greatest art treasures he can get his hand on? Jewish collectors in Poland and France and the Netherlands have already been robbed of their priceless pieces, and there's no reason to believe he'll stop with them.'

She felt her jaw drop. 'You mean he has his sights on Italy and on Florence?'

'That's exactly what I mean. He sees Rome, Venice and Florence as fair game. Thanks to Il Duce and his cronies, all the great works could be in Nazi hands by the end of the war.'

Lina shook her head, trying to digest the enormity of what she'd just been told. 'I can't believe it.'

'I can assure you it's true. I've seen it with my own eyes,' Edoardo told her.

Her head snapped towards him. 'What do you mean, you've seen it with your own eyes?'

The dealer hesitated, checking himself. He'd said too much and bit his lip to play for time. 'I know your opinion of me has been, what can I say, mixed, Signorina Leone, and I was wrong to involve you in all of this. I'm so sorry, but I thought that after your aunt and the other English women were imprisoned …' His gaze dropped.

'You thought what, Signor Bernini?' She was no longer angry. More curious.

'What you did this afternoon with the Cranach was brave. Very brave and I'm hoping my trust is not misplaced when I tell you the truth.'

She shifted in her seat. Was he setting a trap for her? Just as he had at the opera. She'd already exposed her true feelings by lying about the portrait.

'You never cease to surprise me, Signor Bernini,' she replied.

Edoardo cast his eyes down again. 'You have to believe me when I say I loathe fascism and all it stands for.' He shook his head. 'I'm going to tell you something and I hope I can trust you with what I am about to say.'

'Yes,' she told him without hesitation. 'Yes, you can.'

'If it was discovered I had revealed this secret to you, I would not be the only one to pay a high price. You understand?'

Lina tensed, imagining a sword poised above her head. From the way Edoardo was talking it sounded as if he was in jeopardy and sharing this secret, whatever it might be, could also place her in danger. She understood that, but it was a risk she was prepared to take. She braced herself. 'I do.'

'Very well,' he began. 'It involves *Reichsmarschall* Hermann Goering.'

Chapter 22

Lina returned to Villa Mimosa that night a changed person. Just twelve hours before she'd known the fascists were evil. She'd known they were brutal, too, sacrificing Italian lives in pursuit of Mussolini's insane dream to recreate the Roman Empire. Now, even art, it seemed, was caught up in the conflict. She'd no idea the tyrant and his lackies were willing to give away some of the world's most precious treasures for the glory of the Nazi Third Reich. Or that Hitler and Goering considered themselves entitled to possess the work of some of the greatest artists that ever lived. Their greed and thirst for world domination were beyond her wildest imagination. This was a new level of insanity.

The moon was full and instead of going inside immediately, Lina remained in the roadster, gripped by an insidious feeling of dread.

'And you say more art is due to leave for Austria soon,' she said, her gaze fixed ahead of her.

'At the end of the week,' Edoardo replied. No more 'raids' were planned in the immediate future because Manzano had increased security. They'd had to change tack. Rethink their strategy.

'The end of the week?' she cried, switching to face him. 'And you're going with the consignment?' When he nodded, she flashed

131

him a pained look that he caught in the moonlight. 'And if you were to refuse?'

He sighed heavily. 'This isn't about me. If I refuse, I know Manzano will see you and your English ladies suffer.'

Lina pivoted in her seat and shot him a horrified look. Shaking her head, she felt the bile rise in her throat. 'I'm so sorry. I don't understand.'

'Manzano's power is spread far and wide. Whether you like it or not, you and your ladies are caught up in this. I know you thought I was in Manzano's pocket, but you were wrong.'

She began to protest. 'Well, I …' But then her shoulders slumped. He'd tripped her up again. It was exactly how she'd started to regard him – the snake in the Masaccio fresco. And now, just like Eve, she was beginning to feel ashamed.

The moonlight silhouetted Edoardo's profile as he looked straight ahead, one hand remaining on the steering wheel. 'I have to earn my living. Because of my father's mistakes, everything in the gallery was confiscated. Now and again, I may exaggerate a painting's value,' he said, nodding slowly as if agreeing with himself. 'But,' he continued, turning to face her, 'I am not a criminal and I'm certainly not a fascist. I still hold them responsible for the death of my father. Even if he did steal some paintings – and I don't even know if he did because I never heard his side of the story – he didn't deserve to die. I see what the fascists do, and I see what is happening, and I fear for the future. But that doesn't mean I should run away from it.'

Lina bowed her head, still cringing with embarrassment, but Edoardo tilted his face under hers, to catch her attention. 'If I'm on the inside then maybe I can help put things right,' he continued. 'I'm in a privileged position. I have transport. I can move freely within Tuscany. I have access to the art repositories, and I believe I can use my position to ensure the security of the treasures that are at stake. You understand?' He smiled then, not just with his lips, but his eyes too.

Lina smiled back. 'Yes. I understand.'

'So, we can be friends?' he asked. 'Not enemies.'

The sword above her head seemed a little farther away. 'Friends, yes. I'd like that, Signor Bernini.'

'Edoardo, please.'

'Edoardo.'

'But if news of Goering's gifts gets out, Manzano will trace the source to me. What you have heard is strictly secret.'

'I understand.' The consequences, she knew, would be dire.

'In the meantime, you will write a report on the Cranach. Yes?'

Her stomach lurched at the prospect. Committing lies to paper somehow seemed even worse than telling them, but she knew it was what she must do. 'The fake Cranach, you mean?' she said with a shaky breath. 'Manzano will have it shortly.'

Edoardo nodded then and got out of the car to open the passenger door for Lina.

'I'm sorry,' she said as she stepped out onto the drive, and they faced each other in the moonlight. 'I misjudged you.'

'Please. Let's put that behind us. From now on we should work together.' He shook his head. 'There has to be a way to protect what we have and stop the Nazi looting.'

'Yes,' Lina agreed, looking deep into his eyes. 'Yes, you are right. There has to be a way, and I want to help you.'

He didn't respond at first; just kept his eyes on hers until he leaned over, and she felt his lips, soft and warm on hers. They must have stayed there for a few seconds, but she wasn't counting. She was lost in the moment until he leaned back, and she breathed again.

'Was that wrong of me?' he asked when she remained silent.

'No. No, not wrong at all,' she replied, her heart still thrashing frantically inside her chest. She wasn't sure what had just happened. All she knew was it felt so right, and she'd never experienced anything like it before.

He took her hand then and kissed it tenderly. 'Goodnight, Lina.'

'Goodnight, Edoardo,' she replied, watching him return to his car. As he started the engine, she raised her hand and under her breath added, 'Please take care.'

The key made a horrible scraping sound in the front door lock. Lina had never noticed it before, but then she'd barely ever crept in just before midnight. Not wishing to rouse Agatha or Donna, she tiptoed quietly upstairs, even avoiding the fifth stair which she knew to creak. But it was all in vain. As soon as she reached the first-floor landing, Agatha was awaiting her, a candle aloft and her grey hair under a white nightcap.

'I was getting worried about you, my dear,' she said, remaining on the threshold of her bedroom.

Lina bit her lip. 'No need, Aunt,' she replied. 'I told you I'd be late.'

In the candle's glow she could see Agatha was frowning. 'And the painting at Forte dei Marmi?'

The painting. She'd never told a blatant untruth to her aunt before. Never needed to. Reluctantly she would have to start. 'Not a Cranach,' she replied.

Agatha shrugged. 'Oh well, I expect it was pleasant to visit the coast, anyway.'

'Yes. Yes, it was,' Lina said, hoping their conversation had come to a natural conclusion.

'Did that gross podesta fellow accompany you?' *A leading question. Had Agatha seen Edoardo's sports car in the drive?* Lina took a gamble.

'No. One of his men drove me out there,' was all she said. 'Goodnight, Aunt.' And with that she turned and walked to her room, dragging her guilt behind her. Not only had she gone behind Agatha's back to accompany Edoardo, if her aunt were ever to discover what he'd told her that night, it could put all their lives in danger.

Chapter 23

The rising sun glinted on the snow-capped Austrian peaks, turning them a pale shade of pink. Day had just broken as the Florence train pulled into Innsbruck. But the night had seemed interminable. It was the first run to Innsbruck since the raid where two crates of art were taken. Inevitably, Manzano had tightened security, so Edoardo had been forced to come up with another, more sustainable solution. He'd managed to get men on the inside to load the crates, and in so doing substitute some of them for ones containing forgeries. If Goering were to ask questions, he could feign ignorance. Florence was awash with fakes; good fakes at that.

So, while the locomotive clattered and jolted, guards shouted and carriage doors slammed, Edoardo's thoughts turned to Angelina Leone. There'd been other beautiful women, it was true, but none like her. Although now that she had uncovered a genuine Cranach, it added another complication. What should he do with the portrait? He'd left it in his safe at the gallery, but it wasn't secure at all. He needed to figure out where to store it until it could be returned to its rightful owner.

It was just another reason he arrived in Austria feeling he'd gone ten rounds with one of Mussolini's bulldogs. His tongue was like sandpaper and his eyes sore. There was no time to wash or eat. Immediately he was supervising the offloading of the crates of art onto a lorry. From there they would begin their northward journey to Berlin and ultimately to Goering's lodge at Carinhall. But before that he was told of a hold-up. Some junior ranking officer informed him his return journey would be delayed by at least three hours. A connecting train had broken down. Edoardo took the news badly. He cursed under his breath.

'If I'm wanted, you'll find me over there,' he snapped, tossing a glance at the city's best hotel. He'd send Manzano the bill. A hearty breakfast was the least the ugly beast could do for him after the night he'd had.

It was a short walk from the station to the Imperial Hotel. A pleasant one, too. Like walking through a toy town – all bright colours, gables and clocks, and spring flowers spilling from window boxes. It made him think of Lina and how when she smiled her eyes sparkled like gemstones washed by rain. As he was about to cross a main road someone broke into his thoughts. He heard his name called.

'Bernini.'

Edoardo turned to see a black fur hat and a well-upholstered man underneath it, approaching along the pavement. When he drew close, Edoardo realised it was Franz Decker – one of the last people he'd wanted to see.

'Decker! I hardly recognised you in that.' Edoardo's eyes lifted to the crown of the hat the businessman was wearing.

Decker laughed and took it off to reveal his thinning hair. 'I am glad of it in the cold weather,' he replied. 'Fancy seeing you again so soon.'

'Yes. Fancy that,' replied Edoardo less than enthusiastically.

'So, what devilish task are you really up to? Or can't you say?' He slapped his old associate on the back.

Edoardo paused for a moment. He may not trust Decker but, as a former art dealer, he might be useful to him. 'Just an errand for a client but my train back to Florence has been delayed. I haven't had any breakfast, or much sleep for that matter, so what do you say to a coffee and some *wurst*?' He pointed to the hotel. 'Then we can have a proper catch up?'

On the opposite side of the boulevard outside the station, a huge red and black swastika hung from the hotel's facade – a constant reminder to the people of Austria that Germany was now its master. The two men walked into the foyer. It was full of Nazi officers – Wehrmacht and a few SS.

Once they'd handed over their coats and hats to the cloakroom attendant, they entered the bustling dining room. The lofty salon was grandiose, with pillars and an elaborate gold leaf ceiling. Up ahead lay a long table groaning with food. Edoardo thought of the queues in Florence. Bread and sugar were already in short supply, but here there were bagels and pastries aplenty. Plates of salami and sliced speck vied alongside wedges of smoked cheese and fat *swatbrots*.

A waiter showed them to a table in the furthest corner. *That's good*, Edoardo thought. A seat up against the wall. He wouldn't have to keep looking over his shoulder as he sounded out his new best friend.

Decker leaned forwards across the table. 'The bacon is excellent. I always have it.'

'So, you come here often?'

Decker chuckled and patted his large belly. 'Recently it's been every month. Besides, it gets me away from home. I have a child now, a two-year-old, and there's another on the way.' He winked. 'A man needs a break in such circumstances. But you! That woman at the opera.' He made a crude gesture. 'Now she was something else.' He clicked his fingers at a passing waiter. 'You are doing well. Yes?'

Without waiting for Edoardo to reply, he ordered bacon,

sausages and eggs. When it came to his turn, the dealer seemed to have lost his appetite. 'Just a coffee,' he said.

Decker leaned over the table. 'You need to broaden your markets, yes? Is that why you are here? We Swiss may loathe the Nazis, but we've nothing against their money.' He leaned back and chuckled. 'We have a warehouse here, too, so if you want to lease storage, it is yours.'

They made small talk over the food. Decker chewed with his mouth open, and now and again a crumb of bread would hurtle across the table. But Edoardo humoured him while toying with an idea at the same time. As he downed his espresso, Edoardo ruminated about the offer that had just been made. He may have just been handed a solution to storing the Cranach and, as long as the Swiss dealer thought it worth his while, he'd be satisfied.

Chapter 24

While Agatha and her ladies were hard at work in the airless basement of the Uffizi, typing and filing and checking inventories, Lina took advantage of the stillness of Villa Mimosa. She was writing her report on the Cranach for Podesta Manzano, or at least trying to. The gardens, sporting their spring colours of lush green, cobalt blue and yellow, so often inspired her. But that day, as she sat at the large desk in the study, the muse had deserted her. A framed photograph of Agatha's little daughter, Jane, only added to her woes.

With its hedges of pink oleander tumbling over walls and purple fronds of sage and deep blue ceanothus, the garden was the very picture of calm and tranquillity – the opposite of how Lina was feeling inside. For the past hour, she'd written only a half dozen sentences, then, dissatisfied, crossed them out. When she'd studied for her doctorate, it had been a pleasure to write her thesis, her words poured across the pages effortlessly. Now, however, her pen scratched at the paper. Her words and phrases were bogged down by lies and deceit. She was finding it harder than she'd imagined committing blatant falsehoods in ink, even though she knew they were necessary to protect the painting.

Snatching at the messily written sheet of paper in front of

her, she screwed it up and hurled it disdainfully into the nearby wastepaper basket. Angry with herself, she slumped back into her chair. It would have been so easy to tell the truth; to confirm to Manzano that the portrait was a genuine Cranach. But if she did, the podesta would surely put it on the next train to Austria. From there Goering would get his greedy hands on it and the painting would be lost to civilisation forever, never mind its rightful owner. Her sense of natural justice just wouldn't permit that.

Lina's thoughts strayed to Edoardo then, and that kiss. She should have kept their relationship purely professional, but after the visit to Forte dei Marmi she realised it was out of the question. Not only that, she'd been less than truthful to Agatha last night as well. Her words wouldn't stop bouncing around in her skull.

Forcing herself to return to the report, she studied the photographs of the portrait that Miss Giltrap had developed for her. Her eyes played on the sumptuous fabrics and heavy gold jewellery, and that wistful, slightly imperious look on the woman's face. *Who was she?* Lina wondered. The *fleur-de-lys* was fashioned in opals across her bodice. That suggested the subject came from the city and was a real person, but her facial features were surely idealised. Lina supposed she could have been a mistress of one of the Medici. As she examined the incredible detail of the embroidery once more, her eye travelled to the top corner of the portrait, to something she hadn't spotted before. The turret of a castle, painted in miniature, peeped out from a cluster of vine leaves. It seemed strangely familiar to her. Then she remembered. Jumping up from the desk, she hurried over to Agatha's bookshelves, running her hand across numerous spines until she came across what she was looking for. Frantically she thumbed the pages of a thick history book until she found a chapter on Cosimo I de' Medici. With her heart in her mouth she read, '*His illegitimate daughter, La Bia, was born in 1539. Her mother remains unknown, although it is believed she may have been a Florentine gentlewoman. However, the child was brought up at Villa di Castello, away from court.*'

She felt an odd tingling sensation in her fingers. The time period stacked up with Cranach the Elder and the location. Could she have stumbled on a portrait of Cosimo de' Medici's unknown lover before he married Eleanor de Toledo? If she had, it would be a huge discovery in the art world. But none of this mattered right now, she told herself. The most important thing was to convince Manzano that this portrait was a poor, worthless copy. She plucked a date from the air. Nineteenth century, possibly. Definitely a fake. Not even by one of Cranach's pupils. Of no use to anyone, least of all *Reichsmarschall* Hermann Goering.

She reached for her notebook. It contained the observations on the painting she'd made at the villa. She underlined certain words and phrases with a pencil. Perhaps it was her anxiety, or just carelessness but she pressed on the paper much harder than usual. The lead snapped. Cursing under her breath she searched for a sharpener and opened the top drawer of Agatha's desk. There was nothing there, so she looked in the next, and rifling through old letters she reached the back, her hand landing on what felt like a newspaper cutting. Curiosity got the better of Lina and, fishing it out, she noticed the scrap was from an Italian newspaper – surprising since Agatha maintained she'd never learned the language. Opening it up, Lina noted the date: October 13th, 1938. But when she read it, she felt the hairs on the back of her neck stiffen. The headline ran: *Respected art dealer sentenced*. She frowned as she read on. *Henrico Bernini, the renowned Florentine art dealer has been found guilty of stealing several paintings from the city's museums and art galleries. Sentencing him to twenty years in prison, Judge Enzo Tucci, described Bernini as 'little better than a common thief'.*

She re-read the cutting to make sure she understood the report. It came as no surprise to her that Henrico Bernini was a convicted crook. Edoardo had been open about it. The question was, why had Agatha kept the newspaper cutting about his trial? It certainly helped explain her attitude towards him and to Edoardo. She was tarring his son with the same brush; perhaps even suspecting he was in league with his father at the time. That was surely why Agatha didn't want her to fall for Edoardo's undoubted charms. But it still didn't explain why she felt it so necessary to hang on to the cutting. It was just one more question in an ocean of them that threatened to flood Lina's head. She returned the scrap of newspaper to the drawer and shut it, knowing she had to focus on the report. Transferring her gaze to the blank sheet before her on the desk, somehow, she steeled herself to commit her pen to paper once more.

After my detailed examination, I conclude this portrait of an unknown woman, purportedly by Lucas Cranach the Elder, is a forgery.

Chapter 25

The note in Signora Bianchi's shaky hand read: *Call Podesta Manzano as soon as you return.* It was the last thing Edoardo wanted to see the moment he walked back into the gallery. The latest substitution of the paintings had gone smoothly at the stockyards at his end. Surely it was too soon for any of the consignment to have been verified at Carinhall? He frowned as he sat back into his chair and dialled Manzano's number. If Lina had stuck to her word, and he had no reason to believe she would not, then she would have delivered her report on the Cranach by now. Perhaps it was regarding that.

The line clicked and soon he was through to Manzano.

'Ah, Bernini, good.'

'You wanted to speak urgently, Excellency.'

'I have some news that will no doubt be of interest to you.'

'Oh?' Edoardo reached for a notepad and pen.

'Yes. Colonel Fischer is paying us a visit.'

'Fischer.' Edoardo dropped the pen and sat upright. The very name of the Third Reich's art expert made his stomach clench. Colonel Alexander Fischer was widely respected, but he was also a notorious Nazi, and a member of the feared Waffen-SS. 'Really? When?'

'At the end of next week. Good timing, yes?'

'I don't follow.'

A deep laugh travelled down the line. 'He can verify whether the portrait of the girl from Forte dei Marmi really is a fake, of course! I will arrange to have it brought up here from the villa.'

The blood leached from Edoardo's face as he glanced across at his safe. Thinking on his feet he said, 'That won't be necessary, Excellency.'

'No? Why not?'

He gulped down his fear. 'I anticipated you'd want to see it for yourself, so I took the liberty of bringing the portrait back with me. It's here at the gallery.'

'Is it, indeed?' replied Manzano. *Was that a hint of suspicion in his voice?*

Now it was Edoardo's turn to force out a casual laugh. 'So there is no need for the colonel to travel all the way to the coast. Besides, is his opinion really necessary? You've read Signorina Leone's report. There's no doubt in her mind. It's not a Cranach.'

'Yes, I've read her report, but when one of Germany's top art advisers pays a visit, it would be madness not to take advantage of his expertise.' He paused, waiting for Edoardo to agree, but when he hesitated Manzano added, 'You think your little she-wolf can be trusted?'

'Of course she can,' Edoardo shot back. Too quickly, on reflection. 'She is working on a book on Cranach, remember? Her opinion is unimpeachable.'

'Then she has nothing to worry about. Her reputation will remain intact if she is proved right.'

And if she isn't? Edoardo thought to himself. The podesta may have swallowed his excuse for taking the portrait from the villa, but when Alexander Fischer realised the painting was a genuine Cranach, and a previously unknown one at that, as he surely would, then it would be more than Lina's reputation at stake. It could be her life. Not to mention his own.

'You mean *when* she is proved right,' Edoardo countered emphatically, even though inside he knew this could signal the end of the line.

Lina took the tram into the city, then zig-zagged through the back streets just in case she was being followed. Edoardo had warned her the OVRA were on his case, but he'd said he needed to see her. She'd heard nothing from Manzano since she'd submitted her report, three days before, and with every day of silence her anxiety grew.

As soon as Edoardo laid eyes on her he leapt up from his desk at the gallery.

Lina snatched off the scarf covering her head. She'd wanted to avoid the secret police at all costs.

'This way,' he said, eyes clamped on the front door. Ushering her into a small room at the back, he bade her sit.

'What is it? Something's happened?' she asked. Her gaze darted to the safe in the corner of the room. 'The Cranach is in there?'

'Yes. For the time being,' he replied. 'What is it?'

He could tell from the way she looked at him so eagerly she was excited.

'The Cranach,' she began breathlessly. 'I think it could be Cosimo de' Medici's unknown lover. Scholars have been looking for a portrait of the woman who bore his first child, but they've always drawn a blank.'

Edoardo raised a brow. 'Until now?'

Her whole face lit up as she nodded. 'It all stacks up, Edoardo. This is huge!'

'I am happy for you,' he said. 'I really am, but I also have something to tell you.' He perched on the edge of his desk and Lina's smile disappeared. 'Alexander Fischer is coming to examine it.'

The news hit her like a blow to the stomach. 'Fischer!' She repeated the dreaded name, so respected yet feared in the art world, as if it scorched her tongue. 'Manzano doesn't trust me, or why else would that man be coming?'

'You're jumping to conclusions, Lina. He was visiting anyway. A scouting trip. He'll go back to Hitler with a long list of potential exhibits for his *Führermuseum.*'

He laid a hand on her shoulder, but Lina didn't feel in the least reassured.

'Don't you see, Edoardo?' She leaned in aware she was dancing on a knife edge. 'Manzano could easily accuse me of falsifying that report, which of course I did. If he suspects my error was deliberate, that I was trying to stop the Cranach going to Germany, he could accuse me of being a traitor, and you know what that means.'

Of course, Edoardo knew men had faced the firing squad for less. He flinched at the thought but continued to let Lina unpack her fears.

'I should never have got involved in the first place,' she went on, shaking her head. 'And now I'm trapped.' Edoardo kept his eyes on her but didn't respond. His silence only disturbed her. 'Why don't you say something?' she pressed.

'It's my fault,' admitted Edoardo. 'I got you into this and I've been trying to think of a way out.'

'And?' Lina snapped, although she instantly regretted it.

'Perhaps you should leave the city for a while. Say you've been called away.'

Lina shot him an incredulous look. 'You mean go on the run? Where would I go? There has to be another way, Edoardo.' She dropped back into the chair opposite and an uneasy silence hung between them until her gaze settled on the safe in the wall once more. 'Does Manzano know you have it? The portrait.'

He nodded. 'I had to tell him, otherwise he would have sent for it from the villa.' A deep frown creased his forehead. 'But there's something else I need to tell you, Lina.'

She shifted in her seat, preparing for the worst. 'Whatever it is, I can tell it's not good.'

Taking a deep breath, he said, 'Another consignment of art leaves next Tuesday. I have to go to Innsbruck again.'

She swallowed down the news like a bitter pill. 'So, I'm on my own? Is that what you're saying?'

'I'll only be gone two days,' he countered. 'I'll be back before Fischer arrives, but I'll give you these, just in case.' He held out two keys on a ring: one large and rusting, the other newer.

'In case what?'

'In case something happens to me.'

'Do you think Manzano suspects you?' Her voice pulsed with fear.

'I have to consider all eventualities.'

She examined the keys in her palm. 'What are they for?'

He rose. 'Let's walk, shall we?' he suggested.

'But what if we're followed?'

'They only watch the front door. They don't know about the back. And that key there …' He pointed to the old one. '… is for the wine cellar.' He glanced through the window at an ancient door, accessed via some steps in the rear courtyard. 'Come.' He held out his hand.

It was a warm, still evening, and despite the presence of troops on the streets, the sound of music and laughter fluttered on the spring air. A queue had gathered outside the butcher's after rumours of a meat delivery, but despite food shortages and discouraging news from the Front, Florentines battled on with their everyday lives.

Side by side, they walked to the river where the Arno was turned liquid gold by the setting sun. They strolled across the Ponte Santa Trinita, passing the famous statues of the four seasons that were commissioned for a Medici wedding. 'They say this is the most beautiful bridge in the world,' remarked Edoardo, as they stopped to watch the sunlight reflected in the water. He turned to face Lina. 'And I am with the most beautiful woman in the world.'

Before she could say anything, Edoardo kissed her so tenderly that ripples charged through her entire body. She felt herself being lifted above the bridge and she didn't want the sensation to stop. But when his lips left hers and she opened her eyes, he told her, 'You know I have to go. To Austria. Otherwise, I'll be suspected. We'll work something out. I won't let anything bad happen to you.' She nodded and he coaxed a smile from her. 'Am I forgiven?' he asked.

At that moment he could have been guilty of anything and she would have forgiven him. 'Yes, Edoardo,' she replied, 'I forgive you.' But it still didn't stop her mounting dread.

Chapter 26

June 1941

The case was slightly larger than Edoardo's usual valise, but not so big as to attract attention. The portrait, wrapped in brown paper and tied with string, fitted neatly inside. It had sat on the luggage rack opposite his seat ever since the train left Florence for Innsbruck the day before. He'd taken it down and rested against it when he'd grabbed a couple of hours' sleep, otherwise it had journeyed unremarked and undisturbed.

He lit a cigarette and watched the landscape fly by. This time he wasn't on a mission for Manzano. He hadn't been expecting to return to Austria for at least another month. But after the warning he'd decided to act immediately, while the Cranach was still in his possession, and it had been easy to mislead Lina.

On this journey Edoardo planned to transact his own business. During his last encounter with Decker, he'd been offered warehouse space. There were documents, Edoardo told him, which needed storing. Sensitive documents. Decker always had an eye to the main chance. He'd seen the earnings potential and run with it. In exchange for a fee, it was agreed these papers could be kept in the highly secure armaments warehouse in Austria.

The train came to a halt at Innsbruck Station. Edoardo planned to meet Decker at the Imperial Hotel for dinner. He stood, placed his fedora on his head, and hefted the case off the rack. Draping his folded raincoat over his arm, he slid open the compartment door and strode down the corridor. Alighting on the platform, he had just begun the short walk to the boarding gate when he spotted a familiar outline powering towards him. He stopped in his tracks. Decker? Surely not? Why would he be meeting the train?

As he drew closer, he saw the look on his associate's face: an odd mixture of nervousness and fury. He didn't like either.

'What are you doing here, you old devil?' Edoardo asked jovially, masking his own nerves. But Decker didn't reply. Instead, he flashed a glare then pulled to one side as two heavily built thugs emerged from behind him.

'These men would like to ask you the same question,' the businessman growled.

'What the—' Edoardo spluttered as two hands clamped on to both his shoulders and the cold steel of handcuffs encircled his wrists.

'I don't do business with thieves, Bernini,' hissed Decker. 'Or traitors.'

Lina and Agatha had been summoned to Professor Loggi's office in the Uffizi. They found him standing halfway up a ladder by a large bookcase.

'Come in, dear ladies. Please take a seat,' he invited. 'I am most grateful to you for coming,' he said, manoeuvring cautiously down the rungs to reach *terra firma*. 'I have some news to share with you.' He glanced over at the door to make sure it was firmly shut.

'Good news, I hope,' said Agatha, settling herself on a chair in front of Loggi's desk. Lina sat next to her.

'I think so,' he replied, pulling out a folder from among a set of encyclopedias on one of his many bookshelves. Limping back to his desk, he inserted his monocle and, opening the file, took out a letter.

'I have received word from someone who is as concerned about the fate of our glorious Italian treasures as we are,' he told them.

The two women swapped intrigued looks.

'Pray tell,' urged Agatha.

'He's a former Harvard colleague,' Loggi continued. 'An expert art conservator by the name of George Stout. As you may be aware, because America has not joined the war, our two countries can still communicate. Stout is as troubled as we are about the potential damage this frightful conflict is having on works of art in Europe and has alerted authorities in both the United States and Britain to his concerns.'

'Is he influential? Will he be heard?' asked Lina, sensing from the professor's expression he was holding something back.

Loggi frowned. 'Stout is pressing for the formation of some sort of commission to help protect historic pieces and buildings all over Europe.' He shook his head. 'But unfortunately, so far, he is not garnering much enthusiasm, apart from among professionals and academics like us. Naturally, I replied but could say nothing to reassure him.'

Ever since Edoardo had told her about the consignments Manzano was sending to Germany, Lina had wondered if the professor knew about the illicit traffic in art. She decided now was the time to test the waters. Taking a breath, she dived in. 'It's not only the Allied bombs we need to fear, Professor, is it?'

Loggi looked at her intently and she saw his brow furrow. 'If you are asking me if I know what Podesta Manzano is up to? That he's been sending artworks from Florence into German hands, then, yes, I fear I do.'

A mix of frustration and anger flooded her body. If the professor was aware what was happening, why didn't he do anything to stop the consignments? 'You knew?' she queried, trying to suppress her misgivings.

Loggi inhaled deeply, removed his monocle, and leaned back in his seat. 'Let's say I suspected, then I did some checking of my own,' he replied. 'And yes. It's true.'

'But that's quite shocking,' intervened Agatha. 'May I ask what you propose to do about it?' she snapped, rather unhelpfully, thought Lina.

Loggi clasped his hands in front of him on the desk. 'My dear Mrs Fortescue-Smythe, my country is at war. I am powerless in many regards, although, I do have a proposal that involves you and your ladies.'

Agatha's brow arched. 'Which is?'

'There are cellars below the basement of the Uffizi. They were only discovered about ten years ago and hardly anyone, apart from myself and three other staff members, knows of their existence.'

'Intriguing,' she replied with a nod. 'And these cellars are accessible and usable?'

'Exactly so,' assured Loggi. 'And less than a tenth of the movable artworks of the city's galleries and museums have been evacuated so far.'

'I see where this is going, Professor,' said Agatha. 'My ladies and I would be more than happy to help with such an operation.'

While she was encouraged that the professor intended to rescue more art and hide it out of reach of Manzano, Lina was aware it still didn't solve the immediate problem of the consignments to Germany.

'I'm afraid I can't concern myself with things I cannot control, Signorina Leone,' Loggi replied when she challenged him. 'Podesta Manzano is in charge, and I fear Bernini is doing his bidding.'

'Bernini,' repeated Agatha, unable to hide the disdain in her voice.

Lina bit her lip, knowing there was little she could say or do to persuade her aunt that Edoardo was not the deceitful wheeler-dealer she believed him to be. Even though she was tempted to fly to his defence, she knew she must not. She would never betray him, so she would have to accept the insults and aspersions thrown at him, no matter how hurtful.

'I understand you found the painting at Forte di Marmi to be a fake, Signorina Leone. Podesta Manzano showed me your report,' said Loggi, fixing Lina with an odd look. 'Or is that not the case?'

When she hesitated, the professor placed a thoughtful finger to his lips. 'There is no need to answer that question, although I am also told Colonel Fischer is due to pay us a visit in the coming days. Do you know about that?'

This time Lina did nod. The visit loomed large in her consciousness, but she'd still not been able to think of a way out of the situation. 'Yes, I know, Professor.'

'So, you see, ladies, I fear all you can do is carry on your excellent work. Thanks to your efforts, hundreds of masterpieces are now in repositories and, with your help, many more will be even safer in the cellars of the Uffizi. We can only hope that most of them will remain there until this terrible war is over. But in the meantime, I shall carry on corresponding with my American colleagues, in the hope that sanity will prevail, and Italy's treasures will be saved.' Loggi nodded first at Lina, then at Agatha, as a smile spread across his face. 'Those Cranachs belong to Italy, not in Germany. And if you can stop Goering and Adolf Hitler getting their hands on them, dear ladies, I can assure you, I will do nothing to stop you.'

After the meeting, Lina left Agatha and headed for the Bernini Gallery. So, Professor Loggi knew about the portrait she'd declared a fake. She felt as if she'd put her head on the block and the axe was poised. She needed to see Edoardo again, if only for reassurance that everything would be all right, even though she knew it probably wouldn't be. He should be due back from Innsbruck by now, she calculated.

Walking briskly along the fashionable Via Tornabuoni, it struck her how down-at-heel everything looked, but then most places did, thanks to the war. The only people who had any money these days were those who kowtowed to the fascists, and even they were finding it hard to make ends meet. No wonder the black market for art was flourishing.

Soon she came to the gallery. It looked closed. The sign on the door confirmed her worries and made her frown. Edoardo must have been held up in Austria. Perhaps she would see if Signora Bianchi was at the apartment next door. Maybe the housekeeper had some news. She was just about to pull the doorbell rope when she heard the rumble of an engine. A truck had stopped at the top of the street and out poured four or five *Carabinieri*. Rooted to the spot, she watched in horror as they approached. Luckily she skulked into a doorway for cover just as they stopped outside the gallery. The violent thuds of a battering ram assaulted her ears before she peered round to see the men smash through the front door and burst inside. Cowering unseen opposite, the sound of glass smashing, and furniture being tossed aside was all she could hear. Then it dawned on her. The police must be looking for the Cranach. Manzano had read her report and was furious that she'd declared the work a fake and not a previously unknown work by Hitler's favourite artist.

Briefly she even considered following the men inside and telling them the portrait was in the safe to avoid any further destruction. But common sense – or was it cowardice – prevailed. She could easily be arrested on the spot and that would serve no purpose. If they found the painting, so be it. She would have to stand her corner and justify her conclusion. It would not be easy, but she might be able to convince Manzano of her conviction. But her first concern was for Edoardo. Where was he? Surely he'd gone to Austria on the podesta's orders? He was accompanying another consignment for Goering. Her head throbbed as the *Carabinieri* continued their search, leaving her little choice but to retreat down the street, sick with dread and worry.

Chapter 27

At the dining table in Villa Mimosa that evening, Agatha seemed to be her old sprightly, albeit rather acerbic, self again. She even complained the soup was too thin. It was almost as if Professor Loggi's clandestine plan to store more treasures in the gallery's cellars had reinvigorated her, while the notion of thwarting Goering's designs on the Cranachs seemed a rallying cry. But though her aunt's mood appeared greatly improved, Lina's fear gnawed away at her. She ate mechanically as she considered the situation. Edoardo was missing. Where was he? If Manzano and his henchmen didn't know, then who did? It was all very well for some Americans to be concerned about treasures, but the more people who knew about the *Reichsmarschall*'s looting, the more dangerous Edoardo's position became. So did hers for that matter. Then, more immediately, there was Colonel Fischer's arrival. Questions and worries jostled for space in her crowded mind.

'Oh, my dear,' Agatha commented, observing Lina toy with her stewed rabbit. 'You're so troubled, aren't you?' She laid down her knife and fork. 'It's not just this German's visit that's worrying you, is it?'

Lina hesitated then pushed away her plate. 'You're right.'

'I thought so,' replied Agatha. 'I may wear these to read,' she said, lifting up her lorgnettes 'but I'm not blind. I saw your expression when Professor Loggi mentioned Signor Bernini's name, when he accused him of being the podesta's puppet. You still have feelings for him, don't you?'

Lina's pent-up tears welled up inside her. 'He's not the bad person you think he is, Aunt. He really isn't,' she insisted.

Agatha pursed her lips, then reaching out across the table for Lina's hand, she said, 'There's something you ought to know. Something I should've told you a while ago before things got, well …' She shrugged. 'Before they got difficult.'

'Really?' asked Lina, mopping up a wayward tear with her napkin. Her aunt's tone sounded ominous. 'What's that?'

Agatha cleared her throat and sighed deeply. 'You see, Signor Bernini Senior and I were—' she hesitated.

'You and Signor Bernini were what?' Lina was reminded of the newspaper cutting she'd found in the desk drawer.

'We were, well, friends.'

'Friends?'

Agatha gave a little cough to clear her throat. 'I was seventy when Reginald, your great-uncle, passed away,' she began. 'While that might sound very old to you, when I reached that age I still felt quite young, despite my aches and pains. I was lonely. I met Henrico Bernini at an embassy party. We began to visit museums and galleries together, and a friendship developed.' She paused. 'A deep friendship. I didn't enquire about his business dealings but one day he told me he would have to go away for a while. He ended our relationship for no apparent reason, and although I asked him to explain, he refused. I was in a state of shock. Then, a day or so later, I read in the newspaper he'd been arrested. Of course, at first, I thought there'd been a ghastly mistake. I even tried to visit him in jail – oh, the indignity of it – but I wasn't allowed. His case came to trial the following week and the evidence, according to the newspaper reports, was irrefutable. Over several months, he'd been stealing from the Uffizi, where, of course, Professor Loggi was, and still is, in charge.'

Lina had so far listened with her mouth agape. Reading the newspaper cutting had filled in a few of the blanks that Edoardo had omitted to tell her. But to think her aunt had been in a romantic relationship with Bernini Senior was beyond her imagination. 'What did you do?' she pressed.

Agatha's lip trembled slightly in the candlelight. 'He broke my heart and shattered my faith in men,' she replied. 'The deception, the betrayal, I felt so wounded.' She placed a palm on her heart and then, seeing the sadness in her aunt's face, Lina felt her own heart ache. 'It's only because I don't want to see you hurt in the same way that I've tried to dissuade you, my dear.'

Lina put a comforting arm around Agatha as a tear broke loose from her aunt's eye. With her free hand, she wiped away her own tears.

'And you never saw him again?'

'No. Never. He died in jail.'

It all made more sense now; why Agatha had been so opposed to her relationship with Edoardo. She'd been burnt in the fire of the Bernini flame herself and didn't want the same to happen to her great-niece. Lina was just trying to process what she'd learned when a loud knock at the front door broke into her thoughts. With Agatha under house arrest, only official visitors were allowed.

'Who on earth can it be?' asked Lina hurrying to the front window. She turned back with a look of horror on her face. 'It's Manzano and Commander Parissi!' she exclaimed. 'And they've got four *Carabinieri* with them.'

Donna scampered to answer the front door. Words were exchanged, then heavy footsteps powered along the tiles until the dining-room door was flung open. Agatha remained seated and didn't turn a hair when the Podesta of Florence appeared on the threshold. Lina stood behind her, a hand on her shoulder, trying her hardest to look equally composed. Inside she was quaking.

'Mrs Fortescue-Smythe,' said Manzano. 'I am—'

Seemingly undeterred by the huge man in military uniform now confronting her, Agatha raised a hand. 'I know who you are, Your Excellency, but you haven't been invited into my home, so please state your business.'

Manzano baulked at being greeted in such a hostile manner. Agatha seemed to take the wind from his sails. He glanced at Parissi, who knew from experience that this aged English scorpion had a sting in her tail.

'Your companion and I are, however, already acquainted,' added Agatha, pinning a glare on the police chief.

Lina admired her aunt's bravura performance, but she wasn't sure it was the right approach. Looking down at her hand on Agatha's shoulder, she noticed it was shaking. Agatha must've felt it because she placed her own hand on top to steady it.

The podesta stuck out his chin. His authority had been challenged and he wanted to re-establish it. 'We are here because we have reason to believe you may be harbouring a criminal, *signora*,' he announced.

Lina turned to stone. Was he looking for Edoardo? But before she could say anything, her aunt intervened.

'Someone has escaped from jail?' Agatha asked disingenuously. 'If that is the case, I can assure you we are not harbouring a criminal,' she continued, but Manzano's manners seemed to desert him as he marched forwards and held up his palm in front of her face.

'You will not speak unless I ask a question, old woman.'

'Well, really!' muttered Agatha, shocked. She stiffened her neck and gave him one of her withering glares.

Parissi seemed uncomfortable, hitching from one foot to the other and stroking his moustache as his eyes continued casting around the room.

Lina feared she would be next in Manzano's sights. He rounded abruptly on her. 'Where is he?'

Time stood still as she felt the heat of Manzano's glower sear

158

into her. She swallowed hard. 'I don't know who you mean.'

His small eyes tapered as he moved closer. She could smell his stale sweat. 'Don't play games with me, Signorina Leone. Bernini will be here, somewhere. We went to the gallery to collect the painting – the portrait you declared a fake – but his housekeeper said he'd gone away.'

She frowned. Edoardo had told her he was absent at Manzano's own bidding, supervising the delivery of the looted artwork. Why would he be looking for him? 'I'm afraid I don't understand.'

'The painting wasn't at the gallery. Nor was Bernini.' He nodded to Parissi. 'Tell your men to search this place!' he ordered the commander.

'No! No, you do not!' blurted Agatha. The scorpion's tail was up, ready to strike. Rising as quickly as her arthritic knees permitted, she drew herself to her full height.

'Commander Parissi. I am disappointed in you. Where is your search warrant?' She held out a stern hand. 'Well? Let me see it.'

Parissi's eyes slid towards the podesta in an appeal, but Manzano rebuffed him with a shake of his head. Emboldened, the commander declared, 'I do not need one,' before signalling to his men with a nod. The four policemen sprang into action.

'But this is preposterous!' fumed Agatha, directing her ire at the police chief.

'Please, *signor*, I don't understand,' protested Lina. 'There must be some mistake. Signor Bernini is in Innsbruck on your orders,' she told Manzano, before immediately regretting her outburst.

Manzano spiked her with a startled gaze. 'Innsbruck. He told you that, did he? So, what else did he say?'

Lina floundered. She'd said too much. The ground had been taken away from under her feet.

The podesta shook his head and tutted for dramatic effect. 'Bernini is a traitor, and you know what happens to traitors, *signorina*.'

A thud on the ceiling set the glass chandelier tinkling overhead.

It was followed by the sound of doors opening and shutting, and the creaking of floorboards under the weight of the *Carabinieri's* heavy treads. More orders were roared downstairs, and Donna wailed as crockery smashed on the terracotta floor in the kitchen.

At the sound, Agatha tried to elbow her way out of the door. 'If that's my Crown Derby!' she cried.

Lina snatched her back by the arm and guided her, still railing about her dinner service, to her chair.

'Please. Don't make things worse than they are,' she pleaded.

Sitting by Agatha once again, Lina's head continued to spin, only faster. This couldn't be how it sounded. Edoardo wouldn't have made off with the Cranach, leaving her to face the fallout alone. Surely there'd been some mistake? Some misunderstanding? Rising panic clenched her throat. Her head began to reel as she gripped the edge of a nearby table to steady herself.

Countless door slams and thuds later, the policemen returned to Parissi to report there was no sign of the wanted man. The commander regarded Manzano apologetically, while the thwarted podesta tugged at his tunic as if the fruitless search was a personal assault.

'Very well,' he sneered. 'We shall leave you now, Mrs Fortescue-Smythe. But let this be a warning to you. If Bernini approaches you, I must be the first to hear. If I find he has been in touch and you have not notified me, you will be the one to suffer.' He looked at Lina intently and added in Italian, 'The penalties will be severe.'

Agatha gave him a withering look. 'I can assure you, Podesta Manzano, I want nothing to do with Signor Bernini.'

Commander Parissi nodded, seemingly satisfied the visit would serve as a warning to the women. He turned to leave but then noticed Manzano remained rooted.

'As for you, Signorina Leone, you must go with the commander.'

Lina's head shot up. 'What?' Her eyes darted to Parissi, who seemed equally shocked.

'Absolutely not!' bridled Agatha.

'Your cooperation would be appreciated, Signorina Leone,' declared Manzano.

Despite the order being sprung on Parissi, he nodded to two of his men. They took hold of Lina, one on either side.

Agatha was on her feet once more, but this time she was armed. 'This is outrageous,' she cried, shaking her umbrella at the nearest *Carabiniere*. 'Why are you arresting Signorina Leone?'

'Not arresting. Merely taking in for questioning,' came Manzano's slippery reply.

Lina knew there was little point in resisting. 'Please, Aunt. Don't make a fuss,' she pleaded, feeling the *Carabiniere*'s grip tighten.

Agatha lowered her parasol but persisted in her protest. 'Why are you taking my great-niece?'

The podesta regarded her with irritation. 'Bernini is a traitor, and your niece is a close friend of his. I would appreciate a little chat. She may have information that is helpful to us, *signora*.'

Lina managed to nod to her aunt, even though the shock made her light-headed. 'I'm sure I'll be back soon,' she assured her, before being frogmarched out of the dining room.

As they took her out into the hall, Lina glimpsed Donna sweeping up the broken porcelain. Just like the Crown Derby plates, her emotions had been shattered. Not ten minutes ago she was defending a man she thought trustworthy and decent, who was working to stop the wholesale looting of the city's most precious art treasures. But what if Podesta Manzano was telling the truth? What if Edoardo had left with the Cranach? Not only would he have betrayed Manzano and the fascist government, he'd have betrayed her too; taken her trust and torn it up like a piece of paper.

Had Edoardo betrayed her, like his father did Agatha, then gone on the run? After all, wasn't that what he'd suggested to her when he'd heard about Fischer's visit? Wasn't his own home lined with copies, not original paintings? She didn't want to believe it, but the phrase *like father, like son* echoed in her head, and as much as she tried, she couldn't block it out. As she was shoved into a waiting police car and driven to the *questura*, Lina questioned which version of Edoardo Bernini was real and which a fake.

Chapter 28

Waiting in the windowless interrogation room, Lina wrapped her arms around her shivering body. Despite the soaring temperatures outside, the sunless basement was damp and cold. She'd lost count of just how long she'd been in custody. Some time ago they'd brought her from her cell to this room, where a pair of eyes would glower periodically through an iron grille. Twice, when she'd seen them and sprung up to ask a question, they'd vanished, and she'd slumped down again onto the chair bolted to the floor. All she could do was stare at the brown stains round her feet and the scuff marks on the wall, trying not to imagine how they got there. All she knew was inside she felt hollow; as if her heart and soul had been gouged out, leaving behind an empty shell. The more she thought about it, the more she convinced herself she'd been betrayed. How could Edoardo have done this to her?

It'll be safe, he'd told her. *The capitano at Forte dei Marmi won't talk. I paid him well.* She'd had her reservations about keeping the portrait in the gallery. It was obviously the first place Manzano would look if he were to discover they'd double-crossed him. Edoardo had fobbed her off with some excuse because he knew he'd won her trust. Now she realised he may well have been lying to her all along. Had he found a buyer for the Cranach already?

Or was he planning to sell it on the black market in Austria? She recalled all those copies of masterpieces on his apartment wall. He could well have commissioned a forgery. Had he even gone to Innsbruck? He must have known she would be left to face the podestà's wrath. He'd thrown her to the wolves, and she was about to be torn to pieces. All these thoughts whirled and barrelled inside her head as the enormity of his betrayal threatened to overwhelm her like a giant wave. Just when she thought she could stand it no longer and wanted to vent her fury and bitterness in a scream, she heard the jailer's key in the lock.

Turning swiftly, she saw Manzano enter. 'Signorina Leone,' he greeted her with a razor-blade smile, as if he'd bumped into her at the Gran Caffè Doney. He lumbered towards the table where she sat. Under his arm he carried a folder. 'As you know, I need to ask you a few questions.' The chair creaked under his weight. 'So,' he said, settling himself opposite. 'This needn't take long. But it does depend on you.' He fixed her with steely eyes. 'Signor Bernini,' he began. 'Did he tell you why he was in Innsbruck?'

Lina straightened her back to sit upright in her chair. 'No. No, he didn't.'

She hesitated. A large pit was gaping at her feet. One false move and she would fall into it. If she told Manzano she was aware of the truth – that he, the most powerful man in Florence, was delivering prized Italian art to the Germans while raking off some of the profits – the pit could become her grave. She mustn't make it deeper. 'No. I've no idea.'

'But why do you think he went?'

'On business, I presume.'

'What sort of business?'

'Gallery business, I suppose. I didn't ask and he didn't tell me.'

'Strange,' said Manzano, opening the folder in front of him. 'I was under the impression your relationship with Bernini was more than merely a professional one, and yet you did not discuss his travel plans.'

'I'm sorry. I don't know what you mean,' she said, inviting him to reveal his hand.

Manzano drummed his fat fingers on the table, then said, 'I'll tell you what I mean.' Flicking through the file, he dipped his grey eyes. 'Last week on the Ponte Santa Trinita. You were seen in an intimate embrace.' He raised his gaze and regarded her like a child with an insect trapped under a glass. 'Or does he offer such services to all his female clients?'

A look of dismay spread across Lina's face as Manzano read out the dates. She felt violated. She'd been afraid they might be followed, but Edoardo seemed prepared to run the risk. Was that all part of his plan? Guilt and shame fought it out in her head, and Manzano knew it. He carried on, 'Bernini is a person of influence in the art world, but, like his father, he has a reputation for being less than trustworthy. We also found this in his apartment,' he told her, a smug grin widening his mouth. He slid a sheet of paper over to her. It was the charcoal sketch Edoardo had made of her. Her eyes flared before Manzano snatched it back. 'Rather charming,' he said, studying it closely. 'Although I think he got your nose wrong.' He looked up at her face. 'It should have been longer.'

Lina responded with a contemptuous look. But Manzano continued to fire arrows from his quiver of accusations. 'No more lies now.' He glanced down at the sketch. 'It's clear you were in his confidence. And he in yours, I presume. You recognised that painting was a genuine Cranach at Forte dei Marmi, didn't you? You lied deliberately in that report. You told Bernini, thinking he would help you hide it before Colonel Fischer could verify it. But you never thought he'd steal it, did you? Your lover is a common crook. Just like his father.' He shook his head. 'And it seems that, like his father, his greed has got the better of him. He wanted to keep the Cranach for himself.'

'No, Edoardo isn't a thief. He would never do something like that,' she protested, even though she feared what he said could

165

be true.

Manzano let out a laugh, clamping a hand on his unruly belly. 'You really don't know, do you?' he replied. 'Not only has he stolen the Cranach, but he's also been filching from the consignments to Innsbruck, too. He and his gang of thieves have stolen dozens of priceless paintings destined for Carinhall. He spun me some story about a heist this side of the Austrian border, and I swallowed it at the time. But now I know the truth, that your lover is a thief – a clever one, I'll give him that, but a thief, nonetheless. And while we are still missing some crates bound for Herr Goering, at least he has been relieved of the Cranach.'

Her head shot up. 'What do you mean?'

Another smug grin. 'Unbeknownst to me, an associate of ours was waiting for Bernini when he arrived in Austria. He was caught red-handed.'

Her eyes bulged.

'So, it looks like Colonel Fischer will be able to examine the portrait himself after all.' He grinned. 'And a room has been reserved for your lover at Villa Triste, where you probably know we make our guests as uncomfortable as possible.'

Lina had certainly heard of the dreaded Villa Triste. It was where music played to drown out the prisoners' screams. She could barely lift her head to look at the grotesque, smirking beast opposite her. It certainly appeared Edoardo had intercepted some of the crates he was supposed to deliver to Innsbruck. But more than that, he'd planned to sell the portrait of the gentlewoman without telling her. If that were true, it was more painful than any torture Manzano could inflict. As a rush of adrenaline flooded her body, Lina's fury boiled over. It thrust her across the table to slap the podesta hard across his cheek. The blow forced his head to the right and reddened his skin. Holding her breath, she waited for the aftermath. He rubbed his jaw, and she braced herself, but then he simply laughed, deep and low.

'I think we are done, Signorina Leone,' he said. 'Guard.'

The jailer marched in and grabbed Lina by the arm. 'No, wait please,' she cried. 'What's happening? Am I to be released?'

'Released?' repeated Manzano. 'From here, yes.'

'Where will you take me?' she cried, trepidation in every sinew. Did Villa Triste await her, too?

'No need to be afraid, Miss Leone. You'll be in good company.'

'What? What are you talking about?' Lina frowned at the cryptic remark.

'You'll find out soon enough. Take her away.'

With that, she was manhandled back down the basement stairs and into the cells of the *questura*. The last laugh had gone to Manzano.

Chapter 29

In another godless cell, a few hundred kilometres north of Florence, Edoardo Bernini was also waiting, trying to suppress the nausea welling in his chest. He'd been told some top-notch Nazi would shortly begin his interrogation. The German thugs who'd arrested him at the railway station had done a good job of softening him up. A punch to his gut had been a mere *amuse-bouche*. When he'd fallen to his knees, one of them had kicked him in the face, sending him flying backwards. His head thudded against the wall and now his right eye was so swollen he couldn't see out of it. That had been the appetiser. He didn't like to dwell on the entrée, but he guessed he wouldn't have to wait too long to find out.

Footsteps echoed along the corridor, keys jangled, and the cell door screeched open. A tall, lean officer, eyes hidden by the shiny peak of his colonel's cap, entered. He wore the field grey tunic with the death's head insignia of the SS on his collar and cuffs.

'Stand!' yelled the guard.

But Edoardo, slumped against the wall, couldn't find the strength to heave his body upright. On the colonel's order he was hauled up unceremoniously and deposited roughly on a chair by a table. Edoardo flinched as he shifted the weight off his bruised buttocks. He expected no sympathy. None was given.

'So, Signor Bernini,' the colonel began, taking off his cap to reveal a receding hairline and a hooked nose. 'Do you know who I am?'

Even though he could only see through one eye, Edoardo had no doubt, but before he replied he felt the need to empty his mouth. Turning his head, he spat blood on the floor. 'Forgive me, Colonel Fischer,' he said pointedly. 'I find it a little painful to speak when I've just had two teeth knocked out of my skull.'

Unmoved, Fischer stared at the bruises on Edoardo's face. 'Not a pretty sight, I agree,' he remarked in a measured voice. 'However, I am told you arrived here with a very pretty picture in your possession.'

If his shoulders hadn't hurt so much, Edoardo would have shrugged, instead he replied, 'Pretty? I'm not sure about that.'

Fischer flared his nostrils. 'Come, come. They told me you are an art connoisseur. You brought the Cranach here to give to your Swiss associate for storage until you found a buyer.' He leaned back in his chair and snapped his fingers as if he was ordering food in a restaurant.

Right on cue, another guard stepped in, carrying the brown paper parcel that Edoardo had transported so carefully from Florence. 'I thought I'd open it in your presence. A sort of grand unveiling. A great artist deserves such reverence, don't you think, Signor Bernini?'

Edoardo remained silent, the taste of blood still strong in his mouth. The guard placed the rectangular parcel on the table and handed Fischer a pair of scissors. Turning the package over, he snipped the string and carefully unwrapped it to reveal the back of a wooden panel. The portrait was face down.

Fischer's eyes flicked up to Edoardo. 'So, the moment of truth,' he said with a smirk as he turned over the painting with an exaggerated gesture. But then his jaw dropped, his mouth puckered, and an outraged scowl darkened his Aryan features. 'What is the meaning of this?'

The mounted image was not Cranach's enigmatic young Renaissance woman, as he'd anticipated, but a charcoal caricature of Franz Decker, complete with a large fur hat. In the bottom right-hand corner, the artist had signed the portrait with a flourish: *Edoardo Bernini.*

Lina awoke to the sound of someone shouting. Man or woman? She couldn't be sure. Blinking open her eyes, it hit her that last night hadn't been a nightmare. Her limbs were stiff with cold as she eased her aching body away from the corner of the squalid cell and edged to the grille. The noise was growing louder by the second. A woman's voice. She listened intently. Was she shouting in English? Another protester joined in. That was when the terrible thought struck and soon manifested itself before her very eyes. First Mrs Clutterbuck, then Miss Harrowby emerged, herded along the corridor by two *Carabinieri*, ranting and raving as they went.

'Get your filthy hands off me!' boomed Mrs Clutterbuck.

'This really is insufferable,' muttered Miss Harrowby, as both women stopped outside the remand cell.

'Angelina! Good heavens!' cried Mrs Clutterbuck, hefting a large suitcase.

One of the guards unlocked the grille and slid it open. 'You. In,' he barked, shoving Miss Harrowby's shoulder.

'How dare you!' she exclaimed, being uncharacteristically challenging.

As the two women railed and huffed and continued to voice their outrage, Lina clutched the bars. 'What's going on?'

'We're being interned. That's what's going on,' growled Mrs Clutterbuck, fluffing up her bouffant hair, flattened in the mêlée.

'They told us this morning when the truck came to pick us up. We were given five minutes to pack our bags,' explained Miss Harrowby, her bottom lip quivering.

Lina's thoughts flew to Agatha and Lady Felstein. Would they shortly follow suit? As if on cue, Lady Felstein appeared down the corridor.

'Oh, Miss Leone. This really is very upsetting,' she wailed, as she too was pushed into the cell. Her eyes were red-rimmed, and her coat buttoned incorrectly, as if she'd dressed hurriedly.

'Is my aunt with you, Lady Felstein?' she asked, putting a comforting arm around her, and speaking directly into her ear.

'She's making a last stand,' she volunteered. 'She'll be along shortly, no doubt.'

Sure enough, a few minutes later, Agatha's not-so-dulcet tones bellowed along the corridor. She was in high dudgeon. 'Wait until I tell the ambassador about this,' she threatened, even though the British Embassy in Italy had long shut. 'It's prepost—' She stopped mid-flow as soon as she saw her niece behind bars.

'Oh, my dear girl!' she cried. Then, suddenly impatient to gain access to the cell, she called, 'Hurry up with that lock, man!' Leaving the guard to take care of her suitcase, she rushed inside with outstretched arms.

'I've been out of my mind with worry,' she exclaimed, clutching Lina with all her might. 'When you didn't return last night, I'd no idea what to think.' She pushed her back abruptly to study her. 'Are you all right? They didn't hurt you?'

'I'm fine, yes,' replied Lina, trying to brush off her ordeal for Agatha's sake. 'But what about you? Mrs Clutterbuck said you're all going to be interned.'

'It seems we are,' she replied. 'Although, of course, I could get no sense out of that Commander Parissi. Such an objectionable little man.' She shook her head as if the very thought of him irked her. 'And as for poor Mr Ponting, he was arrested yesterday, and taken goodness knows where.'

Lina's heart sank even further. She knew men like Mr Ponting had even more to fear from Mussolini's regime. With the four British women now present in the remand cell, all they could do was wait to see what would happen next.

'We're in the lap of the gods,' remarked Lady Felstein.

'I'd say the fascists, more like,' corrected Mrs Clutterbuck.

Miss Harrowby paced up and down, fidgeting with her hands, while Lady Felstein had wisely slipped a copy of *Pride and Prejudice* into her suitcase. She read, while Mrs Clutterbuck attended to her make-up in the mirror of her powder compact.

Meanwhile, Lina gratefully accepted Agatha's offer of a cardigan from her suitcase. Slipping it on, she sat down to update her.

'They've arrested Edoardo,' she croaked, her voice thick with anxiety. 'They say he's stolen a Cranach.'

An uneasy look scudded across Agatha's face. 'What? A Cranach? I don't understand.'

Lina knew she'd have to come clean. 'The one I went to verify in Forte dei Marmi.'

'The one you said was a fake.'

The look Lina handed her aunt was enough to show her the report was a lie. 'Oh, my dear, why would you say that when it wasn't true?' asked Agatha.

She shook her head. 'I didn't want Manzano to steal it and give it to the Nazis,' she replied. 'I didn't know how naive I was being.'

Realising the grave implications, Agatha tried to pull her towards her, but Lina fended her off with a shake of her head.

'They'll torture him until he tells them where it is. I know they will.'

This time when Agatha wound her arms around her, Lina didn't resist. 'What mess have you got yourself into?' she asked with a sigh, kissing her niece's head, and not expecting an answer. 'I know how much he meant to you, means to you, but I also knew … well.'

Even though Lina was grateful Agatha hadn't actually said *I told you so*, her words were still of little comfort. And barely had she finished drying her tears with her aunt's handkerchief when more shouts came down the corridor. Three more guards appeared, barking orders.

'What are they saying?' asked Lady Felstein, grabbing her ear trumpet.

'We have to leave now,' Lina translated. 'It's time to go.'

'Go? Go where precisely?' asked Agatha to anyone who was listening.

The trouble was no one knew where they would be taken. Despite protestations, the women were herded outside to a troop carrier. Its engine was running, belching out black diesel fumes.

'*Avanti! Avanti!*' shouted the guards, jabbing the air with their rifles. Another guard stood in the truck, yanking at Lady Felstein's spindly arms. Miss Harrowby stumbled on the tailboard, while Mrs Clutterbuck batted away a pimply youth who tried to heave her up. Lina was the last to board the vehicle. But the fight had gone out of her. She didn't clench her fists or rail, she didn't even weep. Edoardo had been exposed as a liar and a thief and the world had come crashing down around her. Right then she didn't fear the future, because nothing mattered anymore.

Edoardo Bernini sat on the floor of a cattle truck, guarded by two Nazis. His wrists were rubbed raw by handcuffs and every jolt jarred his bruised body. At least this way, no paying passengers would be subjected to the unedifying sight of a badly beaten prisoner. And, on the bright side, the long ride, however painful, gave him plenty of time to contemplate his next move.

His plan had backfired spectacularly. He knew that Manzano would have the gallery searched, but thankfully, it seemed his bungling henchmen hadn't found the radio transmitter stashed in the cellar. The one he used to communicate with his fellow resistance fighters.

Decker's cartoon portrait was a test. He'd drawn it from memory on the train journey back from Innsbruck the last time they'd met. He wanted to see if he could trust his old colleague not to open any package he presented for storage. He'd guessed his ego was such that if he'd seen the unflattering caricature of himself, he would have blown a fuse. But the double-crossing goon never even got to see the sketch. Casting his mind back to the night of the opera, Edoardo realised the dealer wasn't there as an opportunist. He was already in Il Duce's pay. They must've wired ahead and told the Germans to meet the train. There was, however, one comforting thought amid all this betrayal and pain. Cranach's beautiful young gentlewoman was still safe. But what of his own beautiful young woman? What of his Angelina?

Chapter 30

Torselli

July 1941

From the back of the troop carrier, Lina could only see what they were leaving behind; the city she loved and called home. What lay ahead – the dark unknown – was too fearful to contemplate. The weather was warm in Florence but the further north they were driven, and the higher into the mountains they went, the cooler it became. Lady Felstein shivered, and she, Miss Harrowby and Mrs Clutterbuck all huddled together for both comfort and warmth. Lina found herself nuzzled against Agatha, as she had done as a child. Inhaling deeply, she smelled her reassuring lavender scent, still detectable despite the reek of diesel.

'At least the English Ladies' Arts Appreciation Society is all together,' mused Agatha after a half hour on the road.

'But poor Mr Ponting isn't here,' pointed out Miss Harrowby.

'And neither is Miss Giltrap,' said Mrs Clutterbuck.

'True,' agreed Agatha. The realisation plunged everyone into a deeper depression until Miss Harrowby made a suggestion. 'Why don't we sing something?'

'What did she say?' Lady Felstein asked Lina over the engine's rattle.

'She suggested we sing,' replied Lina.

'What a splendid idea!' agreed her ladyship. 'But what?'

'My Bernard's favourite was "It's a Long Way to Tipperary"', shared Mrs Clutterbuck. So that is what they sang, along with several other rousing tunes from the Great War designed to keep spirits up. Despite their best efforts, Lina's sense of despair and isolation remained.

Pine trees had long ago replaced the poplars of the plains and fertile ground had given way to rocky outcrops when the truck turned onto an even rougher track. It rose steeply through dark green forests until finally a few crumbling houses came into view. Scrawny sheep and goats foraged on the scant grass around the modest dwellings that clung precariously to the hillside. A group of ragged children stopped by the roadside to watch the women pass, while a half-dead donkey struggled under a burden of firewood.

They were entering a sizable village, high up in the Apennines, dominated by a tall tower. A church bell tolled two o'clock as the truck squeezed into a narrow street then turned through large gates to clatter into a courtyard.

'Where the hell are we?' mumbled Mrs Clutterbuck the moment the engine noise died down. She leaned forwards to stick her head out of the back of the vehicle.

'Language, please, Mrs Clutterbuck. We have to maintain standards,' chided Agatha.

'Out!' came the call from one of the guards, as the tailgate was unlocked. The other two guards gathered round to help the women disembark. Agatha's arthritis was plaguing her again and poor Lady Felstein's stiff joints proved particularly intractable. In the end they both had to be lifted off the truck in a most undignified fashion.

The women were decanted into a large courtyard surrounded

by a building with a tall, thin campanile at one end with a cross on top of it. At first Lina thought they'd been brought to a convent, but then she saw some rough markings in the dirt and guessed they were made by children. Raising her gaze, she saw a plaque near the main entrance. They were to be housed in a former school.

'You. In,' shouted one of the guards, catching Lina trying to get her bearings. He was pointing to a door through which all the other women were being herded.

Once inside they were directed into a large, lofty room with a stone floor and high windows. Lina noted the ubiquitous portrait of Il Duce and next to him a much larger map of the world, without a trace of the pink of the British Empire on it. An empty wood burner at one end of the hall offered a little hope, but there were only two chairs and much of the space was empty. It was where the women's suitcases were dumped.

'Be careful with that!' chided Mrs Clutterbuck, scowling at a young man roughly the same age as her grandson. He merely curled his lip and scoffed at her.

'A school,' muttered Miss Harrowby, looking around her.

'And this is to be our dormitory by the looks of it,' said Agatha, lifting back a moth-eaten curtain that divided the hall in half. A row of single beds was ranged on the far wall.

Just then a sour-faced guard barked out an order.

'What's he saying?' Agatha asked, turning to Lina.

'He's telling us to choose our beds,' she translated.

'Is he indeed?' huffed her aunt. 'He could have asked politely,' she insisted, proceeding to voice her disgust. 'How dare you treat us like this?'

The young man blinked and took a step back, but his superior wasn't so easily frightened. 'Shut up, old woman,' he growled in English and shoved her hard in the chest – so hard, she flew backwards, lost her footing and landed in a heap on the floor.

Miss Harrowby gasped, and Mrs Clutterbuck let loose an expletive. Meanwhile, Lina hurried forwards to see if Agatha was hurt.

As it turned out, the only thing that was bruised appeared to be her ego, but everyone knew she could have broken a bone. As Lina helped her to her feet, the other women looked on stunned.

'*Silenzio!*' barked a loud Italian voice. A slightly built man with gold-rimmed spectacles appeared on the threshold. His hands were behind his back, and his legs planted wide. Seeing him, the men fell into line.

'What is the meaning of this?' he cried, angrily. 'I will report you to your superiors immediately,' he told them.

As the guards skulked off with their tails between their legs like dogs, the man approached. Agatha, on her feet once more, and still rather shaken, arched a brow. 'And who, may I ask, are you?' she asked imperiously.

The man, wearing a suit patched at the elbows but generally quite dapper, gave a low bow. 'Allow me to introduce myself, ladies,' he began in passable English. He turned to address the whole room. 'I am the mayor of this *commune*, and my name is Arturo Cetti. I also used to be a headmaster, and this was my school.' He lifted his gaze to the rafters, as if remembering happier times. 'Now, sadly, war has meant my pupils no longer attend classes.' He sighed heavily, as if the absence of the children pained him deeply. 'We are a humble people, and I know this is not what you are accustomed to, but, despite our two countries' differences, you are most welcome here.'

Agatha, however, had other ideas. 'Thank you, Signor Cetti,' she said after a moment. 'We appreciate your welcome, even though the accommodation is not to our …' she cleared her throat '… usual standards. But you must understand we were brought here against our will, and we must insist you find us more appropriate lodgings elsewhere.'

The mayor's face dropped. 'I'm afraid that is impossible, *signora*. We Italians suffer, too, and this is the best we can offer. Please.' He held out a hand. 'I hope we can be friends. Yes?'

Lina pinioned her aunt with a determined look, willing her to agree. *Take the poor man's hand*. The last thing they should do would be to offend the mayor. But despite counting the British ambassador among her closest friends, diplomacy was never Agatha's strong suit. She simply arched an imperious brow, as if this very minor Italian dignitary was taking liberties, and regarded his hand as if it were an oily rag. 'Friendship,' she replied, 'has to be earned. Until such times, Signor Cetti, you will remain a mere acquaintance.'

'Quite right,' echoed Mrs Clutterbuck.

Miss Harrowby nodded.

Lina, however, was cringing at her aunt's rebuff. She'd hoped, given their strained circumstances, that a little more humility might have come to the fore among the group. The *Scorpioni*, it seemed, still had stings in their tails. Knowing she ran the risk of getting herself into trouble, she stepped forwards.

'*Grazie, Signor Cetti*,' she said in Italian. 'We are very grateful for your courtesy. My aunt and her friends do appreciate these are hard times and we all do what we can.'

If the mayor felt insulted by Agatha, he was heartened by Lina. A smile spread across his careworn face, and he nodded. 'You are most welcome in Torselli,' he told her, clapping his hands and rubbing them together. 'You must not regard this place as a prison. You will be free to come and go in the village as you choose. All we ask is that you register daily at the town hall.'

He turned to the women and carried on in English. 'Ladies, you must be hungry. We do not have much here in the mountains, but we share what little we have. You will find some supplies in the kitchen.' He pointed to a door at the far end of the hall.

Recalling the shoeless children by the roadside and the half-starved livestock in the field on the way up the mountainside, Lina knew what the mayor said to be true. War had cast a long shadow over a country where the light was once so bright.

'*Grazie mille, Signor Cetti*,' said Lina without waiting for Agatha to respond. 'We really appreciate your kindness in such difficult circumstances,' she told him, walking him back to the front door.

Agatha and the other English ladies could be frightfully pompous at times, thinking they were entitled to respect from foreigners when they were surrounded by wealth and privilege in Florence. But Lina knew respect needed to be earned and in this poor mountain village, war made everyone equal. Here, at least, she hoped the *Scorpioni* might learn a little humility.

Chapter 31

Florence

Podesta Manzano sat at his desk feeling distinctly the worse for wear. Despite the food shortages suffered by most Florentines, the previous day the podesta had attended his nephew's wedding and eaten far too much, not to mention the alcohol he'd downed. Consequently, he had ordered Silvia, his secretary, to fetch him a concoction from the pharmacy.

Yet his indigestion and hangover were the least of his problems. Fischer, the Nazi art expert, was breathing down his neck. The colonel had been called to Innsbruck to interview Bernini shortly after his arrest, but instead of the anticipated Cranach, he'd uncovered a crude caricature. He'd been made to look a fool and there was no trace of the Cranach. A very awkward telephone call between Manzano and the SS officer had ensued. The Italian had felt his toes curl inside his shiny boots. The whole episode was excruciatingly embarrassing, but even before Silvia returned with his hangover remedy, Fischer was on the line again.

The podesta lifted his chin and jutted out his jaw as soon as he heard the Nazi's voice. With the Cranach still missing, he knew their conversation would not be easy.

'I fear the circumstances of my planned visit are a little more challenging than either of us originally thought,' said Fischer. His tone was such that anything but agreement from Manzano was unthinkable.

The podesta let slip a nervous laugh. 'We will find the Cranach soon enough, you can rest assured, Colonel. Bernini is near breaking point.'

'Good,' he replied. 'The photograph you sent me of the original was certainly interesting.'

'Ah, yes. That smile. And those come-to-bed eyes,' joked Manzano.

The remark, however, fell like a lead weight, and after a brief silence Fischer continued, 'And this woman, this expert, who declared it a fake, I assume she was in league with Bernini.'

'Yes. She is being taken care of.' It was a euphemism the podesta used quite frequently these days.

'Good. We might use her as leverage later on. But as for Bernini,' the Nazi continued, 'he's played us all for idiots. He was supposed to be working for you, was he not?' Fischer was clearly trying to push the blame for the debacle on to Manzano.

'*Reichsmarschall* Goering was certainly impressed by him,' offered the podesta by way of an excuse.

Mention of Hitler's deputy only exposed another shortcoming. 'Ah, yes, the consignments to Innsbruck,' Fischer butted in. 'How many have there been now? Five, six? The *Reichsmarschall* is appreciative of them, but the last ones are still awaiting authentication. And then there is this Cranach. There would have been great excitement about the possibility of a previously unknown work by the master.'

If it was possible for a threatening glare to travel down a telephone line, it just had, thought Manzano. He stuffed two fingers down the neck of his tunic collar. He needed air. 'I am taking care of the matter as we speak,' he replied. 'Bernini is at Villa Triste, and you know we make our guests' stay as uncomfortable as possible.'

That was another trope he frequently trotted out these days, but once again his attempt at humour seemed to fall on deaf ears.

'I want to see that Cranach for myself, and I want to see it soon. I'll give you three days to make Bernini talk. If he doesn't, it's you who'll have to tell Herr Hitler, personally, that a rare artwork by the Reich's greatest master has gone missing on your watch.'

'Three days,' repeated Manzano.

'Yes. Three days,' Fischer reiterated. 'I want answers and so will the Führer.'

Naturally Manzano had heard about what went on at Villa Triste, but he'd never actually seen how it operated for himself. He imagined it was all very messy and might even put him off his food. But this was war, and everyone had to make sacrifices. Biting the bullet, he ordered his driver to take him to the Via Bolognese to the unremarkable apartment block where so many opponents of fascism entered, yet so few left.

As the podesta was guided down the stairs to the basement, the stench became overwhelming, forcing him to hold his handkerchief over his face. It was then that he caught the sound of a piano. The strains of a classical composition seemed strangely at odds in such an environment.

'What's that?' he asked the guard.

'That's Father Ildefonso,' came the reply. 'The Schubert helps drown the cries.' Just then a terrible wailing sound came from a room they were passing.

'It doesn't always work,' remarked Manzano under his breath.

Another flight of stairs took them to the cells. Rows of doors with small grilles. The podesta was escorted to one of the furthest. He peered in through the bars to see Edoardo Bernini – handsome, charming, Edoardo Bernini – reduced to a similar state as his father the day before he died. Bruised, bloodied and broken, but hopefully not so much that he would throw away his last chance to reveal the whereabouts of the Cranach.

183

At the sound of the cell door, Edoardo raised his head a fraction, and caught sight of Manzano through his one functioning eye. The guard shut the door and the podesta lumbered up to him as he wallowed in his own vomit in a corner. Staring down at him, Manzano clicked his tongue like a disappointed parent.

'You've been a stupid boy,' he said. 'You think you're so clever. Just like your father. So, I suggest if you want to avoid a similar fate, you tell me what you've done with the Cranach.'

Edoardo grunted out a laugh. 'Why would you want it?' he asked. 'It's a fake.'

'According to the girl. But why would you have hidden it if it's worthless? Don't mess with me, Bernini. Just tell me where it is, and you can walk out of here.' He regarded his broken body, then chuckled. 'Well, maybe not walk exactly.'

'Go to hell, Manzano,' cried Edoardo, his head hitting the wall as he slumped back exhausted by venting his own anger.

The podesta's lips curled in a snarl. 'Is there nothing I can say or do, short of having your eyes gouged out – which I'm told they do regularly here – to make you give that painting up? Surely, it's not worth your life?'

Edoardo shook his head. 'No painting is worth a man's life,' he agreed.

'Or a woman's?'

Forgetting his pain, Edoardo's head shot up. 'What do you mean?'

Manzano had hoped mentioning Lina might get results. 'The girl has been interned with the rest of the *Scorpioni*.'

'What?' snarled Edoardo, a look of horror spreading across his bruised face. 'You've sent her and the English women to a camp?'

Manzano pouted. 'Conditions in the village where they are held are harsh, but bearable.' He tilted his head. 'But what if I brought Signorina Leone back here?'

'Here? But she knows nothing, I tell you!' His voice gathered strength and volume as the terror took hold. 'Nothing!'

'If that is the case, perhaps it is she who might persuade you to reveal where you've hidden the Cranach.'

Edoardo pulled away from the wall, his whole body on fire. 'No. She'd never do that.'

Manzano threw his head back in a laugh. 'You'd be surprised what a woman will do to stop her lover suffering.'

'But how many more times do I need to tell you? She doesn't know where it is.' His fists were clenched.

Silence hung on the fetid air until Manzano said, 'And what would you do to save her from suffering?'

The rage that had been bubbling up inside Edoardo spilled over. With every gram of strength in his body he forced himself to his feet and lunged at his tormentor. But all the podesta had to do was lean sideways and Edoardo went crashing to his knees on the floor.

Manzano watched him writhing in agony. 'Hmmm,' he mumbled. 'I think, Signor Bernini, you've just given me your answer.'

Chapter 32

'Good God, Bernini!' exclaimed Professor Loggi, his monocle falling out of its socket with the shock. 'What have they done to you?'

It was early morning in an interrogation room at Villa Triste and the guards had just carried in the prisoner and slung him on the floor, like a piece of meat on a butcher's slab.

'I thought that was obvious, Professor,' croaked Edoardo, slowly stirring. Now his left eye was half-closed, and the area around it a deep shade of purple. He crawled towards the chair, and with Loggi's help managed to haul himself onto it.

Through his red-misted vision, Edoardo noticed the professor glancing back towards the grille, as if unease was tapping on his shoulder. 'How come you were allowed to visit?' he asked.

'I was fortunate.'

Edoardo was suspicious. 'Manzano sent you, didn't he? To ask about the Cranach. He knows you don't want any harm to come to it.'

Loggi nodded and lowered his voice. 'He is like a dog with a bone. Of course he asked me. He's desperate. It doesn't look good in front of the Germans if he can't get his hands on the painting. Fischer wants an answer and he's given him three days to get it.'

A sudden gasp flicked pain across Edoardo's face. 'Three days?'

The professor bit his lip. The next piece of news wouldn't be easy to swallow, either. 'He now believes you made Signorina Leone write a false report.'

Mention of Lina set Edoardo alight. He seized on the professor's words. 'Have you heard how she is?' His bloody fingers combed through his matted hair. 'Manzano said she'd been interned.'

'As far as I know she is with the other English women. They've been sent to the mountains in the north.'

Lurching forwards, Edoardo clutched at Loggi's arm. 'That bastard says he'll bring her here if I don't talk. They'll tor—' he swallowed down the word he couldn't bring himself to say. 'I can't bear the thought of it.' Tears escaped from his badly bruised lids and mixed with the dried blood on his face. 'You understand?'

The professor grasped Edoardo's hand and held it tight. 'Oh, my dear fellow. So, you'll let him have the Cranach, surely?' It seemed the nightmarish vision of Lina lying in a fascist torture cell was also too much for him to contemplate.

A soldier entered the cell then, carrying a tin mug of water. He set it down on the table and left. Edoardo waited until he was out of the room and snatched the mug, gulping down its contents in one. He wiped his cracked lips with the back of his bruised hand as the professor looked on with a mixture of pity and horror.

Edoardo shook his head. 'I never meant her to get caught up in this.'

Loggi elbowed the table and leaned in. 'I know, but I did warn you.'

A grudging nod. 'You did,' admitted Edoardo. The professor had recruited him to the Tuscan Liberation Committee a few months before war was declared. The dealer had joined knowing the risks he would run, but he'd been prepared to do anything to defeat the fascists. And now that commitment was being sorely tested. 'It was Lina's idea to say the Cranach was a fake. She wanted it left at the villa at Forte dei Marmi. I suppose she thought the

187

Jewish family may have been allowed to keep it.' He looked up. 'She's a good person.'

'I don't doubt that.' Loggi shook his head.

'I hid the Cranach to protect her. I knew Fischer was coming to see it, and she was terrified her lie would be exposed.' From somewhere Edoardo found the strength to clench his fist. Without warning, his hand swept across the table, sending the tin mug clattering onto the filthy floor. 'This wasn't meant to happen.'

The silence between them was broken by screams coming from a nearby cell. Edoardo clamped his hands over his ears to block them out. Loggi cast around the room, desperate to find some way out of the situation.

'Perhaps it needn't.' he said. 'I'm assuming when they searched the gallery they didn't find any proof.'

'No.' Edoardo shut him down. 'They'd have said if they had.'

Loggi nodded. 'That's a relief. Then there's room to strike a deal.'

Edoardo's hands dropped to the table, and he looked up. 'A deal?' he repeated and followed it with a scoffing laugh. 'I'm hardly in a position to make a deal' He looked down at his torn shirt and the spatters of blood across his chest.

'On the contrary,' argued Loggi. 'You have what Manzano wants. I'm no dealer, but I'd say that puts you in a position to bargain on behalf of Dr Leone.'

Edoardo scoffed. 'You think if I told Manzano where the Cranach was, he would release Lina? I would tell him in a heartbeat if I could trust him to let her go.'

'I do,' the professor said with a nod. 'Think about it. If you don't tell him where the portrait is hidden, he will be true to his word. He will bring her back here and make her suffer in whatever perverted way he chooses. But if you do tell, Dr Leone might just be granted immunity. And it would give us time, Bernini.' He lowered his voice to a whisper. 'Valuable time to plan.' Loggi tilted his head, trying to hook his gaze under Edoardo's swollen lids. 'That could be worth more than any Renaissance painting to you and to the resistance until we find a solution. It could be worth your life.'

'Perhaps you're right,' agreed Edoardo after a long pause. 'I've been blind.' His thoughts had been so clouded by suffering, he couldn't see a way through the fog of pain, but now the professor was showing him a way. He'd reminded him he was a dealer. And dealers did deals.

'Very well. We are agreed,' said Loggi, planting his hands on his thighs and easing himself up. 'Let me see what I can do.'

Edoardo's eyes burned intently. 'You will get word to Manzano that I'm willing to talk.'

'I will.'

Hobbling over to the grille the professor tapped on it with his stick. 'Ready,' he called.

When the guards entered to return him to his cell, Edoardo needed no help getting up.

'Thank you, Professor,' he said, stretching out his manacled hand.

Loggi took it in his, glad he had offered a ray of hope.

'I wish you luck, Bernini,' he said as Edoardo was led from the room to walk slowly, but unaided, down the corridor. The professor knew he was going to need all the luck in the world if he was ever to leave Villa Triste alive.

Chapter 33

Torselli

At the end of another interminable day, Lina and the other women were eating a meagre supper of stale bread and cheese. Apart from the mayor, there was little contact with the villagers. They didn't seem hostile towards them, merely indifferent. Besides, they had their own struggles to overcome, and these foreign strangers were of no interest.

Miss Harrowby, looking forlornly at the mould on her cheese, was bemoaning how she missed English Stilton, when a loud banging disturbed the women's meal. Everyone sat upright, alarmed. This wasn't a curious village woman or one of the children playing tricks. This was thunderous and brutish and terrifying. The doors shook. Whoever was outside was trying to break in. More hammering, then a voice.

'*Apri subito! Apri la porta ora!* Open up! Open now!'

Anxious glances were exchanged, and before Lina could see who it was, four *fascisti* burst in, pointing their rifles at the terrified women.

'Angelina Leone?' one barked, his weapon aimed at her.

'Yes,' she replied warily. 'What's wrong? What is it?'

Without saying another word, two soldiers were upon her; one yanking her arms behind her back while the other locked steel cuffs around her wrists.

'Get away from her!' shouted a voice from behind. Agatha's, she knew.

'Stop! You can't do this!'

'Leave her alone!'

'No! What's this about?' Lina cried as she was dragged outside.

A chorus of protests rose as the women flooded out into the courtyard to surround the waiting truck.

'Where are you taking her?' cried Agatha, pummelling a soldier's back.

Miss Harrowby burst into tears, while Mrs Clutterbuck surged towards the truck, arms outstretched, trying to reach Lina as she was bundled into the back.

'Stay strong!' she boomed, clinging on to the tailgate, until a guard yanked her out of the way.

Lina, in a daze, looked down from the truck at the outraged women being fended off by the guards. Their fury was so hot it could have melted an iceberg. But the *fascisti*, guns still prone, jumped back into their vehicle and sped off through the school gates. Everyone knew the situation was hopeless. Lina had been wrenched from them and the future had imploded before their very eyes.

A cold sweat broke out on Lina's skin as, with her hands tied securely behind her back, she was led into the blindingly white room. She blinked furiously. The dazzling light was a huge shock after the gloom of the cell where she'd been thrown the night before. She'd already guessed she was at Villa Triste, the place whose name struck terror in everyone's hearts The stench of sweat and blood had made her gag, and the distant sound of a Schubert symphony had sent a chill streaking down her spine. She'd heard they sometimes played music to drown out the prisoners' screams.

191

Could such a fate await her?

Nothing made sense. Why was she back in Florence? She couldn't pose any threat in Torselli. That's why Manzano had sent her there in the first place. So why return her to the city? It had to be to do with Edoardo. Was he here, too? He'd broken her heart already. She tried to comfort herself with the thought that whatever the fascists chose to do to her couldn't be as painful.

Soon the door creaked open and in walked Manzano. Lina felt her legs buckle under her. But one of the guards caught her before she fell and propped her up like a trophy on display.

Manzano smiled. 'It's good to know I can still make women swoon,' he joked. He turned to the guard seeking appreciation and got it in a forced laugh. But his voice pulled Lina from the darkness that blurred her vision. His face swam in front of hers, as she lifted her head, fighting the dizziness.

'Why have you brought me here?'

Another smile from the podesta. 'I thought you'd like to see the man who betrayed you one last time,' he replied. Standing aside, he turned towards the open door to reveal Edoardo, flanked by two more guards. 'Not so handsome now, is he? No longer the dashing young heartthrob.'

'Edoardo!' she heard herself cry as he was dragged into the room. Only it wasn't the same man who'd kissed her on the Ponte Santa Trinita. His beautiful features were so distorted he was almost unrecognisable. Blood smeared his swollen cheeks, and his eyes had disappeared into purple sockets.

'Cara mia!' he called out, but a guard struck him with a rifle in the guts and he doubled over.

'How touching,' remarked Manzano, before ordering, 'Bring her over.'

'No, what are you doing?' screamed Edoardo, pitching towards Lina. 'I said I'd tell you! I said!' But another blow, this time to the head, silenced him. Manzano seemed oblivious to his entreaties, taking great pleasure in watching Lina being dragged towards another man who stared at her blankly as he rolled up his shirt sleeves.

'No. No!' she cried, as he picked up a cosh and hit his palm with it.

Terror registered on Lina's face as soon as she realised what was about to happen.

Manzano looked over at Edoardo, beginning to stir again in the guard's grip. 'The way I see it, you are a dealer, Bernini. So, you and I can strike a bargain. I understand you have already agreed to reveal the painting's whereabouts. But just in case you were tempted to lie once more, I thought Signorina Leone might persuade you otherwise.' He was grinning as his gaze switched to Lina, pain and terror etched on her face. 'So, you can tell me truthfully where you have hidden the Cranach, or you can watch this pretty little lady get a good beating.'

'I'll tell,' cried Edoardo, still flailing in vain.

'Edoardo!' cried Lina, her hands now held behind her back by another guard. Was she really being used as a bargaining tool? Like some pawn in a grotesque game of chess. Confusion and horror clashed inside her head. 'How could you? How could you have used me like this?' But before Edoardo could reply to her, Manzano signalled to the expressionless man. Pulling back his arm, he aimed the cosh at her stomach.

'No! No!' Edoardo begged, thrashing against the guard. 'I'll tell you.'

All Lina's muscles shrieked as she tensed so hard she thought she might explode.

'So you'll talk?' said Manzano slowly, looking directly at Edoardo. He seemed in no hurry. 'Yes?'

'Yes. Yes. For Christ's sake. Yes,' he pleaded, tears streaking his face.

Another signal and the guard holding Lina pulled back and let her fall to the floor.

'Enough!' cried Edoardo, as she knelt doubled over gasping

for breath. 'I will tell you where the Cranach is. I will tell you, but for pity's sake let her go.'

A victorious smile spread across Manzano's face. 'Very well,' he replied, nodding to the guard. 'The girl can go,' he paused, 'but only after my men have brought the portrait to me.' Glaring at Edoardo he said, 'Well, Bernini?'

'Tell them, Edoardo,' croaked Lina. At that moment she didn't care if he had stolen it for his own gain, she just wanted this nightmare to be over.

With his chest heaving, and still in the guard's grip, Edoardo lurched towards her. 'I'm so truly sorry,' he cried. Shutting his eyes, he forced his tongue to deliver the words he never wanted Manzano to hear. 'The portrait is at the railway station. In a left luggage locker.'

Lina, trembling, looked up. 'What?'

'I was going to take it to Innsbruck for safekeeping but had second thoughts,' he told her.

The podesta lifted his brows and shrugged. 'We'll soon see if you're lying,' he said. 'Now take them both away.'

'No! Edoardo!' cried Lina, glancing back as she was jostled out of the room. Even if he had betrayed her, the sudden thought she may never see him again was unbearable.

'What a touching apology,' Manzano remarked to Edoardo as he passed him. 'She may not have accepted it but at least you will have a clear conscience when you go to your grave.'

The hours dragged as Lina waited in the squalid cell for news of her release. If Edoardo was telling the truth and the portrait was at the train station, then Manzano should release her. But Edoardo's fate seemed sealed. Even though he'd gone behind her back and lied to her, even though he'd broken her heart into a thousand pieces and stamped on them, the thought of what he was about to endure at Manzano's cruel hands was intolerable. Again, she wrapped her arms around her quivering body. But even if she were freed shortly, her mind would remain in this hellish place, and on the memory of Edoardo's anguished face. His image was etched on her brain, and it could be the last she had of him. Manzano was intent on his execution, she didn't doubt it for a second.

The cathedral bell tolled three before Lina heard boots outside her cell. A bolt was shot, and a key clanked in the lock.

'Out,' barked a guard, opening wide the door.

Still trembling and weak, she managed to get to her feet and stumbled forwards, reaching out to the wall to steady herself. But she was alive and about to walk out of Villa Triste free.

'This way,' shouted the guard who unlocked her cell. She supposed they were sending her back to Torselli. Or perhaps they'd take her to some wooded area to be shot and toss her corpse into a shallow grave. Her whole body was still in shock. As she was led outside towards a waiting truck, she saw Manzano's car drive through the compound's gates. She wanted to hope that he was going to free Edoardo, too; now that he had the painting. But something inside her told her the podesta wouldn't let Edoardo slip through his hands without wreaking some revenge. They'd searched the gallery and his home – she knew that because they'd shown her the charcoal sketch he'd done. They had no reason to keep holding him, did they?

'Excellency!' she called out suddenly with the little breath still in her lungs. 'Podesta Manzano!' Why had he returned? Had he come to save Edoardo or to condemn him? As she was bundled inside the waiting truck, she hated herself for ever returning to the colour and warmth of Florence to escape her mother's indifference and her new stepfather's arrogance. At least in Scotland she would have been safe, cocooned from the war in his cold castle. She hated herself for ever taking a stand against the fascists, too; for thinking she could stand up for those oppressed by Mussolini's regime. But most of all she hated herself for ever giving her heart to Edoardo Bernini, because if he died in Villa Triste, deep down, despite his betrayal, she knew he'd still take a piece of her with him.

Meanwhile, in Torselli, Lina remained very much at the centre of everyone's thoughts.

'We pray for our dear Angelina, alone and frightened and away from the people who care about her most,' intoned Agatha. Her hands were clasped, and her head bowed as she led the other members of the society in their daily prayers at the schoolhouse. 'Bring her back safely to us, dear Lord. Through Jesus Christ our Lord. Amen.'

'Amen,' chorused the other women.

Three days had passed since Lina had been so cruelly snatched from them. Three days in which the women were left lost and bereft. Agatha, feeling her great-niece's absence the keenest, was comforted by the others, but she'd still found it hard to rally any enthusiasm for daily tasks. It seemed they were all in mourning for someone departed but not, they very much hoped, dead.

Mrs Clutterbuck was the only one who tried to remain remotely positive. 'She'll be back here in no time,' she would say glibly. 'Miss Leone can certainly take care of herself.' But then Miss Harrowby would start to cry, and her tears would trigger an avalanche.

Then, later that same day, Miss Harrowby's keen hearing picked out the rumble of a motor vehicle labouring up the mountain road. In Lina's absence, it had been up to her to collect firewood for cooking. Shielding her eyes against the bright light, she'd managed to make out a heavy truck, slowly coughing its way up a steep incline.

When she returned to the schoolhouse with a basket heavy with firewood, she reported what she'd spotted. 'I've just seen a truck. Coming up from the valley.'

'What sort of truck?' asked Mrs Clutterbuck, nursing a bad cold.

Miss Harrowby shrugged. 'I don't know. Military, I suppose.'

Mrs Clutterbuck harrumphed. 'Come to check on us most probably.'

'Or to bring supplies,' suggested Lady Felstein, sounding unusually positive.

The rumble grew loader. Agatha cupped her ear. 'I can hear it now.'

'Hear what?' asked Lady Felstein, reaching for her ear trumpet.

Miss Harrowby scampered over to the window. 'There it is,' she cried excitedly. 'And it's coming here.'

Agatha, heaving herself up from a bench, limped over to the window to see a vehicle, clearly emblazoned with the fascist emblem, rumbling along the dusty road. A frown pinched her brows. 'Oh, dear,' she said to the other women as they clustered around the window. 'It seems we have visitors.'

The truck came to a halt right in the middle of the schoolyard. The soldiers went straight to the back and unbolted its doors. One climbed inside, while the other looked on.

'What's happening?' asked Lady Felstein, searching for her spectacles.

'I can't be sure,' replied Miss Harrowby, squinting.

'We'll find out soon enough,' replied Mrs Clutterbuck, nodding towards the window as everyone switched back to the misted glass and the figure emerging from the army truck.

'Angelina!' gasped Agatha. 'Oh, my dear!'

'She's back! Oh, thank God,' declared Miss Harrowby, looking heavenwards.

'Oh, Miss Leone!' cried Mr Clutterbuck and Lady Felstein in unison.

There was a rush towards the door and there, standing outside and flanked by two soldiers, stood Lina. Under her eyes were dark circles and her lustrous black hair was lank. She appeared dazed, as if she couldn't quite believe what was happening to her. But before the guards would allow her to be welcomed with open arms, Signor Cetti appeared, powering through the school gates, shrugging on his jacket as he went.

'I am the mayor of this region,' he told the senior soldier. 'I will take this woman into my custody.'

The soldier bowed and flung out an arm in salute. A few words were exchanged before the men were signalled to leave.

'Welcome back to Torselli, Signorina Leone,' said the mayor, smiling broadly and holding out a hand. But Lina didn't take it. Her head was whirling, and dots and sparks flew in front of her eyes. The journey up parched mountain roads and through rocky passes had been treacherous, but it was nothing compared with what she had endured over the past few hours. When, however, the moment to be handed over arrived, her willpower deserted her. She caught sight of Agatha, of Lady Felstein, of Miss Harrowby and Mrs Clutterbuck and that was enough. Finally feeling safe, she let her knees fold beneath her, and her eyes close, knowing this time when she fell, she'd be caught by those who cared.

Chapter 34

Manzano's bulk loomed over the prisoner as he lay on the floor of his cell. When Edoardo didn't respond to his greeting, the podesta kicked him hard in the ribs. He groaned.

'So, you are still alive,' Manzano mumbled. 'Good. I was afraid I might be too late.'

Edoardo struggled to prop himself up against the wall. 'I'm still here, podesta,' he replied, squinting through bruised sockets. 'You've come to release me, I assume. You've got the painting. Why else would you keep me here?'

Manzano boomed out a laugh. 'Why else?' he repeated. He eased himself onto a chair a guard had brought in for him. 'Yes, we have the painting, but that wasn't the only thing we found.'

Edoardo's blackened forehead puckered in a frown. 'I don't understand. What do you mean?' he asked, clutching his side.

'I mean,' said Manzano, reaching into his breast pocket and pulling out a small notebook, 'I sent my men back to search not just your gallery, but your apartment, too.'

Edoardo's eyes flinched under blackened lids. 'Signora Bianchi. She's not harmed?'

199

'Your housekeeper is quite safe,' replied Manzano. 'For the moment. But my men did find this.' He brandished the notebook in the air. 'Proof, Bernini. Proof you are a traitor.'

Edoardo tried to focus, tried to ignore the pain that seared into his head and stabbed at his ribs. He recognised the notebook all right. It was hidden in a frame in his study. It contained codenames of all the other members of the Tuscan Liberation Committee. No one else knew it was there. No one.

He needed to think quickly. 'It's an inventory. I've given codewords to all my stock in the gallery.'

'Nice try,' replied Manzano with a nod. 'But your game is up, Bernini.'

'Why don't you believe me? I've been loyal to you,' Edoardo growled through gritted teeth. With the codenames in Manzano's possession, he was as good as dead. But before they killed him, they'd want the names of all the others in the resistance group. They'd wring every last drop of information from him before they finally put him out of his misery with a bullet through his head.

The podesta leaned forwards, lowering his sloppy mouth towards Edoardo's ear. 'Now will you tell me everything, or shall I call Major Carita to give you his special hospitality?' Carita's very name filled decent Florentines with dread. A crazed cocaine addict, he was chief torturer at Villa Triste. The podesta licked his slack lips. 'Or even, perhaps, Signora Leone? I can always bring her back, you know.'

Edoardo groaned. 'There is nothing to tell,' he insisted.

The podesta pulled his face into a grimace. 'Strange,' he said, shaking his head. 'You really don't take after your father, do you?'

'What?' Edoardo snapped, anger abruptly fuelling his broken body.

Manzano shrugged. 'His problem was he talked too much, but now you say you won't talk at all.' Heaving himself up from the chair, he called for the guard to open the door before turning towards his prisoner once again. 'We'll just have to see if Major

Carita can persuade you, won't we?' he said, and he lumbered out of the cell, a smile hovering on his loose mouth.

News of Lina's return spread like wildfire. It seemed her ordeal at the hands of the fascists had rallied the villagers and made them more sympathetic towards the foreign women. They were all victims of Mussolini's cruel regime. A steady stream of well-wishers left broth and bread at the schoolhouse door.

'They are saying prayers for Signorina Leone in the church,' Signor Cetti told Agatha as she accepted a gift of bread on the doorstep.

'I think they are working,' she reassured him with a smile. She glanced over her shoulder to see Lina sitting on a chair looking wanly out of the window. 'She is much stronger,' she assured the well-meaning mayor, even though she couldn't be so sure about her niece's emotional state.

As soon as Signor Cetti was gone, Agatha sat down by Lina.

'Everyone wishes you a speedy recovery,' she relayed, taking her hand in hers.

Lina forced her lips into a weak smile, but it was going to take more than good wishes and prayers to heal her. There was a gaping hole in her chest where Edoardo had ripped out her heart and yet, at the same time, seeing his once beautiful face so bruised and bloodied, filled the empty void with dread. No one, no matter their crime, deserved to be tortured like that.

'It's Bernini, isn't it?' said Agatha. Lina had told her she'd seen him at Villa Triste. 'Don't forget he is the one who put you through all this. I should never have allowed you to see him.' She closed her eyes.

'I'm a grown woman, Aunt. I have no one to blame but myself.'

Agatha patted her hand. 'But you don't deserve this. You're hurting and I feel your pain.'

Reminded of Edoardo's pain, Lina lifted her gaze and regarded her aunt with eyes sore from crying. 'I'm afraid they'll kill him,' she whispered as she felt Agatha's arms wrap around her tormented body once more.

Chapter 35

Florence

The elderly man in a deerstalker looked up at the large clock over the reception desk at Villa Triste. The minutes were fast ticking away and as each one passed, Edoardo Bernini's lifeline grew shorter. Professor Loggi tapped his walking stick on the tiles as he waited. If his joints weren't so stiff, he'd have paced up and down.

'This is highly irregular,' said the young officer. He squinted at the papers then lifted his gaze to add, 'Professor Loggi.' He'd been handed a written request to visit one of the prisoners. 'Only a priest is usually allowed to see a condemned man,' he explained.

The professor nodded. He needed to remain calm. 'But if the order is signed by the podesta himself ...' His plea trailed off into a smile. In his fifty years in the world of art conservation, he'd picked up some useful skills. It had been easy to forge Manzano's signature on official notepaper.

The officer sighed. 'Very well.'

The professor nodded then lifted up both his arms. 'Surely you're going to search me?'

A wave of the hand. 'That won't be necessary.'

'Thank you, officer,' Loggi replied. 'One more thing.' He glanced at his walking stick. 'Perhaps the prisoner could be brought upstairs. My joints are very stiff.' He looked down at his legs.

'Very well,' the officer repeated. 'You can see him in there.' He gestured to a door opposite. 'But I warn you, he is not in a good way.'

The professor tilted his head. 'I understand.' He'd been told Carita had got his evil hands on Edoardo. But he'd already been tried and sentenced in Manzano's court and found guilty of treason. Even if he survived the torture chamber, he'd be executed. Time was slipping away, and Loggi had been given the go-ahead. Another day and it could be too late.

The officer unlocked the door. The room was bare, apart from a table and two chairs. Paint peeled off the walls and there was an acrid smell of carbolic. Nevertheless, a small, barred window high up made it infinitely preferable to the downstairs reek of blood and other bodily fluids. Taking the weight off his feet on a simple wooden chair, the professor sat as time continued to tick away until finally, heavy footsteps stopped outside, and an apparition appeared in the open doorway.

'The prisoner,' said a guard, ripping off Edoardo's blindfold then shoving him in the small of his back to fall at Loggi's feet.

The professor looked aghast at the bundle of bone and bloody rags in front of him. 'Leave us,' he snapped, appalled by the dealer's condition. Since their last encounter, he'd clearly been thrown to Carita's band of depraved psychopaths. He leaned over and offered a helping hand, but then noticed Edoardo's was caked in blood.

'Can you stand?' he asked.

Blinking furiously, Edoardo lifted his bruised face and gritted his teeth. 'Yes,' he replied, clutching his side, and levering himself up on the chair. 'A few broken ribs never hurt anyone.'

The professor was amazed at this man's tenacity. He glanced at the grille to see the guard's head outside the door.

Edoardo breathed as deeply as his cracked ribs allowed. 'Signorina Leone – is she still being held?'

Loggi shook his head. 'I believe she was returned to internment. I am sure she will recover. You, on the other hand …'

'I'm not dead yet, Professor, but I will be soon if I stay around here much longer.' He'd endured two sessions at Carita's mercy and lost three fingernails from his left hand in the bargain. Now, thanks to Professor Loggi, he hoped he wouldn't be spending any more time in the sadist's company. He turned his back away from the grille, so the guard couldn't see what was happening.

'Good luck,' whispered Loggi, handing over his walking stick.

Edoardo clutched it and took a shallow breath. 'Ready?'

The professor braced himself, closed his eyes, then nodded. 'Arrgghhh!'

The punch, although not hard, sent him off balance, so that he stumbled backwards and knocked over a chair.

At the sound of crashing furniture, the guard, pistol poised, flung open the cell door but was immediately knocked out cold from behind by the unseen walking stick. Edoardo snatched the soldier's gun and fled the room, just as another guard appeared from nowhere, taking aim and firing. The shot nicked the wall behind, but it alerted the sentries at the front entrance. With eyes focused on the main door, Edoardo charged towards it as more guards opened fire. Dodging behind a pillar in the hall, he took aim, shouts and gunshots ringing in his ears. On target. Another guard down, but then a cascade of automatic fire rained from somewhere above. Diving headlong to the floor, he blanked out the searing pain in his ribs to crawl the next ten paces to the door, bullets ricocheting off the tiles. He got lucky. A bullet bounced back up to hit one of the soldiers in the leg, bringing him crashing to the ground.

Blood now streamed over Edoardo's right eye from a split wound, but still, he kept going until he reached the main exit. With all his strength he pulled himself upright and lunged for the door handle, as another shot hit the frame, but he didn't falter. Staggering outside, he saw two sentries standing between him and the high gates. He dispatched the first quickly, but the second had time to take cover and was tracking him from a low wall. Edoardo dropped and rolled towards him, catching him unawares before he could fire again.

Ahead lay the iron gates. They were locked. Grabbing the railings Edoardo shook them as hard as he could, out of anger more than anything else. *Where were they? They should be here by now.* He turned back to the building. More guards streamed out, firing randomly. He ducked just as a pick-up truck screeched to a halt outside. A shot to the padlock and the gates opened. Hands reached from the flatbed and hauled him onto it, just as a hail of bullets peppered the gates. As the truck weaved through the back streets of Florence, Edoardo lay on his back, jinking from side to side as each corner was cut. But he could see the sky. And he was alive. Now the fightback could begin.

PART TWO

Chapter 36

Torselli

July 1943

'Mussolini has been arrested! I heard it from the BBC, on Radio Londra!' Signor Cetti was so excited he could barely get the words out as he barged into the schoolhouse one hot July evening. He'd been secretly listening to the banned station throughout the war, giving Lina regular updates. And now, finally, after more than three long years, there was good news for those who despised the fascists.

'What?' cried Lina, hurrying towards him.

Aware that something momentous was happening, Lady Felstein searched for her ear trumpet. Miss Harrowby stopped dusting and Miss Giltrap abandoned peeling potatoes. A chorus of gasps and exclamations filled the room as Agatha also emerged from the kitchen to join the others.

'The Allies have invaded Sicily, and we have a new prime minister,' relayed Signor Cetti.

'Thank God!' cried Mrs Clutterbuck, looking heavenwards. Miss Harrowby's lips trembled as Miss Giltrap hugged her, while

Lina embraced Lady Felstein.

'I knew we could do it!' exclaimed an excitable Miss Giltrap, slapping her thigh. America had joined the war eighteen months before and Manzano had seen to it she was also interned in Torselli.

But Agatha, it seemed, wasn't quite so elated. 'That's all well and good, but what does that mean exactly for us?' she asked when the commotion died down. It was a question no one could answer.

As soon as word got out about Il Duce's arrest, some of the villagers draped red, white and green tricolour flags from window ledges. An old man played an accordion in the square and the children, sensing a lifting of the sombre mood, skipped and danced in the street. The English ladies, however, after their initial excitement, were in a state of limbo. In the schoolhouse later that day, they sat drinking a nettle infusion, introduced by Lina as a substitute for tea, and weighed up all sorts of scenarios.

'We might still be told to stay here,' said Agatha.

'But we have work to do in Florence,' pointed out Lady Felstein, clearly thinking about the cataloguing at the Uffizi.

'And our bombs can do as much damage as Jerry's,' said the ever-practical Mrs Clutterbuck.

'Meaning?' asked Miss Harrowby.

'I think what Mrs Clutterbuck means,' intervened Agatha, 'is that if the Allies bomb the city, they will have no more regard for its treasures than the Germans.'

'Exactly,' chimed in Miss Giltrap emphatically, as if she were speaking on behalf of the American government.

'I agree,' said Lady Felstein with a nod. 'Besides, surely we all want to get back to our homes.'

Agatha was of the same mindset. 'I, for one, can't wait to sleep in my own bed again.' Her remark prompted a spate of head nodding and agreement.

Everyone was dreaming of a return to normality, but Lina understood that as long as the war continued, nothing could be certain. 'All we can do is wait,' she said.

'At least we know Professor Loggi won't abandon us,' piped up Agatha. 'I have complete faith in him.'

A week later, she was proven right. A troop carrier was sent by the new regime to collect the women. It seemed Professor Loggi had pulled strings and championed their immediate return. But when the truck rolled up outside the schoolhouse to ferry the women back to the city the departure was bittersweet. Lina worried some of their villas and apartments might have been commandeered, and without pay, all the members of staff would certainly have left. She'd no idea how much damage had been wrought by Allied bombing raids, let alone whether the works of art in various galleries and museums had been spared. Suddenly she feared what they were leaving behind might be preferable to what they were about to walk into.

'We will miss you ladies,' said Signor Cetti.

'And we, you, *signor*,' said Agatha, offering her hand. Her initial animosity had long ago given way to respect for the good-hearted mayor.

Several villagers gathered to wave off the *Inglesi*. Some brought bread for the journey back to the city and in return the ladies left items of clothing. There were tearful farewells and promises to meet again one day.

Back in Florence, an unmistakable bullish face stared out at Lina from a burned-out frame. Il Duce's portrait lay on top of a smouldering bonfire in the middle of the piazza, as the troop carrier chugged through the city. Over the rattle of the engine, Agatha and the ladies chatted eagerly about their homecoming, but as Lina listened to their banter about clean sheets, roast beef, and whether or not the household staff might have remained, she only had one thing on her mind. Edoardo.

Signs of change were everywhere. As well as smashed busts and destroyed portraits of Mussolini, tricolours hung from many government buildings. But as the truck progressed slowly through the city centre, Lina noted the people looked worn down. Many were in rags and painfully thin and the good news didn't seem to have changed anything. It was then she caught sight of a placard by a newspaper vendor and her heart missed a beat. It read: *War to Continue*.

Mercifully, Villa Mimosa had been left locked and secure, although Donna was nowhere to be seen. However, in Agatha's absence a neighbour had kindly kept an eye on the property, and everything seemed to be in order, if rather unloved. That night Lina kissed Agatha on the cheek, then went to her own room. Apart from the film of dust and the cobwebs, it was just as she'd left it and, for that, she felt very grateful. But instead of flopping down between the crisp cotton sheets she'd so missed, she went straight to the drawer in her bedside table, her heart beating wildly.

While she'd never mentioned Edoardo's name again in Torselli and done her best to block him from her thoughts during the day, she'd still thought about him every night alone in her bed. Closing her eyes, she would try to shut out the pain of a loss she couldn't quite accept. But she'd never succeeded. She always fell asleep not only wondering if he was alive or dead, but also questioning if he really had betrayed her.

As they'd watched that memorable sunset at Forte dei Marmi, hadn't he told her he hated fascism and Mussolini and Hitler? Was that all lies, too? Was he really like one of those Old Master copies on his wall or a cheap religious fake touted around the *duomo*. Her hot Italian blood boiled at the memory, but then lately, she'd noticed her English reason had started to re-emerge. The more she thought, the more she'd wondered if there was a way to prove the accusations against Edoardo. Before she'd felt utterly powerless, but time had given her strength. And then, as they were driven down the mountainside towards the city, earlier that day, it had returned – the memory of the keys.

Opening the drawer, she gulped down her relief to see they were still there. Two of them – one relatively modern, and the other old and rusty. Edoardo had slipped them into her hand just before he'd taken her to the Ponte Santa Trinita that magical evening. They could hold the answer.

Creeping unseen from the villa in the warm dusk of a July evening, Lina headed towards the Gallery Bernini. There were still patrols on the streets; *Carabinieri* and soldiers. She had to be careful. Curfew remained in place, even though windows closed before were now opened, and music blared from gramophones. Fascism seemed to have loosened its grip. After all, Mussolini and a lot of his cronies were in prison. She hoped Podesta Manzano was now behind bars, too.

Apart from the street patrols, the only other living creatures she encountered were half-starved cats and dogs on the prowl. Keeping to the shadows, she made it unchallenged to the gallery and from there through the arch and to the cellar. With the flashlight quivering, she took out the old key and tried the lock. It clicked after the first turn, and she pushed against the door. Taking a deep breath, she stole inside. As soon as her eyes adjusted to the darkness, she saw she was in a low, vaulted cellar. It was cool, but not damp. The ceiling was draped with cobwebs, and the floor paved with large, flat stones scattered with sawdust. Against the length of one wall stood a metal rack filled with wine bottles.

A sudden sound made her jump, and glancing down, a rat scuttled by her feet and disappeared behind a large barrel. With the torch beam she traced its path and saw it slide into a gap in the floor. It was then she noticed the sawdust had been disturbed around the barrel's base. There was something else. A footprint.

She gave the barrel a shove. It didn't budge, but she could tell it was empty. Bending her knees, she wrapped her arms around its girth and pulled it towards her. It shifted. Only a little, but she repeated the same action again and again until she had shunted it a few inches. She shone the torch on the ground once more.

A grate. There was a space below the cellar floor. Grabbing the iron bars of the grille with both hands, she tugged hard. It lifted. Below was a ladder. Kneeling down, she directed the light to its foot. Boxes? Was Edoardo storing something down there?

Easing herself through the narrow opening, gingerly Lina felt her way down the rungs of the ladder, the torch clamped between her teeth. It wasn't long before she reached the ground, where the air was much cooler. She shivered. The torch beam picked out the low ceiling of bare rock. She was at the mouth of a tunnel. Dipping the light to the ground, she saw more footprints. Her stomach clenched with fear as she edged towards the boxes she'd spotted. Now she could see they were crates, and by the looks of them, they'd been abandoned in a hurry. Some of the lids weren't secured at all. She lifted one easily and with her heart in her mouth, peered inside.

Setting down the torch on a nearby ledge in the rock, so that it's beam illuminated the crate's contents, she knelt down and steeled herself to delve inside. Her probing fingers traced something hard-edged. A wooden panel? With both hands she pulled hard. It was a painting, as she'd guessed. A religious painting of Christ as a child in the Temple. It was vaguely familiar to her. Where had she seen it before? Then she remembered. In the monastery of San Giacomo, just two blocks away from the gallery. Carefully she set down the painting, then pulled out the next item in the crate. A jewel-encrusted candlestick. Next came a silver goblet. Peering in again she saw a bronze statuette. The booty just kept on coming until finally she rocked back on her heels in a state of shock. So Manzano, Professor Loggi, and Agatha had been right all along. Edoardo was a thief. Why else would these treasures be hidden in his cellar? He'd even stolen from a monastery.

At this last realisation, her lips began to tremble, then slumping down on the ledge in the darkness, she gave herself permission to cry. Her tears fell freely and swelled into sobs. Somewhere deep inside she had wanted to believe Edoardo's innocence; that

Manzano had framed him for the theft of the Cranach; that the accusations against him were all false. But now she had discovered the spoils of his career of crime, that last seed of hope had shrivelled and died. Throwing back her head and clenching her fists, she screamed his name into the void, expecting only the echoes to scream back. Then she saw him.

Chapter 37

Florence

At first, she thought he was an apparition; his ghost returned to haunt her. In the darkness she'd screamed out his name and he'd come. But then she jumped up and grabbed the torch, shining it at him. Edoardo's hands shot up to shield his eyes from the blinding light, but Lina's recognition was instant. He'd lost weight and when he brought down his hands once more, she saw his chin was stubbled, but his smile was the same.

'Oh, my love!' he cried, rushing towards her, his arms opening wide. But stunned and confused, her first instinct was to back off. 'It's me, Lina,' he told her, still edging towards her.

'Get away from me, Edoardo,' she said, anger now replacing her shock. His stash of stolen treasures was plain to see. 'Manzano was right. You're a thief.'

'No! No, that's not true.' This time he didn't hesitate, but launched himself towards her.

With hands now clasped he pleaded, but she side-stepped. 'You stole the Cranach, and you stole all these things.' She flashed the torch at the crates. 'You lied to me, and you betrayed me.'

He shook his head. 'You've got it all wrong,' he told her, holding his hands up in surrender. 'I know what it looks like, but please hear me out.'

Her torch beam cast his face in a soft glow. She noticed his eyes were glassy with tears.

'I would never do anything to hurt you.' He palmed his chest. 'I love you.'

She gritted her teeth, knowing she needed to be strong to resist him. 'You're lying now. How could you have loved me? You just used me.'

He sprang forwards again. 'Used you? No. No. I never wanted you to get trapped in this mess.'

Once more she avoided his embrace, shrugging her shoulder as he reached out for her arm. 'I'm getting out of here.' She scowled, snatching the torch and barging her way to the ladder.

'Don't go, please,' he called after her and she felt his hand tug her arm and wheel her around to face him. His touch, so familiar, should have carried a threat. Instead, it sent a thrill charging through her and she hesitated. Once he saw she might be prepared to listen, he said, 'At least let me explain.'

She paused. 'Explain?' she repeated, before slowly nodding her head. 'Yes,' she said firmly. 'I deserve an explanation.'

A soft smile lifted his lips at her acceptance. 'Thank you,' he replied, adding with an appeal, 'Where to start?'

'You could start here, perhaps,' she said, shining her torch on the open crate, the candlestick's diamonds and rubies dazzling in the beam.

Edoardo raked a hand through his hair. 'That's easy,' he replied, 'I didn't steal them, if that's what you're thinking. They are there for safekeeping. There are other crates from the monastery next door, too.'

Lina's eyes widened. 'From San Giacomo?'

'Yes. My father helped the monks store their valuable artwork during the Great War, and they asked me if I'd do the same again. They didn't want to entrust their treasures to outsiders. This tunnel connects both our cellars, so here was the obvious place to put them, in case the monastery was ever looted. I've been hiding here for months. The monks have been smuggling me supplies.'

For a moment she was silent. What she'd just been told made perfect sense, but it still didn't explain why he'd taken the Cranach portrait. Doubt remained, filling the space between them, and he sensed it.

'But why did you go to Austria without telling me, and why did you hide the Cranach?' she pressed, her eyes never leaving his.

He shook his head. 'That is a very long story. But before I tell it, I want to show you something.'

She narrowed her eyes. 'Oh?'

'Please,' he said, moving away from her and towards the pitch black of the tunnel. She grabbed the torch and followed for a few metres.

'Here,' he said, stopping at a niche in the rock. 'More light, please,' he said, and she directed the torch beam on his arms as they delved inside a hole and pulled out something bulky and obviously quite weighty wrapped in green material.

'What is this?' she asked, expecting to see yet another priceless treasure he just happened to have in his possession. She didn't have to wait long before Edoardo unwrapped the cloth. 'A radio set!' she gasped, then shifting her startled gaze, she asked, 'What are you doing with a radio set?'

'Is this the proof you wanted?' he asked her.

She reached out and ran her hands over the dials and knobs, just to make sure she wasn't dreaming. 'So, you're not a th—' All of a sudden she couldn't bring herself to say the word. 'You're a member of the resistance?'

'It's true. I really am,' he replied, his eyes glistening.

A wave of relief swept over her. It was all she needed to see and all she needed to hear.

'Oh, Edoardo. Thank God,' she cried, falling into his arms. 'I'm so sorry to have doubted you. Forgive me, my love. Forgive me, please.'

With his thumb he wiped away new tears. 'The thought of you doubting me was worse than anything Carita did to me,' he told her, holding her close. 'But now you understand why.'

She nodded, swallowing down her guilt. 'Can you ever forgive me?' she sobbed.

'There is nothing to forgive,' he told her as, in the gloom, his lips found hers and she felt herself melting into his warmth once more. Nothing else mattered. When they finally broke apart, she rested her head on his shoulder.

Still in his embrace, she leaned back and, in the half-light, saw him smile. His smooth face was lined, and his black hair stood out at all angles, but his smile still lit up the darkness and she traced his lips with her finger, not knowing whether to laugh or cry as questions flew around like bats in her skull.

'How did you escape from Villa Triste? When?' Words tumbled in a torrent from her tongue. 'And the Cranach! Where is it?' She switched to the crates. Before she'd found Edoardo, a long-lost hope had flared in the darkness, when she'd imagined the portrait stashed nearby. But no. She read his crestfallen look as an apology and knew instantly the young gentlewoman of Florence was gone.

'So, the Cranach was at the train station?' she asked, recalling his words the last time she'd seen him at Villa Triste.

A nod. 'I wasn't sure I could trust Decker, so I left the portrait in a locker and substituted it for a sketch I'd done. If I'd not gone to Innsbruck, he'd have been suspicious, but I hadn't bargained on being met by the SS. The OVRA must have telephoned ahead when they raided the gallery and left empty-handed.'

'So Manzano still has the painting, or has Fischer got his hands on it yet? He'll give it to Hitler or Goering, won't he?' Her voice was tinged with bitterness as she summarised the situation.

Edoardo sighed deeply and stroked her hair as he spoke. 'I don't know where it is right now, and I feel I've let you down. I understand how much it means to you, but I couldn't watch you suffer.'

'I know, my love,' she broke in, her hand resting on his heart, feeling it pump beneath his shirt. 'And I'm so grateful. It still destroys me to think of something so beautiful and so unique being violated by those evil men, but I've got you now.'

He nodded but struggled to find any words of comfort. He knew what the portrait symbolised; purity over corruption, beauty over ugliness, truth over lies. 'We'll find it and get it back,' he told her. 'That beautiful young woman belongs to Tuscany.' He looked into her eyes and added, 'That beautiful young woman is you.'

But right then, in that moment, she didn't care about the portrait. She didn't care about anything else. All she wanted was to relish the joy of being in Edoardo Bernini's arms.

Once they resurfaced out into the courtyard, Edoardo managed to lever off a wooden plank nailed across one of the smaller casements at the back of the gallery. Lina squeezed through the narrow aperture to open a window from the inside, and he joined her. The torch's beam traced the devastation. The back office had been ransacked and the wall safe left wide open. Most of the paintings had been hurled to the floor and several sculptures were smashed.

'They searched here again,' he told her, surveying the chaos. 'After they'd finished with you.'

'Why would they do that? They had the painting.' She looked at him quizzically.

'You should see my apartment,' he replied.

'Your apartment?' She shook her head. 'What about Signora Bianchi? Is she all right?'

'Yes. I found out she's staying somewhere else. I can't blame her.' He shook his head. 'I can't blame anyone but myself.'

Lina baulked. 'What do you mean? Of course you can't blame yourself.'

He looked at her wide-eyed, then, with a heavy sigh, grabbed an overturned chair and righted it for her. 'Sit, please,' he said, while he balanced on the corner of his desk. 'I can explain, but in return, you must swear on your life you will not tell another living soul what you're about to hear.'

Without hesitation Lina shook her head. 'We're on the same side, Edoardo. Please tell me what's going on. You promised me an explanation, remember?'

His chest heaved as he took a deep breath and nodded slowly. 'You've been through so much and I don't want to put you in any more danger.'

Her thoughts flew back to the interrogation room with Manzano leering over her. She'd already felt the horror of imprisonment and faced the terror of a cosh, but her suffering had been mild compared with Edoardo's. As well as both having wayward fathers, it was another bond they shared. 'Tell me, please,' she said.

He cupped the back of his neck, then fixed her with a stare. 'Very well,' he conceded. 'I've been a member of the Tuscan Liberation Committee for a long time.'

She'd known his views on Hitler and fascism, known he hated working for Goering and Manzano, but until then Lina hadn't realised he was involved in any organised resistance. 'All the time I've known you?'

'Months before.' He shrugged. 'There are many of us working underground in the city, and Manzano found my notebook of codenames to prove it, but thankfully not the radio in the cellar. That's how we communicate with other resistance groups across the region and as far as Verona. It's how—' He hesitated.

'What Edoardo? Please tell me.' She rose and took his face in her hands, so that he had to look into her eyes.

'So, is that how you escaped from Villa Triste? With the help of your contacts?'

He nodded and winked. 'Yes,' he told her, touching the side of his nose. 'You could say, I have friends in high places. But you know I can't tell you any more.'

Lina nodded her understanding. She was being kept in the dark for her own safety and for the sake of Edoardo's contacts. 'But what if I were to join the resistance, too?' she asked. 'Formally, I mean.' Edoardo frowned, but she wasn't deterred. 'I want to fight alongside you, my love. You can't deny I know what I'm letting myself in for now.'

He sighed again and kissed her head. 'You're just like your aunt,' he told her.

She replied with a smile. 'Fearless, you mean?'

Edoardo grinned. 'No. I mean stubborn as a mule.'

Chapter 38

Professor Loggi called on Agatha and Lina at Villa Mimosa a day later. Over a cup of tea – real tea – which Agatha had secreted in her bureau for 'emergencies', he outlined what had happened in their absence.

'Without the members of your society, progress has slowed considerably,' he lamented, a bone china cup poised near his lips.

Agatha nodded, slanting her head to one side. 'I like to think we've played our part, Professor,' she acknowledged, glancing at her niece for support.

Lina nodded politely. She'd not told anyone about her reunion with Edoardo the previous night. It remained too dangerous. His secret was safe with her.

Loggi's bushy brows rose in agreement. 'I can assure you that is the case,' he replied. 'We are down to a skeleton staff at the Uffizi. Some museums and galleries have closed. And now that the Allies have reached Sicily, the threat of aerial bombardments is even more real.'

'But the most important works are safe, surely,' said Agatha with a concerned frown.

'Most, but of course those are the ones that can be moved.'

'You're talking about the frescoes,' said Lina, setting down her cup.

The professor looked at her earnestly. 'I'm talking about the frescoes, yes, but also the churches, the palaces, even the Vasari Corridor. They are treasures themselves that could soon be at the mercy of British and American bombers.'

Lina thought about the raids on Turin, Genoa and Milan she'd heard about on Signor Cetti's hidden radio. Already many historic buildings had been damaged or destroyed, not to mention the civilian deaths and casualties.

Agatha's back stiffened. 'Then what can be done to protect them?'

Lina could tell the professor had something up his sleeve. He leaned forwards and spoke quietly, even though there was no one else around.

'You remember I told you about my contact in America?' he began.

'The one at Harvard,' replied Agatha eagerly.

'Indeed, well now General Eisenhower himself is said to be deeply concerned about the possible damage to our historic cities and their treasures.'

Agatha shifted in her seat. 'That is something, I suppose.'

Loggi continued, 'I am also told an article has appeared in the *New York Times*. Apparently, it carries details of a new commission to be formed.'

'A commission for what exactly, Professor?' asked Lina.

He looked at her pointedly, but his expression remained grave. 'To save Europe's art.'

Both Agatha's brows rose simultaneously. 'It does indeed sound encouraging, but how exactly do they propose to do that?' she asked.

'As I understand it, there will be art experts drafted into the Allied armies to advise on how best to protect cultural treasures,' replied Loggi.

Agatha flapped a hand. 'That's all very well, but they will need

224

a lot more than a handful of experts if they are going to succeed.'

'I agree,' replied the professor. 'And that is why your help is needed more than ever,' he added bluntly.

Arching her brow, Agatha's lips lifted wryly. 'You think General Eisenhower needs assistance from the English Ladies' Art Appreciation Society?' she suggested with a flirtatious giggle. The idea clearly amused her, but when her eyes met the stern expression on the professor's face, her smile disappeared.

'You're serious, aren't you?' said Lina.

'This is not a trifling matter, Signorina Leone.' He cleared his throat and leaned even further forwards. 'As you know, Milan has suffered greatly in the bombings. There have been many deaths, and several churches have also been destroyed.'

'And the same could happen to us,' said Lina, paling at the thought.

Loggi nodded. 'Precisely, Signorina Leone, and that's where you ladies come in.'

'We're all ears, Professor,' said Agatha, this time in all seriousness. Setting down her teacup and craning her neck, she added, 'Do tell.'

Chapter 39

August 1943

Agatha called it Operation Medici – the secret mission Professor Loggi had set the women. It swung into action as soon as everyone in the English Ladies' Arts Appreciation Society felt strong enough to report for duty in the conservatory at Villa Mimosa. Fortified by tea and lemon drizzle cake, the members rallied.

'I've been sleeping like a dead woman,' announced Mrs Clutterbuck, pouring a dash of milk into her brew.

'It is good to be back in one's own bed,' agreed Lady Felstein, helping herself to another slice of cake.

'Sure is,' exclaimed Miss Giltrap, slapping her thigh. 'And I can't wait to get back snapping again.' She aimed an imaginary camera at Miss Harrowby seated on a Lloyd Loom chair and mimed pressing the shutter. 'Say cheese!'

'About that,' intervened Agatha.

'About cheese?' asked Miss Giltrap, puzzled. 'If you know where to get some gorgonzola, then I'm putting in an order.'

'No. I don't know where to buy any decent cheese,' reprimanded Agatha. 'I want to talk to you about taking photographs. The other day we had a meeting with Professor Loggi.' She nodded to Lina. 'What he told us is of a most sensitive nature and not a word of it may leave this villa.'

'You mean it's top secret?' asked Miss Giltrap.

'Indeed, it is, and possessing such knowledge carries grave risk,' replied Agatha solemnly. 'Therefore, if anyone does not wish to be privy to this information, I must ask you to leave now.'

Brows arched, necks lengthened, two teacups clattered, and a few 'Good griefs' and 'I says' were expelled. But no one left their seats, and Miss Harrowby seemed to speak on everyone's behalf when she said, 'We are as one on this, Mrs Fortescue-Smythe. None of us is leaving.'

'Very well. I shall begin,' said Agatha with a satisfied nod. 'As you know, British and American troops have landed in Sicily and are advancing on to the mainland. Regrettably, this means more bombing raids, and our beloved city may well be a target. However, all is not lost. Apparently, the damage the bombs do may be minimised by something called expert precision bombing.'

'By what?' asked Mrs Clutterbuck.

'I don't believe I'm familiar with the term,' agreed Miss Harrowby.

Lina intervened. 'It means instead of being dropped randomly, the bombs are aimed at very specific strategic targets, like airfields and ports. That way, fewer civilians will be killed and, hopefully, historic buildings won't be destroyed.'

'How will they know which buildings to avoid?' asked Lady Felstein.

Agatha took over again. 'That's where we come in, ladies. We have been asked to supply a detailed plan of the city centre, showing clearly all the buildings of historic importance, together with a list of their significant contents.'

'Have we indeed?' Mrs Clutterbuck inhaled deeply as she processed what she'd just been told.

The cogs of Lina's mind had long been set in motion on the idea. She'd already told Professor Loggi about Miss Giltrap's detailed photographs, and discussed using Agatha's research notes to pinpoint the most notable pieces of art.

'That's a pretty tall order,' said the American, scratching her head.

Agatha nodded. 'I realise what is asked of us is a task of Herculean proportions, but our precious city is in peril,' she pointed out.

'I suppose what Professor Loggi asks could be done, in theory, but one imagines it'll take a considerable amount of work to produce an accurate plan,' ventured Miss Harrowby, once again sporting a flower in her hair – a red carnation on this occasion.

Looking around the room, and watching everyone's reaction to Agatha's announcement, Lina could see internment had taken its toll on some of the ladies. All of them had aged in Torselli. Lady Felstein's hearing was even worse, Miss Harrowby had developed a widow's hump and Mrs Clutterbuck's eyesight had deteriorated. But their physical deterioration had been compensated for in other ways. They'd all grown in character. They'd all become more tolerant and open in their natures. No longer scorpions, they were better, kinder human beings. She liked to think – hope – she was, too. But now they faced one of the biggest challenges of their lives. Were they up to it?

'What you say is true, Miss Harrowby,' replied Agatha. 'But I certainly have no intention of going anywhere in the near future, so I choose to put my time to a great cause. The question is, who will join me?' Her hawkish eyes roamed around the room, then settled on the person to her right.

'Are you with me, Lady Felstein?'

Lady Felstein was seated so close she hadn't needed her ear trumpet to follow Agatha's words. 'You can count on me, Mrs Fortescue-Smythe,' she replied.

'And me,' said Miss Harrowby, on her other side.

'And me too,' replied Mrs Clutterbuck.

'Me four.' That from Miss Giltrap.

Agatha took a deep breath, and a smile broadened her features. 'Thank you, ladies,' she said, nodding as she spoke. 'I knew Professor Loggi's trust wasn't misplaced. Now that we're all committed to Operation Medici, I suggest we get down to business. Tomorrow at the Uffizi. Ten o'clock sharp.'

Lina saw the newspaper headlines screaming about the bombing raid the following day. The Allies had hit Milan, badly damaging the refectory of Santa Maria delle Grazie. Agatha was incensed by the news.

'They hit *The Last Supper*!' she fumed when they met Professor Loggi at the Uffizi. 'How could they?'

'I fear you're right, Mrs Fortescue-Smythe,' he replied. 'Sandbags and scaffolding had been placed around it for protection, but right now no one can get near enough to assess the damage.'

'Such dreadful news,' wailed Miss Harrowby.

Lady Felstein shook her head. 'Surely Leonardo's finest,' she muttered in disbelief.

The bombing may have come as a terrible blow, but Agatha used her members' reactions to spur them on. The prospect of losing da Vinci's iconic painting forever was unthinkable. 'It makes our mapping even more urgent,' she told the shocked basement room. 'I propose we divide ourselves into teams. We are most grateful to Miss Giltrap for all her excellent photographs.' Her prints of the many historic buildings in the city would form the basis of the work. Agatha nodded at the American who was perching on the table edge, a wide smile on her face. 'I have outlined what is involved, so now I need volunteers to undertake the various tasks.' She smiled as her gaze travelled over the women, sitting demurely at the long table.

Mrs Clutterbuck, whose previously flattened coif had returned to its full height, was first to raise her hand.

'I can type up the inventories,' she volunteered.

'And I propose I draw on my archaeological experience,' said

Miss Harrowby.

'Oh?' said Agatha, intrigued. 'Please elaborate.'

'I worked on an excavation in Africa a few years ago,' she began.

'Well, you're a dark horse, Marjorie,' muttered Mrs Clutterbuck.

Undeterred, Miss Harrowby continued. 'There was a Professor Shinnie, who devised a method of marking maps, and I believe his technique could be applied to the task in hand.'

'If you think it would help,' replied Agatha.

Miss Harrowby, who seemed to have gained more confidence in Torselli, nodded. 'I feel it's what's required for the pilots to be able to identify buildings,' she added. 'The ones to avoid would be outlined in white.'

Lady Felstein, so often the calm and dignified presence in the room, had followed the meeting carefully. 'I could do that. My hearing may be unreliable, but these are not,' she announced, holding out steady hands to demonstrate her point.

So, it was agreed. Each member had been assigned a task and Operation Medici was launched.

'If anyone can do this, we can,' declared Miss Giltrap, slapping her thigh in her familiar gesture. 'Sisters together! Right?' She looked about her for support and found her exhortation to be quite infectious. Instead of being on the receiving end of haughty glares, as so often the case before the start of the war, the other women were nodding and smiling. Lina smiled, too. The ladies it seemed were no longer a mere society, but a sisterhood bound by their shared hardships, experiences, and a will to protect something they all cared about so deeply. She knew it was the only way they could succeed.

Chapter 40

They met at the Gran Caffè Doney. Edoardo suggested the venue. It was only a few doors away from his gallery, and now he knew Manzano himself was behind bars, he'd decided it was safe to emerge from hiding. Lina was happy to return to the café, too. So many memories flooded back; the teas, the genteel conversations and her aunt's penchant for cucumber sandwiches. And of course, there was that fateful day, more than three years ago, when a red-faced Mr Ponting had announced that war was declared.

Signor Rossi, the manager, was still there, looking as though he'd stepped off the stage at the opera house. He beamed as he showed Lina to her seat. Pulling out her chair he bent low and whispered, 'The English ladies. How are they?'

Lina smiled. 'They are surviving,' she answered in a soft voice, then instantly regretted the reply. They weren't merely surviving. These days the women had real purpose. She corrected herself. 'No, more than that,' she added, 'they are thriving, thank you, Signor Rossi.'

The manager angled his head. 'That makes me glad,' he said.

Me, too, she thought.

Lina looked around the high-ceilinged room. The decor may have been the same, but the clientele certainly wasn't. A little over a month ago the café would have been filled with the wives of the *fascisti*, taking tea and enjoying the pastries that most ordinary Florentines only dreamed of. Today, however, they were nowhere in evidence. Lawyers and journalists had taken their places at tables covered in white linen cloths and were making plans for a free and fairer Italy. Some members of the resistance were daring to put their heads above the parapet, but uncertainty and danger still lingered. Manzano may be behind bars, but many of his henchmen weren't. The fascists were still in charge, even though the new government was teetering on the edge of collapse. Chaos threatened.

Edoardo ordered two espressos, knowing they would be made from ground coffee beans, not acorns. Lina looked across the table at him, studying him properly in the daylight for the first time since they were reunited. Gone was the dusky tan that once made his skin glow, but the glimmer in his eyes hadn't been extinguished. He was wearing a suit again – dark blue, double-breasted – and looked immaculate. It was only when the coffee arrived, and he lifted his cup to his lips, Lina noticed his hands. Three of his fingernails hadn't grown back, reminding her of what he had suffered in jail.

'You look beautiful,' he told her softly, aware she was studying his hands.

Her head shot up and she touched her hair, self-consciously. 'Thank you,' she replied with a smile, 'and you. What's it like to be back in a suit?'

He paused for a moment. 'It makes me feel in control again. I like that.'

'Yes,' she said with a nod. She understood what he meant. Since Mussolini's arrest, freedom was certainly in the air. Even if the fascists were still officially in charge, they'd been weakened and the Germans were circling, ready to step in and take charge. 'This is good,' she added. 'Being back here. Being with you.'

He reached across to hold her hand. She clasped it tightly

and an overwhelming desire to kiss him rushed over her. But decorum prevailed.

'I missed you,' he said softly, squeezing her hand.

'And I you,' she replied. But no sooner had the words left her mouth Edoardo's expression changed. He reared his head. Someone he knew was approaching and he let go of her hand.

'Signora Bianchi,' he said, rising from the table. 'It is good to see you again,' he said, kissing the housekeeper on either cheek. 'Won't you join us?'

The woman, her grey hair hidden under a headscarf, nodded unsmilingly and darted a wary look at Lina before accepting the offer to join them.

'I got your message,' she told Edoardo.

'I'm glad you have been safe. When I knew they'd raided the apartment I feared the worst.' His voice trailed off. 'How are you?'

She cast about her and fidgeted in her seat. Lina thought she seemed uncomfortable, nervous even. 'I am well, thank you,' she replied.

'And you are back at the apartment?' she asked Edoardo.

'Yes, and I hope you'll come back just as soon as I've straightened a few things,' he said, picturing the mayhem wrought by Manzano's men. 'Thankfully your room wasn't searched.' He broke off noticing the housekeeper was looking disapprovingly at Lina. 'You remember Signorina Leone?' he asked.

Another nod. 'Yes, of course.' This time her lips twitched in a half smile, but her eyes remained suspicious.

Edoardo raised his arm to attract a waiter's attention. 'What will you have?'

But the housekeeper shook her head. 'I shan't stay,' she said. 'I wanted to tell you about a meeting.' She looked around, and satisfied no eavesdroppers were nearby, she added, 'An important meeting at Bocci's house next Friday at noon.'

Lina realised the housekeeper must be talking about resistance business.

Edoardo was nodding. 'I'll be there,' he said.

'*Bene*,' replied Signora Bianchi, rising from the table.

Lina watched her leave, scurrying out of the café like a cautious mouse.

'She is one of your contacts?'

'Yes,' he replied. 'Has been for a while now.'

So, Signora Bianchi was a member of the resistance, too. How many more would come out of hiding now that Il Duce was behind bars, she asked herself. She looked around the café, wondering which of its customers were secret opponents of fascism. Black and white suddenly merged into grey and the thought unsettled her. 'Please be careful, Edoardo,' she said.

He gave her one of his looks; trying to reassure her. 'At the very least it's the beginning of the end. Remember?' He reached out and took her hand once more. 'Plans need to be in place for when the war is over.'

Lina was yet to be convinced. 'But Professor Loggi says there is still a long way to go.'

'Yes,' Edoardo agreed. 'He's said the same to me.'

His words came as a surprise and brought her up sharply. 'You are in contact with the professor again?'

A smile spread across his face, and he shot her a knowing look. 'That's right. He and I, well,' his eyes cast around the room as he spoke, 'the professor has always wanted to protect the region's heritage. He has contacts in the art world in America and Britain who wanted to help, as you probably know. He already understood I was of the same mind when he recruited me to the Tuscan Liberation Committee.'

'Wait. So, you're telling me he knew all along that you were against the fascists?' Edoardo gave her a flat smile. 'But he made me believe …'

'He did that to throw everyone off my scent.' He lowered his voice. 'Including Manzano.'

Lina shook her head. 'Including me and Aunt Agatha.'

'Of course,' he agreed with a wide smile.

'So that first time at Montegufoni? What was that about?'

'I informed him Hitler was returning to the city for talks with Mussolini. It was safer to tell him there without fear of Manzano's thugs listening in.'

Her eyebrows lifted towards her hairline. 'And I'm guessing he helped you escape, too.'

'You could say that.'

'You really are a man of mystery,' she told him with another shake of her head.

Edoardo's smile disappeared then to be replaced by an earnest stare. 'There's nothing mysterious about my feelings for you, Lina,' he whispered. Lifting her hand, he kissed it gently. 'Let's go for a walk, shall we?'

They headed for the river, passing under a stretch of the Vasari Corridor that ran along the embankment of the River Arno. At the end of a searing summer, the water levels were low. A few scruffy children played on the sandy banks, salvaging tin cans or bottles as they floated by. The soft colours of the Ponte Vecchio glowed gold in the sun as its arches framed a view of the river and the blue sky above.

'It's so good to see the bridge again,' said Edoardo as they linked arms and continued walking along the embankment.

'Is Goering still looting what he can?' she asked.

He didn't look at her. 'I fear so, but at least we managed to stop some of it falling into his hands.'

'What do you mean?'

'We managed to intercept some of it.' He stopped. 'As I said, we are doing our best. We had information about which trains to target. The crates from the monastery aren't the only ones in the cellar.'

'What?' She could barely believe what she was hearing. When Manzano told her about the theft of the Austrian consignments she'd assumed, to her own great shame, that Edoardo had stolen them for his own financial gain, aided by his own organised gang of criminals. Now she understood he'd been working with the resistance to save the artworks all along. Like the complex pieces of a jigsaw, Edoardo Bernini's jumbled, murky past was finally fitting together. She held her tongue, knowing now was neither the time nor place to launch into the myriad of questions assailing her mind. Just being with him, being able to touch him and feel his love again, was enough.

He turned to her then and put his arms around her. 'So, you see, all is not lost, my love.'

'No, all is not lost,' she agreed. *Not yet*, she thought. She loved how Edoardo was always so optimistic. How he could buoy up her spirits with a smile or a throwaway remark. So why did she have this terrible feeling that despite Mussolini's arrest and perhaps even a turn in the political tide, they were still in danger of being swept further from the shore. She stopped dead and turned to face him, wordlessly cupping his face with her hands, and kissing him tenderly. He yielded and they held each other, suspended in time, both in a world where nothing else mattered.

'You mustn't worry,' Edoardo told her softly when they eventually broke apart. His lips brushed her ear. 'Everything will work out fine. But right now, all we can do is be ready to act the moment we are needed.'

But as Lina nuzzled her head in Edoardo's neck on the Ponte Santa Trinita that late summer afternoon, neither of them realised that moment would come quite so soon.

Chapter 41

September 1943

Agatha woke with a start. She'd dozed off in the conservatory at Villa Mimosa after another long day in the Uffizi, only to be rudely interrupted by loud shouts from the street.

'What's that noise?' she asked, shaking the sleep from her head.

Lina, hearing her aunt's call, left the study where she'd been working to see what was wrong. She, too, was aware of a commotion outside. It wasn't a feast day or a popular saint's day. Puzzled, the next thing she heard was Donna yelling at the top of her voice from the kitchen.

'*Che sta succendeno, Donna*?' Lina called, dashing towards the door. 'What's happened?'

'*Oh, Signorina Leone! Armistizio. La guerra è finita!*' The maid practically dived at her to give her a hug.

'An armistice?' repeated Lina. 'But that's wonderful.' Now it was her turn to fling her arms around Donna. The two of them started to whirl round and round until Agatha, her grey hair slightly dishevelled, appeared at the kitchen door. 'Good Lord!' she muttered. 'What's going on?'

Lina, herself still reeling from the news and the dancing, turned to look at her aunt, a smile splitting her face. 'Donna says it's over. An armistice has been called.' She rushed over to her. But Agatha still seemed half-asleep. Her head shook violently, as if she thought she might be dreaming and was trying to shock herself awake.

'The war is over?' she asked tremulously. 'Is it true? You're certain?'

'*Si! Si, signora!*' exclaimed Donna, throwing off her apron. 'I must go and see!' she cried breathlessly, dashing through the back door.

'Well, I never,' mumbled Agatha.

Lina felt light-headed, as if all her Christmases and birthdays were rolled into one. Rushing into the hall, she checked herself in the mirror.

'And I suppose you want to see what's going on for yourself, too?' asked Agatha.

'Of course,' replied Lina looking at her aunt's reflection in the mirror. 'Surely, if the war is over, you'll want to come too?'

Agatha, noticing a few wiry strands of her own hair had broken loose from her bun, patted them down. 'I don't think so, my dear. I'm far too old to dance in the street, or anywhere else for that matter.' She smiled, then. 'But I'll never forget when the armistice was declared at the end of the Great War, and I wouldn't have missed that for the world. So off you go.'

Lina kissed her aunt on the cheek. 'I won't be long, then I'll come back and tell you what's happening,' she promised, checking her excitement. Lina only had Donna's word that hostilities had ended. Her only fear was the news of an armistice was too good to be true.

In the city, celebrations had already begun. Clusters of excited people were gathering outside their homes. Any soldiers on patrol had thrown down their weapons or abandoned their military vehicles to join in the merrymaking. Young boys climbed lamp-posts or sat on the tops of walls for a better view. An impromptu orchestra sprang up on a street corner and played popular folk tunes. Tricolours were everywhere, and bars and cafés threw open their shutters. Cyclists rang their bells and even though there was no fuel for motor cars, horns were sounded on parked vehicles and strangers hugged each other in the street. Lina even had to prise the arms of a tiny old lady from around her waist as she made slow progress along the packed Via de Tornabuoni towards the Bernini Gallery. She couldn't wait to see Edoardo. But when she did, much to her surprise, he was seated at his desk, his head in his hands. When he heard her approach and lifted his gaze, his expression told her he was in no mood for celebration.

'Edoardo, what is it?' she asked, hurrying towards him. Without a word, he stood and swept her up in his arms. After a moment holding her, she stepped back and said, 'Tell me what's wrong. There is no armistice. Is that it?' She wrapped her arms around his neck. 'Please, my love, please,' she implored him.

Clutching one of her hands, he nodded. 'There is an armistice. It's true.'

Lina's concern was replaced by a cautious smile. 'Then why that look? I thought we could go out dancing.'

He resisted her tug towards the street. 'The Germans feel betrayed,' he told her.

She let go of his hand. 'What do you mean?'

'They're out for revenge. We were their allies and now we have surrendered to the enemy without consulting them.'

'Revenge? How? What are you saying?' Her shoulders slumped.

'I mean they've mobilised. They've already started massacring Italians, and their troops and tanks are spilling over the border as we speak. I heard it on the radio. They're going to occupy Italy.'

Lina shook her head. 'No. No. It can't be true.' Glancing outside at the elated crowd, she wanted to weep. A small girl was being carried on her father's shoulders. Throwing back her tousled head and laughing, she was happy. But for how much longer? A week? A day? An hour?

Seeing her alarm, Edoardo walked behind her as she dropped into a chair. His touch against her skin released her shock. 'What shall we do?' she asked, as he stroked her hair.

Turning, she saw he was working his jaw determinedly. He crouched down beside her and took her hand. 'I must leave. It's no longer safe here,' he said.

'Leave? But I've only just found you again.' She clutched at his other hand.

He closed his eyes for a moment. 'I know. I know,' he acknowledged. 'But I have to.'

'And go where?'

This time, his gaze did meet hers. 'You know I can't tell you that, *cara mia*.'

'I'll go with you,' she said, taking his face in her hands, but he prised them away.

'Don't make this any harder for me. You can't come with me. It's complicated.'

Of course, in her heart of hearts, she knew he would be organising the resistance, and she had no training. She also knew the next question she was about to ask was impossible for him to answer, as well, but she persisted.

'Promise me one thing,' she said, tracing his lips with her finger.

'What's that?'

'You'll come back.'

She saw his shoulders lift in a laugh then. 'I promise,' he replied, pulling her close and holding her tight, even though she knew he couldn't say whether he would return alive or dead.

Three days later, from a top-floor window at Villa Mimosa, Lina watched the German tanks roll in. They were accompanied by columns of goose-stepping troops brandishing black and red swastikas. The soldiers who only the week before were considered brothers-in-arms now became occupiers. They'd disarmed hundreds of thousands of Italian soldiers – and murdered almost as many – while the government had fled to territory taken by the Allies in southern Italy. She'd heard reports of a growing numbers of Italian soldiers taking up arms against the fascists to form their own partisan brigades. Despite this thread of hope, dread had seeped into Lina's veins as she'd watched the Nazi occupation unfold. The columns of armoured vehicles and troops had marched into the ancient city of Michelangelo and Raphael with such terrifying speed, that its citizens had barely had time to draw breath, let alone protect their treasures.

The early September sun beat down unrelentingly on to the streets of the city. But, as women queued for hours to buy bread and fruit, and fuel for cooking was in short supply, the members of the English Ladies' Arts Appreciation Society knew they had to carry on their work mapping the city's treasures. With the Nazi occupation, a bus ferrying the ladies to the gallery was out of the question. But such was their commitment that no one failed to report for duty. Everyone made their own way, by tram, on foot, or by bicycle to the Uffizi.

Agatha remained hopeful that neither the Allies nor the Germans could be so brutish as to flatten Florence. Lina, however, was not at all convinced. Naples had suffered terribly. Who was to say that after the Allies had reached Rome her city wouldn't be next?

Professor Loggi studied the master map by the light of an unreliable oil lamp, watched by six nervous women. They'd gathered round the fruits of their labours in the basement at the Uffizi in tense anticipation of the professor's verdict.

The map itself was so large it stretched the entire length of the long table and had to be rolled up to be stored. Miss Giltrap had worked hard in her dark room. While she'd managed to send the photographic originals of dozens of artworks and buildings to the Frick Institute in New York before America joined the war, she'd wisely kept the negatives in her studio. She'd produced copies that gave a visual context for Miss Harrowby to work on.

Lady Felstein sorted through them, indexing them according to an existing tourist map of the city centre, while Mrs Clutterbuck typed up the names and grid references.

The air in the basement was also hot and stale, and despite the occasional wafts of lavender there was also the unwelcome rancid odour of sweat. Mrs Clutterbuck fiddled with her rings. Miss Harrowby chewed her lip and Miss Giltrap started to drum on the table, until she was silenced by an uncharacteristic glare from Lady Felstein. Even Agatha, her tongue normally poised to deliver a reprimand in such flagrant breaches of etiquette, was twisting her lace handkerchief this way and that, as she too stared at the map.

After what seemed to Lina like an eternity, the professor popped out his monocle and looked up to address them all. 'This is excellent work, ladies,' he announced. 'The plan, the cross references. All very good.'

Agatha puffed out her chest and stepped forwards. 'The next step will be to divide this map into more detailed quadrants.'

Loggi nodded. 'That will be crucial,' he agreed.

Lina knew from Edoardo that the Allies would need to fly over the city to identify targets before any bombardment was given the go-ahead. He'd told her in all probability that the bombers would be targeting the stockyards and railway lines leading in and out of the city. The intention was to preserve the historic buildings, not hit them. Even so, there was always a risk. Accidents often happened in war.

'You are doing a magnificent job,' Professor Loggi told the women, bringing the meeting to a close, but as the other ladies resumed their duties he beckoned to Lina. 'A word, if I may, in private,' he mumbled, taking her aside.

'What is it, Professor? Is something wrong?' she asked with a frown.

'Yes. Manzano has been freed from jail.'

'What?' Even though she'd heard Mussolini had been freed by

the Nazis, shock bolted through her body like lightning.

'My reaction was similar,' admitted Loggi. 'In fact, I didn't believe it until I saw him myself.'

'You mean he's back in the city?'

Loggi nodded. 'And he's looking for you. When his men went to Villa Mimosa this morning and got no answer, he asked me if I knew your whereabouts. Naturally, I said I did not, but I fear for you, Signorina Leone.'

By the way he furrowed his brow, Lina could tell he wasn't finished. 'There's something else, isn't there?'

'I hate to say it, but Colonel Fischer is here, too. He's heading up the Nazi's ironically named Art Protection Unit, the *Kunstschutz*.'

It was as if she'd been kicked in the ribs. 'Fischer is here?' she gasped. The name continued to fill her with dread. She'd avoided him before when he'd wanted to verify the Cranach, but Edoardo hadn't been so lucky and had suffered the full force of his wrath.

They both knew that instead of *protecting* Italy's treasures, he would continue to see they were sent wholesale over the border to his Fatherland.

Lina, unable to accept the irony of it, shook her head. 'The Third Reich's looter-in-chief in Florence.'

'That's not his only job,' said Loggi.

'What do you mean?'

He leaned in. 'He's also head of the SS here and every member of the resistance is in his sights. But it's Bernini he and Manzano will want to get their hands on first.'

'Edoardo,' she muttered, shivering suddenly at the thought.

The professor looked grave. 'I fear so, Signorina Leone,' he replied. 'And the easiest way to do that, it pains me to say, is through you.'

Chapter 42

In a room in Villa Triste, a parish priest lay curled up like a newborn baby, semiconscious on the floor. His hair was flecked with grey and his white collar with blood. He barely responded to a kick from Major Carita's boot. A quiet moan was all that came from between his bruised lips after hours of interrogation.

Podesta Manzano winced at the kick. 'So has he given anything away yet?' he asked, his forehead shiny with sweat. 'Names. Locations? I know there's a cell working in the city's sewers. Intelligence says the British and Americans are reaching out to the resistance rats over the airwaves. They need to be found and exterminated.'

He'd arrived back in the city after several days being briefed at the headquarters of Il Duce's new Italian Social Republic at Lake Garda. He hadn't even returned to his old office at the town hall yet, preferring instead to pay a visit to the city's thriving torture chambers. Not only was he relishing his new-found freedom, he was also looking forwards to settling some old scores. Edoardo Bernini was top of his list.

'Not yet, although we know he's had access to a radio. One of his parishioners informed us,' replied Carita with a careless shrug.

The Germans had established radio patrols around the city.

They'd detected activity – unauthorised activity – coming from various buildings. They'd received reliable intelligence that two enemy agents were in their midst, parachuted in to liaise with the resistance, and set up a clandestine radio frequency to transmit information about Nazi activities. Once the source was traced and stopped, Manzano hoped the regular consignments of art to Innsbruk then on to Berlin could resume. As it stood, somehow the resistance kept disrupting the trains carrying the crates and he suspected a mole. A signal had been detected coming from the priest's church.

The podesta nodded, took out a handkerchief and held it over his nose. 'The stench,' he explained.

'You get used to it, my friend,' replied Carita with a laugh.

'How long have you had him?' asked Manzano, trying to change the subject and really hoping they could carry on their conversation somewhere more congenial.

'Five days.'

Manzano nodded. 'Will he last much longer?'

Carita shrugged. 'Probably not, but at least he thinks he'll go to heaven.' Cynically, he pointed to the ceiling.

The podesta managed to raise a smile at this remark. If he seemed ambivalent about the priest's fate, there was a reason. It was because he had other means of finding out information up his sleeve, too.

'What on earth?' Agatha looked askance at the canvas bag on Lina's bed, as her niece threw several items of clothing into it.

Lina stopped what she was doing and sighed heavily as her eyes grazed the blouses, scarves, soap and hairbrush laid out on the bedspread. 'I'm sorry, but it's the only way.' Her voice was thick with emotion.

'Sorry?' repeated Agatha, moving towards her. 'For what? What are you doing?'

Throwing another dress on the bed, Lina wrapped her

outstretched arms around her aunt's small body. 'I'm not safe here. Professor Loggi warned me. Manzano is after me and—' she broke off as Agatha's hands flew to her mouth at the prospect of her niece's rearrest.

'Oh, no. No,' she said, grabbing hold of Lina's arms as she shook her head. 'You can't go through that again. You must heed the professor's warning. But where will you go?'

Lina knew she didn't have much choice, but she still had the key to the cellar below the Bernini Gallery. As reluctant as she was to spend days, weeks or even months below ground, she knew she might have to.

'I have plans,' was all she would say, aware that Manzano could also target her aunt.

Agatha's shoulders juddered and her eyes moistened. 'Very well,' she replied stoically. 'But first let Donna cook you a decent meal.'

'Yes,' she replied. 'Yes, I'd like that very much.'

As soon as Agatha was out of the door, Lina resumed packing until, a moment later, she heard a noise. She stopped dead to listen. By now it was dusk, and at first, she put the sound down to large moths bouncing against the wooden shutters, attracted to her oil lamp. Yet again it came. A tapping. She followed it to the window and, frowning, flung open the French doors to walk out onto the balcony.

From out of nowhere, an arm encircled her waist, and a gentle hand was placed over her mouth. But she made no attempt to struggle free.

'*Cara mia.*'

She felt herself being wheeled around to face her unexpected visitor.

'Edoardo! Edoardo!' she mouthed, muffling her joy. 'Oh, it's so good to see you,' she gasped in a whisper. 'Quick. Inside.' She squinted into the gloom, praying there were no patrols in the area, as he dived into the bedroom. But once inside, she unleashed her shock.

'Are you mad?' she exclaimed, braiding her delight at seeing him again with incredulity.

'I've missed you,' he replied, taking her into his arms again. 'I just had to see that you're all right. Let me look at you.' His eyes swept hungrily over her face, taking in the confused tears running down her cheeks. 'You are so beautiful,' he told her.

'And you are out of your mind!' she replied, aware of the utter folly of his visit. 'You know the OVRA could be watching? It's too risky.'

'I don't care. It's worth it just to see you.' He smiled broadly, then clamping his arms back around her waist, he lifted her in the air and whirled her round. 'Love makes men do crazy things,' he told her.

But Lina wasn't laughing. Even before Edoardo had set her down again, she heard the banging on the front door and a German voice booming orders to open up.

Alarmed, Edoardo shook his head. 'Oh, God! I'm sorry,' he gasped, thinking he'd led the Nazis to her door. But Lina knew they'd come for her.

'Go! Go now!' she mouthed. 'Over the back wall!'

He kissed her quickly and turned towards the shutters as Donna's protests were lost amid the sound of shouts in the hall.

'Signorina Leone!' she heard a German bark. '*Du ist heren*?'

Lina knew it was now or never. Grabbing her bag from the bed, she followed Edoardo out through the French doors. Hurdling over the balcony railings, he landed on a ledge and turned to see her slinging the strap of her bag over her head to follow him.

'I'll explain later,' she whispered, as she too negotiated the railings and found a foothold on a nearby windowsill. Taking the lead, she reached for an overhanging branch and pulled herself onto the high garden wall nearby. She turned to make sure Edoardo was close behind, then edged out to a tall tree stump, finally landing on a footpath skirting the villa.

'Which way?' she asked breathlessly, taking in Edoardo's stunned expression.

Whether he liked it or not, she was coming with him. There was no turning back.

Chapter 43

The safe house lay in a suburb of Florence. An ordinary dwelling, in an ordinary street, that had become home to some extraordinary people. It was pitch black when they arrived, but Lina had never been more relieved to hear a door lock behind her. Yet it wasn't until Edoardo led her into the kitchen and lit an oil lamp she realised who had let them in.

'Signora Bianchi!' she gasped, as the housekeeper's face emerged from the shadows.

From her look, the elderly woman was equally surprised to see Lina. In unison they turned to Edoardo. He scratched the back of his head.

'Please sit,' he asked Lina. 'I need to explain.' His eyes travelled to the older woman. 'To both of you.'

'Yes, you do,' replied the housekeeper, scowling.

Edoardo pulled out another chair, flipped it round and sat astride it.

'Lina was in trouble,' he began. 'Manzano was going to take her in.'

Signora Bianchi's nostrils flared. 'I said you shouldn't go to her villa,' she hissed.

Edoardo nodded. 'I know. I know, I should've taken your advice but I just had to see her.'

This time it was Lina's turn to scowl. They were making her feel like an unwelcome intruder. 'If it wasn't for me, Edoardo, you'd be in Villa Triste again,' she pointed out.

He took her by the hand, then. 'You're right,' he agreed before turning back to the housekeeper. 'And that's why I think Signorina Leone should join us.'

Lina frowned. 'Join you?' she repeated. 'You mean the resistance?'

Edoardo's gaze returned to Signora Bianchi. 'You need to know,' he said.

'Need to know what?' Lina was growing impatient.

He motioned to a lumpy sofa and sat down beside her. 'A few weeks ago, Signora Bianchi's parish priest was approached by two Italian resistance agents who wanted to get a radio station up and running, so the Allies could communicate with the partisans.'

'A radio station?' she repeated.

'You remember you saw the radio in the cellar.'

She nodded. 'Yes, I do.'

'We are a small team,' continued Edoardo. 'As well as the agents, we have a lawyer who owns this house, two radio operators, and three *staffettas*, two women and a young boy who deliver messages.'

The revelations just kept coming and Lina realised she knew very little about the man who held her heart in his hands. Looking deep into his eyes she told him, 'If you need more people, then I want to be a part of this.'

Another nod, slow this time. He glanced over to see Signor Bianchi watching them, then back again to Lina. 'Yes. *I* need you,' he replied softly. 'The Nazis are less likely to stop women, so now, Signora Bianchi delivers messages from the partisans to the radio operators, who put them into code to transmit to the Allies. But the messengers have too much work,' said Edoardo. 'Don't they, Signora Bianchi?' he asked pointedly.

In the glow of the oil lamp, Lina saw the frowning housekeeper baulk at the idea. It was as if the woman regarded her as a threat. Raising her gaze, Signora Bianchi paused, then after a moment, she nodded. 'Yes,' she replied. 'Yes, there is too much.'

Edoardo clapped his hands together. 'That's settled, then,' he said, turning abruptly to Lina. 'If you're happy to be a messenger, too?'

Lina looked at the housekeeper, then at Edoardo. What they were asking her to do was dangerous. She realised she had jumped out of the frying pan and into the fire. This was anything but a safe house. The risk to all their lives, her own included, was now huge, but despite the fear coursing through her, she swallowed down her reluctance.

'Yes,' she replied, fixing her gaze on Edoardo. 'Of course I will join you.'

Lina looked quizzically at the face that stared back at her in the mirror. She'd pulled her black hair from her face into a chignon and was twisting a wayward strand of it to clip it up.

'You look even more like her,' said Edoardo, smiling at her reflection. She knew exactly who he meant. The young woman in the portrait. The young gentlewoman of Florence. She could see what he meant. Her new hair style made her eyes look even bigger and accentuated her lips. He pecked her on the cheek as her gaze remained in the glass. 'We'll get it back, you know.'

Her eyes locked on to his. This time she truly believed him. This time it mattered to her again. But then she thought of Agatha, and he noticed her sudden sorrow.

'But you also look sad.'

The comment made her pull up the corners of her mouth, but yes. He was right. Now and again, she felt sad. She missed the constant light-hearted banter the sisterhood gave her, but most of all she missed her aunt. A month had passed since she'd last seen her, although she had managed to smuggle a note to her via a *staffetta* to assure her she was alive and well. She reached for a pair of gold-framed spectacles that made her look older and more earnest. The disguise had been Signora Bianchi's idea. Lina was a wanted woman, just as Edoardo was a wanted man. He'd already adopted the clothes of a labourer so he could move about the city more easily. Lina had become a housewife, running her daily errands, unremarked and unnoticed by the regular *fascisti* street patrols. Only what she was doing was far from mundane. In the soles of her shoes, she carried messages from partisans, collected from various market stalls or shops. These she would take to the appointed building – never the same place two days running. There, the radio operator would be waiting, fingers poised over the keys of his transmitter, ready to tap out his encoded 'tune'.

There'd been teething troubles, naturally. A second transmitter had arrived damaged and needed repairing. An engineering student lent his expertise. Only the two radio operators, known by the codenames Swallow and Raven, were in possession of the quartz crystals, but replacements were hard to come by.

Once technical difficulties were overcome, logistical ones surfaced. It was Edoardo's job to find suitable safe spots from which to broadcast. They had to be changed all the time so the Nazis couldn't pinpoint the station with their radio locators, and it was hard to find the right locations where the signal was good.

The Germans had begun patrols a few weeks back. Each evening their specially equipped vehicles would cruise along the streets with long antennas prone like huge insects listening for ghostly signals across the ether. They would stop at every main crossroads to set up a transceiver before driving a short distance to erect an aerial and turn on a primary receiver. That way they could track the source and arrest the radio operator.

'They are methodical, these Germans,' Edoardo remarked as he explained the basics of how a radio worked to Lina. He was drawing a diagram on a large piece of paper on the kitchen table in the safe house. 'The Nazis' skulls are packed with numbers and angles and calculations that tell them how best to destroy a building from two hundred metres away, or how much explosive it'll take to blow up a bridge.' He winked at her then, trying to make light of what he'd said, but she understood there was some truth in his statement. 'They're not artistic like us Florentines,' he added. 'Our heads are filled with poetry and light.'

Just then, Signora Bianchi entered the room, carrying a net bag containing a few vegetables. Lina's first instinct was to pull away from Edoardo. There was disapproval in the housekeeper's sour look. She supposed it was because she thought women should confine their love for their men to the bedroom.

'Now clear this away,' she snapped, waving a hand over Edoardo's diagram. 'We eat soon.'

Word came through of a new pick-up point for messages. The radio station, now in its third month, was growing. Lina abided by the golden rule. She didn't ask questions. That way she couldn't give answers if the worst were to happen, and she fell into the bloody hands of Major Carita and his gang. No, she didn't ask questions, but that didn't mean she couldn't draw her own conclusions. She suspected the resistance mole was in Manzano's department at the Palazzo Vecchio, feeding the partisans information about the art consignments to Innsbruck. How else could they know? The fascist press reported certain railway lines had been sabotaged. She knew several trains loaded with artworks had been forced to turn back. She also knew it was an unlikely coincidence.

That day she was headed for the new rendezvous by the opera house. She wore a headscarf and was wheeling a bicycle with a wicker basket at its front. On the way she stopped off at the market to queue for fruit, throwing any OVRA off the scent. After that she took a left through a small square, then a right bringing her to the front of the *duomo* with its wide piazza and Giotto's bell tower. The red-and-white-striped awning of a flower stall rippled in the sharp February breeze. The seller, an elderly woman, sat swathed in a scarf surrounded by early spring blooms. Lina asked for a single yellow iris. 'For my sick grandmother,' she added. That was the pass phrase.

A note was palmed, and a stem duly handed over. The transaction complete, Lina popped the iris in her basket and calmly cycled away, even though her pulse was racing. Her next rendezvous was among the hills to the south of the city. A lecturer at the Physics Institute, who knew Edoardo through the Tuscan Liberation Committee, had offered access to the building's attic for a transmission.

Lina found his office easily enough and handed over the bloom, but not before she had read the message written on a strip of green paper wound tightly round the stem. *Shinnie expelled by Adam and Eve. 10.W.* Of course, the message would be scrambled into a jumble of letters and numbers by Swallow before it was sent, yet even in its current state, it meant a lot to her. She smiled at the bespectacled lecturer as she handed over the iris, knowing that the English Ladies' Arts Appreciation Society had completed its mammoth task. The map, painstakingly marking out all the buildings of historic interest in the city centre, was ready for collection. It would be at the Brancacci Chapel at ten o'clock on Wednesday. Operation Medici was on standby.

Chapter 44

October 1943

Colonel Alexander Fischer, SS officer, renowned art expert, and now head of the reformed *Kunstschutz*, the so-called Art Protection Unit, strode into the Palazzo Vecchio looking the very model of German arrogance. The new appointment made him the most powerful man in Italy when it came to handling works of art.

'*Heil Hitler!*' he greeted, clicking his heels, and thrusting out his right arm as he entered Manzano's office. Since the *fascisti* had welcomed the Germans into the city, the two men had liaised closely over the 'welfare' of Tuscany's many art treasures. But right at the top of Fischer's list of priorities were, of course, any works by Cranach the Elder.

Manzano managed to raise his corpulent frame slightly from his chair but couldn't stretch to an all-out salute. Instead, he bobbed his head and offered a hand that only a few seconds ago had been holding a cream-filled cannoli. The German hesitated when he saw a flake of pastry on Manzano's thumb. When it came to getting what he wanted from the Italian mayor, the colonel left his charm at the door. He had little time for Manzano's slippery ways.

Ignoring the hand and casting round the office he said, 'I'm here about the portrait of the young woman. The Cranach I authenticated. You remember?'

How could Manzano forget it? It was the only thing he'd managed to salvage from the Bernini debacle. Naturally, after the dealer's escape there'd been a manhunt. But all it had yielded was low hanging fruit – three or four bit players in the resistance, but no trace of Bernini himself. Fischer had been furious, but at least the Cranach was retrieved. He'd examined it and declared it genuine, and a masterpiece, although almost immediately he'd been summoned to Berlin on another errand for the Führer. It meant he was forced to leave the portrait in Manzano's custody. The young woman of Florence had stayed in the darkness of the podesta's safe for the past few months – a hostage to fortune.

'Have you spoken to anyone about it?' Fischer asked.

Manzano squirmed in his seat. *What did this arrogant German take him for?* 'No,' he replied. His eyes slid towards Mussolini's portrait, now reinstated on the wall. Behind it was the safe. He was rather hoping the colonel would have forgotten about it so that, sometime in the future, he'd be able to sell the painting and make a very handsome profit.

Fischer followed his gaze. 'I wish to see it. Perhaps you could get it,' he said, adding with a false smile, 'if you would be so kind.'

Manzano grunted and lumbered over to the new portrait of Il Duce – the original having been unceremoniously jettisoned from the window. Tripping a catch, the frame opened like a door to reveal the large safe. He fumbled with the combination for a while until he carefully lifted out the wooden panel and set it upright on a low bookshelf.

'Here she is,' he announced.

Fischer stalked across to inspect the painting once more. The subject's beauty was as enticing as ever. 'Superb,' he muttered under his breath.

Manzano had realised too late his error in inviting Fischer to verify the portrait in the first place. If he'd kept quiet about it, no one would have been any the wiser. He considered it an opportunity squandered.

'Herr Goering wants it for Carinhall, yes?' he asked.

Fischer's reply surprised him. 'I think not. Hermann Goering already has an embarrassment of riches. No, this one, I propose we keep for someone else. Someone supremely more important than the *Reichsmarschall*.' He arched a brow as he spoke.

Manzano's jowls wobbled. 'You mean your Führer?'

The colonel nodded. 'Indeed, I do. There are other masterpieces that would sit well on the walls of Carinhall, but this one, well' – his eyes played on the young woman's sensuous face – 'this one is special, don't you agree? Even more enigmatic than the *Mona Lisa*.'

'Yes. Yes, I see what you mean.' Manzano peered at the image. As light slanted through the window illuminating the brush work and the mysterious, fleeting look captured forever, he could appreciate its appeal. 'A she-wolf,' he said smugly, rather pleased at recalling Lina's description of Cranach's women.

Fischer ignored him. 'So, will you have your secretary prepare it for transportation?'

Manzano frowned. *Just when he thought he might have got away with it. Just when he thought he might keep the portrait for himself.* 'You will send it directly to the Führer?'

The colonel laughed at the suggestion. 'Not right away, no. I intend to keep it in reserve. Until we have defeated the advancing Allies, and I can present it to him to mark our victory.'

While Manzano understood the logic of the German's proposal, he could also see the painting slipping further out of his grasp. Surely the Cranach was his to give? Finders keepers, and all that. He needed some compensation. Still staring at the portrait, the cogs in Manzano's mind started to whir more quickly and he said, 'Such a painting must be worth a lot, don't you agree?'

Fischer shot him a mocking glance. 'It's all about money with

257

you Italians, isn't it? But, yes, millions, my friend. Have no fear. A single Cranach is worth more to Germany than two paintings by da Vinci and I will see that you are justly rewarded.'

Manzano grinned at the thought. 'If that is the case, then perhaps …'

'Perhaps what?' Fischer teased. He knew precisely what this odious Italian wanted, but he was going to have to work for his money.

'I wondered if …' he licked his lips, '… if you could name a figure.'

'For what?'

'For taking the Cranach out of Italy.'

'For taking what rightfully belongs to the Fatherland, you mean?'

'Well, it has probably been here for four hundred years, so I was hoping we could reach a gentleman's agreement.'

What the colonel said next took Manzano completely by surprise.

'An agreement?' he repeated. 'Hmm.' He pulled an exaggerated frown. 'How does an estate in the country sound?' he suggested. 'Castello Di Montegufoni, perhaps.'

A summer breeze could have blown the podesta over at that moment. He shook his head, thinking he'd misheard. 'Did you just say an estate? At Montegufoni?'

Fischer nodded. 'When we win this war, it will be within my gift. As I said, to the Fatherland and to the Führer, this painting is priceless.'

Manzano nodded vigorously. 'Well, yes, but I hadn't expected such generosity.'

'Save your thanks for Hitler himself when you are presented to him in Berlin after our victory. But before that, I feel the portrait will be safer here in Florence. In my office on the Ponte Vecchio.'

After the reward he'd been offered, Manzano would let the German keep it in his own water closet, or under his bed. He didn't care anymore. 'Yes,' he agreed. ·

'The bridge is the safest place in all of Florence. The Führer has a deep affection for the Ponte Vecchio. It is close to his heart. He has insisted it remains unscathed, and the British and Americans wouldn't dare touch it,' concluded Fischer. 'No. You will have the honour of accompanying me to Germany to hand over the portrait to the Führer in person. We will both receive the highest honours the Reich can bestow.' He lifted his long arm, pointing to some imaginary ceremony taking place in a huge sun-lit hall. 'I can see it now – the fanfare, the Iron Crosses.'

Manzano smiled at the thought of adding yet another medal to his collection. 'In that case, it will be my pleasure to see the painting is delivered to the Ponte Vecchio for safekeeping,' he agreed. To seal the deal, he held out his hand once more. This time the German didn't hesitate. And the podesta was rather pleased with the outcome.

'Good to do business with you,' he said.

Fischer nodded but did not reply. Instead, he withdrew his hand as quickly as possible and made a point of wiping it with his own handkerchief.

Chapter 45

March 1944

Lina looked up at the vault of cloudless sky. It reminded her of the blue in da Vinci's *Madonna Litta*. Winter was coming to an end. Food had been in short supply and the nights long and cold, but any day now, she told herself, the same sky would be filled with airplanes. Allied bombers. Edoardo had told her there had been talks to make Florence a 'free' city to protect its priceless treasures; to save its buildings and monuments from air attack. But so far these had failed. *That meant it was a legitimate target for the Allies and open season for the Germans.*

Once again, she was on her way to the flower stall. For the past six months it had been her job to collect messages from the partisans and deliver them to the radio operators to encode and send to the Allies. The information from resistance fighters on the ground, she knew, was vital to the Americans and British. But still the bitter fighting continued in the south of the country, with few gains being made. So many lives had been lost on both sides over the winter and the Allies' progress north was slow and painful. Now and again, she would hear a village had been taken, or that the Germans had been forced to retreat a little way, but the longed-for defeat of the Nazis still seemed like a distant dream.

On that particular morning, however, just as she crossed the Piazza del Duomo, she heard an odd humming overhead. Like the thrum of a thousand bees. Glancing around, she saw she wasn't the only one bemused by the sound. Street vendors and pedestrians, too, raised their eyes to the sky as the buzz grew louder and turned into more of a rumble. Women called their children to them. Old men seated by the fountain stirred. Old women crossed themselves. Then, as a dark shadow fell across the piazza's golden stones, those who could, hurried inside. Screams and shouts carried across the square as the air-raid siren wailed, launching flocks of pigeons into the sky.

Nearby someone shouted. 'Bombers! Take cover!'

For a moment Lina stood transfixed. This was it – this was what Operation Medici had been for and now she was finally witnessing it. All those hours; all those sleepless nights Agatha and the other women had endured came down to this. She felt both terrified and elated as she tilted back her head to see the sky filled with giant hornets. Each one carried a deadly sting.

'Get down!' shouted a man careening past her, but she stood her ground. This had to work. The pilots would never drop their payloads so close to the cathedral. They all had their Shinnie maps; the areas to avoid clearly marked in white. Their targets lay to the north-west – the railway station and its tracks. These pilots knew what they were doing, *didn't they?*

With each passing second, Lina's doubts started to crowd in. The target area was a little over one hundred metres wide and six hundred metres long. Their ground speed left the bombers no room for error, and they only had a few moments to drop their payloads. Stray seconds could easily lead to the immediate destruction of the *duomo*, the Uffizi or the Ponte Vecchio, not to mention the death of hundreds of innocent civilians.

Moments later came the first explosion. The ground shook. Lina staggered a little. Then came a second and a third, forcing her to clamp her hands over her ears. They were too close for comfort. People were screaming, running helter-skelter across the square. Doubling back to the *duomo*, she joined the crowds pushing through the huge eastern portico to flood the cathedral's aisles. It wasn't supposed to be like this. The raw panic. The terror on faces. Helpless against the onslaught, citizens crammed into pews, away from the stained-glass windows in case they were blown in.

Babies and children bawled each time the building shook, and the votive lamps flickered as the explosions continued for what seemed like an age, until the fury of the bombs stopped and the humming of dozens of aero-engines died away. The siren sounded the all-clear and slowly and carefully everyone began to move, stretching out limbs and taking deep breaths, as if they'd recently woken from a nightmare.

Lina looked about her. The *duomo* seemed unscathed. Its windows and pediments untouched. *Now let's see about the rest.* Cautiously she moved towards the huge doors and stepped out into the sunlight. Only, she could no longer see the sun. A pall of smoke had turned the blue sky grey and the air acrid. Pressing a handkerchief over her mouth, she hurried towards the Uffizi with a mounting sense of dread.

From cellars, basements and churches' crypts, dazed men, women, and children emerged blinking into daylight. In one street, Lina saw glass strewn on the cobbles and a wooden beam across another, but there seemed to be hardly any damage to the buildings she passed. She began to pray. 'Please, God, let the Uffizi be spared.'

Hurrying on, she saw huge plumes of smoke rising from over by the railway station. A man covered in soot was running from the direction of the stockyards, shouting at the top of his voice.

'*Hanno colpito la stazione ferroviaria!*'

They've hit the railway station, she repeated to herself. The more she listened to the cries, the more she understood many people

262

had been injured or killed. Women with blood on their clothes were running away from the scene, screaming. The bombs may not have hit the stones and mortar of the historic city, but they'd still maimed and killed innocent civilians. The news sickened her as she headed across the Piazza della Signoria, past the Palazzo Vecchio, but she knew she had to carry on.

Everything seemed as it was. Nothing had suffered damage, on the outside at least. A moment later the Uffizi came into view. It remained unscathed. She wondered if Agatha and the other women were there as she made her way down to the basement. But a quick glance told her it was deserted. She was about to leave when a wheezing sound made her turn back to catch sight of someone emerging on all fours from under the table.

'Miss Leone is that you?' puffed Miss Harrowby, in the throes of an asthma attack.

'Yes. Yes, it is,' she cried, offering her hand, and pulling her up.

'Oh, my dear!' Agatha's unmistakable voice sounded from the stationery cupboard.

Lina ran forwards to hug her just as Miss Giltrap and Lady Felstein also appeared, both with bemused expressions on their faces, followed by Mrs Clutterbuck.

'Well, I'll be damned!' cried the American, embracing Lina energetically.

'It's so good to see you all again,' she replied, turning to see the familiar faces that wore expressions of both relief and anxiety.

'We've been so worried about you,' said Agatha. 'Oh, my dear, are you all right? You look so thin.'

'I'm fine,' she replied. 'It's you I care about. And you did it!'

'What? The air raid, you mean?' queried Lady Felstein.

'But did we?' asked Mrs Clutterbuck, rather aggressively.

'What news is there?' asked Agatha.

'The bombs,' said Miss Harrowby, clearly in shock. 'Oh, quite terrible.'

'It'll be a miracle if there's anything left?' wailed Lady Felstein.

'They came so close. We thought we were doomed.'

Lina shook her head. 'Yes, quite terrible,' she agreed, thinking of those injured and killed at the station. 'But the bombers hit the railway tracks and destroyed the warehouses and repair shops, as they were supposed to. It looks like all the bombs stayed in the target area.'

'In the target area?' repeated Agatha, casting around at the other women to gauge their reaction.

'Yes, the area you mapped,' Lina confirmed. 'Don't you see?' She took Agatha's hand and turned to face everyone. 'You did it, ladies.' she told them, a seam of relief running through her voice, even though she knew there'd still been a terrible human cost. 'You helped save the city's treasures.'

Chapter 46

Two days after the bombing of the train station, Professor Loggi received a summons from Podesta Manzano. Now the Americans had flattened the city's railway network and destroyed the tracks, lines from Florence were cut. Not only did that stop German supplies reaching the battlefront near Monte Cassino, it also meant no more convoys of art could leave by train. Any future sabotage plans Edoardo and his group had planned were made redundant, for the time being at least. But Loggi knew the Germans would find other ways round the problem. Florentine art was too valuable to leave to the mercy of the Americans and British. So, when he was called to a meeting, he'd already calculated Manzano and his new Nazi SS-colonel friend had something up their repulsive sleeves. He was right.

'Colonel Fischer is growing very concerned,' Manzano told the professor, standing in his office gazing out over the Piazza della Signoria. 'He fears for the safety of all this art in these various repositories.'

'Oh?' was all Loggi replied. He would let the podesta do the talking.

Turning on his heels, Manzano plodded back to his desk to glance at an open folder. 'We have thirty-eight in Tuscany, I understand.'

'That is correct,' agreed the professor, aware that his palms were growing clammy, even though the room was relatively cool.

'Therefore,' Manzano continued, 'the colonel and I are agreed the most valuable pieces from the Uffizi and the Pitti Palace should be taken further north.' He nodded. 'For their protection, you understand.'

'North?' queried Loggi. The podesta smiled – the smarmy, infuriating smile of a man who knows he holds a trump card. 'Our German brothers have created a repository on the island of Isola Bella.'

'What?' Loggi's monocle popped out of his left eye as his brows shot up.

'No need to be alarmed, Professor,' Manzano assured. 'It's one of three islands in Lake Maggiore and only accessible by boat. All the art will be secure there.'

Secure, behind the Gothic Line, the Nazi's defensive belt of fortifications, and much closer to the German border, the professor realised. The suggestion brought to mind the inventories the English ladies had compiled. Their work suddenly took on a new significance. If Fischer and his cronies were to get their hands on all those sheets of information so carefully curated, then they would behave like spoilt children in a sweet shop. They could help themselves to some of the most precious works of art in the world. Montegufoni may be housing *Primavera*, but there were many other repositories. *Minerva and the Centaur*, also by Botticelli and Caravaggio's *Sleeping Amor* were at Villa Bossi-Pucci, and Villa di Torre a Cona contained many of Michelangelo's works. And, as for the Cranachs, there were several dotted around the region.

Men like Fischer needed their egos massaging – Loggi had learned that in his dealings with fascists over the years – and Manzano was in his pocket. Yet, it was hard to argue with the colonel's logic without showing his own deep mistrust. Calmly he explained. 'The city officials have already agreed with my recommendations. Unless the paintings are in urgent peril, they should remain where they are, Your Excellency.' He squeezed a sudden smile.

'And if they are in urgent peril, as you put it, Professor, what happens then?'

Loggi leaned his head to one side, as if trying to explain something to a child. 'Then they should be returned to Florence. On no account should they be taken across the Apennines.'

The podesta flexed his jaw and sighed heavily. 'So, you are rejecting Colonel Fischer's generous offer?' Having his Nazi friend's backing seemed to give Manzano a new, bullish confidence. His tone was ominously threatening.

The professor smiled another smile, this time one perfected for such tricky encounters. 'Rejecting? Not at all, podesta. Please tell Colonel Fischer I am most grateful for the offer. It's just that it has already been agreed by a panel of experts that the city would be the best place for the artworks to be stored should they be in jeopardy.'

Manzano nodded, but remained seated, flipping closed the folder on his desk. 'I see,' he said finally, tapping his lips with a flabby finger. 'That will be all, Professor.'

It seemed he had heard Loggi's views on the subject and already chosen to ignore them without saying so blatantly. The professor suspected that when the SS colonel received answers from Manzano that weren't to his liking, it made no difference. The Nazi would always act as he wanted to, regardless.

Meanwhile, the atmosphere in the safe house had turned almost as acrid as the bombed-out warehouses by the train station. The success of the Allied bombing raid and of Operation Medici had heartened Edoardo, but in the aftermath the Nazis had further tightened security. A ring of steel now surrounded the city centre, subjecting ordinary citizens to even more rigorous checks. Lina had been late back from a delivery and the tension hit her the moment she crossed the threshold. She may have escaped injury during the Allied bombing raid, but she felt like she'd walked into a war zone. Signora Bianchi was pacing the room, venting her anger as Edoardo looked on.

He rushed to the door as soon as he noticed Lina walk in. 'Thank God you're all right,' he told her, taking her hands in his. 'I was worried.'

She'd had to queue to have her bags searched by *fascisti* but she always carried her messages in the heel of her shoe. 'No need,' she assured him, kissing him on the cheek.

But then she saw Signora Bianchi's angry expression. A suitcase stood by the table. 'What's going on?'

The housekeeper gritted her teeth and picked up the case. 'I'm leaving,' she announced.

'Leaving?' repeated Lina. She glanced across at Edoardo for an explanation.

He nodded. 'It's bad news,' he began with a sigh. 'The body of her parish priest washed ashore near the Ponte alla Carraia last night.'

Lina closed her eyes. 'You mean he was murdered?'

'Tortured to death by Carita's men, yes,' confirmed Edoardo. 'We broadcast from his church once. They picked up the signal.'

Signora Bianchi's expression blazed with fury. 'I can't stand it here anymore,' she hissed, glaring at Edoardo. 'Your father was a fool and so are you. You got Father Nicolo into this. I hope you rot in hell,' she fumed, and with those words she stormed out of the house.

For a moment Lina was stunned. She shook her head. 'Oh, Edoardo, that's terrible.'

He nodded. 'Father Nicolo was a good man. Someone betrayed him, but he won't have cracked.'

'So, he knew about the radio network? He knew names?'

'Yes. Yes, he did. But he was strong. He would never talk.' Shaking his head he walked towards her with arms outstretched.

268

Lina lifted her gaze and looked into his eyes. 'But there's still a risk, isn't there?'

'There's always a risk,' he agreed, pulling her close to him once more. 'That's why a meeting's been called.'

'A meeting about the radios?'

'Yes. We need to be across town within the next hour.'

Chapter 47

The ash trees in the Piazza d'Azeglio swayed gently in the breeze as they arrived in the square. It was good to get away from the bustle of the city centre and find respite in the tranquil surroundings of a respectable neighbourhood. Orienting herself, Lina realised Villa Mimosa was just around the corner.

The man who lived in the top-floor apartment at number twelve was not only a lawyer, but a resistance leader called Enrico Bocci. Two more radio operators had been parachuted in a few days earlier. It was time they were briefed. Father Nicolo's death was also on the agenda. A traitor could be in their midst.

Standing on the corner of Via Vittorio Alfieri, Lina and Edoardo waited in the shade. The group's arrival would be staggered over the next half hour. According to Edoardo, Swallow and Raven would already be there, followed by the two new radio operators. Now it was their turn.

'Are you ready?' he asked.

She took a deep breath. 'As I'll ever be,' she replied, grasping the hand he held out to her.

The block's communal hallway was empty. Side by side they made their way to the top floor and pressed the doorbell. An eye appeared at the spy hole, and they were admitted. They were the last to arrive and were led wordlessly into a large salon. Over in the corner the man Lina assumed was Swallow sat hunched by the transmitter, his finger tapping frantically as the illuminated dials swung this way and that. A blonde-haired woman wearing headphones – Raven, she wondered – was at his side, scribbling madly. But when she glanced up, Lina took a step backwards.

'You!' she muttered, unable to hide her shock.

'Yes, Signorina Leone,' replied Manzano's secretary.

Edoardo smiled. 'I think you've already met Signorina Silvia Corvo,' he said. 'Or Raven, as we know her,' he explained, drawing out a chair for Lina. 'How else do you think we got details of the art consignments in advance?'

Once again, Lina had rushed to judgement and been blindsided by an unseen hero. The woman she thought was the podesta's plaything, who did his bidding without question, was also working for the resistance. She was the mole in the Palazzo Vecchio. Lina smiled at Silvia as she left the radio and sat down next to her, just as an older man in horn-rimmed spectacles began to speak.

'Greetings, everyone,' he began. Lina assumed he was Signor Bocci, although there were no more introductions. Introductions were too dangerous. 'Swallow will join us shortly,' he added, glancing over at the lone operator by the transmitter.

'So, the first item on the agenda today is to update you on the progress of the Allies. As you already know two British agents were dropped in the last week and—' He paused. 'Did anyone hear that?'

An undercurrent of unease rippled around the table. No one spoke. Silence. Lina's ears strained to listen, but all she could hear was the sound of her own heart battling against anxiety.

'No? Then please forgive my natural state of alertness. It comes with the territory these days,' said Bocci with a smile.

Edoardo nodded and nervous looks were exchanged. The lawyer began again. 'We now have two radios at our disposal and—'

A heavy thud had Edoardo leap to his feet in a second.

'What the hell?' exclaimed one of the other men, as he too jumped from his seat.

There was no mistaking the sound now. Boots thundering up the stairs, followed by guttural German shouts, punching the air. Edoardo drew a pistol and gripped Lina's arm. 'This way,' he cried, knocking over a chair as he thrust her towards a far door. Bocci scrambled up and Silvia followed, while Edoardo stayed on with Swallow. They were joined by the two other men training their guns on the salon door, while the others fled into adjacent room.

There had to be a back exit, Lina knew. Rushing into the next room, she'd only covered a few paces when she heard a crash and realised Signor Bocci had stumbled. Offering him a hand, he righted himself awkwardly and followed her, but they'd barely made it to the far side when she heard the Germans burst into the salon and begin firing. One moment Bocci was behind her, the next his eyes flashed, and he dropped like a stone. Silvia screamed and Lina seized her hand and started to run again, as another rifle shot ripped through the room.

With burning lungs, she managed to make it to another door. Behind them more shots followed thick and fast. So did the blood-curdling screams. *Edoardo? Please God, not Edoardo.* Gripping the handle, she stopped for a split second, then saw Silvia's face puckered with anguish. There was no time to lose. Flinging open the door she saw a steep metal fire escape. It was their only chance. Down the two women went, taking two or three steps at a time, until finally they reached the hallway, only to see two German sentries at the entrance. As soon as they'd hidden under the staircase, they realised they were trapped, until Silvia stumbled backwards against a door behind. It opened without warning.

Wordlessly Lina pushed her inside, and was about to follow, when she saw more boots flying down the stairs through the rungs of the fire escape. Not polished military boots, but familiar working men's boots.

'Here,' she called in a loud whisper, as Edoardo careened round the corner and dashed through the door into the semi-gloom of the janitor's cupboard. 'God, you're hurt!' she cried seeing splashes of crimson hit the floor. Blood oozed through Edoardo's fingers. Grabbing a towel from a nearby shelf, she pressed hard against the wound. 'We'll get you out of here,' she told him.

A window high up offered hope of an escape. Silvia balanced on an upturned bucket to open it. Cupping both hands together Lina gave her a leg-up and a moment later she'd sprung onto the ledge. Half in and half out, the secretary reached down and heaved Lina up, then together they used all their might to heft Edoardo through the narrow gap. One by one they dropped onto the lawn below.

Two German trucks awaited in the square, their engines rattling, in readiness to whisk away their prisoners – alive or dead. Lina spotted a nearby shrubbery, and they crawled to its shelter. Behind her, she could hear orders snarled in German and then saw the first of the bodies being dragged out, a red ribbon of blood in its wake. Edoardo, his face plastered in sweat, saw it, too. 'Swallow,' he mouthed. 'Quick.' He bounded up to make a break for it, tugging Lina as he went. Silvia followed and together they scrambled round the corner, before Edoardo, exhausted, finally slid down against the wall.

'Here,' said Lina, untying the scarf she'd worn around her neck and pressing it on his wound. 'To stop the bleeding.' Then, gritting her teeth, she coiled one of his arms over her shoulder, taking his weight before nodding to Silvia. She knew exactly where they were going.

Somehow, keeping to the shade of the trees that bordered the avenue, they made it to the back gate of Villa Mimosa. Donna saw them from the kitchen window. '*Mamma mia!*' she cried at the sight of Edoardo.

'He's badly hurt,' cried Lina, as he lolled against her.

The maid, her hands flaring in shock, helped them inside. '*Si, si, signorina!*'

Alerted by the commotion, Agatha called through from the conservatory. 'Donna, are you talking to someone?' She rang her little bell and when no reply came, she rose, irritated that she'd been ignored and walked stiffly through to the kitchen.

'Donna, I need your help.' Agatha arrived in time to see Edoardo stagger inside from the garden. Her jaw fell open and an odd sound emerged.

'He's been shot,' Lina grunted, sharing Edoardo's weight with Silvia.

'Good grief!' cried Agatha, suddenly finding her voice. 'What is that man doing here?' she asked, alarmed.

'Please, Aunt. He needs our help,' pleaded Lina. 'It's not what you think. I can explain, but for God's sake let us stay.'

Agatha took a deep breath, her alarm sliding into an acceptance of the dire situation.

'Please,' begged Lina.

'Very well. If you're sure. In here,' she conceded, flapping a hand towards a small utility room off the kitchen. Meanwhile, Donna appeared with her arms struggling to contain a bulging eiderdown and pillows which she lay on a long bench running the length of the wall.

'Come,' said Lina, putting her arm around Edoardo's waist and guiding him into the room. As he sank onto the makeshift bed, she eased off his boots and Silvia lifted his legs.

'I'll leave you now,' she said.

Lina hugged her. 'Thank you and God bless you,' she whispered as the girl left. Returning to Edoardo, she squeezed his hand and wiped the sweat from his brow. 'We'll get a doctor to you.'

'And what about you, Angelina?' gasped Agatha on the threshold. 'You're hurt!'

Lina looked down at her dress, caked in blood. 'No. It's not mine,' she replied, but her face crumpled. 'The Nazis raided our meeting and began shooting. I didn't know where else to go.' She snorted back tears. 'Here was the nearest place. I'm so sorry.'

'Oh, dear girl,' Agatha cried, holding out her arms as she marched into the room. 'You did the right thing, my dear,' she soothed, drawing her close and patting her niece on the back. 'So, you're saying Signor Bernini is in the resistance?' She glanced at Edoardo, teeth gritted against his pain.

'Yes. Yes, he is. I couldn't tell you before.'

'But we must get him a doctor,' Agatha insisted, sweeping the past behind her with a no-nonsense gesture. 'But it has to be someone we can trust.'

A moan came from the bed. 'Tacci. Dr Tacci is one of us,' muttered Edoardo.

'Tacci?' repeated Agatha, frowning and gently taking Edoardo's hand in hers. 'You are in safe hands here, Signor Bernini,' she assured him.

Edoardo managed a weak smile then and Lina squeezed her aunt's arm. 'Thank you,' she whispered.

Agatha returned a soft look then said, 'I play bridge with Dr Tacci's wife.'

Donna returned to the room with a bottle of iodine, a wad of lint and a roll of bandages. She'd already filled a bowl of water and set it down at Edoardo's side, together with a sponge.

'I'll take care of him, thank you,' Lina instructed. 'Go and fetch the doctor. He needs to come as quickly as he can.'

The Germans had cut all the telephone lines in the city, but Agatha assured Donna that Dr Tacci lived less than half a mile away.

'Please hurry,' Lina called, returning to Edoardo as she knelt by his side. 'You're going to be all right, my love,' she whispered, dipping the sponge into the water.

Edoardo grasped her wrist. 'The others,' he mumbled. 'They took the others. Swallow is dead, but they've got the others.' He gulped back a sob.

Lina stroked his forehead, as tears rolled down his cheeks. Biting her lips to stave off her own tears, she knew the fate of those captured was sealed.

'You must rest. Dr Tacci will come soon,' she told him, kissing his forehead gently and dabbing his wound.

'But I can't stay here long. I have to warn the Allies,' he said.

'You'll stay here as long as it takes,' Agatha told him, as Lina squeezed out the bloodied sponge. The water in the bowl turned a deep pink as she spoke.

'But they'll be after us,' he protested.

Lina and Agatha swapped anxious looks. They both understood what Edoardo said was true. Agatha nodded and left the room as, without a word, Lina poured iodine onto a pad of lint. Of course the Nazis would have men searching for them. It was only a matter of time before the fateful banging was heard at the door of Villa Mimosa, but until then, she and Agatha would care for him.

'Do you think it was Signora Bianchi who informed on us?' Lina asked as she worked, voicing the nagging doubts she'd held so long. 'Perhaps it wasn't just luck that Manzano's men didn't search her room for the Cranach at your apartment, or that her parish priest was murdered by Carita.'

Edoardo closed his eyes for a moment as if the thought of the housekeeper's betrayal was too painful. 'Perhaps,' he whispered.

With hindsight, Lina suspected the die was cast when the woman had stormed out of the safe house the other day. She should have realised then she was an informant. She'd likely told the authorities that Edoardo was taking the Cranach to Innsbruck, too. How would Decker and the Nazis have known otherwise? It made sense now. And because of her, at least one man, who less than an hour before had sat at the same table, was dead. The remaining would be tortured, then killed. But she couldn't let her rage blind her to the moment. All her energy must focus on making sure Edoardo recovered quickly.

'We must start—' his jaw snapped shut and he flinched as she dabbed his wound, '—we must start transmitting again.'

Lina looked at him in horror. 'But we've no radio. How can we?'

He stayed her hand as she patted his wound and looked her straight in the eye. 'You know this is bigger than me and you. It's the only way the partisans and Allies can communicate. Somehow, I'll find one. I have to carry on.'

She closed her eyes as she felt his fingers brush her cheek and clamped his hand on her face. Of course she understood what he had to do.

'I know, my love,' she replied. 'I know what you have to do, but you won't do it alone.'

That night Lina made a bed up on the floor and slept – or tried to sleep – at Edoardo's side. Mercifully, Dr Tacci had arrived within the hour and declared the bullet had passed clean through Edoardo's abdomen. By some miracle it had not punctured any vital organs. But, despite the good news, a fever took hold. Edoardo kept calling out, reliving the moment the Germans burst into the apartment and rounded up his comrades. 'No! No! Get away from me!' he'd cried, thrashing about. Lina had tried to soothe him and kept wiping his forehead with a cold flannel, fearing the wound might turn sceptic. But as dawn broke, so too did Edoardo's fever, and finally he fell into a sound sleep.

Those bleak hours gave her a chance to think about what needed to be done. Overnight her role had become clear. With the added threat that one of the team might crack in Carita's torture chamber, there was no time to lose. She would help Edoardo re-establish communications between the approaching Allies and the partisans. The radio frequency had to begin broadcasting again – the sooner the better.

Chapter 48

May 1944

The green Lancia sputtered to a halt by the checkpoint on the north bank of the Ponte Santa Trinita. The moon was high, and its reflection rippled like a silver ribbon on the Arno. It may have been a cool spring night, but from underneath the man's deer-stalker a bead of sweat surfaced as a lanky German approached his car window.

'Papers!' ordered the guard charily, noticing the sheen on the driver's face.

The elderly man reached into the glove compartment and handed them over quickly, hoping the guard wouldn't notice he was shaking. 'A warm night,' he remarked in perfect German, even though he knew it wasn't. He pulled out a handkerchief from his breast pocket and dabbed his cheeks.

Ever since the raid on Bocci's house four days before, the city had been on even higher alert and the OVRA was working over-time. He'd known there would be roadblocks, but he was banking on not being asked to open the boot of his car. Inside were six boxes, each containing around twenty files, detailing every work of art from the Uffizi and several other city galleries that had been transported to various repositories. In Colonel Fischer's hands they would be worth their weight in gold.

The soldier continued to eye him suspiciously. 'And the purpose of your visit,' – he checked the name on the document – 'Professor Loggi?'

'I am on urgent business for the Uffizi,' he replied, drumming the steering wheel. From the blank look, it seemed the Nazi guard had never heard of the gallery. He scrutinised the document in sullen silence. 'You can ask Colonel Fischer, if you like?' Loggi suggested. He felt a little extra kudos might be needed to beat the curfew. 'He has sanctioned my meeting.'

'That won't be necessary, Professor,' came a voice. It seemed a young officer with a long scar down his cheek was listening to the exchange. He strode over from the guard post. With the beam of his torch trained on the papers he gave them a cursory glance and handed them back with a click of heels. 'You are Professor Loggi of the Uffizi?'

His mouth went dry. 'Yes. Yes, I am.'

'I am honoured to meet you, sir. I have visited your wonderful gallery several times.'

Loggi felt the tension build in his chest. He had to remain calm. 'So, you are an art lover.'

The officer nodded. 'Caravaggio, Reubens, but of course Cranach the Elder is the best.'

'Of course.' With every passing moment the professor felt his heart beat faster. 'I could discuss art all night, but ...'

'Where is your meeting?'

The professor's stomach lurched. 'What?'

'Tell me where your meeting is, and I will arrange an escort.' He leaned in. 'There are partisans everywhere.'

'No, really.'

'I insist. The address if you please.'

The professor's tongue felt like a lead weight in his mouth. He wasn't used to thinking on his feet. 'Villa Mimosa. Via Venezia.'

The officer clicked his fingers and snapped an order. Within a minute a motorcycle outrider appeared.

'You will escort the professor to his destination.'

As he shifted the gear, Loggi felt he was driving a Trojan horse, not a Lancia. He was bringing the enemy to Agatha's gate. His sweaty hands gripped the steering wheel tightly. At least he was thankful not to be asked to open the car's boot. The motorcyclist moved off a few metres ahead of the car and drove at a sedate pace through the near-deserted streets of central Florence. After another five minutes they reached the leafier outskirts. Stopping outside Villa Mimosa, Loggi prayed he'd be left to enter the grounds alone, but his heart sank when instead of going, the motorcyclist opened the gates. Mercifully, he did no more and saluted as the professor drove through them.

'*Danke Schoen*,' Loggi called. Seconds later he'd pulled up outside the front door of the villa, unable to believe what just happened.

Agatha awaited him in the drawing room. 'I was getting worried, Professor,' she told him, easing herself out of her armchair.

'A minor delay.' He wasn't going to let on just how close he'd come to being searched.

'And you have them?'

'The files are all outside,' he twisted round to point to his car.

'I'll get Donna to deal with them immediately.'

'I can't thank you enough for offering to store them, Mrs Fortescue-Smythe,' said the professor. But his intense look carried with it something more than gratitude.

Agatha sensed it and absorbed it for a moment, before seemingly brushing it away. 'Think nothing of it. As cultural attaché my late husband had a secret storage space built for important documents. I'm glad it will be put to good use again.' She shrugged. 'And we couldn't have my ladies' hard work fall into the wrong hands, could we, Professor?' she replied with a coquettish tilt of her head.

'Indeed not, Mrs Fortescue-Smythe.'

'Please, do call me Agatha.'

'Agatha,' he repeated slowly, as if he'd never heard the name before. 'And I am Giuseppe.'

Together they went to the Lancia and Donna unloaded the boxes, stacking them on a hand cart, and taking them directly to the icehouse in the grounds.

'You'll stay for some refreshment?' Agatha asked as they stood in the hall.

'I'd like that very much, Mrs Fortescue-Smythe,' replied the professor. He dabbed the back of his neck with a handkerchief, before correcting himself. 'Agatha, I mean.'

'Then come into the drawing room,' she said. 'Donna will bring us something to drink. A sherry, perhaps?'

Loggi nodded and settled himself in an armchair opposite Agatha. 'You have news of Signorina Leone?' he asked.

He noticed Agatha shifted uneasily in her chair. 'She is—'

'I am well, thank you, Professor.' A voice broke in from the threshold.

Loggi was stunned to see Lina standing in the doorway.

'Signorina Leone,' he said rising. 'I feared you'd been arrested,' he began, shaking his head.

Lina's stomach was churning. 'You heard about the raid? How are the others? Do you know?'

The professor's gaze sank.

'They were shot, weren't they?' she said, her voice shaky. The rumours in the city that Donna had told her were true.

A despondent nod sufficed as a reply. She didn't want to know the details. Couldn't bear to hear them. All she knew was that more brave men had sacrificed themselves for freedom. It could so easily have been Edoardo. Or her.

'And Signor Bernini?' asked Loggi softly. 'He escaped?'

'I did,' came another voice. Edoardo stood by Lina, leaning on the door lintel. He looked pale and thin, but he was very much alive. His loose shirt was unbuttoned, and a swathe of bandage could be seen around his torso.

'Bernini!' Loggi could barely contain his shock.

'You should be resting,' Lina scolded, taking him by the arm.

'I've rested long enough,' he told her. He edged forwards slowly and held out a hand to the professor.

'It is such a relief. I feared … we all feared …' Loggi began, taking Edoardo's hand in his.

'We were the lucky ones, Professor. But tell me, what news has there been?'

Loggi's face lightened. 'Monte Cassino has been won, and the Allies are advancing on Rome as we speak.'

Edoardo took a deep breath and nodded. 'Then it's time for me to leave. I have to go.'

Lina regarded him with dismay. 'You can't. You're—' But just as she was about to launch into a dozen reasons why he was in no fit state to leave, there was a loud knock at the door.

Loggi looked at Agatha alarmed, while Lina took Edoardo by the hand and led him back towards the utility room, crossing over Donna running from the kitchen. She needed instructions.

'Stall them for as long as you can,' ordered Agatha. Then, catching the professor shambling towards the door, she asked, 'And where do you think you're going, Giuseppe?'

'To hide of course,' he replied, before realising he had no idea where to go.

Meanwhile, the banging on the door continued, until Donna, playing for time, finally answered it. Two German soldiers stood on the front step; the young officer with a long scar on his cheek and a private.

'*Si*,' she greeted them in Italian, trying to sound confident.

They said nothing but simply barged past her into the hallway and stopped by the first door they came to – the drawing room. Not bothering to knock, the officer burst inside, his subordinate giving cover with a prone rifle. But the scene that confronted them was totally unexpected. An elderly woman with unkempt hair was sitting with her arm around a gentleman of similar age, wearing neither jacket nor tie, and with his top three shirt buttons undone. Perhaps most startlingly, his cheeks were covered in lipstick marks.

Agatha let out a very plausible cry at being caught practically *in flagrante*. The officer's jaw dropped in shock when he saw what the professor from the Uffizi was really up to, while the young soldier smirked.

'What do you think you're doing?' cried Agatha in remarkably good Italian, rearranging her blouse and shifting her weight.

The officer was still too alarmed to offer resistance. He nodded his head and shot a look of disbelief at the professor. 'Forgive me, madam. Sir,' he said, saving a glare for the lanky soldier. 'When I checked with Colonel Fischer, he said he had not been informed of your *urgent business* at Villa Mimosa. Now I see why.'

'As you should know by now,' said the professor in German, 'we Italians don't let anything stand in the way of our passion.'

'So I see,' agreed the officer, arching his brow. 'All the same, you will show me what you have in your car.'

Happy to oblige the officer, the professor was able to demonstrate that his boot was empty, and that the purpose of his visit had been purely to satisfy an urgent impulse. The Germans retreated as soon as they could; the officer too angry and embarrassed to search the premises.

'I must say that was a virtuoso performance,' remarked Loggi, wiping off Agatha's lipstick from his face with his handkerchief.

'Yes, it was,' she replied, looking pleased with herself as she tidied her hair in the mirror over the fireplace. She shrugged and added, 'But I have to say I rather enjoyed it.'

Loggi looked at her reflection and smiled. He had to admit that he did, too.

Meanwhile, Edoardo and Lina had managed to slip out of the villa and into the garden unremarked. If it hadn't been for

Agatha's quick thinking, the Germans would have searched the house, and they'd both have been as good as dead.

'You promise you'll come for me soon,' whispered Lina as they stood by the back gate.

'You know I will,' he told her. She felt his breath mist over her in a deep sigh. 'I'll get word to you, somehow. I love you too much to let you go.'

'I will always love you, too, Edoardo. And when this is over,' – her voice began to crack – 'we must never be apart again.'

He drew her towards him again and kissed the top of her head. 'Never,' he whispered.

Chapter 49

June 1944

In the elegant dining room of the Hotel Excelsior, Podesta Manzano and Colonel Alexander Fischer were enjoying an excellent luncheon of pork casserole, washed down with a good Chianti. The colonel, a tall man with a gaunt face, was the exact opposite of his Italian counterpart. Yet they did share at least one thing in common – their interest in Renaissance art – albeit for different reasons. The talk, on this occasion, however, was dominated, at first, by the Allied advance northwards. It was only afterwards, over cigars in the smoking room, the conversation veered into territory closer to home.

Lighting his Havana, Fischer sniffed and inspected the stub of his cigar. 'I hear Professor Loggi is giving you grief.'

Manzano's jowls quivered. 'Not a bit of it,' he protested. 'I am the one who dispenses the grief around here.' He leaned towards an outheld flame. 'The old fool wasn't happy when I told him you'd dispatched several trucks to bring back the most precious pieces from the repositories.'

'And you told him about Isola Bella – the ultimate refuge?'

'Of course, but he didn't seem too impressed by your special island.' Manzano puffed on his cigar. 'He knows what you're up to.'

'Up to?' Fischer shot back. 'You make me sound like a thief, Manzano. These paintings deserve to be in the finest art gallery ever created and that is where they will go.'

The podesta was keen not to offend. 'I didn't mean to cast aspersions on your good character.'

'Did he ask to see the inventories?' Fischer cut him off, his lips twitching.

'Just as you said.'

'But you ordered new ones.' The colonel's eyes narrowed. 'Ones that suited our purpose.'

'I did. But he's a wily old fox. The first thing he did was check for the Cranachs, as we thought.'

'You mean as *I* thought,' corrected Fischer. He paused for a moment, taking another puff of his cigar. 'And what about the portrait of the young woman of Florence? The new Cranach?'

'*Our* Cranach, you mean,' Manzano jumped in, a sly look on his face.

The German arched an imperious brow. 'You are too presumptuous, Manzano. May I remind you, you are merely a custodian of the work? It belongs to the Fatherland now.'

Manzano challenged the statement by inclining his head. 'But what if Goering were to hear of it?'

The colonel stiffened. 'You're not threatening me, are you Manzano? That would be very foolish. The portrait must remain our secret until I say otherwise.'

The podesta frowned disingenuously. 'I was just pointing out that technically the portrait belongs to Italy, and to Florence, and that it is' – he shrugged – 'arguably the new Socialist Republic's to give.'

'The Socialist Republic's?' repeated Fischer mockingly. 'I think you'll find the Third Reich's claim on it is far greater.'

Manzano opened his mouth to say something, like a disgruntled fish, then closed it again. He had to trust Fischer – after all he'd been promised a country estate for his loyal service, hadn't he? His thoughts switched to the castle, the vineyards and the wine cellars – but it didn't mean he had to like the German. Instead, he settled on asking, 'But the portrait is still in your office on the Ponte Vecchio? Yes?'

'It is, and as safe as any artwork can be,' he replied. 'The Ponte Vecchio is not in danger. It enjoys the Führer's special protection.'

Manzano grunted his approval. 'So you have not told your Führer about it?'

'Not yet, no. I think it should be a marvellous surprise, don't you? The look of sheer joy when I present him with a hitherto unknown Cranach will be priceless.'

The podesta nodded. He didn't set much store by what the Nazi said, but he did like the idea of reflected glory. He'd happily settle for that and the financial rewards that would come with it. 'Then let us drink to your wonderful German painter,' he suggested, raising his brandy glass.

'To Lucas Cranach the Elder,' said Fischer, his own glass also aloft. 'May his homecoming be glorious and imminent.'

The sick feeling in the pit of Lina's stomach grew as she made her way down the steps into the basement of the Uffizi. Going to the gallery was a terrible risk, but she couldn't simply stay at Villa Mimosa and do nothing. She felt like a coiled spring. Knowing that Edoardo was out there, somewhere, in this city of bridges, trying to build his very own bridge between the partisans and the Allies, spurred her into action.

Professor Loggi was in his office and surprised to see her. She'd donned a black headscarf and dress to blend in with the ordinary Florentine women and managed to make it to his door unchallenged.

'Signorina Leone!' he exclaimed, looking up from his desk. Instantly he stalked over to the door and craned his neck down the hall to make sure no one was about.

'You were lucky you were not stopped,' Loggi told her, half scolding, half admiring her audacity. 'Does your aunt know you are here?'

Lina shook her head and slumped into a chair. 'No, Agatha would have a fit if she knew I'd left the villa. But I need to do something.'

'You can stay alive,' the professor reminded her. 'You know they shot the others in the team.'

Lina shook her head. 'I am fully aware,' she replied, pushing back the fear and deep sorrow she felt when she thought of the fate of Swallow and Signor Bocci. 'But if I can't help the resistance on my own, I can help you. I can help save the art.'

Yet her intention only made Loggi's face darken even more. 'Well, I'm not so sure about that.'

'What is it, Professor?' she asked, frowning.

He shook his head and sighed. 'My dear Signorina Leone, I fear you are not going to like what I am about to say.'

'Something's happened? Please, Professor. What is it?'

He took a deep breath. 'Earlier this evening I was to have had a meeting with Colonel Fischer at the Hotel Excelsior,' he began. 'He has ordered the return of many of the masterpieces into the city.'

'Back to the city? Why? Are the repositories under threat?' she asked, alarmed.

'If they are, it's not from the Allies,' he told her with a shake of his head. 'No, Fischer insists he wants them back because Florence has become a mere staging post.'

'Staging post,' Lina repeated.

'He plans to load all the returning artworks onto lorries and take them to his island.'

'Island? What island?' Lina pressed.

'Somewhere Fischer insists is safe and secure in the middle of Lake Maggiore, where they won't be bombed.'

Lina nodded as the professor's revelation made more sense. 'Closer to the German border, you mean.'

'Precisely.'

'And what of the two Cranachs at Montegufoni? Did he mention those?'

'No, he didn't. But I did.'

'And?'

'He assured me they remain at the castle.'

'And the other one? The portrait of a young woman? What has he done with that?'

'It wasn't on the inventory of work bound for the island, so I asked him outright.'

'And? What did he say?'

'He said she was far too precious to transport, so he'd left her in the only safe place in Florence. In his office on the Ponte Vecchio.'

'On the Ponte Vecchio,' she repeated. 'And you think that's true?'

'I doubted him at first, but it might make sense. Hitler has apparently said the bridge must remain unharmed. Having said that, Fischer will want every Cranach out of Italy as soon as possible if I know him, but only when it's safe to do so. That's why I asked for a meeting to discuss their return to the gallery, here.'

'So, what happened?'

Loggi's shoulders slumped. 'I went to the hotel at the agreed time, but I arrived too late.'

Lina shook her head. 'You mean you didn't see him?'

'No, I regret to say I didn't. He'd already checked out. And what's more, I heard a convoy of trucks left the city earlier today, carrying a consignment from another repository at Villa Bossi-Pucci.'

A look of disbelief scudded across her face at the mention of one of the other repositories. 'You mean to tell me Fischer has stolen them? Just like that.' She snapped her fingers.

The professor bowed his head, like a man defeated. 'I feel such a fool. He duped me. I am so sorry,' he muttered.

Lina sympathised. 'It's not your fault.'

The professor replied through gritted teeth, trying to bridle his frustration. 'This man is head of the Art Protection Unit, yet he thinks it gives him a licence to loot.'

She understood the professor had been placed in an impossible position. Like a diplomat, he had been called upon to tread a fine line. The Germans were strict masters. He had been obliged to do their bidding, while at the same time trying to protect what he cared about so deeply. 'I have let you down,' he said disconsolately, his face dropping into his hands. 'And I have let down my country.'

This time Lina reached out and placed her hand on his arm. 'You haven't let anyone down, Professor. You did what you could. Thanks to you, Agatha and the other ladies, hundreds of works of art have been saved. You must never lose sight of that.'

Slowly he lifted his face to reveal glistening eyes. He nodded in slow agreement. 'You're right, Signorina Leone,' he replied, his lips lifting into a smile. 'Your aunt really is a most remarkable woman.'

Chapter 50

August 1944

A ragged boy stood on the doorstep of Villa Mimosa, his cheeks caved in and his large eyes sunken into their sockets. Donna was keen to shoo him away.

'We have no spare food. Go!' she cried, waving a tea towel at the urchin. Lina, however, suspected he wasn't just begging for something to eat.

'What is it?' she asked, coming to the door and bending down level with the boy's face.

'She won't listen to me!' he cried, scowling at Donna, who was scowling back at him and cursing.

There was something about the child that made Lina take notice of him. They regularly had youngsters come to the door at the villa to beg for food, but this one was different. More self-assured. Could he be a *staffetta*? 'I will listen,' said Lina. 'Come in.'

The child shot a triumphant glance at the maid, before being shepherded inside and shown into the study. 'Please fetch him something to eat,' Lina called to Donna before closing the door firmly behind her. 'Now,' she said, crouching down by the boy, 'you have something to tell me. Is that right?'

The child looked at her, nervously wringing his hands and nodded. 'I am hungry,' he told her.

Lina smiled and pushed a lock of matted hair back off his grimy forehead. 'Food is on its way, but first you must deliver your message. You have one, yes?'

He glanced down at his bare feet. 'Yes,' he replied. Then, looking straight ahead, as if reciting a poem learned by rote, he launched in. 'I am to tell you friends are coming, but before they do, the bridges will be destroyed. Everyone in the city is in great danger.'

A knock at the door came just as he finished his delivery. Donna walked in carrying a tray with bread and cheese on it and a glass of lemonade. As soon as he saw it, the child bolted and was wolfing down the bread even before Donna had set down the plate. The maid looked at the child with mild disgust.

'That'll be all. Thank you, Donna,' said Lina. It was sorrow she felt, rather than disgust. She thought of the fruit trees in the garden, laid down with apples, plums and pears. The boy would leave the villa with more food, but for now she needed to know if he had anything else to say.

'Who sent you here?' she asked.

The urchin, his jaw working hard, looked up. 'A man,' he replied through a hunk of bread. 'A nice man. He said he is safe, that he gives you his love and you will always be his young woman of Florence.'

Lina's heart leapt. Edoardo's message somehow made the warning about the Nazi's intentions easier to bear. Knowing she was still in his thoughts despite the looming devastation, gave her renewed courage.

'Thank you,' she told the child. 'Now, you must go into the orchard and help yourself to as much fruit as you can carry.' The child's eyes lit up. 'What are you waiting for?' she asked with a smile and, opening the study door, directed him towards the kitchen, while she went over to the window and looked out across the gardens.

Clasping her hands together, as if in prayer, she tried to digest what Edoardo had just told her. The Allied forces were advancing on Florence. That was the good news, but much destruction would be wrought, and much blood shed in the city before they could liberate it. By blowing up the six bridges, the Nazis were thinking the unthinkable. It meant Agatha and her ladies were in danger, too. The message had made up her mind. It was a call to defend the city. Somehow, she had to find a way to thwart the Nazi's intention to blow up the bridges. The English Ladies' Arts Appreciation Society needed to reconvene. But when she hurried to the kitchen to see if the child was still in the orchard, she spotted Donna slumped over the kitchen table, sobbing.

'What's wrong?' she asked, laying a hand on the girl's heaving shoulder.

'Oh! Signorina Leone,' she wailed. 'The boy, he told me—' She broke off in a sob.

'What did he tell you?'

'He said the Germans are ordering everyone living near the river to leave their homes. My parents, my brothers and sisters.' She took the handkerchief Lina offered.

'You mean to evacuate? But where will they go?'

'They say the Pitti Palace on the south bank.' Donna dabbed her eyes.

'There are German paratroopers everywhere. If they don't do as they say, they will kill them all.'

If the Germans were forcing everyone living near the north bank of the Arno to leave their homes, it could only mean one thing. Edoardo's warning had to be heeded. The Nazis intended to carry out their terrible threat.

The members of the English Ladies' Arts Appreciation Society reconvened for the first time in many months at Miss Giltrap's first-floor apartment. The venue was chosen because it was more central than anyone else's. It was also less conspicuous. The modest residence fronted on to a busy thoroughfare, and the women were less likely to attract the unwanted attention of a German or Italian patrol. The ladies had been advised to wear the ubiquitous black of Italian women over a certain age, too. Only their speech would betray them should they be stopped and questioned – something to be avoided at all costs.

Lady Felstein, looking even more fragile than usual, arrived on the arm of the equally delicate Miss Harrowby. Both managed the stairs with difficulty, and arrived out of breath and exhausted. Mrs Clutterbuck, who couldn't look Italian if she tried, had opted to cover her head with a black lace mantilla. Their hostess, Miss Giltrap, was in an unusually sober mood too, as Agatha rose to address the meeting.

'Ladies, ladies, please,' she called, raising her voice above the din, as the women sat huddled in the relatively small salon. 'Thank you for coming today. I know we have all put ourselves at considerable risk to be here and it is heartening to see everyone again after all this time. But there is news. Alarming news. We have it on good authority' – she turned to defer to Lina, sitting to her right – 'that the British, the Americans and various others in His Majesty's forces are making their way north from Rome. They are, however, meeting with strong resistance from the Germans and *fascisti*, and there is much destruction and, sadly, loss of life. Their progress also puts the bridges of our beloved city in the firing line and my niece would like to update us with some information gleaned from Professor Loggi.' She gestured towards her niece.

As she surveyed the women's faces, Lina saw the worry and the weariness that war had etched into their skin. They were all eager for news, but she was going to have to break it to them gently. Standing to address them she began, 'We did not call this meeting lightly, ladies. I apologise for the late notice, but—' She broke off almost immediately. Someone outside was shouting at the top of their voice. Heads turned to the window, then back again. 'As I was saying,' Lina resumed with a shrug, 'I—' Another cry, followed by more, until dozens of voices were buffeting the hot air, making the sound swell. She hurried to the window. The normally busy street was busier. Much busier. In fact, it was verging on chaos. People were bumping into each other, clambering around a German soldier standing on the steps of a church on the other side of the piazza. He was nailing a notice on the door as a second soldier kept the crowds at bay.

Miss Giltrap joined Lina at the window.

'What the deuce?' cried the American.

'Some sort of announcement,' ventured Mrs Clutterbuck at her shoulder, but Miss Giltrap didn't wait for a reply. Grabbing her camera from the table, she scrambled out of her front door and down the stairs to see what was going on.

'Hadn't one of us better go with her?' asked Miss Harrowby.

'No, indeed,' Agatha called as Mrs Clutterbuck made a move. 'Remember what happened the last time we got caught in a mob?' she reminded. 'And sadly, Signor Bernini isn't around to rescue us this time.' She caught Lina's eye as she spoke.

'But everyone seems in such a panic!' protested Mrs Clutterbuck.

'What?' exclaimed Lady Felstein, as soon as she registered the word 'panic'. 'What's happening?'

'Nothing to worry about, your ladyship,' Miss Harrowby assured her. But Lina wasn't so certain. She'd kept an eye on the soldier posting the notice and now that he was gone, the throng surged forwards, and one man took it upon himself to tear down the poster and read it aloud to the crowd. Lina opened the shutters to listen.

'What's he saying?' asked an anxious Lady Felstein, as the others clustered around, and Lina began translating.

'The Germans have declared a state of emergency.'

'Oh, no!' gasped Miss Harrowby.

'What does that mean?' boomed Mrs Clutterbuck.

'Listen and we'll find out,' snapped Agatha.

'*From noon today, it will be prohibited for anyone to leave their homes and walk in the streets or piazzas of the City of Florence.'*

'What?' exclaimed a horrified Miss Harrowby.

'Sssh!' scolded Mrs Clutterbuck.

'*All windows, even those in cellars, together with the entrance and hallways of houses, shall remain closed day and night,*' continued Lina.

'Preposterous!' Agatha cried.

There was more. Lina held up her hand for silence. '*The population is advised to stay in their cellars. Where there isn't one, go to a church or other big building. German patrols will shoot at anyone found on the street or who appears at the windows. Military operations begin at ten o'clock tonight.*'

'Oh, my goodness,' mumbled Miss Harrowby with trembling lips, looking very distressed. 'What shall we do, Mrs Fortescue-Smyth? What should we do?'

Agatha's complexion was the colour of ash. For a moment Lina feared her aunt might faint, but then she seemed to rally. As four pairs of expectant eyes turned upon her, reaching for her white parasol, she eased herself to her feet and said calmly, 'We act like the dignified English women we are. We neither panic, nor surrender. We shall simply ride out the coming storm.'

A short pause for reflection was followed by a 'That's the spirit!' from Mrs Clutterbuck and a 'Brava!' from Miss Harrowby. Lady Felstein, not entirely certain what Agatha had said, but sensing the general mood of approval, clapped.

Just then the door was flung open and in stormed a furious Miss Giltrap. 'Bastard Nazis!' she cried, kicking a cupboard door hard with her boot. 'Who the hell do they think they are!?'

While such behaviour wasn't at all becoming, no one batted an eyelid. Despite Agatha's order to remain calm, they all shared their American sister's sentiment, but were too polite to say so. Lina replied first.

'They're in control and it looks like we're stuck here,' she said. 'Do you have a cellar?'

Gloria Giltrap dropped into one of her vacant chairs, her camera still slung around her neck. 'Yeah. But it's tiny. And they're saying we have to share it with everyone else in the goddamn block.'

'Then we'll have to stay put in here. We don't have any choice in the matter,' replied Agatha. 'As you know from my previous record, I have never been one to kowtow to foreign authorities in such circumstances, but on this occasion, I fear it would be prudent to do so.'

'But what about our beloved bridges?' bemoaned Miss Harrowby.

There was a short pause as everyone contemplated the horror such destruction would bring until finally Miss Giltrap leapt to her feet. 'And we're just going to let them do that?' she protested, clearly spoiling for a fight.

'They can and I fear they will,' replied Lina. 'Why else would they evacuate everyone living within a mile of the river? Why else would they confine everyone else to their homes?'

'But if they blow up the bridges,' said Miss Harrowby, 'they may as well blow up our hearts.' She dabbed at a wayward tear.

'You're so soft,' muttered Mrs Clutterbuck, but Agatha agreed with her sentimental friend.

'Those bridges aren't only strategically important. They are symbols of Florence, of Italy,' she said, her features taut with indignation. Then, transferring her gaze to her niece she said, 'Surely there must be something we can do to stop their destruction?'

Lina shifted and thought of Edoardo. She wondered if he'd managed to find another radio to contact the advancing Allies. If that was the case, he would have notified them of the Germans' devastating intentions. The Americans and British would at least try to prevent the Nazis blowing up all six of the bridges across the Arno. The look on the older women's faces reminded her of the night they all found themselves behind bars at the questura. That same bewildered expression, worn by vulnerable people who have no control over their own fate, had returned.

'Signor Bernini will be doing all he can,' she replied.

'But the Ponte Vecchio,' blurted Miss Harrowby, hands clasped in supplication. 'They wouldn't. They couldn't,' she wailed before dissolving into tears again.

Lina thought of Professor Loggi and how horrified he must also be at the prospect of the bridges' destruction. Hitler himself had been particularly taken with the Ponte Vecchio. What did Edoardo say he'd called it? *The jewel in Florence's crown.* Surely no German commander would want to incur his wrath by blowing it up. There had to be something she could do as they waited like tethered goats in the path of the oncoming assault on the city.

As Mrs Clutterbuck wrapped a comforting arm around Miss Harrowby, and Agatha patted Lady Felstein's hand, Lina turned to Miss Giltrap and enquired quietly, 'Do you have any binoculars?'

'Sure I do.'

The American strode over to a drawer and pulled out a pair of field glasses, but before Lina could take them, they were snatched back.

'What are you up to?' Miss Giltrap teased, narrowing her eyes.

Lina didn't want to play games, nor did she want to attract the others' attention. She sighed deeply and replied through clenched teeth, 'I'm going up onto the roof to see if I can find out what's happening.' As she spoke, she opened her palm. 'Now may I have them?'

'Only if I come with you.'

Another heavy sigh. 'Very well. But we have to be very careful.'

Miss Giltrap's face broke into a grin. 'I can do careful.'

There were rumours the Germans were about to cut off the water supply, so Agatha proposed the ladies fill up as many buckets and bowls they could. The women were so engaged in the task, they didn't notice Lina and Miss Giltrap slip out of the room to climb the stairs. On the fourth floor the treads grew steeper and narrowed – Miss Giltrap had to pause for a breather – while on the fifth they stopped altogether when a ladder presented itself. Above it was the wooden square of a hatch. A nod from the American confirmed this was the only way to the roof. Standing on the sixth rung of the ladder, Lina slid the bolt back, and pushed hard until the door opened. They both knew if they were seen, they would be targets for the Germans.

Lina went first, heaving herself up, but stopped with her feet on the fourth rung from the top. Only her head and shoulders were exposed. Quickly she raised the binoculars and scanned the skyline towards the river. On the far bank she could see crowds of people corralled in the Boboli Gardens by the Pitti Palace. Slightly to the right was the Ponte Santa Trinita. In contrast to the chaos of the gardens, it looked majestic in the golden glow of sunset.

Somehow, she needed to talk to Professor Loggi, to see if anything could be done to save the bridges, but all civilian telephone lines were down. If only German High Command could be persuaded they didn't have to destroy the bridges; that mindless vandalism served no purpose. But then again, a voice inside her pointed out that the Nazis had shown so little regard for human life, why should they think twice about destroying stone and mortar? Edoardo would be doing all he could to thwart the Nazis, but he and his resistance group were small, and the might of the Germans so great.

'Is this a private party or can anyone join in?' came a whine from below.

Lina looked down to see Miss Giltrap. 'I was just checking for snipers,' she said. 'But it seems all clear.' First heaving herself out of the hatch door, she turned back and clasped the American's arm to ease her up.

Brushing the dust from her trousers, Gloria Giltrap looked out across the terracotta rooftops of Florence towards the Arno. Holding out her hand she said, 'My binoculars, if you please.' Lina obliged and she scanned the river. From her vantage point she had a reasonable view of the Ponte Vecchio. 'What's going on down there?' she asked. Something had caught her eye. 'There's movement under one of the bridge's spans. Two Germans. No, four. They're heaving boxes down the riverbank.'

'Let me,' Lina said, prising the binoculars out of the American's hands and training them on the Ponte Vecchio. So, it was true. Despite Professor Loggi's best efforts and the clamour from many influential people, Florence wasn't classified as a *'Free'* city. That meant nothing was off limits. Not even its iconic bridges. But then Miss Giltrap spotted something else.

'Isn't that the podesta's?' she asked, watching a limousine progress towards the bridge.

'What?' asked Lina, switching her sights on to the road below. Focusing on the car, she spotted, alongside the city's pennant, it was flying the new Italian Social Republic's, too. 'Manzano,' she mumbled to herself. He must be up to something, and she needed to find out exactly what before it was too late.

Chapter 51

A crimson wound gashed the glowering sky as the sun set on the Arno. The distant rumble of advancing tanks and the sound of shell fire grew ever louder. In the city, the Germans were preparing to retreat, but not until they'd deliberately left a trail of devastation and suffering in their wake.

Podesta Manzano's driver had taken him to the northern end of the Ponte Vecchio. To his surprise, soldiers were laying charges around all the buildings within a few metres of the bridge. The sight both puzzled and troubled him. He had expected to see Germans at work on the other bridges, but not here. Metres of wire were being laid and crates hoisted down to the river. He'd been right not to trust Fischer. If this bridge was to be blown up at both ends, then the head of the *Kunstschutz* certainly wouldn't have deposited the priceless Cranach in a safe in the middle of it. No. Manzano smelled a rat. But no sooner had the driver held open his door and he'd set foot on the bridge, he was challenged.

'*Halt!*' cried the sentry.

Manzano resented the order and pointed to the insignia on his uniform. An apologetic salute was delivered, and he was granted access to the bridge. But the sight that greeted him on the walkway was one of chaos and confusion. All the jewellery shops that lined it were boarded up and soldiers were heading across the bridge to the north side. Cries of 'Schnell! Schnell!' rained down like ack-ack fire.

Manzano made his way as fast as his heavily laden legs would carry him to the SS colonel's headquarters. Surreptitiously, he fingered his holster. The Beretta was there. The Germans were evacuating in a hurry. No doubt about it. Boxes and crates were being heaved along the corridor as the podesta entered the building and ploughed his way towards Fischer's office. But then a lieutenant stopped him in his tracks.

'Sir, you should not be here. I have orders.'

Manzano sneered. 'Where is Colonel Fischer?'

'I am not at liberty to tell you, sir. Now please go, or I shall have to arrest you.'

'Arrest me? I demand to see Fischer. Where is he?' Manzano side-stepped and tried to barge further down the corridor, but the officer was too quick and blocked his way.

'Sir, no,' he cried.

'Let him pass,' called a voice nearby. The colonel was standing bareheaded in the corridor, holding open his office door. 'Come in, Excellency. Please. I apologise for my officer's zeal.'

Manzano snarled at the officer, then marched in. The door was shut behind him.

'Take a seat,' said Fischer, pointing to one of only two that remained in the room, alongside empty filing cabinets and a globe. Manzano's eyes swept over the bare walls once covered with maps. Even the portraits of Hitler and Mussolini had been removed, although, he noted, a single telephone remained.

'I don't understand,' he began. 'You said this bridge was safe. That's why the Cranach is here.' He paused for a moment to gauge Fischer's reaction. 'It is still here. Yes?'

The German exhaled through flared nostrils. 'Of course it is. Is that why you're here? Did you think I might remove the precious young woman without informing you first?'

Manzano laughed, although nervously. 'I trust you, of course,' he lied. 'We have a deal.'

'A country estate, as I recall,' Fischer said, as if the podesta needed reminding. He pointed to a large safe in the corner of the room and rose from his seat. 'Come, let me show her to you.' He invited the podesta to join him.

'That is not necessary,' said Manzano. 'I believe you, although, I admit when I saw your men mining either side of the bridge, it worried me. What good will it do if the painting is safe and yet the Ponte Vecchio is inaccessible?'

Fischer nodded. 'You are right, my friend. But if we can't get to it, nor can anyone else.' His lips broadened, and although Manzano also smiled, he couldn't really follow the logic.

'Come,' said the colonel, beckoning. 'Surely you want a glimpse of her again?'

'Very well,' said Manzano with a shrug. He had to admit he was eager to see the painting that held the key to a bright and glorious future for him. But on his own terms.

As Fischer clicked the dial on the safe, and opened it with a theatrical gesture, Manzano stomped towards him and drew his gun.

'You may think me a Philistine, Fischer, but I know the worth of that painting to your Führer,' he began. 'And I'm not letting you take it anywhere.'

When the colonel turned back from the safe to see the Beretta pointed at him, his first reaction was to arch a brow. But he said nothing. It was almost as if he had been expecting the confrontation. He let Manzano have the floor.

'You arrogant bastard,' he began. 'You have a poor opinion of me, don't you? I'm just a low-down Italian who'd sell my own mother if I could profit from her, but you're very wrong. That painting doesn't belong to Germany. It is not yours. It never has been, and it never will be. If anyone presents it to anyone, it'll be me to Il Duce. Farewell, Fischer.'

Yet before the Italian's fat finger could squeeze the trigger, a shot from another gun blasted from behind. The bullet, fired by one of Fischer's men, hit Manzano in the shoulder with such force his great mass was launched forwards, a look of abject horror on his face. He opened his mouth to speak but only a grunt emerged just before he hit the wall. A split second later he slid to the ground with a thud, landing in a large, unruly heap on the office floor.

Fischer leaned over to inspect the soldier's handiwork. The bullet seemed to have gone clean through and blood flowed freely down the front of the podesta's uniform. The solider felt for a pulse. Manzano wasn't dead, but he would be – shortly, he assured.

'Good work,' Fischer said, before returning to the safe.

Satisfied his adversary would cause no further trouble, Colonel Fischer retrieved the painting and scanned his office for what he knew would be the last time. Ignoring the groans of the dying Italian, he merely curled his lips.

'*Arrivederci*, you fool,' he said with a gratified nod, stalking out with the Cranach tucked firmly under his arm.

Chapter 52

Even though the sun had set an hour before, inside Miss Giltrap's apartment it remained insufferably hot. Banned from opening the windows, the ladies were breathing in stale air, and without electricity there were no fans.

'I think this is what Dante meant when he wrote about the first circle of hell in his *Inferno*,' announced Miss Harrowby, fanning herself with a tourist guide to the *duomo*.

Everyone knew the night would be long. 'We've weathered a storm before, ladies,' Agatha exhorted. But this time, no one was under any illusion. They'd stared into the abyss in the *questura*, but then they'd had clear sight of their enemy. Now, however, as well as the Italian fascists, the Germans, and not to mention the Allies who might inadvertently cause civilian casualties, the twin threats of hunger and dehydration also loomed.

The ladies began to organise their sleeping arrangements, despite knowing they would be lucky to grab any rest at all that night. The windows may be shutting out any fresh air, but they were failing to deaden the sound of sudden bursts of artillery fire from the river. Both the suffocating heat and the fear pressed down on them all.

Rumours had been running round like rats all day about what

the Nazis intended to do. But no one dared set a foot outside, let alone open a window. Anyone seen leaving their home would be shot on sight.

Lina took herself into the small kitchen with a small cushion, but she had no intention of staying there. Shortly before ten o'clock she slipped out of the apartment once more and clambered up the ladder to the roof. This time, under cover of thickening darkness, there was no holding back. Heaving herself out of the trap door, but keeping her head low, she crept out onto the edge of the roof terrace and surveyed the scene before her.

The great River Arno lay somewhere below, flowing through a yawning chasm too dark to see because the Nazis had sabotaged the local power plant. And over the river spanned the six world-famous bridges, joining the two sides of Florence. Each of them a work of art in their own right, a testament to man's ingenuity and creativity. They stood as symbols of the city's history, its beauty and its power. But tonight, they lay like condemned prisoners, shackled by fuses, and weighed down by hundreds of tons of high explosives. Like Agatha and her ladies, and the countless other residents of Florence, they were left to await their fate.

The first detonation was scheduled for ten o'clock. When morning came, Lina wondered, would they really all be gone? She understood she was risking her life to watch this catastrophe unfold. Turning her head to where she knew the Ponte Vecchio lay, she recalled its expensive jewellers' shops, now looted and vandalised, and the ramshackle houses huddling on the bridge, with their windows blown. But then she glanced up at the starless sky, as if searching the heavens for an answer.

When she didn't find one, she decided it was time to join the other women below. Either that or be shot. Keeping her body low, she'd just started back when she saw something move up ahead. The hatch door. *Miss Giltrap?* Maybe. Come to check on her. But no. The smudged figure that emerged wasn't a woman. It was a man. A man with a gun.

Panic swept through her body, but she was too afraid to gulp down air for fear the slightest movement could alert this Nazi sniper. Silently she watched as he moved through the darkness towards her. There was nowhere to hide. On the way up she'd realised she was vulnerable on the roof, so she'd grabbed the thick wooden stick holding open the trapdoor. It would make a weapon, she'd told herself, although no match for a German bullet. She felt the heft of it in her hand as she flattened herself against the chimney stack in the shadows. Glass now crunched under the intruder's feet as she readied herself to take a swipe. Nearly in reach. Raising her arm to shoulder height she drew a deep breath and struck blindly, but hard. The soldier yelped and doubled over, dropping to his knees. Seeing she'd winded him, she bent over him, snatching his pistol. But when he didn't put up a fight, she thought it odd.

'Hands up, you coward,' she growled as the gun trembled in her grasp.

But instead of obeying her, her victim lifted his head and looked her in the eye.

'Lina,' he groaned. His voice sounded far away. 'Oh, Lina. It's me.'

Flinging down the baton, she dropped to her knees and took his head in her arms. 'Edoardo,' she cried. 'I'm so sorry.'

Edoardo simply shook his head and leaned on her as together they got up. 'There's no time for apologies. Come, quick. The first bridge will go at any moment,' he warned. But his voice was a target, and a bullet cracked from out of the blackness. They'd been spotted by a German sniper. The shot nicked the roof ridge near the chimney stack. It also snapped Lina out of her own shock. She grabbed Edoardo's hand and together they ducked down to crawl across the terrace. They'd almost reached the door when another bullet ricocheted off the guttering. A near miss. But just as Edoardo grasped the latch on the trapdoor, it happened …

No one heard the sound of Martinella, the most famous bell in

Florence, strike ten. It was drowned out by the roar of the explosion. The block beneath them trembled, and from the sky rained down wood and rubble. Splinters of glass pricked her skin like tiny spears. All around, the noise of pandemonium flowed like a great cascade, until a few seconds later it settled, to be followed by an eerie silence.

'Oh, Edoardo,' she mouthed. 'What have they done?'

'The Ponte alle Grazie,' he muttered, as they finally made it to the door.

Flinging the hatch wide, Edoardo piled in, pulling Lina down with him, but her foot slipped and she fell, clutching frantically at the rungs. Edoardo tried to break her fall, grabbing her by the arm, but she pulled him down with her and they both ended up flat on their backs at the foot of the ladder, shocked and bruised, but grateful to be alive.

Slowly she sat up. 'Edoardo. I didn't know you were still in the city.' A moment before she had been tumbling down the ladder, now words tumbled from her mouth in a tangle of shock.

'None of that matters now,' he told her, easing himself to his feet. 'Donna told me you were here. I just needed to see you before I go.' A ribbon of red trickled down his forehead.

'Go? Go where?' she asked, standing once more. Seeing he was hurt, she lifted a finger to wipe away the blood, but Edoardo only took her hand and held it tight. A metal case lay on the landing. His eyes settled on it. She followed his gaze and when she saw it, she knew instantly what was inside. She'd seen one before. A transmitter.

'I'm going to the Ponte Vecchio,' he replied. 'Raven overheard a telephone call earlier today. Fischer assured Manzano the bridge was safe.'

Her body stiffened. 'If you go, then I'm coming with you.'

His eyes narrowed. 'No. No, you can't. It's not possible. It's dangerous.'

'I'm going to the bridge with or without you,' she told him.

Reading the resistance in his face, she took his hand. 'Whatever it is you're planning, it will be easier with the two of us. Tell me what's in that case.' Breaking free from his grasp she leaned over to snatch it. He tried to stay her hand, but she was too quick for him. The clasps flew up. But when she opened the lid, she frowned.

'What's this?' she asked, expecting a transmitter, but finding something quite different.

'A field telephone,' he replied, staring at the contents of the neatly packed case, 'and about two hundred metres of line.'

Lina studied the device for a moment, trying to figure out what Edoardo might be doing with it. Then a thought occurred to her, and her eyes widened as the possibility took root. 'Tell me you're not going to try and run this over the Ponte Vecchio, Edoardo.'

Her astuteness made him smile. 'Very clever,' he replied. 'With this beauty,' he said, patting the telephone, 'the partisans can liaise with the Allies on the other side of the river. And' – he tapped the breast pocket of his suit – 'my mission is official. I have papers from the Tuscan Liberation Committee.'

'Then that's settled,' she replied emphatically.

'What do you mean?'

'I can help you lay the line.'

'But that's madness,' he shot back.

'Maybe, but while we're at it I can check in on Fischer's office. If there's a chance of saving the portrait, I have to take it.'

He looked into her eyes. 'Yes. Yes, I know that nothing could stop you.' Slowly Edoardo nodded. 'At least Vasari's Corridor is still open,' he told her. The famous covered passage ran from the Palazzo Vecchio to the Palazzo Pitti and was the best way to get onto the bridge without being spotted by the Germans.

'Still open? Surely the Nazis wouldn't be that stupid?' she snapped.

'Wouldn't they?' He smirked. 'We've got a man inside, in the Palazzo Vecchio. He's told us it's clear.'

Taking a deep breath, she squared up to Edoardo and asked,

'So what are we waiting for?'

He opened his mouth to reason with her one more time, but seeing the determination on her face, thought better of it. Instead, he said, 'Do you remember when I told you you're just like your aunt?' he reminded her.

She replied on a smile. 'Stubborn as a mule. Yes, I remember, and that's why I'm not taking no for an answer.'

While Edoardo waited for her on the landing, Lina returned to the apartment to find everyone wide awake. Miss Giltrap was pacing the floor. In the candlelight Miss Harrowby and Mrs Clutterbuck were deep in conversation. Lady Felstein, largely oblivious to the noise, was the only one managing to rest on the chaise longue, while Agatha stalked up and down like an ill-sitting hen.

'Oh, there you are,' she said sternly when she saw Lina. 'Miss Giltrap said you were up on the roof. What on earth were you thinking? Look at you!' Taking out her handkerchief, she began to dust off some of the splinters and powder that had settled on Lina's clothes and hair. 'You could have been killed.' Then, quickly softening, she added with a shake of her head, 'Then where would we all be?'

'I'm sorry if I worried you,' replied Lina with a reassuring smile. But before she could break her next move to her aunt another huge explosion rattled the window frames. Hard on its heels came a mighty repercussion that tore through the room. Everything and everybody was thrown off balance. Miss Harrowby lurched forwards and fell on top of Mrs Clutterbuck on the sofa. Agatha gripped the side of an armchair, while Lady Felstein was rudely awoken when the chaise longue literally jumped into the air.

'Another bridge by the sound of it,' muttered Lina, even before the dust had settled. She began to pick herself up from the floor.

'Is everyone all right?' asked Edoardo, holding out a helping hand. In all the commotion, no one had noticed him walk into the room.

'Signor Bernini,' cried Agatha. She stopped brushing the dust from her shoulders in shock. 'What are you doing here?'

He gave a shallow bow. 'I wanted to see how everyone was bearing up,' he told her.

His presence lightened the mood and seemed to cheer everyone's spirits. Even poor Miss Harrowby, who'd been in tears once more, stifled her sobs.

'Do you have any news for us, Signor Bernini?' asked Mrs Clutterbuck, straightening her blouse.

Edoardo sighed heavily. 'The Germans are retreating, but we still have a long fight ahead,' he replied. 'The bridges are all mined.' His head shook mournfully at the tragedy of their impending destruction.

'Why are the Germans destroying them?' asked Miss Harrowby, fretfully.

'To slow down the Allies' advance and allow themselves to regroup in the north.'

Agatha shook her head. 'It really is heartbreaking.'

'It is,' agreed Lina. 'But we can't give up, Aunt. You of all people know that.'

'Not while there's a breath in my body,' replied Agatha defiantly.

'And that's why I must go,' said Lina. She hated to spring her departure on her aunt like this, but she had to go to carry on fighting.

'You're not leaving us?' croaked Lady Felstein, suddenly more alert.

'I'm afraid I must.' Lina looked pointedly at Edoardo. 'But I will be with Signor Bernini.'

'She will be safe with me now,' he assured, laying both hands squarely on Lina's shoulders. 'I will take good care of her.'

'It'll only be for a short time,' she added, trying to lessen the blow.

Agatha's lips quivered. 'Please don't take any unnecessary risks, my dear,' she told her niece, grasping both her hands and giving them a squeeze.

'I won't,' she replied, despite knowing what she was about to do was the riskiest thing she'd ever done. 'I love you,' she mouthed to Agatha, as, holding Edoardo's hand, she closed the apartment door. Somewhere, in the back of her mind, she failed to suppress the darkest of thoughts from snaking its way back in. She might never see Agatha again.

Chapter 53

Only the fires and the red arcs of tracer bullets lit up the night sky. The street itself was in total darkness, but the noise was all around, and the smoke was choking. German sentries were at most junctions, their rifles primed and ready to shoot on sight. In the early hours of the morning, Lina and Edoardo picked their way over shards of glass, edging along street by street, alley by alley. They were on their way to the Palazzo Vecchio – a route Lina had taken so many times, she could do it blindfolded. It was just as well. Knowing every nook and cranny was vital if they encountered a German patrol.

Some of the streets were blocked off with barbed wire. Others were only accessible via checkpoints. The shadows were their allies, doorways and stairwells their saviours. Overhead, airplanes crawled like giant insects across the sky and the screeching of shells became almost incessant. But sticking to the back streets, they had almost reached the Piazza della Repubblica, a few hundred metres north the Palazzo Vecchio, when the buildings surrounding them were rocked by another almighty explosion. Lina clamped her hands over her ears and hit the ground. Edoardo fell beside her.

'Let's hope that wasn't the Ponte Vecchio,' he murmured as he hauled her to her feet. But no sooner had he spoken than Lina noticed a pall of smoke rising from near the river in the bridge's direction.

'Oh, God!' she exclaimed. She started to bolt but Edoardo pulled her back.

'Where do you think you're going?'

'To see if the bridge is still standing, of course.'

'It's not worth the risk.'

'But if we plan to get to the Ponte Vecchio via the Vasari Corridor and they've blown it already, we'll be trapped.'

Edoardo shook his head. The plan, he told her as they began walking again, was simple. There was a trusted man on duty on the inside of the Palazzo Vecchio. He would give them access to the Vasari Corridor and from there they would cross over the Ponte Vecchio onto the south bank of the Arno where the Allies were waiting.

Minutes later they reached their destination. The Palazzo Vecchio loomed above them. For a while longer they watched from the shadows as two German soldiers paced up and down outside.

'Ready?' Edoardo asked.

She nodded.

'Fire! Fire!' he yelled, running through the main entrance and pointing back down the street. 'Quick!'

The soldiers reacted as planned, running away from the main entrance. With her heart racing, Lina dashed inside with Edoardo, praying the insider would stick to his word, so they could reach the Vasari Corridor without being challenged. As they rounded a corner a *Carabiniere* barred their way, but then smiled at Edoardo.

'Quickly,' he said, leading them unchallenged into the first courtyard. Normally, Lina would have marvelled at its beauty and its fountain and arches but there was no time to linger. They were headed straight up the monumental staircase to a balcony. Gasping for breath and constantly looking around them, they arrived at the door they were seeking.

'This is it,' said the contact. 'Good luck.'

Lina stared into the dark void ahead of them. Taking a deep breath, she went first. Edoardo, suitcase still in hand, followed. Gaining entrance was the easy part. Too easy. As Lina held a torch, he set down the metal carry case and brought out the field telephone.

'*Abracadabra*,' he said triumphantly as he inserted a crystal. Within moments the device sprang into life, dials lighting up and needles swivelling. 'Right, now to start laying the wire.' Returning to the suitcase, he pulled out the spool of cable. 'I'll lead and you make sure it's hidden,' he instructed.

With Lina's torch lighting the way, they set off. On either side of a narrow corridor, self-portraits of the great masters stared down at them until they rounded a corner. A staircase leading to the riverside passageway lay ahead. Less than two minutes later, they were on the covered walkway adjoining the palace to the top gallery of the Uffizi. Below them, the unsuspecting Nazis were training their guns along the river, unaware their defensive plans were being unravelled under their very noses.

The first window they came to let in the cold light of early dawn. Hugging the wall, Lina dared to glimpse out across the Arno. It was five o'clock in the morning, and she shivered as she looked out at the Ponte Santa Trinita. A sick feeling rose in her stomach when she realised the magnificent statues of the four seasons were bound by wires like sacrificial victims.

'Oh, Edoardo. They couldn't, could they?' she asked wanly, but no sooner had she spoken than the answer came in a tremendous roar. The explosion thrust her backwards across the passageway, rocking the building and sending a blizzard of plaster across the corridor. Edoardo, also knocked off balance, landed by her in a heap on the floor.

For a moment she lay still, too afraid to move, as she listened to the sound of massive stone blocks hurtling into the river, followed by the waves washing up the banks. Then gathering her courage, she crawled to the window and hauled herself up to peer over the sill.

'What can you see?' asked Edoardo, as she strained her eyes to look out into the half-light. She didn't answer. Couldn't answer. The shock was too great.

Edoardo edged his way over. 'Oh, God,' he muttered, surveying the smoking ruins below. What many called the most beautiful bridge in the world, designed by Michaelangelo himself, was fatally wounded. Only two piers remained steadfastly defiant in the water.

'She's not dead yet,' said Edoardo, putting his arm around her shoulder.

'You mean they'll carry on with the explosives until she's completely gone?' she asked, horrified.

Edoardo nodded, but then Lina turned to her right to catch an even more troubling sight. The shattered remains of the Ponte Santa Trinita were enough to make anyone weep, but the bank where the northern entrance to the Ponte Vecchio once lay was a devastated wasteland.

'My God, Edoardo. What have they done?' she cried.

A massive pile of rubble lay in front of it, making the bridge impossible to access. Small fires burned among the remains. Smoke wafted in gusts but now and again it cleared to reveal the devastation. Where medieval houses had once crammed the ancient streets like crooked teeth, there were jagged stumps. A mountain of splinters and stone pierced the dark sky. Hundreds of years of history simply vaporised. Their plans were up in smoke, too.

Lina's body slumped. 'The Cranach isn't there,' she muttered. 'Fischer would have taken it with him if he intended to do this.'

'You're right,' Edoardo agreed with a long sigh. 'And there's no way we can get to the other side anyway. We may as well turn back now. It's over.'

Lina stood at his shoulder now, surveying the seemingly hopeless scene, trying to salvage something from the wreckage. Staring out at the horror, she had to find a shard of hope. But just as she, too, thought they might have to double back, she called out, 'Look, Edoardo.' She was pointing to the dawn light splitting the sky over the river and beyond that a silhouette. 'The bridge!' she cried. 'The Ponte Vecchio is still standing.' She grasped him by both arms. 'We can still do this.'

Even though the area at the south bank had been completely ravaged too, the central spans remained mainly intact. Edoardo squinted into the gloom, then, after a moment he hugged her tightly and said, 'Yes. Yes, we can.'

Broken glass crunched underfoot, and plaster fell from the ceiling, as they made their way along the corridor past a door smaller than the others. They'd reached the section running parallel along the river and at right angles to the Ponte Vecchio. Lina pictured the series of high arches along the river beneath them. Inside, the beams supporting the structure were badly damaged, but what about outside? What if the arches were mined? If that was the case, the demolition charges hadn't yet been fired. The damage they'd seen was caused by the earlier explosions, but all it would take was for them to be spotted at a window and the Nazis could detonate their mines. The whole bridge could go sky-high.

They edged forwards where the windows were blown out, knowing rifles would react to any shadows. Dropping to their knees, they wrapped strips of cloth from the shredded drapes around their hands to protect them from the broken glass scattered over the floor and started to crawl.

The sound of battle continued to rage all around. German parachutist machine-gunners and mortar crews had their sights trained on anything and anyone that moved, opening fire with no questions asked. Edoardo knew even the debris blocking either side of the bridge could be mined. They were crawling into a death trap. Every metre they covered could be their last.

They made it to the stretch of the corridor bordering the river and, finding cover, stood upright. Now, ahead of them lay the bridge itself. Although from afar most of its buildings had appeared relatively unscathed, up close it was a different matter. Tons of masonry had been launched into the air by the nearby explosions at both ends. Some of it had landed on the bridge itself, shearing through pediments, exposing wooden planks, and weakening the supporting beams which didn't look as though they'd hold out much longer. Right then, the most immediate problem was the gap between the planks directly in their path. It was only about a metre wide, but the drop below was more than thirty. Lina looked down to see the churned-up river, swollen by mud and debris, swirling beneath them.

'This isn't going to be easy,' said Edoardo, clasping her hand, as, on the count of three, they jumped across the gap. But at least the looted shops and buildings on either side, while badly damaged, offered some protection from artillery fire. Keeping her head low and her eyes down, Lina tiptoed forwards behind him. Her stomach was pitching, but it was too late to turn back. Yet despite knowing they were past the point of no return, something made Lina stop in her tracks as she trod across the spans. They were standing by a plaque on the wall proclaiming they'd reached the headquarters of the *Kunstschutz*. She needed to satisfy herself the portrait wasn't inside Fischer's office.

'Can we just check, Edoardo? To make sure.'

A smile grazed his lips. 'I couldn't stop you if I wanted to.'

The Nazis had left in a hurry. The door at the main entrance was ajar, but as soon as she stepped forwards, Lina baulked. 'What's wrong?' whispered Edoardo, whipping round when he felt her recoil. He followed her horrified gaze.

'Blood,' she replied, eyes wide at a bright red footprint on the front steps.

Without another word, he drew his pistol from its holster,

cocked it and peered into the entrance. No one in the hallway, but the occupants had left a trail in their wake. Dislodged drawers and discarded papers were strewn across the floor. Cautiously, they crept along the corridor, when something else caught Lina's eye. More bloody footprints. Edoardo followed her gaze to a closed door where the sign on it told them it was Fischer's office. He nodded a warning as, pistol at the ready, he kicked the door. It burst open, revealing abandoned filing cabinets and two upturned chairs by a desk. Scanning the room quickly, he strode inside and returned his gun into its holster.

'It's safe,' he called to Lina, a little way behind. But just as she stepped inside, a shot cracked the air. Edoardo dived for cover, and she dropped to her knees as the bullet hit the far wall. It was only when Lina saw who'd fired the gun, she screamed. Propped against the wall in the corner, his dark green fascist tunic caked in blood and his slack face an ashen grey, was the last person either of them wanted to see. And the Beretta he held in his shaky hand was pointed at her.

'Put the gun down, or the she-wolf gets it!' ordered a familiar voice.

'Manzano,' muttered Edoardo. 'What the hell?'

'Hands up!' he called. 'Up, where I can see them!'

Edoardo obeyed, raising both arms, but his unblinking eyes were fixed on the dark red stain on the podesta's uniform. 'What are you doing here?'

'I could ask you the same, Bernini,' replied the podesta, his face creasing in pain as he spoke.

'You and your German friend Fischer forgot to block off the Vasari Corridor,' retorted Lina, above another loud explosion that rattled the office windows.

Manzano's shoulders twitched at the mention of the colonel's name. 'He's no friend of mine,' he hissed.

'Really?' said Lina, her hands still raised in surrender.

Manzano wheezed and touched his wounded shoulder. 'This is

319

what betrayal looks like,' he came back. 'Fischer double-crossed me.' But the effort of speaking sent a shower of blood spurting from his mouth.

Lina's lips puckered at the sight of the blood. 'You need help.'

'Yes,' Edoardo agreed. 'Tell us where the Cranach is, and we can get you out of here.'

Whipping round to look at him, Lina glimpsed the old Edoardo. He remained a dealer at heart. Despite Manzano's gun, he still thought he could bargain his way out of the situation and get off the bridge alive.

The podesta's rubbery features pulled taut into a grimace. 'I don't want medical help, and I don't want the Cranach,' he growled.

'But you know where it is,' said Lina, taking a step closer.

In reply the podesta only jabbed the gun in the air again. 'The Nazi took it and put a bullet through my shoulder.'

Edoardo's gaze slid towards Lina. 'Fischer? Where did he take it?'

Manzano's Beretta switched to him. 'Do you think I'd tell you where the portrait is?' he asked, half mocking. 'Although there is something I could tell you.'

'There's nothing I want to hear from you, apart from where the painting is,' sneered Edoardo.

Manzano smirked. 'Really? Not even what happened to your father.'

At the mention of Henrico, a fire suddenly burst into flame behind Edoardo's eyes. 'My father? What are you saying?' Ignoring the Beretta, Edoardo lunged towards the podesta and swooped on the gun, wrestling it from his hand. Manzano put up little resistance. His face convulsed as he gasped for breath and another trickle of sweat ran down his cheek.

'I should put you out of your misery now,' yelled Edoardo, pointing his own weapon at him.

Lina held him back. 'Let him speak,' she urged, snatching the discarded Beretta.

Manzano flinched as he took a breath. 'Or maybe you don't want to know how your father died?' he taunted.

Edoardo thrust the gun to his temple. 'All right. Tell me. Tell me now or I'll blow your brains out!'

The podesta shifted his weight, trying to make himself more comfortable. 'I had a nice little racket going,' he began. 'Small pieces from the galleries. Nothing to attract attention. That's how I got away with it for so long. Bernini was my art adviser, but thanks to Signora Bianchi, I found out he had a conscience.' His face twitched in a sneer.

'Signora Bianchi,' yelled Edoardo. 'What did she have to do with it?'

Manzano's lips pouted. 'It must hurt to know your loyal house-keeper was in my pay for all those years.'

Edoardo's face erupted in fury but once again, Lina managed to thrust herself between the two men before he could attack. 'Let him speak!' she ordered. Turning to Manzano, she said, 'Go on.'

The podesta smirked and continued. 'When he found out I was helping myself to the paintings and other trinkets, he was shocked, and planned to tell Mussolini.' He sniffed. 'Not that Il Duce would have minded my little sideline, but it would have caused me problems locally, you understand. So, I decided it was best to dispense with his services. For good.'

Edoardo shook his head. 'You framed him for the thefts, then had him killed in jail.' He lurched towards Manzano again.

The jolting set the podesta coughing. 'He was … he was a threat, even behind bars. Wha … What else c … could I have done?'

But Edoardo wasn't listening. Enraged, he flew at his tormentor. Again, Lina stopped him. 'No, Edoardo!' she cried. 'Leave him. Don't waste time. He's not going anywhere soon.' Then turning to the podesta she told him, 'The game is over, Manzano. And you have lost.'

'Wait,' said Edoardo, more calmly. He'd come to read the ugly fiend like a book. 'If you don't want the Cranach, what do you want?'

Manzano flinched again and lifted his palm to press against the bullet wound. His lips twisted and as he drew breath to speak, Lina noticed something different about him. His expression had changed, as if the helplessness of his own situation had only just dawned on him. 'You're right,' he gulped after a moment, 'I am dying, I know, but maybe you could grant me one final wish.'

Lina swapped a glance with Edoardo. Perhaps he didn't even know where Fischer had taken it. She tried to hide the suspicion in her voice when she asked, 'And then you'll tell us where the portrait is?'

'I will if I can have one final cigar.'

Edoardo blurted out a laugh. 'What?'

'It could be our only chance,' Lina reminded him. She nodded to the podesta.

With his uninjured arm, Manzano reached up to pat the breast pocket of his uniform jacket. The cigar was just out of his reach. 'In here,' he said.

Still pointing the pistol at him, Edoardo fished out the cigar with his other hand.

Manzano nodded. 'A light?'

Flicking his own lighter into life, Edoardo held the flame to the stub and lit the cigar.

Manzano smiled as he took a puff.

'I don't get it,' said Lina watching the self-satisfied expression on the podesta's face.

Ignoring her, Manzano looked at Edoardo. 'Why don't you join me in a cigarette?' he asked.

'You know the game is over, you said so yourself,' Edoardo reminded him, glancing at Lina. 'So why this act?'

Another long puff on the cigar. 'Oh, this isn't an act,' he smirked.

His lingering look told Lina he was up to something. 'He's playing for time,' she blurted. 'He's stalling.' The question was why.

'You're not just a pretty face, are you?' said Manzano, his gaze playing on her. 'You're right, she-wolf. I am truly savouring this moment before I tell you what is about to happen.'

'What do you mean?' she asked warily.

'I am looking forward to seeing the look on both your faces,' Manzano replied, his gaze switching from Edoardo to Lina before settling on the safe.

They both followed his gaze and Lina jumped up. The safe door was open. Setting down the Beretta on the desk, she strode towards it and placed her hand inside. It was empty, so, like a child trying to fathom a magician's trick, she tapped the sides. For a second, she'd dared to think this was all a charade. The portrait had remained there all the time. But no. 'There's nothing there,' she said.

Another smirk from the podesta. 'When Fischer abandoned me to die, he left me with a much bigger prize than the painting.'

Edoardo cocked his pistol. 'What's that?' He was fast losing patience.

'He's left me with this bridge. The most famous bridge in the world.'

'What are you talking about?' asked Lina, wafting a puff of smoke away from her face.

Manzano licked his lips and trained his bloodshot eyes on Edoardo. 'You suspected I wanted something,' he said. 'You were right. I want revenge.'

'Revenge?' repeated Lina.

Manzano nodded weakly. 'They say it's a dish best served cold, and I've been lying here for the last twelve hours dreaming of how it will be delivered to Fischer.'

'You want revenge on Fischer. How?' she asked.

The podesta coughed out a laugh, more blood trickling from between his lips. 'He told me he had express orders from Adolf Hitler himself not to blow up this bridge. He said it was the safest place in the city.'

'That's why he was storing the portrait here,' Lina cut in.

'Correct. But then it seems he decided to go back on one of our arrangements. So, I decided I would do the same.'

'What do you mean?' snarled Edoardo.

'I mean the Ponte Santa Trinita will not be the last bridge to be blown today.'

It was as if Manzano had just lobbed a hand grenade into the room. He planned to blow up the Ponte Vecchio.

'What?' Edoardo screamed. 'You're mad! Why would you do that?' He raised his arm, intent on striking Manzano across the face.

'Wait!' Lina cried. A thought had suddenly dropped into her head. 'If you blow up this bridge, it'll look as if Fischer has directly countermanded Hitler's orders.'

Manzano gave a self-satisfied nod. 'Precisely. A very public crime, punishable by a very public death. He will be disgraced forever.' He raised his head, fixing his piggy eyes into the distance as if picturing the Nazi's suffering.

'You can't. You wouldn't,' she muttered in disbelief.

The podesta suddenly turned his head to face them both. 'I can and I have.' Broadening his mouth in a bloody grin, he said, 'Just before they disabled the telephone lines to High Command, I called through and gave them this. It was left in the safe. Fischer thought he had no need of it.' Manzano broke into a low laugh as he reached for a sheet of paper and waved it in front of his face. Lina snatched at it and a look of sheer horror swept over her as she read it.

'The passcode,' she gasped. 'The passcode to detonate this bridge!'

'What?' screamed Edoardo, snatching it back and scanning it. 'No. No.' His face contorted in disbelief as he saw Manzano shrug. This time Lina couldn't stop him delivering a stinging blow across the podesta's face. As he cried out like a wounded animal, she managed to pull Edoardo away.

'We don't have time for this,' she yelled. She took a deep breath, trying to think straight and squared up to Manzano. 'When is the bridge due to detonate?'

More beads of sweat dotted the podesta's brow. He glanced at the clock on the opposite wall. Her eyes followed his. 'At five o'clock.'

'Seven minutes!' she gasped, panic flooding her voice.

Edoardo aimed a glare at Manzano knowing he'd planned all along to stall them. 'You bastard!' he cried again before offering Lina his hand. 'Let's get out of here!'

'But what about him?' she cried, glancing at the bloodied hulk propped up against the wall.

Edoardo tugged at her arm. 'If he's bluffing, the Allies will find him soon enough,' he replied, pulling her towards him.

'And if he's not?'

He shook his head in exasperation. 'If he's not we still have a chance to get this laid before the bridge blows,' he said, replacing his pistol in its holster and picking up the cable spool. 'Part of it could still survive, even if we don't.'

The reality of his words cut deep, but she knew them to be true. They were facing death within the next few minutes, but at least they'd face it together.

'Yes,' she agreed, swallowing down her fear and taking his outstretched hand. 'We can still do this.'

A fiery sun was peering over the battle-worn Tuscan hills, offering Colonel Alexander Fischer as good a view of the Ponte Vecchio as any. The control room was set up in the Palazzo Vecchio on the north bank, and despite the constant shelling and subsequent fires, the Arno remained in sight. Powerful binoculars were, of course, essential. He could see both ends of the bridge were ravaged, and he'd been assured the debris was criss-crossed with mines. Totally impassable. He'd made certain of that. He was also gladdened to see German guns on the heights and mortars on the riverbanks. Working with the Italian fascists meant his men had access to local knowledge and this gave him complete control. The troublesome partisans were being swatted like flies and now that all the bridges were gone – well, almost all – his confidence grew. Crossing the Arno would be impossible for the British forces, or anyone else for that matter. Despite its setbacks in the south, Germany would still triumph.

As for Manzano, the lecherous fool deserved that bullet. And now the portrait of the young girl would join the other two Cranachs he had in his possession. She was the jewel in the crown – a beacon of hope and light for the new Reich that would soon be rising out of the ashes of Florence, and every other European city that lay vanquished under the Nazi jackboot.

The thought stirred him, and he took one more nostalgic look through his binoculars, seeking out the windows of his former office on the Ponte Vecchio. As he did, he recalled the deliciously stupefied look on Podesta Manzano's face as a bullet sliced through his body at almost point-blank range. He scanned the windows, then doubled back to where he thought he'd seen something move inside. *Strange*, he mused. Many of the panes were smashed when the Ponte Santa Trinita was blown sky-high. Perhaps a pigeon had flown in. He kept his sights on the window for the next few seconds. A pigeon. It must have been.

Behind him, a bank of telephones was red hot, and coloured counters were being shunted across a map of the city spread out on a large marble table. His men were pulling back, but very slowly. An organised retreat.

'All quiet on the bridge?' came a voice behind him. It was an old colleague, seconded in for the withdrawal. Fischer loathed him but forced an acknowledgement.

'If you call this quiet,' he quipped, artillery fire still booming in the background. He rarely smiled but judged this as good a time as any.

'May I?' The officer nodded at the binoculars. Fischer handed them over. 'Didn't you have your headquarters on the Ponte

Vecchio?' he asked scanning the bridge.

'I did.'

The officer paused, lowering the lens. 'Pity it has to go.'

Fischer arched a quizzical brow. 'What do you mean? The Führer has given direct orders for it to remain.'

'That's what I thought, but look.' He handed him back the binoculars. 'There are men down there, getting ready to detonate.' He pointed at the bank by the bridge, then at the sky. 'Boom!'

'I can assure you the Ponte Vecchio is not to be blown up,' Fischer insisted. 'Why else do you think it's so heavily defended?'

'Five o'clock,' said the officer. 'That's what I heard.'

'On whose orders?' challenged Fischer, starting to doubt his own sanity.

'Yours, I assume.'

The colonel's normally smooth feathers were starting to ruffle. Fischer snatched back his binoculars and trained them on the bank by the northern end of the bridge. There were men down there, all right. Italians taking cover from Allied fire by an armoured truck. And what were those on the bank? Surely not detonators?

He stalked over to the telephonists, mainly women, seated in front of a wall of wires and flashing lights. Standing by them, he signalled everyone to take off their headphones and listen.

'Did anyone here receive an order from 8375?' he cried. It was the number of the line on the Ponte Vecchio.

Heads were quickly shaken, but then one hand was raised. A young Italian army telephonist dared to answer. 'I took the call,' she replied. 'It was from His Excellency, Podesta Manzano. The password was correct, so I handed it on.'

Fischer's eyes snapped open then narrowed as he cursed through his teeth. He should've finished the job himself. Put a bullet through Manzano's thick skull, not left him to die a slow death while plotting his revenge. He hadn't credited him with the wit to do such a thing. Technically, the podesta did not have the authority to make such an order, but the Italians were lax about following procedures. And now he had to clear up their mess, otherwise he, Colonel Alexander Fischer, could find himself facing a firing squad.

Stalking to the window Fischer snatched at his abandoned binoculars once more. Turning to address the whole room, he called so everyone could hear, 'Which unit is that?'

'Technical troops,' replied a nervous corporal.

The colonel turned a pale shade of grey. 'Get a rider down there immediately,' he ordered. 'They are not to blow the bridge, you hear. On no account must the Ponte Vecchio be destroyed.' Then mumbling to himself he added, 'On pain of my death.'

Chapter 54

Leaving Manzano moaning in the corner, Lina and Edoardo, clutching the spool with the remaining cable, fled the office. They were on the bridge once more. The crack of mortar shells and gunfire continued. A bullet whistled past Edoardo's head. 'Down. Get down,' he cried, pulling Lina into an alcove, as German snipers resumed tracking their every movement from the north bank.

Five seconds passed. Then five more. Only a few metres of the bridge remained. The southern end had already been blown to smithereens, and any second now there'd be another explosion. A momentous, catastrophic one. Edoardo nodded at her to get ready to run for it. But as Lina glanced back for a final check on the wire, a bloody spectre appeared, staggering towards them. With one hand clutching the Beretta Lina had mistakenly left on the desk and the other grabbing at anything he could, Manzano zig-zagged from one side of the bridge to the other. As soon as he caught sight of them he stopped. Then, aiming his gun, he gathered his last breaths and yelled.

'Traitors! Traitors!'

Instinctively Lina ducked as soon as the first shot sounded, but still Manzano lurched closer, blood gushing from his wound. Edoardo fired back, but the podesta wove to the side and the bullet missed. Whether it was his own pain, or his intention to kill, that blinded him to what lay immediately in front of him, they would never know. Whatever it was, the crazed Italian didn't see the gaping hole where the walkway was damaged. One moment Podesta Cesari Manzano was about to shoot his quarry at almost point-blank range, the next he lost his footing and was plunging through the skeleton planks into the roiling depths of the River Arno below.

As the seconds ticked away, they made it to the edge of the bridge. Only a minute or two remained before the bomb was due to explode.

'Look!' cried Lina, pointing to a group of soldiers on the northern side of the bank. It certainly looked like Manzano's dying wish would be carried out. The Ponte Vecchio was about to be blown sky-high, and with it, Colonel Fischer's reputation and life.

Edoardo sidled his way to the jagged edge of the bridge, scoping the piles of rubble below. The Germans had made sure anyone insane enough to venture on it would most likely be blown up. But smoke from the surrounding fires hampered the snipers' view. It kept wafting across their positions. They might just be in with a chance.

'Quick,' he said. With no rope, Edoardo secured a length of the telephone cable around one of the few remaining stanchions, then dropped the spool to the debris beneath. He was going to abseil down to the bottom.

'Have you ever done anything like this before?' he asked her, as Lina watched him tighten the cable. She couldn't quite believe he expected her to follow.

She gulped down her fear. 'Only in gym lessons,' she replied, remembering clambering up and down the high ropes. For once her English boarding school education would come in handy, she told herself.

'I'll go first,' said Edoardo. With one final tug to make sure all was secure, he let the cable take his full weight. But just as he did a mortar exploded nearby, rocking the bridge and blasting Lina off her feet. Lying flat on her stomach she watched in horror as the windows and doors of the SS headquarters were hurled onto the bridge, spraying splinters and glass for metres around. But the bridge itself remained intact.

As soon as the dust settled, she whipped round, then scrambled to the ledge where, just a few seconds earlier, she'd seen Edoardo about to launch himself off the pier. The cable remained but Edoardo wasn't secured to it. On her hands and knees, she peered over the jagged edge of the bridge, scouring the rubble underneath – a pile of sharp stones and twisted metal that could cut as easily as knives. Then she spotted him, about thirty feet below, blown off by the force of the explosion and lying face down, not moving. She had to get to him.

Catching hold of the cable, she inhaled deeply then surrendered. Ignoring her burning palms, she hurtled down hand over fist until, seconds later, she felt jagged stones under her feet. Turning quickly, before lifting up the cable spool, she reminded herself that the debris was riddled with dozens of primed mines and booby traps. Still, keeping low, she edged towards Edoardo, calling out to him. But the cracks of artillery shells seemed louder at ground level and her voice was lost in the thunder of battle. As soon as she reached him, she turned him over, dreading what she might find. There was a deep cut on his forehead, but then, as she held him in her arms, his eyelids flickered into life.

'Am I dead?' he asked, a smile overriding his pain.

Relieved, she kissed him. Even when he was in shock and injured, just one look from him could still bring a smile to her own face. 'No,' she told him, as he levered himself to his feet. 'You are very much alive. And so am I. The bridge didn't blow. It's still standing, and we still have work to do.' She looked at the spool. Most of the line was laid, but most wasn't good enough. It was all or nothing.

Only twenty metres now lay between them and the piazza beyond. But it was by far the most dangerous stretch. Smoke from the nearby fires kept billowing in their direction and screening them from their German watchers. They were still in with a chance.

'I love you,' said Edoardo, hooking his arm around her neck. His ankle was hurt, and she helped take the weight off it.

'I love you, too,' she replied, even though inside her fear reached a new crescendo at the prospect of them both hobbling through a minefield.

Fate would decide. If they were going to die, so be it. There was no point being cautious now. And at least if they went, they'd go together. Still spooling the cable, Lina led Edoardo across the shortest route over the ruins, negotiating twisted beams, mangled metal, and great slabs of serrated stone, all the while trailing the telephone line behind them, until they were stopped in their tracks.

'*Halt!*' commanded a voice.

The game was up. The end of the road. The Germans had caught them. They'd got so close to reaching their goal. With eyes blurry and still stinging from smoke, Lina glanced at Edoardo, bleeding and exhausted. They couldn't make a run for it.

'It's over, isn't it?' she muttered, her heart sinking as she spoke. Yet, despite the automatic rifles aimed at them, when she glanced at Edoardo's face again she realised he was grinning.

'What is it? Why are you smiling?' she asked, the adrenaline still pumping through her. But then she squinted at the soldiers' uniforms ahead of them, and she understood why Edoardo suddenly looked more relaxed. The voice wasn't a German's after all. It belonged to a British officer.

Wearing a khaki uniform and peaked cap, he approached and demanded to see Edoardo's papers. 'Well, well,' he said, examining them, then returning them with a salute. 'Welcome to free Florence, Lieutenant Bernini.'

Chapter 55

'You're in the clear,' said a cut-glass English voice. They were waiting in a commandeered hotel away from the riverbank for Edoardo's credentials to be verified by the commander of a partisan brigade on the south bank. Lina looked up to see an officer with a waxed moustache beaming down on them. 'You were lucky the Ponte Vecchio didn't blow. We were all expecting it. Jerry was down there, but then they were suddenly withdrawn. Bit of a mystery that!' He scratched his neck. 'Anyway, I expect you'd like a wash and something to eat.'

Lina knew they both felt as though they'd taken on the might of the German army, not to mention Manzano, single-handedly. She'd no idea if the podesta had been bluffing or if something had gone wrong for the Nazis. Nor did she care. In torn clothes, and covered in dust and blood, she and Edoardo looked like vagabonds and felt exhausted. But she couldn't rest until she knew Agatha and the others were safe.

'There are four elderly English women and an American trapped in an apartment on the other side. They need help,' she told the officer.

He flinched as a gun fired nearby, then gave an apologetic shrug. 'There are several thousand Florentines trapped on the other side, miss,' he said. 'But we're doing our best.'

All Lina could do was wait until the Allies arrived in force to beat back the remaining Germans. Only then would it be safe to free Agatha and the others. Until that happened, she sat with Edoardo in the hotel occupied by a British advance party. Drinking stewed tea and eating some sort of potted meat, she couldn't quite believe only three hours before she'd been dangling from a cable above a German minefield.

'What happens now?' she asked.

Edoardo smiled. 'What happens now?' he repeated. He'd immediately managed to get a message out to his commanding officer, and the field telephones had been connected. The partisans on the north bank of the Arno were now in touch with the British. The telephone line was vital for communications and meant the Allies could advance even quicker and the Germans leave even sooner. 'They tell me the line is already red hot. The Allies are swapping intelligence and setting up meetings with partisan leaders. We did it.' He leaned forwards, took her hand and kissed it.

'Yes, somehow it seems we did,' she replied, still in a state of shock.

As he leaned back in his upholstered chair in the comparatively luxurious surroundings of the hotel, Lina studied Edoardo. His shirt was dusty and ripped, his face cut and his ankle bandaged, but they'd survived and Manzano was dead. They'd managed to lay a telephone line between the resistance and the Allies, but the fate of the Cranach was still unknown and, more importantly, that of Agatha and the ladies also lay in the balance. Their work was by no means finished.

Still feeling on edge, she had just poured herself a cup of tea to ease her own nerves when she noticed him pull a face. He turned to her then. 'Do you know what I'm thinking?' he asked her.

She let out a little laugh. 'That English tea is terrible?'

He shook his head. 'I'm thinking that your aunt and the other English ladies will be dreaming of just such a cup right now.'

334

She thought of them too, prisoners in the small, airless apartment, fearful for their lives. Tears welled up in her eyes. She set down her tea. 'I can't just sit here, Edoardo, while they suffer,' she told him, shaking her head. 'There must be something we can do to help them.'

They spent the night in a hotel room far enough away from the Arno to be out of enemy reach. The shutters had to remain closed, but there was a double bed. They exchanged looks but said nothing. Lina sat on the edge and slowly took off her shoes. Edoardo, his back to hers, shrugged off his boots, then together, as if they were performing a dance, they lay down in silence, turned to face each other and drew up their legs onto the counterpane in perfect time. Edoardo slipped his arm under Lina's head, so it rested in the crook of his arm. Outside, the war still raged, but despite the shells and the bullets, Lina could hear Edoardo's heartbeat as she rested her head on his chest. Tenderly he stroked her hair.

'I will treasure tonight forever,' he said gently, shifting his body and lowering his head to kiss her so lovingly she thought her heart might break.

Somehow, they managed to grab a few hours' sleep and awoke to fingers of light poking into the room. Edoardo kissed her on the head and rose to walk to the window. 'Let's see what view we have,' he remarked, flinging wide the shutters. Lina, lying naked between cotton sheets, waited for his verdict, but instead of describing what he saw, he remained silent.

'Edoardo?' she called, frowning. Wrapping a towel around her, she slipped out of bed to join him at the window. Shock descended like a veil. The hotel was on the brow of a hill above the city, and while she'd been preparing to see terrible damage, what she actually saw was carnage. A grey haze of smoke merged into the billowing thunder clouds bubbling overhead. They blocked out the sun, casting a suffocating fog over the devastating scene.

The Arno was a gaping, festering wound, encrusted with rubble, mortar and great slabs of stone on either side. Fires still burned. The air above it was gritty and acrid and the few remaining buildings lining its banks were teetering on the brink of collapse. Her hands flew to her mouth to stifle a groan of pain.

Edoardo placed an arm around her as she took in the devastation. So many homes and livelihoods had disappeared under the rubble, but it was the unseen cost that lay beneath the rafters and stones that tore at both their hearts. Hundreds of innocent people lay buried beneath.

After a moment's reflection Edoardo said, 'I once told Manzano that no painting was worth dying for.'

'You did?' asked Lina.

He nodded. 'I did, but I was wrong.'

She turned to him. 'Why have you changed your mind?'

He remained fixed on the devastation. 'Art is the measure of a civilisation. We're fighting for our culture and our way of life.'

His words made her body tingle. Their way of thinking had finally fused. Their experiences had changed them both. Art was no longer a commodity for Edoardo, but something he felt, deep inside.

She turned back. 'When the war's over, people will somehow rebuild their lives,' she told him. 'They always do, but if you destroy their achievements, what they've created over the past centuries, then it's as if they never really existed.' She felt his warm skin against hers then. 'That's why the portrait was so important to me. Her eyes. Her expression. She was so determined. So defiant against all the odds.' She lifted her gaze.

'You mean like you?' said Edoardo, bending to kiss her once more.

'Yes. I suppose like me.' Her eyes followed the line of the river to a pall of smoke above the rubble by the Ponte Vecchio and painful thoughts of the young woman forced themselves in. 'I fear she's lost forever,' she whispered, her chest juddering as she spoke.

'At least the bridge is still standing,' he said, his arms still around her. It rose as a beacon of hope amid the ruins.

'Yes, it is,' she agreed. But then she thought of Agatha and the ladies once more.

'They're down there too, Edoardo,' she whispered as tears stung her eyes. 'We have to help them.'

They dressed in silence and went downstairs. Their meagre rations were eaten in the hotel dining room, alongside military personnel, mainly from the bomb disposal team. They'd almost finished when the officer they'd met the day before interrupted them.

Edoardo dabbed the corners of his mouth with a napkin and rose to salute him. 'Major.'

'Bernini,' came the reply. Lina had to settle for a perfunctory nod. 'Got someone waiting who wants to meet you. American, from some division or other that looks after art.'

The major turned towards a man, in his late forties perhaps, and wearing glasses. He was waiting by the dining-room door.

Edoardo looked puzzled. 'I'd like to meet him, too,' he replied.

The major beckoned, and the man stepped forwards. 'This is Lieutenant Commander Stout,' he said. Lina recognised the name and shot to her feet. 'Not George Stout from Harvard?' she gasped, shaking the outstretched hand.

The crow's feet around the American's eyes crinkled in a smile. 'Yes. Yes. They call me a Monuments Man,' he replied. 'Or a Venus Fixer. Take your pick.'

Lina beamed. 'It is an honour to meet you, Commander Stout. I'm Angelina Leone, a friend of Professor Loggi.'

'Loggi! Of course. So, you must be Dr Leone. The Cranach expert.'

'That's right,' she replied. 'And Signor Bernini here is a dealer in Renaissance art.'

Stout arched a brow. 'Impressive,' he replied. 'We could certainly do with your help sorting out the god-awful mess we've been left.'

Lina swapped looks with Edoardo. 'We'd be happy to help, sir,' she replied.

The American nodded. 'Tell me, how is dear Giuseppe?'

She managed a smile, but in reality she had no idea how Professor Loggi, or Agatha or any of the other ladies had fared overnight. 'He's still in the north of the city, as far as I know,' she replied.

'You'll be able to see him once we've shown the Germans who's boss,' quipped the major, adding, 'but until then, it's all a little bit lairy.' Sounding like an overgrown schoolboy, he slapped on his officer's cap and gave the peak a tug. 'We move out within the hour.'

They tagged on to the small advance party on the southern approach. The Florentines, corralled there for days, lined the route. With arms eager to touch their liberators, they cried '*Benvenuti! Viva Italia!*' at the tops of their voices. Flowers were thrown at the troops. A sudden cheer rose above all others when a raggle-taggle band of men marched by.

'*I partigiani!*' cried Edoardo, picking up Lina and whisking her around. 'The partisans have made it over from the north bank!' he cried.

'You did it!' said Lina, planting a kiss on his cheek.

'We did it!' he told her, returning the kiss on her lips.

But their rejoicing didn't last long. It was cut short by the crack of gunfire which sent the crowds scattering like a startled flock of pigeons.

'Snipers!' Stout called from the truck in front, as they all scrambled to abandon their vehicles. Lina and Edoardo took shelter from the bullets raining down on the road, while the partisans and the advance party dealt with the gunmen.

Dashing into the Pitti Palace, they were met by another crowd. The complex was now home to hundreds of displaced families who'd left their homes with only what they could carry. Women had set up stoves, but there was no fresh water, and the stench of sweat and filth made Lina want to retch. The wounded were being tended in a makeshift hospital in the corner and crying babies and barking dogs added to the pandemonium. But as soon as word spread that more Allies were on their way, the atmosphere changed, and cheers soon drowned out screams and moans.

But while the Germans may have been in retreat, they weren't leaving without a fight.

'We have to get to the north bank,' said Lina, as they stood looking out on to the Arno. By now, the threatened rain was falling hard, and the current was gathering speed. The Ponte Vecchio remained standing but was virtually inaccessible. The only other crossing point was at the demolished Ponte alle Grazie. Broken stumps protruded from the water like felled trees. A few souls were brave enough to try and ford the river as it flowed around them, but the crossing was perilous. One false step, one slip, would mean almost certain drowning. But Lina knew Agatha and the ladies would be in desperate need of help.

They managed to make it to the bank where a few desperate people were lining up to cross.

'I have to do this,' she told Edoardo, staring at the seething river below.

'I know,' he replied, a borrowed rope slung over his arm. 'Ready?' he asked Edoardo, securing the length round his waist.

'Ready,' she replied.

As airplanes flew overhead, as bullets cracked, as water raged all around, Lina kept looking straight ahead. Each step taken over the debris was a journey. Each metre covered a mountain climbed. The soles of her feet slipped as the rain fell faster and the wind got up, threatening to knock her off balance. They were roped together with Edoardo leading the way, but they were only about halfway over when a scream ripped through the air. A woman carrying a bundle lost her footing and fell. Everyone else on the crossing stopped dead. A man tried to grab her, but she was out of reach. The current was too quick and carried her down river, watched by scores of helpless witnesses.

Edoardo turned to take Lina's quivering hand. 'Almost there,' he told her. She steadied herself and filled her lungs before setting one foot in front of the other again. 'Yes, almost,' she whispered, knowing that they may as well have been a million kilometres from arrival.

They made it to the other side just as the rain stopped. Eager hands on the north bank were there to pull them to safety. But alongside the touching reunions, gunshots still fired. Dodging another burst of Nazi bullets, they made it to the Piazza della Signoria, then onwards to the via degli Strozzi. Miss Giltrap's apartment lay two blocks beyond. As they scurried from corner to corner, dodging rooftop snipers, dread swelled inside Lina. And when she finally turned the corner and spied bullet holes in the apartment wall, she took it as an ominous sign. Running up the stairs to the first floor she tried the door. It was locked. She called out, but silence stretched before her. Edoardo was just about to break in when a chink appeared.

'Mrs Clutterbuck!' cried Lina. 'Thank God!'

'Well, don't just stand there,' commanded Agatha, as the door was flung open. 'Come in! Come in! Or the Germans will shoot at you.'

Grabbing Edoardo by the hand Lina dashed inside.

'You made it!' cried Miss Giltrap, slapping Lina on the back.

'It's so wonderful to see you all,' she replied, hugging Agatha first.

'Good to have you back,' exclaimed Mrs Clutterbuck as she waited for a hug.

'I'm so glad, my dear,' said Agatha, 'And just in the nick of time.'

'What do you mean?' asked Lina with a frown. 'What's happened?'

Following Agatha's strained gaze to the chaise longue, she saw Lady Felstein lying motionless, with a tearful Miss Harrowby at her side, sponging her forehead with vinegar. It seemed the heat and lack of water had badly affected her. The women were taking it in turns to sit with her, but everyone was afraid she might slip into unconsciousness and never wake up if she didn't get help soon.

Chapter 56

'She's fading fast. She needs a doctor,' said Lina, feeling Lady Felstein's weak pulse.

'That's easier said than done. It's quite hellish out there,' Agatha pointed out. 'The Germans are shooting at everything that moves.'

'Not to mention the mines they've been laying,' piped up Mrs Clutterbuck.

'What choice do we have?' asked Lina. She looked at poor Lady Felstein, sinking further into oblivion. 'We can't just sit here and watch her die.'

'My doctor has a surgery nearby,' volunteered Miss Giltrap.

'You have the address?' Lina asked as she made for the door. There was no time to lose.

'But you'll get shot,' protested Mrs Clutterbuck.

Edoardo produced his pistol. 'It's all right. I'll go with her,' he said.

'Oh, my goodness,' said Agatha, clasping her hands. 'Please be careful, Signor Bernini,' she implored as they ventured out once more. The doctor only lived four blocks away, but it may as well have been four kilometres. Gunshots shredded the air every minute. Each step was a risk. Even so, they made it safely to the nearest junction with a wider road, accessible to motor vehicles. They waited for a moment to make sure the coast was clear when, from out of nowhere, an ambulance, its bell ringing furiously, came speeding along the rubble-strewn street.

'Edoardo, no!' screamed Lina as she saw him step out into its path, frantically waving his arms. But instead of slowing down, the vehicle's driver speeded up and headed straight for Edoardo, forcing him to dive into a doorway.

'What the hell?' he yelled as he picked himself up.

'It turned down there, by the baker's,' panted Lina, pointing to another junction a little further up the street.

'Right,' said Edoardo, dusting himself down. 'Second time lucky.'

Still hugging the walls, they scurried the few metres to the corner just in time to hear automatic fire. Rounding the baker's shop, they saw to their horror that the ambulance had become a target for gunmen. It weaved across the road, its brakes screeching, before ploughing into the front of a building, its windscreen cracked by bullet holes.

'I don't understand,' cried Lina.

'Nor do I,' agreed Edoardo, his revolver in hand, as they approached.

They were the first on the scene and when Lina opened the ambulance door, she was greeted by a gruesome sight. The driver was lolling in his seat, a bullet between his eyes. But then she noticed something else.

'A Nazi!' she gasped, staring at the dead man's uniform. They were now joined by a small band of partisans, ammunition belts slung over their shoulders. Edoardo didn't recognise any of them, but they seemed only interested in the driver at the wheel. Meanwhile, Lina motioned to Edoardo to go round the back of the vehicle. The double doors were warped by heavy gunshot, but Edoardo yanked hard at the handles. They yielded simultaneously. Neither of them could have guessed what they'd find within.

'Fischer!' cried Edoardo.

There was indeed a patient inside the ambulance, but the man, also in Nazi uniform, looked remarkably healthy, if rather nervous. Beside him, on the floor, lay a crate. He'd just been caught red-handed in the act of theft.

Alerted to the ambulance's very important passenger, half a dozen partisans crowded round and dragged out the Nazi colonel, manhandling him away as he protested loudly. Meanwhile, Lina climbed into the back of the vehicle. There were other matters far more important than taking revenge on Fischer. The crate. A sudden possibility stabbed her brain. Surely, it couldn't be? As if they shared the same thought, she and Edoardo swapped glances. Using his pocketknife, he prised off the lid. Inside, the crate was full of sawdust, but delving deeper Lina could make out three rectangular packages. She pulled out the smallest. Eagerly, but carefully, she tore off its newspaper wrappings. From out of the jagged strips, the face of the young woman stared at her, the *fleur-de-lys* emblem emblazoned on her dress. Lina stared back and a feeling of relief and joy blended inside her, like being reunited with an old friend she'd feared was lost forever. Clutching the portrait's gilt frame with both hands and looking into the young woman's hauntingly beautiful brown eyes, she whispered softly, 'Welcome home.'

'It can't be!' exclaimed Edoardo, fixed on the portrait, but before Lina could reply, the spell cast by the painting was broken.

'Oh, my dear, thank goodness I've found you!' came a voice, followed swiftly by a face peering into the ambulance. Lina's head shot up as her unexpected visitor leaned in. 'And look. Is that your Cranach you've found?'

'Aunt Agatha!' Still holding the portrait, Lina leapt to her feet and scrambled out of the open doors. Her aunt stood before her breathless, clutching her chest with one hand and her parasol with the other. 'You shouldn't be here,' she scolded.

Agatha looked over her shoulder and grimaced disdainfully

as the partisans surrounding Fischer continued to jostle him and shout, then turned back to her stunned niece. 'I'm here to tell you a doctor has come.' She took a deep breath. 'He's tending to Lady Felstein as we speak, so there's no need for you to be out here. Come back now, my dear,' she pleaded. She gestured with her brolly. 'It's really not safe.'

'You're right,' Lina agreed, wrapping a protective arm around Agatha, while the portrait remained under the other. 'Let's get out of here.' They both needed to return to the apartment. But no sooner had she spoken than a crack sounded above their heads, followed by another and another. A sniper, at a top-floor window across the street, was firing at the partisans surrounding Fischer.

'This way!' cried Edoardo, pointing to a nearby alley. But, in the mayhem that followed, as everyone scrambled to safety, Fischer managed to break free. With the German sniper giving him cover, he darted the few steps back to the ambulance, only to discover the young woman was gone. As soon as he realised the painting wasn't there, he cursed and punched the vehicle's door with his fist. Then, still fuming, he turned. As he did, from out of the corner of his eye, he caught sight of Lina, Agatha and Edoardo piling round the corner.

'I know you've got her!' he screamed, suddenly bolting after them. 'Give her to me!'

Edoardo pushed the women to safety in a nearby doorway. 'He means her, doesn't he?' cried Agatha, gulping down air as more gunshots were fired. Her eyes were trained on the portrait that leaned against a wall by her feet as Lina tried to get her to duck down.

'Don't move,' instructed Edoardo as, gun in hand, he peered around the corner only to see Fischer hurtling towards him. Within a second he'd fired, but although he was quick, he wasn't quick enough, as another sniper's bullet from the building opposite whizzed past, nicking the stone by his left ear. Edoardo dropped to the cobbles and the Nazi lurched, kicking the revolver out of his hand. Turning into the alley where Lina and Agatha were cowering in the doorway, his eyes immediately clamped on to the Cranach propped against the wall.

'No!' screamed Lina as Fischer pitched forwards to pounce on it. But just as he grabbed it, he was struck hard on the head by a parasol and the painting was snatched from his grasp.

'Get your filthy hands off it!' yelled Agatha defiantly, back on her feet. She was standing upright and clutching the portrait to her breast. 'It doesn't belong to you. It belongs to—'

Agatha didn't finish what she was about to say because just at that moment another loud crack screeched through the hot air. Something sharp hit her forehead and catapulted her backwards. Yet, instead of frightening her, the violent motion made her feel young again, like the girl she once was at a debutante's ball. She was spinning round and round on the dance floor, surrounded by friends and loved ones. Was that Reginald, her late husband, holding out his hand to her? Somewhere, far off, she heard muffled noises. Lina's voice, perhaps? Was she laughing? All she knew was that a sensation as sublime as the ecstasy she felt whenever she gazed on *Primavera* was washing over her as she left the ground to float effortlessly among the clouds.

Chapter 57

Florence

September 1946

They were gathered in a small room off one of the main galleries in the Uffizi. The front row of seats was reserved for the remaining members of the English Ladies' Arts Appreciation Society. Lady Felstein, frailer but nevertheless serenely elegant, sat next to an emotional Miss Harrowby, on this occasion sporting a white rose in the brim of her hat. At her side was Mrs Clutterbuck, who made sure she sat next to Edoardo on her right. Gloria Giltrap came next, seated by Rodney Ponting, who'd miraculously survived three years in a fascist camp for degenerates. Fittingly, his new suit was in a shade of dusky pink. At the end of the row there was also a vacant seat on which was placed a folded white parasol. It served as a poignant memorial to the society's founder and best-loved member, Mrs Agatha Fortescue-Smythe.

Several city officials were also present, as well as Professor Loggi's special guest, Lieutenant Commander George Stout, otherwise known as one of the Monuments Men. Eighteen months after the war ended, his unit's vital work, reuniting masterpieces with their rightful owners across the length and breadth of Europe, remained as important as ever.

The room was brimming to capacity and filled with a hum of conversation until Professor Loggi appeared to take charge. He strode over to a purple velvet drape which concealed something on the wall. Lina took her place at his side as he addressed his audience.

'Ladies and gentlemen,' he began. 'Welcome to the world-renowned Uffizi Gallery to witness the unveiling of a truly remarkable new exhibit which, if certain German military personnel had had their way, would have taken pride of place in Hitler's planned *Führermuseum* in Linz.'

A ripple of polite laughter ran around the room. Lina smiled and caught Edoardo's eye. The truth about the portrait she was shortly to unveil was a little more complicated than that. As Agatha fell with a bullet through her temple, Lina, distraught, had thrown herself down by her side. Edoardo, recovering his pistol, had taken a shot at Fischer. The colonel had also fallen, badly wounded in the shoulder, and the partisans managed to dispatch both Nazi snipers. After they'd rescued the painting, which had miraculously remained unscathed, the war had raged on as the Germans fought a brutal campaign in the north of Italy. Many thousands more lives were lost until the Allied victory was declared in May the year before. When Lina could finally make enquiries about the Austrian-Jewish businessman who owned the Cranach, she discovered he'd died in Auschwitz. His son had, however, managed to escape to America before the outbreak of war. He'd been delighted to allow the portrait of the young woman to remain in her home city of Florence, and in the Uffizi in particular.

In his speech, Professor Loggi paid tribute to the English Ladies' Arts Appreciation Society, but of course especially to Agatha. 'She was a force of nature,' he told his audience with a tremulous voice. 'I miss her terribly. We all do. How proud she would be today to witness Lina unveil the masterpiece she and her husband saved from the Nazis. Through their tireless endeavours, art lovers all over the world will be able to share in the wonder of this joyous and inspirational masterpiece for generations to come.'

With those words, Lina pulled a golden cord, and the curtain was drawn back to reveal the exquisite face of Lucas Cranach the Elder's *A Young Gentlewoman of Florence* to the public for the first time. A feeling of both joy and sadness welled up inside her as she surveyed the expressions of delight and amazement on the faces of those who gazed at the portrait. Everyone in the room burst into spontaneous applause.

'You did it,' whispered Edoardo, joining her by the painting and planting a kiss on her cheek. 'I'm so very proud of you and so would Agatha be. I'm sure her spirit is with us.'

For a moment there was no one else in the room. 'I couldn't have done it without you, Edoardo,' she replied, kissing him on the lips.

'Signora Bernini! Signora Bernini!' A high-pitched voice broke the spell.

'Yes, Donna. Is everything all right?' asked Lina as the maid approached.

'She will not settle, signora,' the girl complained, as two balled pink fists appeared from out of a noisy white bundle.

Lina looked at her husband and smiled. 'Come here, Agatha,' she said, cradling the infant – the latest honorary member of the English Ladies' Arts Appreciation Society. 'I do believe you're right,' she said to Edoardo. 'Her spirit will always be with us.'

'All right, ladies and gents, everyone bunch up!' came a call from near the back of the room. 'Let's get a photograph of you all,' called Miss Giltrap, waving frantically and fiddling with the very latest model of a Rolleiflex secured to a stand.

Lina, still holding baby Agatha, obeyed. She stood with Edoardo at her side and Professor Loggi on the other. They were joined by Lady Felstein, Miss Harrowby and Mrs Clutterbuck and, of course, Mr Ponting. As soon as Miss Giltrap was satisfied with the composition, she set the timer and rushed to join everyone else.

'One, two, three! Everyone say "*Eee*talia!"' she cried. Three seconds later, there was a great flash, and the moment was recorded on film for posterity.

Not long afterwards, Signor Rossi hung a framed print on the wall of the Gran Caffè Doney. It joined an earlier photograph, also taken by Miss Giltrap, on the day war broke out. That one, of course, included Mrs Agatha Fortescue-Smythe. And if anyone taking tea at the linen-clad tables ever asked about the women in the frame, Signor Rossi would look at them with tears in his eyes, puff out his chest, and declare, 'They were heroines. Each and every one of them. True sisters of Florence.'

A Letter from Tessa Harris

Thank you so much for choosing to read *The Florence Sisters*. If you would like to be the first to know about my new releases then follow me on X.

I really hope you enjoyed *The Florence Sisters* and if you did, I would be so grateful if you would leave a review. I always love to hear what readers think, and it helps new readers discover my books too.

Thanks so much,

Tessa

Facebook: Tessa Harris Author
X: @harris_tessa
Bluesky: @tessaharrisauthor.bsky.social
Instagram: @tessaharrisauthor

The Light We Left Behind

England, 1944: When psychologist **Maddie Gresham** is sent a mysterious message telling her to report to Trent Park mansion, she wonders how she will be helping the war effort from a stately home.

She soon finds captured Nazi generals are being detained at the house. Bugged with listening devices in every room, it's up to Maddie to gain the Nazis' trust and coax them into giving up information.

When **Max Weitzler**, a Jewish refugee, also arrives at Trent Park with the same mission, Maddie finds herself trapped in a dangerous game of chess.

The two met in Germany before the war, and Maddie's heart was his from the moment they locked eyes.

But Maddie has finally gained the trust of the Nazi officers at the house, and her love for Max must remain a secret.

When the walls have ears, who can you trust?

The Paris Notebook

A secret big enough to destroy the Führer's reputation . . .

January 1939: When **Katja Heinz** secures a job as a typist at Doctor Viktor's clinic, she doesn't expect to be copying top secret medical records from a notebook.

At the end of the first world war, Doctor Viktor treated soldiers for psychological disorders. One of the patients was none other than Adolf Hitler . . .

The notes in his possession declare Hitler unfit for office – a secret that could destroy the Führer's reputation, and change the course of the war if exposed . . .

With the notebook hidden in her hat box, Katja and Doctor Viktor travel to Paris. Seeking refuge in the Shakespeare and Company bookshop, they hope to find a publisher brave enough to print the controversial script.

But Katja is being watched. Nazi spies in Paris have discovered her plan. They will stop at nothing to destroy the notebook and silence those who know of the secret hidden inside . . .

The Tuscan Daughter

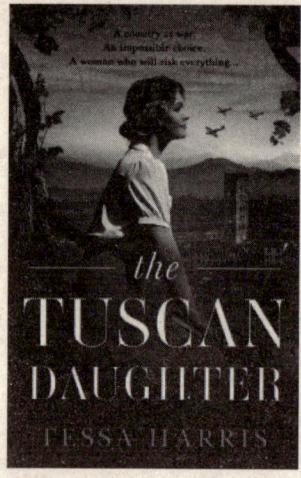

Tuscany, 1942: having moved from England to the beautiful city of Lucca before the outbreak of war, Lizzie Thornton adores her job as tutor to eight-year-old Cristo – despite the fact that his father, Count Antonio de Falco, is a notable fascist and supporter of Mussolini.

Then war is declared, and Lizzie is suddenly regarded as an enemy in the country she loves so much. When new tutor Vincenzo Baldini arrives, Lizzie is exposed to a new secret world; Vincenzo is actually a member of the Italian resistance, running an anti-fascist propaganda magazine. Lizzie, desperate to be part of the fight, joins Vincenzo's unit, and soon she is head over heels in love.

But when someone from her past reappears and threatens to overturn her new life, Lizzie must decide if she has the strength to fight for what, and who, she truly wants.

Acknowledgements

You may already be familiar with the Monuments Men, thanks to the eponymous 2014 George Clooney film telling the true story of a group of professors and curators who saved countless pieces of art from the Nazis after the Second World War. They did the most amazing and painstaking work all over Europe, and, indeed the Pacific, but there were many others who also worked tirelessly to save masterpieces from damage and destruction who are not as well known.

One of my favourite films of the 1990s was *Tea with Mussolini*. It tells the story of an orphan raised among a circle of British women living in Il Duce's Florence. It is loosely based on director Franco Zefferelli's own life. In his autobiography, *Zefferelli*, he says he owes much to his English tutor Mary O'Neill, who was like a mother to him. She belonged to a group of cultured English women whose wit was regarded as so stinging and their demeanour so formidable they were given the nickname the *Scorpioni*. Sadly, the names of the other women remain unknown.

Fast forward two decades and, still fascinated by these enigmatic characters, I decided to do my own research into their fate. My initial findings were disappointing. According to the tourist information office in the Tuscan town where the group was interned in the film, Zefferelli simply 'invented' the *Scorpioni*. They didn't really exist. I knew, however, this was not the case because the women were also mentioned in the memoirs of the writer Violet Trefusis, one of Virginia Woolf's Bloomsbury friends. (Incidentally, she was someone who actually did have tea with Mussolini.) According to Trefusis's memoir, *Don't Look Round*, the women spent their days before the war at the English Cemetery and the Uffizi Gallery, as well as at Gran Caffè Doney, on Via Tornabuoni, a haunt of British nationals in Florence at the time. It seems they were interned outside Florence during the war.

The character of Edoardo Bernini is loosely based on Rodolfo Siviero, an Italian secret agent and art historian who hid various works in Florence to save them from plunder. Although arrested and tortured, he escaped from the notorious Villa Triste. He went on to monitor the Nazi military body known as the *Kunstschutz*, which was supposed to protect cultural heritage, but in reality stole vast numbers of artworks from Italy to Germany. Several of these pieces were destined for the *Führermuseum*, Hitler's unrealised super museum and arts complex planned for Linz. Siviero's former home in Florence is now a museum.

Faced with the possible destruction of their beloved city and all its art treasures, I wondered how the *Scorpioni* might have reacted. Aloof and, at times, reportedly quite arrogant, I wanted to explore what might have happened if they were challenged to protect the thing in life they cared about most – art. That is how the idea of the novel came about, and the more I delved into the efforts of Florentines to protect their priceless treasures, the more amazed I became at their valiant efforts, not just to save paintings and sculptures, but historic buildings too.

On one bombing raid Allied pilots relied on custom 'Shinnie' maps which highlighted the city's chief artistic landmarks. In this they were helped by America's Frick Institute, which had already photographically recorded many historical sites in the city. Numbered white rectangles indicated the buildings not to be harmed under any circumstances. According to Robert Edsell, author of *Saving Italy: The Race to Rescue a Nation's Treasures from the Nazis*, the resulting aerial strike 'may well have been the most precise bombing mission of the war.' Every bomb landed in the target area.

Several resistance fighters associated with the partisan radio station, Radio CORA, were also uncovered and executed by the Nazis in the city. The story of how a telephone line was laid across the Ponte Vecchio by an Italian partisan is certainly stranger than fiction. It is recorded in a book by SOE (Special Operations Executive) agent Charles Macintosh, called *From Cloak to Dagger*.

In my research I am also indebted to Susan Chore, Archives Lead at The Frick Collection/Frick Art Reference Library Archives for digging out several documents for me, and to my fellow author and friend Caroline Montague. For a comprehensive history of Florence itself, look no further than Christopher Hibbert's *Florence, The Biography of a City*.

My thanks also go to my amazing editor Priyal Agrawal and, as ever, to my wonderful husband Simon for his huge support.

Dear Reader,

We hope you enjoyed reading this book. If you did, we'd be so appreciative if you left a review. It really helps us and the author to bring more books like this to you.

Here at HQ Digital we are dedicated to publishing fiction that will keep you turning the pages into the early hours. Don't want to miss a thing? To find out more about our books, promotions, discover exclusive content and enter competitions you can keep in touch in the following ways:

JOIN OUR COMMUNITY:

Sign up to our new email newsletter: http://smarturl.it/SignUpHQ

Read our new blog www.hqstories.co.uk

𝕏 https://twitter.com/HQStories

f www.facebook.com/HQStories

BUDDING WRITER?

We're also looking for authors to join the HQ Digital family!
Find out more here:

https://www.hqstories.co.uk/want-to-write-for-us/

Thanks for reading, from the HQ Digital team